DEMON

"Dark, rich, and sexy, every pa[...]
—*New York Tim[...]*

"Another fantastic book in a beautifully written series. [It] has all the elements I love in Meljean's books—strong, gorgeously drawn characters, a world so real I totally believe it, and the punch of powerful emotion."

—*New York Times* bestselling author Nalini Singh

DEMON BOUND

"An excellent entry in a great series . . . Another winner as the multifaceted Guardian saga continues to expand in complexity while remaining entertaining . . . As complex and beautifully done as always."
—*Book Binge*

"Be prepared for more surprises and more revelations . . . Brook continues to deliver surprising characters, relationships, paranormal elements, and plot twists—the only thing that won't surprise you is your *total* inability to put this book down."

—*Alpha Heroes*

"Raises the bar on paranormal romance for sheer thrills, drama, and world-building, and hands-down cements Brook's place at the top of her field."
—*Romance Junkies*

DEMON NIGHT

"Meljean is now officially one of my favorite authors. And this book's hero? . . . I just went weak at the knees. And the love scenes—wow, just wow."
—*Nalini Singh*

"This is the book for paranormal lovers. It is a phenomenal book by an author who knows how to give her readers exactly what they want. What Brook's readers want is a story that is dangerous, sexy, scary, and smart. *Demon Night* delivers all that and more! . . . [It] is the epitome of what a paranormal romance should be! I didn't want to put it down."
—*Romance Reader at Heart*

continued . . .

"Poignant and compelling with lots of action, and it's very sensual. You'll fall in love with Charlie, and Ethan will cause your thermometer to blow its top. An excellent plot, wonderful dialogue . . . Don't miss reading it or any of Meljean Brook's other novels in this series." —*Fresh Fiction*

"An intense romance that will leave you breathless . . . I was drawn in from the first page." —*Romance Junkies*

DEMON MOON

"The fourth book in Meljean Brook's Guardian series turns up the heat without losing any of the danger." —*Entertainment Weekly*

"A read that goes down hot and sweet—utterly unique—and one hell of a ride." —*New York Times* bestselling author Marjorie M. Liu

"Sensual and intriguing, *Demon Moon* is a simply wonderful book. I was enthralled from the first page!" —Nalini Singh

"Brings a unique freshness to the romantic fantasy realm . . . Action packed from the onset." —*Midwest Book Review*

"Fantastically drawn characters . . . and their passion for each other is palpable in each scene they share. It stews beneath the surface and when it finally reaches boiling point . . . OH WOW!" —*Vampire Romance Books*

DEMON ANGEL

"I've never read anything like this book. *Demon Angel* is brilliant, heartbreaking, genre-bending—even, I dare say, epic. Simply put, I love it." —Marjorie M. Liu

"Brook has crafted a complex, interesting world that goes far beyond your usual . . . paranormal romance. *Demon Angel* truly soars." —Jennifer Estep, author of *Jinx*

"I can honestly say I haven't read many books lately that have kept me guessing and wondering 'what's next' but this is one of them. [Brook has] created a unique and different world . . . Gritty and realistic . . . Incredibly inventive . . . This is a book which makes me think and think about it even days after finishing it."
—*Dear Author*

"Enthralling . . . [A] delightful saga." —*The Best Reviews*

"Extremely engaging . . . A fiendishly good book. *Demon Angel* is outstanding." —*The Romance Reader*

"A surefire winner. This book will captivate you and leave you yearning for more. Don't miss *Demon Angel*."
—*Romance Reviews Today*

"A fascinating romantic fantasy with . . . a delightful pairing of star-crossed lovers." —*Midwest Book Review*

"Complex and compelling . . . A fabulous story."
—*Joyfully Reviewed*

FURTHER PRAISE FOR MELJEAN BROOK AND FOR "FALLING FOR ANTHONY" FROM *HOT SPELL*

"An emotional roller coaster for both the characters and the reader. Brook has penned a story I am sure readers won't soon forget . . . Extraordinary work." —*Romance Junkies*

"In-depth and intriguing. I loved the obvious thought and ideas put into writing this tale. The characters are deep, as is the world that is set up." —*The Romance Readers Connection*

"Brook . . . creates fantastic death-defying love . . . Extremely erotic . . . with a paranormal twist." —*Fresh Fiction*

"Intriguing . . . The sex is piping hot." —*Romance Reviews Today*

"I look forward to many more tales from Ms. Brook."
—*Joyfully Reviewed*

Titles by Meljean Brook

DEMON ANGEL
DEMON MOON
DEMON NIGHT
DEMON BOUND
DEMON FORGED
DEMON BLOOD

Anthologies

HOT SPELL
(with Emma Holly, Lora Leigh, and Shiloh Walker)

WILD THING
(with Maggie Shayne, Marjorie M. Liu, and Alyssa Day)

FIRST BLOOD
(with Susan Sizemore, Erin McCarthy, and Chris Marie Green)

MUST LOVE HELLHOUNDS
(with Charlaine Harris, Nalini Singh, and Ilona Andrews)

DEMON BLOOD

meljean brook

BERKLEY SENSATION, NEW YORK

THE BERKLEY PUBLISHING GROUP
Published by the Penguin Group
Penguin Group (USA) Inc.
375 Hudson Street, New York, New York 10014, USA

Penguin Group (Canada), 90 Eglinton Avenue East, Suite 700, Toronto, Ontario M4P 2Y3, Canada
(a division of Pearson Penguin Canada Inc.)
Penguin Books Ltd., 80 Strand, London WC2R 0RL, England
Penguin Group Ireland, 25 St. Stephen's Green, Dublin 2, Ireland (a division of Penguin Books Ltd.)
Penguin Group (Australia), 250 Camberwell Road, Camberwell, Victoria 3124, Australia
(a division of Pearson Australia Group Pty. Ltd.)
Penguin Books India Pvt. Ltd., 11 Community Centre, Panchsheel Park, New Delhi—110 017, India
Penguin Group (NZ), 67 Apollo Drive, Rosedale, North Shore 0632, New Zealand
(a division of Pearson New Zealand Ltd.)
Penguin Books (South Africa) (Pty.) Ltd., 24 Sturdee Avenue, Rosebank, Johannesburg 2196,
South Africa

Penguin Books Ltd., Registered Offices: 80 Strand, London WC2R 0RL, England

DEMON BLOOD

A Berkley Sensation Book / published by arrangement with the author

PRINTING HISTORY
Berkley Sensation mass-market edition / July 2010

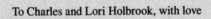

To Charles and Lori Holbrook, with love

A BEDTIME STORY

Three centuries ago, there lived in Florence a little girl beloved by her mother, father, and young brother. Though she was not a princess, as many girls in these stories are, the wealth and power of her family made such distinctions irrelevant.

Unbeknownst to that happy family, their wealth and power also attracted a demon.

When the girl was seven years of age, her father journeyed to Rome and returned a changed man, as if someone else inhabited his skin. The words of love he'd once whispered to her mother became whispers of another sort, until she could bear him no longer. But when he thwarted each assassin she hired and the wounds he received quickly healed, when she poured enough poison to kill an army into his wine and he did not sicken or die, she poisoned her own cup.

Darkness settled over the household. Quiet and frightened, the girl and her brother went largely unnoticed by their father, except for when he subjected them to small torments for his amusement. They noticed him, however, watching his movements as mice will watch a cat until it has left the room, and they saw that he neither slept nor ate. In rare moments, they glimpsed the crimson glow of his eyes, the appearance of scales over his skin, and cloven hooves. They witnessed him move inhumanly fast and fly with bats' wings; they saw him battle and behead a woman who wore wings of white feathers. They watched, and as the years passed, the children understood what their father had become.

The girl shielded her brother from their father when she could, and was relieved when the boy's schooling took him from their home. Though the girl prayed for a similar escape through a good marriage, no happy fate awaited her; eager to form an alliance with a noble family, the demon arranged her wedding to an aged man known for his perversity. The girl fled and found sanctuary in an abbey whose prioress had once been a friend of her mother's, and who pitied her. The girl's father did not pursue her, and she realized that although he had power enough to kill an angel, he dared not cross the Church.

Five years passed. Protected and cloistered, the girl grew into a woman and took her solemn vows. Her brother rarely visited, but they corresponded often, and his missives brought her great joy. Over time, however, his infrequent journeys to the abbey stopped altogether. Dark and melancholy sentiments filled his letters, until they, too, stopped. She still wrote to him daily, begging him to visit her again. Five more years passed before he did, and he was in the company of her father.

They came at night. Despite the hour, she spoke with them in the convent parlor, through the grating that separated the cloister from the outside world. Even obscured by the grating, however, she could see the changes in her brother: his pale appearance, the hunger in his gaze, the teeth that would rival a wolf's—but the greatest alteration was his manner, which had become cold and cruel. He looked upon her with disdain, and she could see no love in him. Alarmed, she began to retreat, but with a few words, her father halted her escape. He told her the abbey offered no protection from her brother and offered her a terrible choice: Either she would die by her brother's hand, or all of her sisters would.

Believing that her brother would stay his hand at the ultimate moment, she chose her own death. Though no longer a girl, she could not help but remember the love she and her brother shared when they had been young, and how they had protected each other. He'd been corrupted by her father, his soul twisted, but she could not believe her brother would truly kill her.

She was wrong. He used his fangs to tear open her throat. As her lifeblood poured onto the floor, she watched her brother walk away from the abbey, leaving her for dead. She heard her father laughing.

He did not laugh long. Just as he had once slain an angel, another appeared in a flare of white light and struck the demon's head from his shoulders. The angel lifted her from where she lay dying, told her he was named Michael, and he, too, offered her a choice: to become as he was, a protector who guarded humans against demons; or to die, and face what awaited her in the afterlife. She chose to live, was transformed and taken to Caelum, a shining realm of light and beauty. There, she learned they were not angels, but Guardians. She heard their story, and years later, she would tell it to children whom she called her own:

The Story of the Guardians

Many years ago, when the universe was old but the world was still new, Lucifer the Morningstar led his angels in a rebellion against Heaven. The rebels battled the seraphim, a small order of warrior angels loyal to Heaven, and they rent the skies with their war. But even as the rebels fought the seraphim, they struggled against one another for their place beneath Lucifer, and it was not long before duplicity and betrayal weakened the rebels' ranks. Though vastly outnumbered, the seraphim had but one purpose—to protect Heaven—and with their combined might, they crushed the rebels.

As their punishment, the rebel angels were transformed into demons. Angels were created of energy and light, and although they could assume the appearance of flesh, it was only an illusion; demons were stripped of their light and bound to flesh. They were turned away from Heaven and tossed into Hell, where they dwelled in darkness.

Some angels, uncertain which side to take in the war, hid in the dark corners of the universe until the victor became apparent. They emerged, swearing fealty to Heaven, but they were too late: The weakness of their faith and their hearts had been revealed. These angels were bound more closely to their flesh than demons, cursed with a deep hunger for blood and a need for sleep. They burned at the touch of sunlight. They were called nosferatu, "those who would not be tolerated."

This was the First Battle.

Demons could travel through the Gates to Earth, where humans lived under the protection of the seraphim and the Rules, which forbade both angels and demons from killing humans and from interfering with human free will. Demons could tempt mankind to sin, however, so that when men died, their souls would not ascend into Heaven, but be tortured in the Pit. From those tortured souls, Lucifer drew much of his power. He reigned in Hell, hoarding knowledge, using angelic symbols and blood to perform experiments on lower creatures from Earth and the Chaos realm, from which he drew even more power. He did not rule uncontested, however. The demon Belial, once Lucifer's lieutenant, promised his fellow demons a return to Grace and escape from their punishment if they helped him overthrow Lucifer's throne. Their civil war has been waged in Hell for millennia.

The seraphim, when they were not on Earth, resided in the realm of Caelum—a shining marble city situated in the center of an endless sea. The creatures of light took *human form when they walked among men, but the seraphim's overwhelming beauty and manner eventually led mankind to regard them as gods. Lucifer's jealousy was great. In his rage, he brought a dragon from Chaos to Earth, declaring another war upon the seraphim.*

This war, the Second Battle, did not take place in the heavens, but on Earth. The demons rode the dragon, and the seraphim fell before it. The world burned. Mankind saw the battle taking place, and one man—Michael—struck his sword into the great beast's heart, slaying the dragon.

With the dragon defeated, the seraphim regrouped and were victorious. But the angels knew that they could never hide their nature from humans; it would only lead to more Earth-bound wars between demons and angels, and offer a false truth to mankind. They were not gods.

So they bestowed upon Michael the power of the angels, and gave unto him the ability to transform any other human who sacrificed his life to save another from the temptations of demons and the terrors of the nosferatu. These men and women would be called Guardians. In addition to immortality, wings, strength, and the ability to alter their appearance, these Guardians were given individual Gifts to assist them in their battles. Because they had once been human, they could walk among men without drawing notice, but like the angels, Guardians had to follow the Rules; they could not interfere with human free will or kill humans, no matter how terrible some men were. If a Guardian broke the Rules, he either had to Fall and return to human form, or Ascend and go on to his afterlife.

Centuries passed, and although the numbers of Guardians increased, many also died. Their lives were fraught with danger, and they often had to defend themselves in combat against demons and nosferatu. They avoided bargains and wagers with demons; if left unfulfilled, a demon's bargain would trap their eternal soul in Hell's frozen field. And they fought to save as many humans as possible, all the while concealing their existence from them.

In time, the Guardians discovered that humans who had been attacked by nosferatu might be saved by drinking the creature's blood. Though much stronger than humans—and a vampire created from nosferatu blood was stronger than one transformed by another vampire's blood—the vampires were weaker than Guardians and could not alter their shapes. Like the nosferatu, these transformed humans were vulnerable to daylight and suffered from a deep and powerful hunger—the bloodlust. Fearing discovery and persecution by humans, vampires formed secret communities, living among humans in their cities, but feeding only from one another.

The vampires' souls were not transformed; their characters were the same in undeath as they had been in life. The vampires were not bound by the Rules, just as nosferatu were not, and so the Guardians took upon themselves another task—to guard humans against vampires should the need arise. For the most part, Guardians allowed the vampires to live as they willed, but there were those vampires who had to be watched more closely than others, and who would be destroyed if they broke the Rules.

So the Guardians fought to keep the influence of those Above and Below from touching humanity. There is no end to this story; the Guardians are still fighting. They will keep fighting for as long as they exist.

When the girl heard this she was overjoyed, for it meant that although her brother had become a vampire, he could still be saved. His transformation had not corrupted his soul; the demon had. She persuaded Michael not to slay her brother and allow her the chance to undo what the demon had done.

She could not immediately begin, however—first, she had to complete one hundred years of training in Caelum. Those years were filled with hope. Even the discovery of her Gift to manipulate darkness and shadows, so painful to use beneath Caelum's sun-filled sky, did not diminish her happiness. After a century, she returned to Earth, her hope still bright within her chest.

It took almost two more centuries for her brother to kill that hope. Then he was killed, too.

And so the tale closes with the girl left alone and her hopes shattered, with no one to save—and the demon, though defeated, ultimately the victor. Unlike other stories, this does not have a happy ending.

Not yet.

CHAPTER I

The string quartet in the corner of the ballroom slipped from a sleepy minuet into a sleepy waltz. Rosalia lifted her champagne flute to her lips to cover her sigh. Thank God for the demons. If not for their conspiring, boredom would have killed her by now.

The small circle of humans she'd joined burst into laughter. Rosalia smiled vacuously in response. She hadn't heard the joke, but no one at the gala would expect a reply, anyway. She'd changed her dark hair to a wispy, baby blond, donned a vapid expression over soft features, and paired them with an insubstantial pink dress for that very reason: She wouldn't be expected to talk. She only needed to stand and look pretty. So she stood with humans she didn't know in the center of a chateau ballroom, watching three of Belial's demons solidify an alliance.

Others watched them, too. Some humans glanced in their direction; some stared. Rosalia could not blame them. Like every demon she'd known, they'd disguised themselves in sinfully handsome human forms—sensual lips and blade-straight noses, black hair glinting under the crystal chandeliers, as if they'd each used an advertisement in a men's fashion magazine as a template. With a backdrop of priceless paintings mounted on gold-painted walls, they formed a would-be triumvirate with Bernard and Gavel as the base and Pierre Theriault at the top.

Of the three, Theriault ranked the highest in both Belial's army and Legion Laboratories, the corporation that both concealed and supported their activities on Earth. Two years ago, when the Gates to Hell had closed, preventing Belial from overseeing the demons that remained on Earth, Legion began to serve as a communication network. Through it, one of Belial's lieutenants issued orders and received reports—until he'd been slain by the Guardians. Now, with no clear successor to the lieutenant and no contact from Hell, Belial's demons were maneuvering for his position, and all of them were arrogant enough to imagine themselves in the spot. But if Bernard and Gavel thought they'd ride the wake of Theriault's ascent, they were as foolish as he was. Theriault's particular brand of arrogance bordered on stupidity.

No, Rosalia amended. Not *bordering* stupidity. He'd flung himself over that line the second he'd begun discussing the alliance in a public room, and using English instead of the demonic language. Good Lord, the idiocy. Though the chateau was just north of Paris, perhaps fifteen people out of the hundreds in the ballroom didn't understand at least rudimentary English.

Even if Theriault imagined that the string music floating over the room and the crowd's chatter would conceal their voices from humans, he hadn't made sure there weren't any Guardians or other demons in the vicinity. Though strong enough for Rosalia to feel, Theriault's psychic sweep hadn't penetrated her mental shields. At that shallow depth, her mind would seem no different from a human's.

Careless. Stupid. Rosalia had many reasons to slay the demons, but at this moment, making the consequences of that carelessness the last thing they ever saw was the most tempting reason to shove her swords through their eyes.

But she wouldn't slay them. Not tonight. She'd come to the gala to observe Theriault, and to judge how much of a threat he'd be if he led Belial's demons. Not much. But it hadn't been a wasted trip. She'd overheard repeated mention of one demon standing in Theriault's way, one he'd considered too powerful to take on alone: Malkvial.

She hadn't yet learned who Malkvial was. Rosalia didn't know many demons by their true name, only by the human identities they used. She needed to find this one out, soon, either by listening in on Theriault or by other means.

A soft crackle sounded in her ear, and her attention shifted. The noise indicated that Gemma had opened the microphone connecting the tiny receiver bud in Rosalia's ear to the surveillance van outside the chateau. Rosalia couldn't perform a psychic sweep without revealing herself to the demons, but she hadn't gone in blind.

Rosalia possessed her share of arrogance. But unlike some demons, she was neither careless nor stupid. At least, not most of the time.

"Mother, infrared is picking up either Davanzati or Murnau approaching the chateau. He's moving south across the grounds. On foot."

Davanzati or Murnau. Code words for vampires and nosferatu. Though the receiver's volume was probably too low for a demon to hear unless he was standing next to her, Rosalia wouldn't risk drawing the demons' attention. Both demons and Guardians could hear everything said in the ballroom, but they couldn't *listen* to everything. Even if whispered, however, certain words and names pierced background noise like a candle lit at midnight.

To cover her reply, Rosalia turned as if searching the crowd. "You don't know which it is?" she murmured.

Both vampires and nosferatu would register a lower temperature on infrared than a human or Guardian, but nosferatu were huge. Most towered at six and a half to seven feet in height.

"He's tall, but I don't think he's tall enough for Murnau. He's not close enough for me to be sure, though."

"When he is, let me know."

A nosferatu posed a problem. People would notice it. Enormous, with pale and hairless skin, pointed ears, and fangs twice as long as a vampire's, nosferatu were bloodthirsty, evil creatures. Even if it dressed to pass as human—difficult beneath the bright lights in the chateau—and even if people refused to believe what they saw, its presence would stir fear and revulsion. But Rosalia doubted a nosferatu would try to blend in. If one was coming, then it was coming to kill. To protect the people here, she'd have to slay it, revealing her presence to the demons. Then she'd have to slay the demons so they couldn't report that a Guardian had been watching them. She didn't want to give Belial's demons any reason to unite against the Guardians, and she'd prefer not to kill Theriault yet. No matter how little his chances of leading his brethren were, the infighting over the lieutenant's position benefited the Guardians. Even an incompetent demon might provide a distraction for Malkvial and prevent him from quickly uniting the others.

If a vampire was coming, though . . .

Rosalia glanced back at the demons. Bernard and Gavel were taking their leave of Theriault, agreeing to circle among the guests. Satisfaction emanated from each. Demon business finished, now they were conducting Legion business, building human contacts.

Perhaps one of them intended to continue demon business, though. Six months ago, Belial's lieutenant had ordered the slaughter of Prague's vampire community; since then, fewer vampires willingly aligned themselves with the demons. But there were still some vampires who sought either power or protection from the demons—and the demons had their own uses for vampires who were willing to break the Rules in exchange.

The Parisian vampire community had resisted Theriault's attempts to make an alliance, but maybe a dissenter was in their ranks. A foolish dissenter, if he'd come alone. A human crowd provided some protection if the demons turned on him, but not much.

The soft crackle came again. *"Mother, I have visual confirmation. It's Davanzati."*

A vampire. "Anyone I know?"

"Yes." The hesitation told Rosalia that Gemma was thinking of a way to describe him without saying his name. *"Six months ago, he stayed one day in your bedroom and left the same night."*

Deacon. Rosalia's champagne flute tilted in nerveless fingers. Her breath corkscrewed painfully through her lungs. Her mind could hardly comprehend it—*Deacon, here*—but the ache filling her chest said her heart had already taken it in.

Deacon was here.

And still alive.

She hadn't known if he was. Once the leader of the Prague vampire community, he'd betrayed the Guardians in a desperate gamble to save his people, and lost. Belial's lieutenant and a second demon, Caym, had done everything to destroy Deacon without actually killing him. Caym had beaten Deacon bloody, crushed his bones and his pride, then held his community and lovers hostage in exchange for information about the Guardians. As a result of that information, a Guardian had been killed—a woman Rosalia hadn't known well, but had liked very much. After learning of the Guardian's death, Rosalia had watched Belial's lieutenant use Deacon to transform a human murderer into a vampire, then finally break him by showing Deacon the ashen remains of his companions. Though Deacon had managed to slay Caym, Belial's lieutenant had stopped the vampire by stabbing an iron spike through his forehead, and had left Deacon for the Guardians to find and kill. But Irena, a Guardian and the friend Deacon had betrayed, had stayed her hand, and Rosalia had taken him to her home in Rome. She hadn't known what she was going to do with him. She only knew why she'd taken him.

Deacon had rescued her. Once, ninety years ago, and again more recently, when she'd had an iron spike through her own head and three nosferatu feeding from her throat. And so she owed him.

When they'd reached Rome, Deacon had still been unconscious, healing from the damage to his brain. She'd taken him to her room and had left him to his daysleep. When she'd returned, night had fallen and Deacon had already gone. Gemma had reported that he'd walked out the door without saying a word.

Rosalia had thought he'd left to die. He'd been broken. She'd felt his despair when he'd realized all that he'd lost; he'd welcomed death when the demon had shoved the spike through his forehead. She'd been certain he'd face the sun the next morning.

But he was here, instead. Why? *Never* would he ally himself with Belial's demons. The launch of a new skin-care line and this party couldn't interest him. She couldn't picture him mingling comfortably. The people glittered; conversation sparkled. Deacon wouldn't.

Had he somehow known *she* would be here? Rosalia's heart gave a heavy, slow thump. Hope bubbled within her bloodstream. Ruthlessly, she squashed it. Deacon couldn't have known she'd intended to observe Theriault tonight.

Or could he?

If he had known, he wouldn't recognize her like this. Not with blond hair and this baby face—

Rosalia closed her eyes. *Stop.* She wouldn't let her thoughts head in this direction. Whatever his reasons, he wasn't here for her.

"He's at the rear of the chateau, Mother. I've lost him on infrared."

A vampire didn't need an invitation to enter a building, but he did to gain admittance into this gala. So did a Guardian. She'd come through the back disguised as one of the caterers. Though Deacon couldn't shape-shift, he could easily climb the exterior wall to the second floor or speed through the doors unseen.

She opened her eyes. The demon Gavel was approaching her group, his gaze fixed on the CEO of a cosmetics company standing beside her. Rosalia excused herself and threaded through the crowd toward the refreshment table, smiling brightly and nodding at anyone who met her eyes. She joined another group of humans at the side of the ballroom. Now that Theriault, Bernard, and Gavel had split up, she needed a wider angle to keep an eye on them. It also let her see both the enormous staircase that led from the second floor, and the main entrance from the gallery—the route Deacon would take if he approached the ballroom from the back of the chateau.

Assuming, of course, that the ballroom was his destination. And if he didn't come, she would *not* seek him out. She'd spent most of her life trying to save her brother, Lorenzo, from himself. She refused to spend the rest of it on another lost cause, no matter how much she owed him.

But she could thank God he was alive. She'd allow herself that.

She waited. Around her, the humans' laughter and voices seemed too loud. The musicians finally switched to an arrangement with a quick tempo, but every draw of their bows sawed across her senses.

She glanced at the wide marble staircase. He wasn't there. Disappointment weighted her chest. Accustomed to the feeling, she ignored it.

Returning her gaze to the ballroom, she watched the demons and saw their calculated expressions and conversation win over their companions. Would they recognize Deacon? Only Belial's lieutenant and Caym had used him, but he'd led Prague's community for more than six decades. Other demons might have seen him before.

If these demons gave any indication that they knew Deacon, she'd kill them—Theriault's alliance and Malkvial be damned. A lone vampire was nothing but sport to their kind. She wouldn't stand by and watch them play.

She looked toward the gallery. Even in this crush of people, Deacon's height would make him easy to spot. He wasn't there.

Had he been delayed? Was another demon or a vampire at the gala, one that neither she nor Gemma had detected? She should wander through the other rooms and see.

Rosalia headed for the gallery, her gaze sweeping the stairs. Sweeping over the vampire descending the steps.

Sweeping past him.

Her heart galloped. She continued walking. *Don't stop. Don't react and draw attention to him.* Her focus traveled the length of the ballroom, but her mind remained locked on that brief glimpse. She'd been right. Even here, Deacon didn't glitter. He stood like an unpolished stone pillar amid sparkling diamonds. His dark dinner jacket stretched over shoulders as wide as a blacksmith's. He'd unbuttoned his shirt at the collar, revealing pale skin that could have belonged to an unfinished marble statue—possessing the strength, but none of the smooth perfection of a completed piece. Before he'd become a vampire, Deacon had earned his money boxing, and his transformation had physically frozen his appearance. His body was still heavily muscled. His dark brows and hard mouth formed uncompromising lines on a face roughly sculpted by both nature and occupation. A beard shadowed his jaw; he obviously hadn't shaved in months. And . . . *had he cut his hair?* She wanted to look again. She forced herself to continue smoothly across the floor. The click of her heels drummed in her ears.

Don't turn around yet. Find one of the servers and—

There. A waiter in a white jacket paused beside a matron wearing gold silk. Rosalia downed her champagne, circled the waiter, and lifted a new glass from his tray, sliding in next to the matron.

Deacon had reached the bottom of the stairs, but remained on the last step. His gaze searched the crowd.

She glanced at the demons. None were looking toward the vampire, and so she did, studying him from beneath her lashes.

He *had* cut his hair. Though it was longer than the first time she'd seen him, a member of the American naval service and his brown hair regulation short, six months ago the dark length had touched his shoulders. Now he had just enough to slide his fingers through, but not enough to grab a handful. A vampire's hair grew slowly; it'd be another ninety years before it reached his shoulders again.

Though the cut was tidier and less distinctive than his long hair, he still appeared slightly disheveled. With his shadowed jaw and unbuttoned collar, many men would look like they'd just come from bed; Deacon looked like he'd prepared for a fight. One side of his shirt collar had escaped the jacket, as if he'd dragged off his tie just before coming here. Now the points of his shirt collar were uneven. It bothered her. Her gaze kept flicking back to them. She wished he'd fix it, if only because an orderly appearance would make him less remarkable amid all of the glossy perfection. But even if he knew how crooked the collar was, she doubted that it would occur to him to adjust it.

In her cache, she carried a tie for her son, Vincente. It would take only an instant to pull it from her mental storage space and into her hands. She could approach Deacon and offer to tidy him up.

To amuse herself, she imagined his reaction. She was still smiling when Deacon's searching gaze touched her and immediately moved on.

Well. She'd expected that, hadn't she? Rosalia swallowed champagne past a throat gone tight. He never recognized her. Not his fault, really. Until six months ago, when he'd led the Guardians to the catacombs where she'd been trapped for a year and a half, an endless fount of blood for a nest of nosferatu, she'd never appeared to him as herself; before that, she'd never approached him with the same face twice. The form she used tonight was new, too.

His jaw flexed as if he'd clenched his teeth. After a moment, she realized he was no longer searching the crowd. She looked to see who he'd focused on.

Theriault.

She should have guessed. A man like Deacon would not rest until he'd avenged his people. The two demons who destroyed his community were dead, but not *all* of Belial's demons were. One by one, he would hunt them down and slay them.

For a vampire, it was an impossible task. Perhaps he might slay two, or ten, or fifty. Eventually, though, one of the demons would kill him first.

Deacon had to know that. And so he was not only seeking revenge. He still sought death. It just wouldn't be in the face of the sun. He'd go out fighting, instead of broken.

Good for you, preacher. Rosalia mentally lifted her glass to him as she took a sip of champagne. She understood the need to avenge her people, no matter how impossible the odds. So she still wouldn't try to save Deacon from himself—she *wouldn't*—but she could help him a little.

And make sure he didn't get in her way.

"Mia piccola bambina?"

"Yes, Mother?"

She heard the laugh in Gemma's response, as she did every time she referred to the young woman as her tiny little girl. In her bare feet, the lanky blonde stood at eye level with Rosalia in heels, and Rosalia's current fashion-model height was only slightly taller than her natural one.

"I want to know where he's staying, his financial situation. Where he's been in the past six months and who he's been with." Rosalia hadn't looked before, afraid that she wouldn't find anything. "He came alone, but does he have a new partner? Who is he feeding from?"

He must have been feeding. After two or three days without blood, a vampire began showing it—pale, tired, and thin. None of those described Deacon. Neither did careless or stupid, so he'd likely already fed that night. His psychic blocks were good, but he wouldn't risk the demons sensing his blood-lust by coming in hungry.

So he'd either found a new vampire partner or was using different human women each night. He'd been forced to do that before, while his consorts had been held hostage. *Offer the women so much to drink that they won't remember. Heal the bite, so that even if they do remember, they won't have evidence.* Rosalia thought he must hate that. To her knowledge, he hadn't been to bed with anyone he didn't want since Camille had transformed him. Soon after he and Camille parted ways and he'd taken over the community in Prague, Eva and Petra became his lovers and companions. But the bloodlust wouldn't give him the same choice if he fed from strangers. If the woman was interested, he wouldn't be able to stop his response. He'd have sex with her.

The bloodlust wouldn't always rise and overwhelm his free will, and not every woman he fed from would desire him. So it wouldn't *always* happen—but it would happen often enough that he must feel as if the bloodlust controlled him.

Her gaze fell to his uneven collar again. Maybe that was where he'd lost his tie. Some woman's bedroom. The restroom in a Parisian bar. An alley.

Her fingers flexed. She *needed* to fix that collar.

Gemma broke in, her voice holding a hint of apology. *"It will take me longer to send that information to you than it used to, Mother."*

Oh, God. Rosalia's throat closed. Grief hit her so hard that only practice and discipline kept it from showing. Once, a team of vampires would have been in the van with Gemma. More would have been at a converted abbey in Rome, which they'd all shared and called home. She'd trained all of them, had raised most of them, and had known some for more than a century.

Not just a team. Her family. And they were all gone. Slaughtered by the nephilim, a race of demons that Rosalia hadn't known existed until six months ago. While she'd been trapped in the catacombs beneath a church, with a spike through her head, the nephilim had killed her friends and family. They'd slain every vampire in Rome, including Lorenzo, and she hadn't been there to protect them. But Gemma had. She'd been in the abbey when the nephilim had come, and because she was human, she'd been the only one to survive.

Gemma still woke up screaming from the nightmares.

"Oh, Gemma, I am so sorry. I was not thinking." Because she could hardly bear to think about it. "Tomorrow morning, we'll begin looking together."

"Vin's coming up tomorrow. He'll help."

"And have it all to me before you've finished breakfast." She forced the lightness into her tone. Her son would help, but only because Gemma would ask him to. Ten years ago, he'd left the abbey without looking back. He'd still be gone if not for his relationship with Gemma—and if he could convince Gemma, he'd disappear from Rosalia's life again. But he hadn't yet, and she thanked God every day that her son had fallen in love with a woman as bullheaded as he was. "Will he be staying the weekend at the hotel with us?"

"Yes. He will, and he'll like it."

Gemma's determined tone brought Rosalia out of her grief, made her smile. She glanced at Deacon, gathering her calm and her courage. "I am on my way to speak to Davanzati."

"And I'm turning into a mouse." Except for an emergency, Gemma would keep radio silence until Rosalia put space between them again. *"Give him hell, Mother."*

She didn't have to. Belial's demons had already put him through hell, first when they'd beaten him, then when they'd killed his people. None of those marks were visible, but Rosalia knew they were there. Just as hers were.

Deacon had remained at his vantage point on the stairs, his posture casual, his elbow braced on the wide marble banister. Though he must have been aware of Rosalia's approach, he didn't acknowledge her until she was a few paces away. He glanced down, his eyes the muted green of the sea lying beneath dark clouds. She put on another dazzling smile and directed it right at him. He looked toward the demon again, dismissing her.

She glided up two steps as if she intended to pass by, then slipped behind him. Propping her hip against the banister, she reached down and rested her hand against his cool fist. Before he could react, she said, "You do not intend to do it here, do you? With so many humans as witnesses?"

His big body stiffened. She could almost feel him weighing his response. Her skin was warm, not the feverish temperature of a demon's or the cold touch of a vampire's. That left human or Guardian. When he inhaled, she knew he was testing her scent—or trying to, beyond the redolence of perfumes and colognes saturating the air. She'd sprayed her own floral fragrance to conceal her lack of odor, and with every breath, she took in the pine and bergamot that masked his. One so earthy, the other a light tingle lifting through her senses.

To her delight, he raised her hand to his lips and sniffed. The tension leaked from his form. His mouth setting into a hard line, he turned his head, looking at her in profile.

"Of course you would not," Rosalia answered for him, though she guessed he was preparing to respond with, *Haul off, lady*—Guardian or not. She withdrew her hand and touched his back, where she could feel the short swords strapped beneath his jacket. Vampires had no cache to store their weapons. They had to physically arm themselves. "You are just observing him, I think. You plan to finish it later, when the element of surprise is yours. And you will defeat him, because he is arrogant . . . and he could not know how strong and fast you have become."

After Irena had slain the nosferatu who had been feeding from Rosalia, she'd given Deacon their blood to drink. It had changed him, strengthened him, as if he'd been given a second transformation. Though he was still not as strong or as quick as one of the rare nosferatu-born, Deacon had a brief, important advantage: A demon expected a normal vampire's strength and speed from him. He was the only vampire to have been strengthened that way, so as long as no Guardians revealed that a second transformation was possible, Deacon would always possess that moment of surprise against a demon, useful for both defense and attack.

She watched his eyes narrow. Had he not expected *her* to know, either? Perhaps no other Guardians but she knew that the second transformation had been successful. Perhaps he'd not realized, until now, who had been speaking to him.

Or perhaps he thought that the Guardian he'd told had spread the information to everyone. If so, she forgave him. He had not known her long enough to understand that she would never rip away a friend's defenses. Particularly when he had so few.

"Yes, I know all of this," she confirmed. "Do *you* know that two of his brethren, who have just sworn to protect him, are also here?"

Deacon's face didn't give anything away, but his quick, searching sweep of the room did. He hadn't known.

"If you struck against him tonight, it would be suicide. Suicide compounded by failure, when you are not able to finish what you set out to do."

Even when he spoke softly, his voice had gravel in it. "Why would you care?"

Some Guardians wouldn't. They'd prefer to see him dead. Rosalia wasn't one of them. "I have many reasons. One is that it benefits my kind to keep these three alive . . . for now. Your chance will come again."

He didn't reply. He didn't ask her reason for delaying the demons' deaths. Did that mean he didn't care what those reasons were, or that he was afraid he might care too much and be dissuaded from his course?

"You at least owe us that, do you not?" she pressed.

"I owe my people more."

A fair point, she conceded. And one she wouldn't argue with, so she would leave him to it. Intending to rejoin the crowd, she moved around him and down the steps. "I doubt you will find your opening tonight, preacher. But if you do, take it. I will not interfere."

He caught her hand, palm to palm. She stopped, staring ahead into the crush of chatting, laughing humans. Her heart jumped against her ribs, pounding. If he hadn't guessed before, he must be certain of her identity now. She'd once told him that she'd known he was a chaplain on his ship, and revealed she'd taken vows of her own. No other Guardian knew him that well. Not even Irena, whom he had called a friend before he'd betrayed them.

His grip tightened. His fingers encompassed hers, seemed to draw her into the palm of his hand with that small movement. Rosalia looked back at him. His gaze delved beneath her skin, as if searching for something familiar. She wanted to offer it to him, to wear her own face. She wanted to tell him, *I have known you for so long. I have waited for so long.*

But there was no reason to make such a confession. Deacon didn't want to know her—and she didn't really know him anymore, either. Thanks to Belial's demons, he was no longer the man he'd been. He sought revenge and death. And she was done with waiting.

He glanced over her head. "Tell me who they are."

The demons. Of course. They were his only concern. They should have been her only concern, too. Unfortunately, she'd been cursed since birth with an overdeveloped sense of gratitude.

"Look to the center of the room," she told him. "The silver-haired woman wearing a floor-length red dress and a fortune in rubies. He is on her left. Very handsome, of course. Do you see him?"

Deacon nodded. "And the other?"

"Four meters behind me. He is the only one in his circle who does not hold a drink."

He blinked, the only indication of his surprise that she'd come to him with the demon so close. His gaze dropped to hers. "You live dangerously, sister."

No. She had never risked enough—and thanks to the nephilim, she'd lost it all anyway. She pulled her hand free. And since she had nothing to lose now, she reached up and tucked his collar into place. She doubted he noticed. "If you need as-sistance tonight—"

"I don't." His tone implied he'd already gotten everything he needed from her. He looked toward the demon. "So you can haul off."

Anger jabbed at her. She'd expected rejection and under-stood his need to go this alone, but she didn't deserve that rude dismissal. "Or, as you once told me, 'Get the fuck out of your face'?" When his startled gaze met hers, she smiled sweetly. "It will be my pleasure. Good luck to you, preacher."

To him, and to her. They were both going to need it.

CHAPTER 2

Deacon returned to his hotel not far ahead of the sun. At his door, he flipped the housekeeping sign to *Veuillez ne pas déranger*, and listened for sounds from inside before slipping through. An empty room greeted him. Above the headboard of the single bed, a framed photograph of the Eiffel Tower provided the room's best view. The flower-sprigged bedspread had been straightened; folded white towels were stacked in the tiny bathroom and the damp ones cleared from the floor. Judging by the wet ring on the sink, the maid hadn't replaced the tumbler he'd used after brushing his teeth, just rinsed it out, but he didn't care. He couldn't taste anything that came out of the glass, and if they didn't wash it for a year, he still wouldn't get sick off it. All that mattered was that they'd done the housekeeping after midnight, just as he'd requested. This wasn't the best hotel in Paris—far from it—but it suited his needs.

Not that he'd ever had too many needs. But he'd whittled them down to a cheap room with heavy drapes and a solid lock, blood, and a mirror. Facing himself every day meant that he'd never forget why he was still going.

It wasn't as bad as it had been, though. Six months ago, every time he'd walked into an empty hotel room the punch of grief and failure had almost leveled him, and after he'd regained his feet, was followed by unexpected jabs. But now he automatically hung up his jacket, instead of slinging it across the back of the chair before realizing that Petra wasn't there to cluck her tongue at him and iron out the wrinkles. The clothes he laid on the bed before showering were always the same as when he finished, not replaced with ones that Eva liked better. He never expected the odor of turpentine and oils from Eva's studio to fill the rooms anymore, only the scents of strangers. The noise of the television was never punctuated by their laughter, but came through the walls or from another floor, accompanied by the sounds of people he didn't know, eating and fucking and living.

Eating and fucking and living. Deacon was still doing all of that, too. But he wasn't doing enough killing.

He laid his swords on the top shelf of the closet. This time, he'd left the gun in the room's lockbox. When he'd had bullets coated in hellhound venom, which could slow a demon, the weapon had been useful. But he'd used two bullets slaying a demon in Madrid, and the rest in London. That one had been close. By the time he'd managed to kill it, he'd bled almost as much as the demon. He'd relied on those bullets too much. He wouldn't make the same mistake with Theriault.

Getting to the demon might be harder than he'd anticipated, though. Deacon had been hoping to get his chance on the sixty miles between the chateau and Paris, but the Guardian had been right. Those other two demons had remained with Theriault until he'd reached his residence on the Champs-Élysées—the best Paris had to offer. There, his protection had left him, but Deacon couldn't take advantage of their absence. The fucker had a human wife. Considering she was pregnant and the baby couldn't be a demon's, maybe she wouldn't care too much when Deacon killed him. But he wasn't bastard enough to kill Theriault in their home where his wife might stumble across them. A few more nights of watching, and maybe he'd find his opening. Trying tonight would have been suicide. And although this journey Deacon was on couldn't end any other way but with him dead, he'd like to take out a few more demons first.

She'd been right about that, too.

He stripped off. His shirt and pants went next to the weapons. No reason to have any of them near his bed. If a demon or human came in, he couldn't defend himself. A bomb could go off during the day and he wouldn't know it. A Guardian could teleport in . . . or slide through the shadows.

He crossed the room toward the window, knowing he should hit the bed instead. Sunrise was almost here, and he'd drop where he stood when the sun came up. He pushed back the drapes. Not much to see. Scooters and chained bicycles lined the cobblestone alley. A few potted flowers folded in on themselves against the night. Deacon studied the shadows. Hell, he'd been watching the shadows all night, expecting her to step out of them.

Rosalia.

When she'd spoken to him on the stairs, he hadn't immediately known it was her. Sure hadn't looked like her. His memory held a vision of long dark hair and crimson lips against pale skin. A fairy-tale princess, locked away by the nosferatu—but she'd been wakened by betrayal rather than a kiss, when Deacon had followed Caym's orders and guided the others down into those catacombs. But at the chateau, she'd been rail-thin, tanned, and blond, like half the models working the floor. She'd walked like one, too, all knees and shoulders. No lush roll of her hips. And whenever he'd seen her, she'd worn a wide-eyed, vacant look in her blue eyes, instead of a warm, soft brown.

But when she'd looked at him, she'd seen right through him. So deep there wasn't anything she didn't lay bare. As if she knew him.

It was a stupid thought. How could she know him? But he'd

barely made it down the stairs before she'd been in his face, telling him exactly why he was there and what he'd planned. And hitting the nail right on the head.

She wasn't out there now. None of the shadows was deep enough; he could see through them. But when they were impenetrable . . . that would be Rosalia.

He curled his fist against the glass, wishing he could smash through it. Why the hell was he looking for her? She was the last person he wanted to run into again. She made him hunger. Made him think about a time when taking blood wasn't just feeding. When it had been a part of something that mattered. But it never would be again. Not for him.

Goddamn her. He'd rather it had been *anyone* but Rosalia. She'd seen him at his lowest. A man couldn't get past that. Other Guardians and vampires might have heard what Caym and the other demon had done, but they hadn't *seen*. But Rosalia had been hiding in her shadows, watching as Belial's lieutenant left him for dead. Deacon had been glad she'd hung back and hadn't saved him. Glad of it. Then for some godforsaken reason, she'd taken him away from Prague and tried to help him. He was beyond that. She should have found someone more deserving.

But tonight she'd stuck her nose in it again. Helping him, when he could barely look at her square on. He hated being near her. He didn't need a mirror when she was around. He couldn't escape his failure or his guilt when she looked at him. Yet he searched the shadows for her. The temptation, the hope, of a single glimpse had drawn him to the window instead of the bed.

Movement beyond his reflection froze Deacon in place. Someone had come into the room. The door hadn't opened—not a demon or vampire, then. So Rosalia had come after all? She wouldn't be staying. He'd run her out of here, the same way he'd run her off before. Uncivil bastards pissed her off. Lucky for him, being one came easy.

Deacon let the drape fall back into place, began to turn.

"Don't move."

He tensed. No. Not Rosalia. The voice was a strange rasping harmony, both male and female and holding too much at once: threat, warning, and terror.

But threats didn't work anymore. Deacon didn't have much to lose. He turned, but he wasn't stupid. He did it slowly.

She crouched in the corner, trembling. Pale as a vampire, but not one. Her clenched teeth formed an even line. No fangs. Tangled red hair framed a face with hollowed cheeks. Solid black filled her eyes where the whites and irises should have been. Deacon stared, unease crawling over his skin. He knew this woman. A detective. One who'd worked with the Guardians. He'd met her once, at a vampire club in San Francisco. She'd been human then. She wasn't anymore. He didn't know *what* she was.

"He wants to kill you," she said, then gasped. Her fingers dug into the wall, her nails gouging the plaster. Her heart beat a rapid pace against his ears. "I'm holding him back. But it's hard . . . when you move."

Someone wanted to kill him? Nothing new. But *she* was new . . . whatever she was. And whoever was inside her. "Who?"

"Michael."

The Guardians' leader? Deacon tried to take it in. No surprise that the man was out for his blood. His only surprise was that it had taken this long. But like *this*?

"He's controlling you?"

Anger flashed through her psychic scent, dark and deep. "Hell . . . no."

From what he could see, that response held more wish than fact. But she'd gotten her breathing down, slow and steady. "Why is he—"

"Shhh." It came out like the hiss of a snake. Or a demon.

Had Michael possessed this woman? Guardians couldn't do that, but Michael was something more: one of the grigori, the son of a human and a demon. But demons couldn't possess humans, either. The nephilim could—but they possessed the dead. The person inside didn't fight their control.

But even if Michael had possessed her somehow, *why*? That wasn't what Deacon knew of Michael, the man who valued human free will above everything, even life. Not even a man, but like a myth. He had power, strength. Michael wouldn't use this woman. Michael wouldn't *need* to use this woman. But apparently, he was, and she was fighting him.

Deacon felt the sun coming, like the clench of hot fingers on the back of his neck. Quietly, he said, "I'm moving to the bed."

She nodded. "Slow." Her voice sounded more like a woman's now. Less male in it, and not so full of threat.

But however stifled, the threat was still there. And he was going to sleep with this in his room. Either he'd wake up, or he wouldn't.

Deacon hoped to God he'd be waking up.

Paris never seemed content with what it had. Even at dawn, the city never allowed the sun its full glory. The day didn't start with the rising sun, but with the warm glow of stone buildings, a glint against glass, and the steady brightening of colors that had been muted by the night. By the time the sun ascended, Paris was already shining.

Rosalia watched the sun rise from her room, surrounded by the sounds of the hotel guests stirring. Gemma had crashed in her suite upstairs as soon as they'd arrived, but Rosalia didn't need to sleep. She'd chosen this room solely for its view of Theriault's apartments, and she'd been able to watch both the demon and the vampire who'd watched *him*. She'd stood on her balcony in her own form, wearing pink silk pajamas that wouldn't look out of place if she was noticed. The demon wouldn't have recognized her regardless, but to Deacon, she would've been as plain as day. Neither had bothered to glance her way. Deacon had left half an hour ago—he must not be staying too far away—but she'd forced herself not to follow him.

On the avenue below, tourists were already ambling down

the tree-lined walks toward the Place de Concordes, where Marie Antoinette had famously lost her head. Though Rosalia lived through those years and had heard news of the revolution, she hadn't witnessed it. She'd still been training in Caelum. When she'd returned to Earth, Napoleon had been in power, and the nation embroiled in war. Ninety years ago, she'd met Deacon near the end of another war, in a situation that would have been laughable if she hadn't been so stupid and careless.

In Brussels, while hunting a demon, she'd been accosted by humans in an alley. Focused on her target, she'd let her guard down, and two drunks grabbed her wrists and manhandled her into a corner. She hadn't been in danger. Unless they cleaved through her heart or chopped off her head, they couldn't have killed her, and Rosalia wouldn't have let them rape her. She couldn't have removed their hands from her wrists without breaking the Rules, but she didn't have to spread her legs. It had been a difficult position, however, one that would have forced her to reveal herself. And although she'd have happily shape-shifted to scare the drunken piss out of her attackers, she hadn't wanted to tip off the demon she'd been trailing.

But Deacon had walked by and seen that she was in trouble. He'd been James Buchanan Knox then, a Presbyterian reverend on shore leave. He hadn't even waited for a plea to help. He'd come quietly into the darkened alley, wearing his chaplain's collar. She could still hear the jeers of the men who'd equated that collar with softness and mercy. But Deacon hadn't been soft. He'd asked them once, had given them one opportunity to let her go, before he began swinging.

He'd easily taken them down, and she'd felt how tightly leashed he was. His anger burned hot, but once they were beaten, he'd stopped. Fascinated, she'd let him escort her to the building she'd told him was her home, and she watched over him after that, repaying the favor. Just making certain that he was all right until he made it back home.

But he hadn't returned to America. The war had taken its

toll on his faith, and after he'd been discharged he also left his vows behind. He'd taken up boxing and drinking, and pursued both with focus and determination. In fighting circles, they'd called him the Deacon. Maybe in the beginning, some had known who he'd been, but later, they said he'd earned the name because he demanded "a tithe in pain." She'd laughed the first time she'd heard that, but not the second or the third, when it became apparent that the only pain he hoped to extract was his own. How many bouts had she watched with her heart in her throat and her fingernails in her palms? He had fought *so* hard, yet always seemed disappointed when he won. As if he'd expected to hurt more. But he'd never managed not to care, which Rosalia thought he'd been aiming for. He'd never managed indifference, or cruelty. He never used women like he did the drink, never hurt anyone who wasn't looking for pain, too. He just didn't have people around him to care about. So Rosalia had sent Camille, and gave him new people.

She glanced at the phone. Camille. She should have contacted the vampire. Too late, now that the sun had risen. Camille would be in her daysleep. Courtesy dictated that a visiting vampire alert the city's elders, especially if he didn't have a partner to feed from. A bloodsharer would be provided to reduce the risk of human discovery. Rosalia wondered if Deacon had bothered to alert Camille and her partner, Yves.

Asking Camille would be particularly hard for him. Not because they'd parted sixty years ago as enemies, but because they'd remained friends. And because Deacon had trouble asking for help from anyone.

Maybe if he had, this would all have turned out differently. No betrayal. His community still alive. And with Lorenzo dead, maybe Rosalia could have come forward and told him how she'd met him so many years ago. Told him why she'd sent Camille.

And maybe it wouldn't have made any difference at all.

A sigh moved through her. Rosalia turned toward her desk, where her computer waited. It was time to find out what Deacon had been doing the past six months.

❧

He had been busy.

Not right away. There had been nothing the first month after Deacon had left Rome. Then he'd spent three months liquidating his assets. They'd amounted to a substantial sum, but he'd been using them carefully. He apparently intended to be doing this a long time.

She leaned back in her chair, pleased by what she'd found. The past two months showed a financial trail through Spain and London. A few demons' deaths she'd thought were a result of the infighting were probably Deacon's kills. Good for him. He'd known where to start—Legion Laboratories. Although not every executive in the company was a demon, careful observation would reveal who was. He'd only been in Paris a week and a half, though, so Theriault must have given himself away quickly. Arrogant and careless.

Her smile faded. So was she. She should have been spending this time trying to discover who Malkvial was.

She glanced at the clock. Only eight in the morning. After such a late night, Gemma would sleep in—until Vincente arrived, and then sleep in more, afterward. Heading up to the suite before noon risked hearing her son engaged in activities that Rosalia preferred to remain ignorant about.

Less than twenty minutes later, however, a scratch sounded at her door, and Rosalia opened it to find both Gemma and Vincente. Her heart immediately leapt into her throat. Vincente looked shell-shocked. His color was ashen beneath his tan.

"Are you all right?" She tucked her hands into her elbows to keep herself from running to him—and to prevent herself from brushing the dark curl that had fallen across his forehead. He'd stepped back too many times for her to try it now, when something might genuinely be wrong. "Is everything all right?"

"Everything is fine, Rosa." Gemma came into the room, pulling Vincente with her. Rosalia finally saw beneath his shock, encountered an emotion that might have been *thrilled*. But surely not. He was within ten feet of her; based on his behavior the past six months, she could expect brooding resentment, not excitement. "We had something to tell you, and wanted to do it together."

"Oh?" Rosalia doubted that. Gemma had wanted to, and Vincente had reluctantly agreed. Then the only reason she could possibly imagine struck her. *Scared. Thrilled.* Her gaze dropped to Gemma's flat stomach. Her hands clapped together. "Oh!"

Gemma sighed. "He said we wouldn't have to *tell* you, that you'd just sniff it out—"

Rosalia stopped that nonsense by flinging her arms around Gemma, laughing. She turned to Vincente. If he stepped back now, she would smack him—and Fall for it, if necessary. But he didn't move as she slid her arms around his waist. She held him tight. Though stiff, he hugged her back. Good. Stubborn boy, but he hadn't forgotten all of his manners.

She stepped back, placed her hands on his cheeks. Her eyes had filmed over. "Congratulations. You will be a wonderful father."

His guard dropped slightly, and his wry humor came out. "Considering who your father was, you would say that to anyone."

"But I would mean it when I say it to you." She laughed again at his expression, and flicked back that distracting curl. This would not last long. She would not push more than this. She faced Gemma again. "May I listen?"

"To the heartbeat?" Gemma's hand flew to her belly, her eyes rounding. "You can do that?"

"Yes." Years of athletic training had firmed Gemma's stomach into a washboard. Rosalia pressed her ear against it. She picked up the heartbeat almost immediately. Oh, sweet child. She tapped her fingers against Gemma's hip in the same rhythm. "It is like this."

"That's not too *fast*?"

She heard the panic in Gemma's voice, made her tone

soothing. "No. She is already strong." She listened for a few more beats, on the edge of crying. She hadn't been this happy in . . . She didn't know.

A long time.

"There's more," Gemma said when Rosalia rocked back on her heels.

Vincente said, "We're moving the wedding up. It'll be in three weeks."

Of course they would. Vincente's father had not married his mother or taken responsibility for him after her death. Vincente would never repeat the same.

"And will you be moving back into the abbey with Gemma and me?"

Immediately, Rosalia saw that she'd pushed too far. Vincente's face took on that brooding expression, a sullen look that might have affected her more if she'd not known it so well from when he'd been five, brought to the abbey by Father Wojcinski, who had been at the end of his considerably long and patient rope with the angry boy. And, ten years later, when Vincente had been denied the right to visit the movie theaters alone after dark. This expression was never permanent, though it had lasted longer than before.

But she remembered how it had been six months ago. She'd returned to the abbey and found it empty. Then Vincente and Gemma had arrived—and she'd seen, *felt* his relief and joy that she hadn't been dead as they'd thought. She held on to that.

When neither answered, she pushed again. Why not? She had nothing to lose. The line had already been crossed. "You don't plan to live at the abbey?"

The look that Gemma and Vincente exchanged told her that was still in dispute.

As if agitated, Vincente pushed his hand through his hair. "I don't think the home of a Guardian is the safest place to raise a child."

He had the grace to look uncomfortable as he said it. Gemma turned away, dropping his hand to stalk over to the balcony.

Rosalia crossed her arms. She would *not* shake sense into him. "It is strange, then, that in two centuries no child has ever been harmed in my home."

"No. But fourteen vampires were."

Gemma spun back around. *"Vin!"*

Rosalia held up her hand. She formed the sole rift between these two. She would not widen it. "Do whatever you feel is best. I hope I will not be completely excluded from your child's life, however."

Vincente's gaze flicked to Gemma, standing rigidly at the balcony doors. Rosalia read that glance and interpreted it all too easily. Hurt speared through her chest. Safety might be an issue, but it wasn't the abbey that worried him: It was *her*. If they lived with her, Rosalia would be too influential a figure in their child's life. Vincente would not be able to control everything she said or did, and she would fill the child's head with stories about the Guardians.

Vincente had heard them. So had Gemma and her brother, Pasquale. But only Pasquale had sacrificed himself to save another's life in an attempt to become a Guardian. The danger he'd saved that woman from hadn't been an otherworldly danger, however, but just a man—and so Michael hadn't been called to transform him. Rosalia still didn't know what angered Vincente more: that she'd inspired a young man to his death at twenty-two years of age, or that Michael hadn't come—even though Michael couldn't have *known* to come, and couldn't have transformed or healed Pasquale if he had.

Rosalia had grieved, too, and had blamed herself—she didn't regret the stories, but that she hadn't succeeded in protecting Pasquale. Her grief and sorrow hadn't been enough for Vincente, however. Ten years ago, before he'd left, he'd asked her, *Have you ever succeeded at anything, Mother?* He never spoke the words now, but she still saw them in his eyes from time to time.

She could have told Vincente that if her goal had been to protect him from emotional upheaval so well that he'd be incapable of coping when tragedy struck—to the extent that he had left his heart vulnerable to only one person in ten years—then yes, she had succeeded spectacularly.

Only Gemma's rigid posture stopped her from saying it now.

She shifted her clothes from the pajamas to her black pants and boots, instead. A heavy cloak formed over her dark shirt. "I am leaving you to celebrate, then. When I return, I'll find an opportunity to wire Theriault's apartments. If Michael has no information, perhaps we will learn more of Malkvial that way."

"Michael?" Gemma blinked. "You're going to Caelum?"

"No. I will be in San Francisco." Where the Guardians kept a base of operations that was connected to American law enforcement. Even if Michael wasn't at the Special Investigations warehouse, someone could find him for her. Rosalia hadn't been to Caelum since Pasquale had died; she wasn't ready to return now. She glanced at Vincente. "I do not know if this matters to you, but I *would* change the stories to include Michael's lie."

He hadn't been a man when he'd killed the dragon in the Second Battle, but a grigori, the son of a demon. Rosalia wouldn't tell the truth through *his* story, however—it would be the story of his sister, Anaria, who'd been the reason the nephilim had slaughtered so many vampires, including those Rosalia loved. Until six months ago, Rosalia hadn't even known about Michael's sister. Now her thoughts were filled with the woman who possessed such terrifying power and good intentions.

Supposedly, the path to Hell was paved with good intentions. Rosalia hoped to make that path an expressway for Anaria and every one of her cursed nephilim children.

Vincente shook his head. "Michael lied, yet you go to him now?"

"Yes." Michael was not perfect as she'd once painted him, yet he always came through when he was needed. But Michael couldn't do that if he didn't know she needed him. Rosalia smiled and flicked her hood up over her hair. "I have a little more faith in him than you do."

CHAPTER 3

Anaria

After the First Battle, Lucifer gained the throne in Hell, and as its ruler, the realm resonated deeply within him, strengthening his already considerable might. As the eons passed, he practiced his magic, using symbols and blood to increase his knowledge and power. He opened Gates to Earth and sent his demons into the world. He made portals to Chaos, where dragons with unharnessed magic reigned over a realm of stone and fire. From the creatures of both realms, Earth and Chaos, he took blood and bodies, and formed new life in Hell—the hellhounds, the basilisks, the nychiptera, and more—each terrifying and hungry. He named the act "creation" and said his powers equaled those Above, yet he was not satisfied. For although some of Lucifer's creatures feared him and a few were loyal to the throne, none worshipped him.

On Earth, however, humans had begun worshipping the

seraphim, despite having little reason to do so. The Rules protected humankind; they did not have to fear the angels, who in their weakness never made examples of men or demanded their obedience. Lucifer was not weak, and so he schemed to create a race superior to humans—a race that did not have to follow the Rules and that could bring humanity to their knees. A race that would obey and worship him, as was his due. To that end, he carved symbols into the flesh of his chosen demons—including his most powerful and loyal lieutenant, Belial—and bade them to drink the blood and eat from the heart of a dragon. The spell transformed the demons; they left Hell and mated with humans. Five sets of twins were conceived, and in each set a child of light and a child of darkness were born. They were the grigori, and they possessed strength and power, just as Lucifer had planned.

But Lucifer had not anticipated that the demons' transformations went deeper than the physical, and that they might love their human mates and their children. The seraphim befriended and loved the children, as well, and so the grigori were raised as a family—not in hatred and fear, but with understanding and kindness.

Of the grigori, Belial's daughter, Anaria, was the most understanding, the most kind. Her goodness shone through to her soul as easily as the sun through glass. Though her dark brother, Michael, possessed greater physical strength and spirit, it was Anaria they each tried to emulate, and to whom they looked as a guide. She was their heart.

Her heart she gave to another grigori—Zakril, one of the light twins and brother to Khavi. They married, and their lives were filled with a happiness that was marred only by the gradual change in their parents. Though the demons' physical forms became more angelic than human or demonic, the corruption in their hearts once again resembled a demon's.

And so when Lucifer brought his dragon from Chaos to

*Earth and the Second Battle began, their parents joined
the demon prince. The grigori, led by Michael and inspired by Anaria, stood with the angels and mankind, instead. Three grigori fell before the dragon and Lucifer's
demons, and much of the world burned. When Michael
was killed while slaying the dragon, Anaria held him and
wept—and when he returned to life, transformed by the
seraphim and made a Guardian, her tears were of joy.*

*Each of the grigori eventually made the necessary
sacrifice to become a Guardian, and for hundreds of
years, they lived in Caelum, training new members of the
Guardian corps, and defending the Earth from demons
and nosferatu.*

*Their lives were full. They had both purpose and fam-
ily. Anaria lacked only one joy, but it became a steadily
growing blight to her happiness: She could not bear
children.*

*For more than a thousand years, she and Zakril tried
to conceive. They Fell; they became Guardians again.
Zakril eventually accepted that they could not have children, and found his joy in what they had.*

Anaria could not, and she would not give up.

*In secret, she went to Lucifer, and they struck a bar-
gain: If he taught her how to create children, they would
serve Hell's throne. Though Lucifer hated to share his
knowledge, he could not resist the temptation of com-
manding the children of a grigori, and so Anaria learned
of the symbols and how to work their magic.*

*They were not immediately successful, however. Anar-
ia's body would not conceive. Finally, they bargained
with the human women suffering in the Pit—women who
were not truly flesh, but spirit that manifested as flesh in
Hell. In exchange for a quick burn and their souls' release
from Hell, they were impregnated with Zakril and Anaria's seed. Hundreds of nephilim were born full-grown
and stronger than most demons—but Anaria was disappointed, for her children could not physically leave the*

realm. Like the women who bore them, the nephilim were only spirit that manifested as flesh in Hell. They could travel to Earth only by possessing a human spirit as it entered Hell and by inhabiting that human's body; on Earth, they could shape-shift into their own form temporarily, but a prolonged transformation risked the host body rejecting the nephil's control. And as long as anyone who had to follow the Rules sat upon the throne, the nephilim also had to follow the Rules.

Lucifer was not disappointed, however. The nephilim became useful to him; when demons on Earth broke the Rules, a nephil was called across the realms to slay them. And when demons within Hell, led by those who had been transformed with the dragon's blood, rebelled against Lucifer's reign, he sent the nephilim to kill them.

Upon learning that her children had been ordered to slay her father, Anaria intervened and led the nephilim against Lucifer. Though the nephilim's numbers were small, their strength devastated Lucifer's armies, until Belial's forces joined with Lucifer's. They defeated Anaria and her nephilim. As punishment, half the nephilim were slain, and the others were imprisoned with their mother.

When Anaria did not return to Caelum, the Guardians began searching for her. For years, they searched. They finally learned of her bargain with Lucifer and the children she had created, the war she had waged. Michael, Zakril, and Khavi journeyed to Hell and, with enormous effort, freed her from her prison. They did not free the nephilim.

Centuries passed. Anaria dreamed of releasing her children. She dreamed of liberating Hell from the tyranny of Lucifer's reign, and of freeing the tortured souls in the Pit. She dreamed that humans would no longer sin and always choose kindness and compassion over hatred and fear. She developed a plan that would fulfill all of her dreams.

As her first step, she led a group of Guardians who

shared the same dreams. Together, they slaughtered a human army.

Michael did not allow her to take any more steps. They'd broken the Rules, and so he forced her Guardian companions to Fall or Ascend. His sister was grigori, however—and even though he stripped Anaria of her Guardian status and Gifts, her strength and power far exceeded a demon's or nosferatu's, and she posed a terrible danger to humankind. When he ordered his sister's execution, his pain was as great as if he'd ripped out his own heart.

Zakril saved Anaria and hid her away, though he told Michael that the deed had been done. For centuries, Zakril, his sister Khavi, Anaria, and the Guardians loyal to her hid from Michael, until a demon who had called himself their friend betrayed them. Zakril was slain. Khavi was trapped in Hell, where Belial killed her husband, Aaron. And Anaria, who had been hidden away in a temple that only Zakril could enter, found the temple had become her prison.

She remained there for two and a half millennia. Imprisoned, just as her children were still imprisoned Below.

In Hell, Khavi, who bore the Gift of foresight, delivered to Belial a prophecy: Anaria would be freed. A dragon would rise from Chaos. Vampire blood would destroy the nephilim. And after the nephilim had been defeated, after Michael's heart was destroyed, Belial would ascend to the throne.

For two and a half thousand years, none of it came to pass. The names Anaria, Zakril, and Khavi were no longer spoken on Earth or Caelum. Guardians knew nothing of the grigori, the nephilim, or the prophecy. Michael continued leading them, never faltering. Civilizations crumbled, and men advanced in fits and spurts. Ancient cities fell to ruins and skyscrapers rose in their place. The Guardian corps carried on, though their numbers fell dangerously low.

With one wager, everything changed. Michael risked Caelum and bet the heart of a Guardian against the heart of a demon, and won. Lucifer was forced to close the Gates to Hell for five hundred years. Many demons remained on Earth, however, and the Rules still had to be enforced— and so Lucifer released the nephilim, who possessed the bodies of humans recently dead and bound for Hell.

Aware that vampire blood weakened them, the nephilim began massacring vampire communities. They freed their mother from her prison, and assisted her attack against the Guardians, where she collected a vampire's blood that allowed her access to the Chaos realm. From there, she hoped to gain entry into Hell, where she would resume her battle for Lucifer's throne. Her portal to Chaos unleashed a dragon that the Guardians fought and destroyed.

Now the Guardians wait for her next move.

Rosalia didn't want to wait. She wanted to strike before Anaria did, though she didn't know what form that strike would take, and she suspected that no one but Michael would be powerful enough to bring it about. She couldn't compose Anaria's ending yet.

The nephilim's end, however—Rosalia imagined that often. And although those scenarios took many forms, the result was always bloody.

How to do it, though? She had nothing but time to contemplate a solution as she flew west, her wings beating a steady course above the Atlantic. Methodically, she reviewed everything she knew about Anaria and her children, went over the grigori's story again and again, but she came up with few ideas.

The nephilim were too powerful. Anaria was too powerful. If the Guardians faced off against them, singly or together, Rosalia saw only disaster.

Halfway across the ocean, Rosalia caught up to the sun, slipped past another dawn and into the night. The moon had already set, deepening the darkness and making the shadows easier to gather. With her Gift, Rosalia congealed the darkness like glue. She wrapped it around her body and stretched the shadows, forcing them to carry her along. The wind roared in her ears; she thickened the shadows into a cocoon of silence. In the quiet, she raced through the dark, across a continent, faster than she could fly. Within ten minutes, she reached the bay east of San Francisco. Though in the early hours of the morning, the city shone brightly, busy with life.

She pulled out of the shadows and spread her wings. Cool air sifted through her white feathers. Not far from the shoreline, a dilapidated warehouse sat inside a large fenced lot—Special Investigations' headquarters.

The exterior of the building had surprised Rosalia the first time she'd seen it. After Deacon had led Irena to the catacombs and Irena had destroyed the nosferatu feeding from Rosalia, they'd brought her here. She'd woken up inside the warehouse, where everything was modern and new. She hadn't expected the disrepair on the outside, but she *should* have. It was the first lesson Michael taught each of them: Appearances were almost always deceiving. It didn't require full-blown cynicism, but a healthy dose of suspicion never hurt.

Or it ended up hurting *less*. Rosalia could've probably exercised her cynicism a little more often.

The warehouse door opened into an empty white corridor. At the end, a novice disguised as an older gentleman in a butler's uniform waited behind thick glass. With her Gift, Rosalia could have slipped into the building without using the entrance or bothering with security, but doing so felt rude. Though every Guardian was welcome at the warehouse, this facility and Special Investigations wasn't *hers*. She presented her identification, instead, and submitted to the retinal scans designed to verify the identity of shape-shifters. Once admitted, she passed into a hallway, walked past offices and conferences rooms. They were mostly quiet now, though a few Guardians and vampires sat at desks, typing on their computers and speaking various languages into their phones.

She reached the warehouse's hub, where corridors headed in four directions and stairs led to the second floor. From the passageway across the hub, the psychic hum of a Gate reverberated through her mind, warm and gentle. With a few steps, she could cross into Caelum, a city of marble shining beneath a never-setting sun. She turned left, instead, seeking either Jake or Selah, two Guardians with the ability to teleport. Rosalia's Gift could carry her through the dark, but she couldn't go to a specific person unless she already knew where they were.

She found Jake in the tech room. The young Guardian stood in front of one of the computers, his hands clasped behind his shaved head, staring at the machine like he wanted to shove his boot through the screen. The scent of fried circuitry hung in the air.

She'd heard he'd picked up another Gift after he'd been transformed a second time. Apparently he was still working through the kinks.

Jake glanced at Rosalia when she said his name, then did a double-take.

She wasn't surprised by his reaction. She hadn't been in contact with any other Guardian since taking Deacon from Prague to her home. She was, however, surprised that he managed to keep his eyes on her face. Whenever she'd seen him before, his gaze had always been glued to her chest.

God had been generous when He'd created her—and He was either kind to the men who looked at her, or cruel enough to test their character every time they did.

"Hello, Jake." She waved her hand, hoping to snap him out of the surprised expression that was rapidly turning into uncertainty. "Ciao. I know I have dropped in on you, but I need to speak with Michael. Will you take me to him?"

His eyes widened. His gaze hadn't dropped yet. Impressive. "Uh, yeah. But I don't know if I can—"

"Will you try? It's important."

"But, you can't— Shit. I need to tell you . . ." Doubt flooded his psychic scent. He ran his hands over his head, obviously flustered. "Hold on, okay?"

He vanished.

Rosalia smiled and closed her eyes. In the darkness, she listened. Upstairs, the novices chatted and played the card games that doubled as practice. Most of the rooms on the second floor were empty. Six months ago, she'd tried to seduce Deacon in one of those rooms, hoping he'd warm to her. It hadn't worked, and she'd left—disappointed, frustrated, angry. She'd thought he'd been beaten by another vampire, rejected by his women, and tossed out of the community he'd once led. She hadn't known his partners Eva and Petra had a demon's knife to their throats.

Now knowing the true circumstances, she respected that he hadn't accepted what she'd offered. Not that she'd been very good at seduction. She'd never included it in her repertoire of talents.

Perhaps she should have. She wasn't likely to get the chance again, and she'd have liked to know what it was to be with him, even once.

She also liked to console herself by imagining that he'd turn in a terrible performance. A suck and a thrust and a *haul off*.

Heartbeats and a rustle of clothing told Rosalia that Jake had returned—but not with Michael. Irena and Alejandro accompanied him, still unsteady on their feet from the teleportation. Rosalia lifted her brows at Jake. Maybe he'd thought she just needed assistance slaying a demon. Alejandro and Irena were undeniably perfect for that. But they weren't who she needed now.

Jake shifted his feet, looked both apologetic and uneasy, so she turned to Alejandro.

"Thank you for coming, but—"

"We aren't Michael," Irena said.

Rosalia glanced at the other woman. She didn't know Irena well—had avoided her, in fact. Though small and compact, Irena's loud laugh, brassy hair, and the serpent tattoos winding her arms drew attention, and Rosalia felt exposed just by proximity. She preferred to wait quietly and watch, unnoticed.

She could not do so next to a woman who wore leather long-stockings and a white fur mantle. Alejandro, however, was more like Rosalia, and the resemblance went deeper than their height and the darkness of their hair. Though Alejandro hadn't been raised by a demon, he'd been a noble during the Spanish Inquisition, and it had taught him subtlety and how to maneuver gracefully around his opponents—in both his speech and his use of the sword. He and Irena were two of the oldest, most respected Guardians, but Irena was right: They were not Michael.

Rosalia tried to frame a response that wouldn't be taken as an insult—then decided Irena probably wouldn't care. "No. You aren't."

Alejandro signaled for Jake to leave them. The young Guardian vanished again, and dread began to rise through Rosalia's heart. Despite her response, Alejandro hadn't asked him to find Michael. Why?

Irena said, "Michael is dead."

Michael was *dead*? Rosalia shook her head. She couldn't have heard that right. What could have killed him? "I do not— No. I don't understand. Where is he?"

Alejandro stepped forward. Rosalia wondered if he thought he'd have to catch her, but his hands remained at his sides. "We couldn't find you to tell you."

A question lay in that statement—*Where have you been?*— but Rosalia couldn't answer. The joy of that morning had turned into the heavy weight of despair. She had to know. "How?"

Irena's eyes flared a venomous green. "Anaria."

That seemed to be enough explanation for Irena. Rosalia looked at her helplessly, hoping for more.

Alejandro elaborated, "Anaria weakened the barrier between Hell and Chaos. If she took the throne, her nephilim would return to Earth and rule over mankind. And if Lucifer broke through to Chaos—"

"He'd bring another dragon," Rosalia whispered. Dragons, demons, hellhounds—the Lord knew what other terrors.

"Yes," Alejandro said. "Michael sacrificed himself to strengthen the barrier. He's in the frozen field now."

In Hell. Tortured, with the dragons eating his body in Chaos, his face frozen into the floor of the territory that surrounded Lucifer's throne. Oh, God.

Rosalia's knees wouldn't hold her. She staggered back. In a blur of movement, Alejandro raced forward and slid a chair behind her. She sat heavily, her elbows on her knees, trying to breathe despite the drowning weight that seemed to be filling her chest.

"We'll get him back," Irena said, and again, Rosalia was at a loss. Get him back? From *death*?

"How?" she repeated, feeling stupid. She didn't like asking questions unless she already knew the answers.

"Khavi."

Khavi, the one powerful grigori the Guardians had left on their side. But was she powerful enough—knowledgeable enough—to pull Michael out of the frozen field? Could it possibly be done?

Once again, Alejandro filled in what Irena had left unexplained. "As we speak, she is searching for a spell that will keep the barrier strong, and to return Michael's spirit to his body." He hesitated before adding, "It may take some time."

Rosalia's every thought seemed sluggish. She forced her mind to work. "She has the Gift of foresight. Has she *seen* his return?"

"Yes. But she does not yet know when or how it is done."

It was a relief, but not a significant one. In the meantime, one grigori and fifty Guardians stood against all of the demons, the nephilim, and the nosferatu. Only the Doyen, Michael, could transform more humans to Guardians. Unless Khavi could do that as well . . .

"Can she make more of us? Can we increase our numbers?"

"Khavi cannot." Irena's sigh seemed to soften her, and was filled with worry. "Michael bound himself to a new Guardian: Detective Taylor. You have met her."

Rosalia had a brief memory of a fragile woman with red hair. Tired, pale. "Yes."

"She can make new Guardians, but no humans are dying."

They were, but not in the manner that called for transformation: self-sacrifice while saving the life or soul of another from a vampire, demon, or nosferatu. With the Gates closed, there were fewer demons now, and Belial's demons weren't focused on tempting humans. Lucifer's demons concentrated on their individual ambitions rather than collecting souls to fuel Hell's throne. And they were all careful around humans, so that they didn't risk breaking the Rules—and calling a nephil, who would slay them.

She felt lost, again. This wasn't what she'd expected to hear when she'd come. Not at all.

Alejandro crouched beside her. "Has something happened, Rosalia? We have not heard from you since you took the vampire."

Although that was Alejandro's subtle way of asking about Deacon, he wasn't why she'd come. Belial's demons were.

Belatedly, she also realized why Jake had brought Irena and Alejandro to her. With Michael gone, Irena—the oldest Guardian and the fiercest warrior—must be leading them. And so Irena and Alejandro were who she needed to speak with after all. "I've come to discover if you know anything about Malkvial."

He nodded. "We have heard some."

"Do you know his human identity?"

"No. Do you?"

She shook her head. "Tell me what you know."

Alejandro rose to his feet again. "We've intercepted communications between other demons. They all play against each other for position, but Malkvial has taken a platform: He wants to slaughter the vampire communities and harvest the blood."

Rosalia couldn't hide her surprise. The prophecy stated that vampire blood would kill the nephilim, which in turn would put Belial on the throne. Unsure how that blood was supposed to be used, Belial's demons had been courting many vampire communities. But just to kill the vampires and store the blood for their use?

Oh, the demons would like that, wouldn't they? Killing instead of courting. Grimly, she asked, "Is there any news from the demon Sammael?"

One of Belial's demons was bound by a bargain to give the Guardians a daily ration of his blood. Living demon blood could feed a vampire without a partner, and so Special Investigations kept it on hand for emergencies. But the Guardians also received information through the demon.

"Aside from the blood, he gives nothing to us but lies." Irena's lips thinned before she said, "Are you returning to us? You have been outside the corps for a decade. We need you, Rosalia. There are not enough of us."

No, there weren't. And with Lorenzo dead, she had no excuse for limiting herself to Rome.

Rome was not where the nephilim were, anyway. "I have one task to finish before I can dedicate myself completely. But if I am needed, I will be available."

She stood and produced her card. Irena took the information, but didn't look at it before passing it to Alejandro.

"Rome?" he read.

"Yes."

Irena frowned at her. "What have you been doing? There are no vampires left there, and your brother is dead."

Rosalia might have been taken aback if the past few minutes hadn't taught her to expect Irena's bluntness. "But that was not all I did. I owed the Church—I have worked for them. For many years."

"Doing what?"

Irena's lips had curled into a sneer. Obviously, she was not a fan of the Church.

"Listening. But they do not concern themselves with kings and emperors so much, and so I do not exist to them anymore.

I never have officially, anyway. But now I do not exist even unofficially."

"You *spied* for them?" Alejandro asked. Rosalia thought he was amused, but wasn't certain. He was a difficult man to read.

"Yes. And trained vampires to do the same."

That surprised them. He and Irena exchanged a quick glance.

"Did Michael know?"

"Oh, yes. Of course. After all, I reported the Church's interests to him."

Irena threw her head back with that loud laugh. Alejandro didn't smile, but stroked his goatee in a gesture that was familiar from Rosalia's days as a novice, when he'd tutored her with swords. She'd thought of it then as his silent laugh; two hundred years had not changed that.

When Irena's laughter faded and she could hear herself speak again, Rosalia continued. "But now that I am back with you, I would like a territory to protect, if possible. I prefer Europe."

"That will work," Irena said. "But you'll have to take all of it."

Perfect. "I will."

Alejandro's gaze sharpened. "And your vampires?"

"They are gone."

"They were in Rome when the nephilim massacred them all?"

Hatred sat bitter on her tongue, her heart. "Yes."

"And Deacon?" Irena asked. Both Rosalia and Alejandro had danced around the vampire. Apparently Irena would not. "Is he still with you?"

"No. He is killing Belial's demons."

Approval flared in Irena's eyes. And realization. "And what task do you need to finish?"

"I'm going to help him." That was not all she intended to do, but she had no plan yet for the nephilim—and even if she had one, what good would it be without Michael? In the meantime, she would assist Deacon. She had her reasons for killing Belial's demons, too.

Alejandro began to shake his head. She cut off his protest.

"I will not reveal myself. I will give Belial's demons no reason to hurry and follow Malkvial, or to strike against us. Not when we are so . . ." She trailed off. *Weak* was not the right word.

"Weak?" Irena's smile had a dangerous edge.

"Not weak. Outnumbered."

"You split hairs," Irena said, but Rosalia didn't think it was an accusation. "You should know that I do not disagree with killing demons at any time."

Alejandro appeared amused again. "We have only held back because the risk was so great," he said. "If you think you can assist Deacon without turning Belial's demons on us, do."

Irena frowned. "Won't they turn on vampires?"

Alejandro gave the same answer that Rosalia would have. "They would never admit that a vampire could damage them. And if the suggestion was made that Malkvial wanted to slay vampires out of fear, the others might balk. It might delay his taking the lieutenant's position."

Rosalia nodded. "What of the nephilim?" she asked. "Has there been any sign of them?"

"No," Irena said. "Not since Michael was killed."

"Has Anaria given up?"

"She is probably regrouping. We killed half the nephilim's number in Chaos."

"Half?" Rosalia could not stop her smile. "Good. That is good." And on that note, she would take her leave. "I will return to Rome, then. And I will keep you abreast, should I learn anything new. Be well, Irena. Alejandro."

"Be safe," Irena said.

Rosalia gathered the shadows, letting them pull her into their dark cocoon. Safe, yes. *She* would be. But the vampires?

Her fear for them would not diminish. She felt so protective of vampires. And although Belial's demons and nephilim were enemies of each other, always it was the Guardians and vampires caught in the middle. The nephilim were focused on slaughtering vampires except when a demon broke the Rules. And now, instead of protecting the vampires in hope of fulfilling the prophecy, the demons would be killing them, too.

Demons. Nephilim. They all had to be stopped. But how would it be done without uniting the demons against the Guardians or the vampires, and without drawing Anaria's wrath? How to remain untouched?

How to stand by, watching and listening, as they destroyed one another?

Rosalia stopped. Darkness swirled around her. Her thoughts raced. Her body was still, though a storm of shadows raged outside and a maelstrom of possibility raged within. What would be the demons' downfall?

Their arrogance.

It was a lightning strike, illuminating the dark. Rosalia ripped apart the shadows, like tearing a veil away from her face. In the tech room, Irena stared at her, two curved knives in her hands. Alejandro stood slightly in front of Irena, his body angled protectively. Rosalia could not imagine what her shadows had looked like from outside, but it must have been terrifying for Alejandro to respond that way.

"I will need you to stay out of Europe," Rosalia said. "All of you. If there is something a Guardian must do, contact me. No Guardian can be near Deacon or me if we are to be safe— if all of us are to be safe. And if you discover who Malkvial is, I will need to know."

Irena vanished her knives. "Do you plan to have Deacon slay him?"

"Not just Malkvial." Rosalia smiled. Her heart shed the despair, was buoyed by hope. "We're going to kill them *all*."

CHAPTER 4

If the vampires following Deacon through the Paris streets were shooting for stealth, they'd missed by a mile. Fine by him. He'd make a meal of them if they came too close. Better than wasting half the night softening up a human woman with a bottle.

A bead of sweat itched from his hairline down over his temple. The sun had set an hour before, but the city still suffocated under its heat. Deacon wiped the sweat away, searching for a suitable bar. Hotels worked best. Businesswomen traveling alone made up a significant portion of his diet, and their bedrooms lay no farther away than an elevator ride.

Just imagining feeding from one seemed to make the air around Deacon heavier, weighing him down. Fuck. He didn't want to play that game tonight. He didn't want to get into another stranger's body—or her head. But without blood, he hadn't a chance in hell of beating Theriault. *If* the opportunity arose. Three days had passed since the gala at the chateau. In the previous two nights, the demon hadn't spent a single moment traveling or alone, and Deacon pissed away time and money while waiting for an opening.

And he spent far too much time watching the shadows. Wondering if Rosalia was still in the city. Planning how to get rid of her if she stuck her do-gooding nose in his face again.

Reminding himself that sucking her dry wasn't part of that plan.

The assholes tracking him were all but asking for it, though. He glanced back along the narrow street. No vampires in sight, but he knew they were near. They'd done a shit job of blocking their psychic scents. Even if Deacon's mind hadn't been stronger than theirs, he'd have felt their contempt. Their anticipation.

Looking for a fight, were they? He'd give them one—

Deacon stopped mid-turn. He'd curled his hands into fists. He forced them to open.

Fighting would call attention to him. It didn't matter if that attention came from demons, Guardians, or his own kind. Once he drew notice, he'd have to abandon the city, leaving Theriault for later. Teaching a few pissant vampires a lesson wasn't worth it. They'd obviously recognized him, but if he got off their radar, they'd move on.

A hotel sat at the end of the street. Constructed with a white stone block façade and large enough to employ several uniformed doormen, it housed a restaurant along with a bar. Deacon battled the temptation to wait near the entrance long enough to catch a look at the vampires' faces. Teeth clenched, he went inside.

He wasn't hiding. Just avoiding a conflict he couldn't afford to have. But god*damn* if it didn't grate on a man's pride.

Resentment rolled through him like a hot and fetid stone as the hostess seated him at a dimly lit corner table. It cooled as he ordered and methodically chewed his way through a richly fragrant meal that was all texture and no taste to his vampire tongue. By the time he sensed Camille and her partner, Yves, entering the hotel, the resentment had become an icy weight, a bitterness at the back of his throat.

A far cry from how he'd been feeling the last time he'd seen Camille. She and Yves had visited Prague, where they'd shared with Deacon everything they knew of the nephilim. Together, they'd made preparations to evacuate their communities if the demons targeted Paris or Prague. When had that been? Ten months ago? A year?

She hadn't changed. Her gaze searched the room for threats as soon as she entered, a habit she'd possessed for as long as he'd known her. Her dark hair still framed her pixie face, making her dark eyes seem huge and guileless.

But the hardness in her gaze was new.

Sixty years ago, they'd parted well, both recognizing that they were better friends than partners. Camille didn't like that she couldn't manage him, and Deacon didn't like being managed. Yves, however, was an easygoing sort. He had to be, the way he let Camille run him. Deacon had never figured out if Yves knew how quietly she could maneuver a man. Perhaps the vampire knew he was the appearance of leadership in Paris, and Camille was the reality of it.

But unlike the last time they'd met with Deacon, Camille and Yves weren't here as his friends. As the Paris elders, they were here to run him out.

Protecting the community came first. It always came first. And when protecting his people went really fucking wrong, friendship didn't matter so much anymore.

One side of Deacon's table stood flush against the wall; a corner lay behind him. When Yves sat across from Deacon and Camille to his left, their backs were exposed to the room. They wouldn't like that. And if it made them edgy and defensive, that suited Deacon just fine. He was heading that way himself.

He'd made a mess of everything else. Might as well start a big fucking mess here, too.

"I am not sure which surprises me more, Deacon," Camille said. "That we had to find out from one of our vampires that you were in Paris, or that when we find you, it is here."

Camille's gaze lingered a second too long on Deacon's

empty plate. When her eyes met his, the conclusion she'd drawn was clear: He'd hidden from them.

Like a coward.

Smiling took effort. Judging by the way Yves shifted his weight, as if reaching for a weapon, that smile hadn't looked friendly.

"In other words, after your boys lost me, they called Mommy and Daddy for help. Can't let the demon-loving bastard get away." They didn't confirm or deny it, but he knew that was how it'd gone down. "Untwist your panties, Camille. I'm just passing through."

"Passing through? But you've stopped." Yves looked Deacon over. "And food obviously isn't all you've been eating. No humans, Deacon. Not in our city."

Not anywhere. No community allowed vampires to drink from humans. "You've got a volunteer willing to feed me?"

"No. Not for you."

"No" would have been enough. But the "Not for you" made it crystal clear.

"We have enough trouble," Camille said. "Watching for the nephilim, demons pressuring us . . . We don't want the Guardians breathing down our necks, too, if they learn you're in our community."

Oh, now, wasn't that clever. Not enough to let him know he was damaged goods. Now he endangered the whole fucking community.

"The Guardians let me go." Deacon still didn't know why Irena had. In her place, he wouldn't have shown mercy. But maybe that was why she was a Guardian, and he was the bastard who'd betrayed her friendship. "They aren't going to come hunting for me."

Except for their leader, in the form of a possessed detective. But even if Michael came for him, the Guardians wouldn't make the community pay.

"You understand that we don't want to take that chance," Yves said as he stood.

Yeah. Deacon *did* understand that. He'd taken chances trying to protect his community, and they'd been slaughtered. Camille and Yves would learn from his mistakes, but they wouldn't tolerate Deacon being around to repeat them.

She rose to her feet. "And I'm sure that you understand that when we say, 'Good-bye, and good luck,' we truly mean it. Good luck to you, Deacon—and good-bye. If we see you in Paris again, it will be for the last time."

So it'd come to this? "You won't see me."

Camille nodded. For an instant, regret flickered through her psychic scent. But she wouldn't have been the woman she was—the community leader that he'd long admired—if she hadn't squashed it. As she left, he felt nothing from her at all.

Blocking, he hoped. Just as he blocked her from sensing the gaping hole in his chest—the hole that used to hold his community, Eva and Petra. It'd started to heal just a little bit, but Camille had ripped it open again.

Fuck them. Fuck *all* of them. Under the table, his fists clenched. He wanted to drive them through the wall. Or head outside, find the pissants, and pound this rotting fury into their bones.

He had only his goddamn self to blame, though. Himself, and too many demons.

Killing Theriault came first, but then he'd make good on his word. Camille wouldn't see him again.

Feeding from humans, though . . . There wasn't anything he could do about that.

A few women had looked him over since he'd entered the restaurant, but none dined alone. The bar, then. Though judging by the wary look the waiter gave him and how quickly he scuttled back with Deacon's check, maybe he ought to wait a while before approaching anyone. If one glance at his expression scared every woman away, it'd be another night wasted.

He moved into the lobby. The lighting was brighter here, but still mellow. A young couple stood at the reservation desk. Near the lobby doors, a man in a suit spoke impatiently into a cell phone. At the seating area to his left, a dark-haired woman waited, facing the entrance. The knee-length black dress she wore hugged luscious curves. Either she was meeting someone . . . or hoping to.

Deacon paused. As if she felt his attention, the woman turned. This time, she wore the face he remembered. Soft brown eyes met his. Lush red lips curved into a smile.

That welcoming curve was a sucker punch to his gut. Rosalia. Not in the shadows, where she belonged. Here, waiting.

Long enough to have heard Camille and Yves?

"Oh, *fuck* no."

His denial echoed. Heads turned.

Rosalia's smile faded. She stood. "Deacon, listen for one—"

"There's only one thing you could say that I'd be interested in listening to, sister." He strode toward her. She could probably hear his heart pounding. So the fuck what? She'd probably heard that *not a single goddamn vampire in Paris* would lower themselves to feed him, too. That the woman he'd lived with for twenty-five years and had been a friend for almost ninety had threatened to slay him if they met again. "But unless you've got a key to a room upstairs and a vein you want to open—"

He broke off when a plastic bag filled with blood appeared in her hand. An instant later, the bag disappeared.

Quietly, she said, "It's not from my vein, but it *is* living blood."

Demon blood. Not many vampires knew that blood drawn from a living demon would feed them as well as blood from a vein. Fewer vampires knew that one demon had made a bargain with the Guardians to provide them with a supply of his blood. A pint a day. That wasn't much.

So why would the Guardians offer it to him?

He only knew of one thing a vampire could do that a Guardian couldn't: kill a human.

This is what it'd come to? They thought he was so fucking low, a dog to lick up scraps and attack on command, to get his paws dirty so their wings could stay clean?

Already pissed, now he was working himself up into a hot rage. "In exchange for *what*?"

He asked, just to hear her say it. To see if she'd lower her gaze as she did.

She continued watching him, her eyes steady. "I need you to win over the European vampire communities."

Was this a joke? He almost laughed—until he thought of the scene she'd just overheard. That wouldn't just happen in Paris. He'd be treated the same way in every single community.

So it was a joke, yeah. *He* was the fucking joke. Not a dog to kill for the Guardians, but one to kick. And when they sent Rosalia to do it, they caught him right in the balls.

Fuck this.

He turned for the door. Her sigh followed him, but he didn't hear her footsteps. The suit on the phone got out of his way. Outside, the night was still hot. Humans crowded the walks. He went left, made it half a block.

"Preacher."

Every man since Lot knew better than to look back. But God help him, he did—and Rosalia was standing not two feet behind him, looking as sweet and sexy and as sad as she always did.

Sweet, sexy, sad. Each one a hook in his skin, pulling him in.

"The blood is yours, preacher, whether you help me or not."

Help her? For fuck's sake. Maybe he'd been quick to jump on thinking she'd ask him to kill someone, but the same two problems still existed. A) There was nothing a vampire could do that a Guardian couldn't, and B) Deacon didn't have any fucking interest in helping anyone, unless it was assisting a few demons on their journey back to Hell. By nature and by choice, he was useless to her. He turned to go again.

Her voice halted him before he'd gotten more than a step. "How many hours will you waste tonight searching for someone to feed from?"

Damn her. Why couldn't she be useless to *him*? Deacon turned back.

"Not that it will matter," she continued. She watched his

approach, and even though he pushed into her space, forcing her to tilt her face up, she didn't back away. "He and his wife have no plans to leave their apartment tonight."

Theriault? "How do you know?"

She smiled faintly, but didn't answer. The bag of blood appeared between her fingers instead.

He took it. God help him. She was so close that he didn't even have to reach out.

"I have a week's supply," she said. "All of it is yours."

"So give me all you've got now."

She shook her head. "I'll find you tomorrow."

"Don't."

"I will." Her eyes and smile didn't seem as soft. Not hard . . . but brittle. Fragile. "You do what you must, preacher. I intend to do the same. And so I *will* see you tomorrow."

She slipped past him. Not into the shadows as he expected, but walking along the street. Heading in the same direction he was. That fragile expression lingered in his mind. That wasn't the look of someone fucking around with him. That was someone at a breaking point.

What was she doing here? Why asking for help? She had Guardian friends who could offer more help than he could.

He glanced down at the blood in his hand, then back after her. So, she was a Guardian. She was also running a bit vulnerable and heading the same way he was. He could hang back, make sure she got where she was going. Then he'd go wait for Theriault again.

Hopefully tomorrow, he wouldn't still be around for her to find.

❧

Well. That had gone as badly as she'd expected. Worse, probably, thanks to Camille's and Yves's unexpected appearance.

He'd been angry when the vampires had forced him into the hotel. She'd waited then for his anger to pass. She should have known better than to approach him after Camille had ripped out a piece of him.

And it didn't help that as soon as she'd faced him, nervousness had taken hold. The enormity of what she had to accomplish struck her—and that she needed to convince *Deacon* to help her, of all people.

But she'd gotten the worst out of the way, and Deacon had been too wrapped up in his anger to notice how nervous she'd been. His rejection had been inevitable, so she'd lobbed at him the reason he'd be least likely to accept. She *did* need him to win over the communities, but he wouldn't think it was possible, and wouldn't want the distraction. Not when he was so focused on killing Belial's demons.

She'd give that to him, too. But she'd wait until he wasn't so primed to reject out of hand whatever she offered.

At least he'd taken the blood, though. It'd keep him strong. He wouldn't have to hunt. She hadn't mistaken his reluctance to find someone to feed from.

And she wouldn't have to know that he was with someone every night—or feed him herself, and risk revealing far too much. Psychic shields weren't much good with vampires when they fed, and if the vampires were nosferatu-born, shields were useless. They couldn't just read emotions, but thoughts.

Deacon wasn't nosferatu-born, but he *had* changed since drinking the nosferatu blood. His psychic senses were stronger. And even though Rosalia wondered what feeding him would feel like, she wasn't ready to let him into her head. He'd already spent far too much time circling around her heart.

Knowing that he was trailing behind her didn't help kick him out of there.

She didn't look back, afraid it might put him on the defensive again. Maybe his following her meant nothing, anyway. Theriault lived in this direction, too.

At her hotel, she went inside. Deacon didn't follow her, but when she reached her room and went out on the balcony, he wasn't watching Theriault's apartment. His gaze found her the moment she stepped outside. He still carried the bag of blood. Well, he'd have nowhere to put it, would he?

She should have considered that. He wouldn't suck on it while walking down the street. While he waited in the shadows, though . . .

Knowing he'd hear her, even from across the street, she said quietly, "Hold out your hand, preacher."

His brows pulled together, but he did as she'd asked. Dropping a small object out of her cache from that distance took concentration, but her aim was true. A drinking glass appeared in his palm.

His gaze found hers again. His brow arched.

"I've heard that fangs snag on the plastic." She caught the amusement that pulled at his mouth. With a smile, she turned for her balcony doors. "Let me know if you want ice."

He didn't ask for any, though the summer night must be uncomfortable for him. Tomorrow, she'd remind him that her room had air-conditioning. For now, though, she'd just work.

Gemma had returned with Vincente to Rome the day before, but they both still searched for Malkvial. Rosalia's equipment that recorded all of the conversations in Theriault's home and over his phones had yielded their first small break: Malkvial had been in London the week previous. It wasn't much to go on, but Gemma had already come up with several possibilities within Legion's roster who'd traveled to England for business, and e-mailed them to Rosalia.

Clayton Conley. Nicholas St. Croix. Karl Geier.

She passed over Geier. Short, slightly overweight, and with thinning blond hair, he kept a modest home in Munich and hadn't been promoted in more than ten years. Demons tended to adhere to a more striking and affluent template. With chiseled features and icy blue eyes, St. Croix certainly fit, and he possessed personal financial holdings that rivaled any tycoon's—yet he'd been employed by Legion for the past three years as a financial consultant. He certainly didn't need the money, but loyalty to Belial might have driven him to take a place at Legion.

But she wanted to look at Conley first. After Deacon had slain Caym, Conley had taken over Caym's position in

Prague. Putting another demon in the same position would be the height of arrogance—or stupidity. Rosalia wondered which had won out. If Theriault had been leading them, she'd have wagered that Conley was a demon. But if Malkvial was calling the shots . . . She didn't know. She doubted, however, that he would be *that* arrogant or stupid.

But there was only one way to make certain: Rosalia would have to personally observe Conley and St. Croix to determine if they were demons. That would take time. She couldn't use a psychic probe to test their shields, or they'd know a Guardian was there.

For as long as she walked this path, she couldn't use her psychic abilities. No moving too fast, never appearing too strong, and remembering to always breathe. Until everything was in place, she might as well be a human.

A human with a cache. She thought of the glass she'd given Deacon, the blood. As long as nobody saw her materialize items from thin air, it wouldn't give her away. Nor would changing her clothes. And if she kept her wings out of sight, those were still available to her, too. Unlike her Gift, a demon, vampire, or nephil wouldn't *feel* her use her cache and her wings—and she was already accustomed to keeping humans from witnessing any of those abilities.

Not using her Gift would be the most difficult. She was too accustomed to hiding in the shadows. Now the only way to conceal herself was to stay out in the open.

The infrared monitors in Theriault's apartment showed that he lay in bed, pretending to sleep for the benefit of his wife. She listened to the recordings from when she'd been out of the room while working. So much of finding demons came from details in financial trails. Travel, with no evidence of tickets. Patterns of purchases that indicated no regular sleep pattern. No evidence that they bought groceries—a sometimes misleading indicator, especially if the demon often sat through business meals or lived with a human.

Some demons were careful about details and appearances.

She suspected Malkvial would be one of them. Belial's previous lieutenant had been.

About two hours before dawn, Theriault rose from bed, but only went as far as his study. Rosalia left her computer and returned to the balcony.

Deacon wasn't in sight.

She frowned, her gaze searching the shadows again. Each night previous, he'd waited outside until about thirty minutes before sunrise. Every night, as she felt his impatience grow, she'd expected him to draw the demon's attention, calling him out. But the vampire continued to wait for an opportunity to take the demon off guard. Surely he hadn't abandoned Theriault now?

The knock at her door shot through her. She stared at it, but could only imagine one person who might be on the other side. Deacon?

She couldn't use a mental probe to find out; Theriault might sense it. Pushing her fingers through her hair, straightening her dress, she made herself walk slowly to the door.

By the time she opened it, her heart had settled down. Not for long. She wasn't accustomed to being so close to him. From a distance, he appeared strong. Tall and big. But now, here, she couldn't help but compare his size to her own, her body informing her impression of his. Tall*er*. Bigg*er*.

Without a word, he held the drinking glass out to her, and she took it—again, comparing. Not just a large hand, but larg*er*. So capable of holding more than hers did.

"Thank you." She opened the door wider, inviting him inside.

He began to shake his head, then stopped, as if something had caught his attention. Perhaps the monitors, she thought. Or he'd heard something from the audio surveillance. Green eyes narrowing, he came inside.

He hadn't always moved so quietly, she knew. Boxing had lightened his feet, and, like the muscle, he'd carried it after his transformation. Despite that quietness, she didn't know whether the surveillance equipment or the vampire looked

more out of place among the blue-silk sofas, the delicate furniture, and the unused bed piled with white lace pillows. He
wasn't exactly a bull in a china shop, but the surroundings
were so feminine, he overwhelmed them, made everything
seem off balance.

Or maybe he just overwhelmed *her*.

At the balcony doors, the filmy white curtains stirred from
a breeze. She closed the doors while Deacon examined the
equipment. Theriault probably wasn't listening, but at this
time of night when few humans were awake, the people who
were up seemed louder by comparison. She wouldn't make it
easy for the demon to hear them.

Deacon looked over when the latch closed. Studying her,
perhaps trying to puzzle her out. Finally, he nodded toward
the door. "A radio would help with that."

Relief rushed through her. Yes, a radio would create background noise—and Deacon's suggestion meant that he intended to have a conversation.

Progress.

Her computer had music. She turned it on low. High volume could completely cover their conversation, but it might
draw attention, too.

"This is one hell of a setup."

She glanced over her shoulder. He'd come to stand next
to her. When she straightened, he leaned over the keyboard
and tabbed through the computer screens. He paused on the
infrared.

"From across the street?"

"Yes." She crossed her arms, tucking her fingers into her
elbows. She told herself that she should be looking at the
screen, too, but his black trousers fit him well. *Very* well.

"You don't need this kind of surveillance to kill him."

"No."

"Why bother, then?"

How many reasons did he want? She offered the simplest
one. "I'm trying to find another demon through him."

He straightened, and she felt how close he was again, how

much bigger and taller. And if she'd been uncertain about how she'd decided to proceed before, it vanished when he said, "So you aren't planning to kill him, but are looking for information. I'm not going to help you with that, sister. And if I get the chance, I'll slay him, even if it means you don't get what you need."

She hadn't said anything about help since he'd come in. So her request had been on his mind.

"I don't need you for information," she said. "I need you to kill Belial's demons."

The look Deacon gave her said she was a lunatic. "What do you think I'm doing?"

"Kill *different* demons. For now."

"Why would I do that?"

She sighed. He'd taken the tone of a man who asked just because he wanted to hear the answer, not because there was any possibility that he might change his mind. "Because if *I* do it, they will have a reason to unite under a new lieutenant and move against the Guardians."

"That's not my problem, sister."

"Then what of this one? The one who will lead them plans to destroy vampire communities and harvest their blood rather than protect them from the nephilim."

"*My* community is already dead. The others can do a better job of protecting theirs." But that one had gotten to him. He shook his head, turned away from her, and just as quickly turned back. "So that's who you're looking for." He gestured at the infrared. "The one who will lead them."

"Yes."

"And you'll slay him?"

"Eventually. Yes."

"But you want me to kill others before that."

"Yes. And when the pieces are in place, we will kill them all."

"All?" He stared at her. "How?"

She almost sighed again. He asked, but only to humor her. Or to humor himself.

"Trap them inside my Gift and blow them up."

Probably. She hadn't worked that through yet. Only the slaughter that came before—only the part where Belial's demons slaughtered the nephilim. How to destroy the demons that remained, however? Without Michael, she didn't know yet how she would slay so many at once—but she wouldn't risk the other Guardians. And if all went well, Deacon would be far away, too.

Rosalia didn't think she would be. She didn't see *how* she could be, and still be certain that no demons escaped. And without Michael, she simply didn't see any other way. But she hoped to God she found one.

"Don't do that," he said roughly.

Startled, she looked up at him. "What?"

"That sad little . . ." He broke off. Looked away. "I don't know what you've got planned, sister, but leave me out of it. I'm not killing demons for *you*."

No. On behalf of his community. "I'm not asking you to do it for me. But how many will you slay before one kills you? Ten? Fifteen? With me, you can see them all die."

He shook his head. "That's not the same."

"You want them dead. Does it really matter if you do it with your sword or arrange it so that they all die at once?"

His fists clenched, as if he was feeling his weapons gripped within them. A deadly smile formed on his lips. "Yeah. It does."

"So it feels better." Crushing bones. Spilling blood. "That's not revenge. That's therapy."

Deacon, when he smiled for real, had a slow, sexy smile. Her breath caught. She could count on one hand the number of times she'd seen it in ninety years. This was the first time it'd ever been aimed at her.

"Sister, there isn't a shrink in this world who wouldn't say therapy is exactly what I need."

That was probably true. "But they wouldn't suggest a form that will end up killing you."

He wasn't bothered by that. His smile didn't fade. "No."

His gaze slipped down her form, then returned to her face, lingering on her mouth. "But the other type of therapy I've been getting hasn't helped."

With the women he'd been feeding from. She couldn't offer him any better. Her sexual skills were limited, and she couldn't judge herself with him. How would she react if he kissed her? She didn't know. She couldn't control her reactions with him as easily as she did around others. Already, her heart beat a little harder, just imagining.

But it was foolish, pointless. Even if she had experience, it wouldn't compare to what he'd had with Eva and Petra. He'd been with them for sixty years. Judging by everything that Rosalia had observed, they'd been bighearted, fun-loving women. Partners even before they'd met Deacon, they'd loved each other in a way that their affection for Deacon hadn't matched. But they'd all shared a deep friendship, and their love for one another was unmistakable, even to an outsider.

When Deacon had witnessed their deaths, it had ripped out a part of his heart. And she wondered if anyone had said they were sorry for his loss in the past six months. A pariah in the vampire community, no condolences were laid at his feet. Only blame.

"I haven't said before, but . . . I am sorry, Deacon. About your community—and your partners."

"Me, too." His shoulders fell. He glanced at the balcony doors, as if they could see through them to Theriault's apartment. Then anger seemed to slip into him again, straightening his back, hardening his face. "All right. Good luck with all this, sister."

He was leaving. Rosalia fought her disappointment. She hadn't expected differently, had she? But when he opened the door, he glanced back.

Hope spurred her on. The words tumbled out. "Deacon, I truly need your help. Please."

He looked at her for a long second. Then he left, closing the door behind him.

CHAPTER 5

The two vampires—one male, one female—lay facedown on the bed, their wrists chained together at the small of their backs. They'd both been sexually violated before their hearts had been cleaved through from behind.

Or perhaps the violation had been afterward. Taylor wasn't certain. Perhaps the physical trauma was telling her, but she didn't know enough about vampires and their rate of bruising, bleeding, and healing to make an educated guess. Not that those details mattered here—those were for the criminal investigation and the courts. And whoever had done this wouldn't face either.

Even knowing that, Taylor still took in the details as she walked through the room. These vampires had led the London community, one of the largest vampire communities in the world, and it showed. The enormous carved bed looked like a prop in a castle from an Elizabethan television drama. The sheets had a designer label. An antique lamp lay in shards on the floor—the only indication that they'd fought their assailant. If they'd had any defensive wounds, those had already healed. But in the end, they hadn't struggled; they'd turned their faces toward each other. To offer strength, to speak of love—Taylor didn't know. But it was the detail that got to her. The one that made her stomach clench with anger and hate, the one that made her want to hunt the motherfucker down and make him pay, to bring these people just a little bit of justice.

"So what do you think?"

Taylor glanced toward the bedroom entrance, where Mariko stood with her shoulder braced against the door frame, her thumbs hooked in the pockets of her low-slung jeans. Dark, solemn eyes watched her from under heavy bangs, and the sharply angled cut of her hair—short at her nape, shoulder-length in front—better suited a comic book convention than a crime scene. Taylor had only met Mariko twenty minutes ago in San Francisco, just before they'd teleported here, and she hadn't been able to shake the impression that a geeky sorority girl lived in that two-hundred-year-old Guardian body.

Two hundred years old. That was a hell of a lot more experience than Taylor had. "Why are you asking me?"

"You're the detective."

Once upon a time, Taylor had been. She didn't know what she was now.

But she looked around, gathered her impressions. "It all happened in here. They've got a ton of furniture and break-ables in the other rooms, but that lamp is the only thing out of place. They weren't chased through the house. They just . . . didn't have time to escape."

Two vampires, the strongest in the community. If another vampire had done this—or even if there had been several others—there would have been more indications of a fight. So someone much faster and stronger had probably done this. Not a nosferatu, though, because there was too much blood, and the bodies weren't torn apart.

Taylor had seen what nosferatu did to their victims. Inves-tigating those murders was how she'd first become tangled up in all this crazy Guardian and vampire shit. God, that felt like forever ago, but it'd only been a little over two years. And she was still feeling her way around.

She glanced at Mariko. "A demon?"

"Even the rapes?"

Demons didn't experience sexual arousal. They could fake it, though. "Rape isn't always about sex."

"Power, right? But that's the problem here—if he was going for pain, to show them he was in charge, he could have done worse. A *lot* worse. And if it was about power, he'd probably have done it in front of their community." Mariko paused, and her troubled gaze landed on the bed. "And I really hope you'll poke holes in what I just said."

Taylor couldn't. And an all-too-familiar darkness seemed to be pushing its way up the back of her head, just under her skull. Sometimes the darkness screamed. Now it was just there, watching and waiting—and when Taylor glanced at the vampires on the bed again, it became coldly, coldly angry.

Her stomach churned. Mariko looked at her, the corners of her mouth suddenly tense.

Taylor knew what she saw. The obsidian eyes.

Not trusting her voice—not trusting that it would be *her* voice—she gestured to the door. When Mariko nodded, Taylor fled through the house, out the front. She stopped on the porch, gulping the cool pre-dawn air. Sinking to the steps, she clutched her stomach, trying not to puke all over the sidewalk.

Get out of me. Get out of me.

He receded, but Taylor could still feel him. She could *always* feel him. And she hated that in six months, she'd become so accustomed to his presence that she only noticed when he pushed harder into her awareness, when he tried to take over. But always, he was there.

A weight in her hand made her look down. She'd called in a dagger. For an instant, she wanted to stab it into her thigh. Into her stomach. Let him drain out with her blood. If that didn't do it, she could cut him out.

She'd tried that before, though. It didn't work.

Vanishing the steel blade, she pushed her hands through her hair, tried to breathe steadily. Breathing was important. Michael never breathed unless he needed to talk. Too many times, she'd become aware of her breath and wondered how long it had been since she'd taken one. Aware of every little detail that said she was herself—that said the demon-spawned fucker hadn't taken her over.

And the brutal thing was, before he'd tethered himself to her from Hell, she'd actually started to like him. Not much. As a big, dark, and scary type, Michael had never been someone she'd felt comfortable around. But he had a protective vibe going on, and she'd appreciated that. In her family, with her partner, when she'd been on the job, they watched each other's backs. That was what she'd grown up with, a code that went down to her bones: You take care of your own people. Michael's people were everybody—and he watched *every-one's* back. That was something she could admire. And it didn't hurt that he was easy on the eyes, and that when she'd been dying, he'd kissed her and the whole fucking world had exploded with light.

But when she'd woken up again, he'd been a dark scream echoing around inside her. Sometimes he was quiet. But when he wasn't . . .

Feeling her gorge rise again, she stared out into the street, breathing deeply. A jogger ran by, ponytail bouncing. Farther down the block, a small car started up and pulled away from the curb. London woke up just like any other city, apparently. A man in a suit and carrying a briefcase poked at his phone as he walked toward the subway station.

No, not subway here. The underground, maybe, or the metro. Tube? Whatever the hell it was, she could feel the train clacking and rumbling beneath the street, could hear it shriek by, then squeal and brake. She'd been able to ignore most of the city's background noise, but that one drilled into her head every time. God.

She lifted her hand to rub at her temple, and paused when

she noticed the guy watching her from across the street and down the block a little way. A good-looking guy, tall and dark-haired, but since Michael hadn't come tearing up through her head, not someone to worry about.

Not really someone she wanted to say hello to, either. That weird little noise in her mind that she'd begun associating with her psychic senses told her the man was curious—maybe wondering whose house the obviously screwed-up redhead had stumbled out of, and would he catch anything if he passed by too close?—but there was coldness there, too. It took a real piece of work to look at a woman hugging herself on a door-step across the street and not feel an ounce of concern.

He turned away, and she thought about flipping the bird after him, then decided it wasn't worth the effort.

The underground train rumbled and squealed. She cupped her hands over her ears, sucked in a long breath, and caught a faint thread of scent—like hot metal, like dried blood.

Then *he* was in her, pushing apart pieces of her mind, overwhelming every thought. She gagged and tried to fight, had a flash of memory—*not hers, not hers*—of a pale hairless monster and long bloodied fangs. Nosferatu.

Kill.

No. She yanked at her hair, trying to yank him out of her brain. Pain pushed him back, as if he wondered where it'd come from and whom he needed to fight, but it wasn't enough. Shoving to her feet, she staggered her way back into the house, where the only scent was blood—fresh blood, vampire blood—and that cold, cold anger swept over her again.

Then he let go. Taylor braced her hands on her knees, her chest heaving. The vampires' murders pissed him off, but she thought there was something more to it—that he had realized something else was going on here. Probably the same reason why Mariko had wanted her to poke holes in the "It's not a demon" theory she'd been forming.

Something bad. Something that was going to kill more than just two people.

"Holy shit, Taylor. Are you okay?"

Taylor looked up. Mariko's brow furrowed, concern sharpening her voice. Taylor nodded, forced herself to straighten.

Mariko's gaze fell to her feet. "Where'd you lose your shoes?"

Oh, damn him. She didn't want to see, but she could already feel the cool hardwood beneath her soles. She looked down. Her pale, narrow feet were bare.

Just like Michael's always were.

Realization softened Mariko's face. "Oh. Damn. Why does he do that?"

I don't know, Taylor thought, and she didn't—but the words came out anyway, "Because even if you can't see or hear them coming, you can feel them."

Mariko tensed. "He thought something was coming?"

"Not coming. Just . . . somewhere."

"What was it?"

Nosferatu. But she didn't get a chance to say it.

On a dark wave, Michael came screaming to the surface and took her away.

❖

Had she thought persuading Deacon would be so easy?

Rosalia had known it wouldn't be. She didn't know why her failure bothered her so. She would convince him to help her, eventually. He'd already come further in one night than she'd expected him to.

And she didn't know why she took his rejection as a personal, emotional blow, when nothing like that existed between them. Yet Rosalia couldn't let it go. She'd spent the past few hours reviewing every word of their conversation in her hotel room, every nuance of his expression, wondering if she could have said anything differently—or if she'd said something better left unspoken. She replayed him closing that door over and over. And each time was a spike through the heart.

She shouldn't do this to herself. Unfortunately, she didn't have much else to do.

Clayton Conley had spent the morning exploring Prague with Nikki Waters, an American who'd moved with him when he'd transferred from Legion's New York offices. Shadowing the couple through the streets of Old Town hadn't been a hardship; Rosalia had always loved this city, the pastel buildings with their delicately ornamented façades; the smoky fragrance of grilled sausages that billowed from restaurant doors and lingered; the people at the sidewalk tables, whose conversations over beer or coffee often sounded both intense and lighthearted, all at once.

Not so Conley and his lover. As they sat for their lunch, Rosalia watched them from a café across the street and listened to their tense silence, broken now and again by her shrill complaints and his insulting replies.

Such had been the entire morning. Though Nikki's continual whining irritated Rosalia, she could dredge up some sympathy for the homesick woman. Her primary complaint cited how often Conley left her on her own in the unfamiliar city; Rosalia could have pointed out dozens of other foreign women on the same street who had been getting by on just a little backbone and initiative, but she understood the loneliness behind the woman's complaints.

Rosalia couldn't feel sympathetic toward Conley. Every word he chose cut like the edge of a poisonous blade. He belittled his lover for her ignorance, made fun of the people around them, and treated the waiter like a servant. When he told Nikki to pass on dessert or risk turning into a fat cow, Rosalia began to hope that he *was* a demon, simply so that she'd have the pleasure of watching him die later.

And his behavior *did* resemble a demon's. Unfortunately, many humans could be just as cruel.

So could vampires.

Only seven years before, she'd sat at a café table similar to this one, in the same city, listening to a young vampire beg Deacon to take him into his community and offer his protection. The vampire had been fleeing Rome after serving Lorenzo for only three of the twenty-five years required by the community contract, unable to withstand any more of her brother's mental cruelties.

Many other community leaders would have refused to protect the vampire from Lorenzo. Before Rosalia had returned from Caelum, her brother had slain community leaders who'd harbored runaways, fearing that leniency would be interpreted as weakness. She'd managed to thwart him since her return, but by that time, vampires throughout Europe had become so terrified of him that few dared try to escape, and fewer communities would harbor those who did.

Deacon had known that Lorenzo would come for him, yet he'd still given the young vampire his protection, confirming every belief she'd had in his goodness and his courage, even in the face of a powerful opponent.

In ninety years, he'd confirmed it many times, so often choosing the right path over the easy or the safe one. She just needed to convince him that her path was just as important, just as right.

Always easier said than done.

A woman passing by Rosalia suddenly dropped into the chair to her left. Taken by surprise, Rosalia called in her bladed fan beneath the table and turned. When she saw Mariko's familiar face framed by black hair cut into an angular fringe, she let out a breath.

"No Gifts," Rosalia said. "No psychic senses."

"I know. I'd heard you were hiding." Mariko looked Rosalia up and down, taking in her jeans, sandals, and red T-shirt. "Not in your usual way."

"No." Because she wasn't hiding. The exposure made her uncomfortable, but she wouldn't be recognized. She'd spent two hundred years wearing other skins, except for when she'd been with Guardians and her vampires in Rome.

Mariko pointed to Rosalia's plate, piled high with pastries. "Are those koláče?"

"Yes." Sampling food from carts and cafés throughout the morning had been the best part of shadowing Conley. Knowing her friend's dislike of anything that had once resembled a fruit, she said, "The ones at the bottom are filled with cheese."

Mariko dug in and snagged two. Quick to laugh, quick to fight, the Guardian had trained in Caelum during the last twenty years that Rosalia had been a novice. Rather than being killed by her brother, Mariko had become a Guardian by saving hers. When Rosalia returned to Earth with the intention of helping Lorenzo, Mariko had been Rosalia's staunchest supporter. By the time Mariko became a full-fledged Guardian, however, only her friendship with Rosalia prevented her from killing the vampire herself.

Rosalia wasn't sorry she hadn't given up on Lorenzo. And she was forever grateful that Mariko hadn't slipped in and killed her brother behind Rosalia's back, like hacking off a gangrenous limb. Mariko preferred to get the pain over quickly, to make clean breaks.

Rosalia admired that. She never managed to do it herself.

"How did you find me?"

"I called Gemma. Is that the one you're looking at?"

"Yes."

Knowing better than to say "demon" aloud, Mariko kept it simple. "Is he?"

"I don't think so. Look at her wrist."

She knew Mariko would immediately recognize the bruises in the shape of fingers on Nikki's wrist.

Mariko whistled through her teeth. "Bastard."

"And still alive," Rosalia pointed out.

Demons couldn't physically hurt humans. If they did and broke the Rules, a nephil would be called—teleporting to the demon's location—to slay him. A demon might fight back, but the nephilim were stronger, faster, than demons. Even most Guardians couldn't defeat a nephil alone.

Rosalia added, "But I'm not certain it was he who hurt her. So I wait."

"And if he did and is human? You're hiding, so you can't pull your 'I'm going to shape-shift into a scary bitch and frighten him straight' routine."

That routine never worked as well as it should, anyway. "Maybe something else."

"This is why we all need dogs," Mariko said, frowning. "We could sic them on the people we don't like."

"Hmm," was Rosalia's only response. She studied her friend. Mariko seemed edgy—making inane comments and picking at her pastry filling, but not yet taking a bite. Was she not doing her usual thing, either? Perhaps putting something off?

"Why would you call Gemma?"

Mariko took a deep breath. "The London community elders were slain last night and no one claimed their position," she said, then crammed the pastry into her mouth.

Oh, God. The slaughter of the vampire communities in every other city had been preceded by the deaths of the communities' leaders. Why the nephilim killed the elders first, no one knew—only that each massacre had those early deaths in common.

"How much time separated the others? How much time between the elders being killed and the entire city?" Rosalia had only heard the stories secondhand. She'd been beneath a church in Rome with a spike through her forehead when her brother had been killed—then a month later, her family. All slaughtered by the nephilim.

"The shortest was two weeks. The longest was three months."

"In Seattle, they stopped the slaughter." More than a year had passed since a Guardian had slain the nephil who'd killed the Seattle elders. That vampire community hadn't been targeted again.

"And we're going to try to stop it in London, too. I'm here to tell you that, although you wanted everyone to stay out of Europe, a few of us will be in London." Mariko held up her hand, though Rosalia hadn't been going to protest. She couldn't look for the nephil in London, find Malkvial, *and* bring the vampire communities together under Deacon. "We're talking about evacuation, but there isn't another community that wants to risk taking them in and moving the target to their cities. So we might bring them here to Prague."

Where many of the vampires' homes and gathering places still lay empty after Caym had slaughtered Deacon's community. Hopefully, it wouldn't come to that.

"So we have two weeks—maybe—until another city is slaughtered," Rosalia said.

Mariko nodded.

London had two hundred and seventy-three vampires in their community. Rosalia knew their names and faces, their stories. And if the Guardians—Rosalia's friends—were in London when the nephilim came, hoping to stop their attack . . . many would die.

Mariko read her face. "So whatever you have planned, Rosa—"

"I need to do it fast."

"Yes. And I'll help—"

"No."

"You don't have to take this on alone."

"I won't be."

Mariko snorted. "Because you'll be with *him*? Turn your back and he'll stab you—"

"Don't." Rosalia couldn't think that way about Deacon. If she didn't trust him, it was all over.

"You think he'll help you? Yes, he was forced to give up the info about us. Yes, he was used. But he didn't ask for help. He didn't think we *could* help him. Why do you think he'll believe you can do this?"

"I don't know." Rosalia heard the despair in her voice. She didn't know if Deacon would believe in her. And now he'd resist her even more, because with the nephilim threatening London, she'd have to force the issue. *Use* him. She couldn't wait for him to soften and agree to help her. And with one word from Deacon to a demon, to another vampire, her game would be up. "I want it done. All at once. And if it goes wrong, he already expects to die seeking his revenge. He's already on this route."

"What route are you on?" When Rosalia didn't answer,

Mariko clenched her teeth and looked away. "We're only supposed to sacrifice once."

"Tell that to Michael."

"He did that so you wouldn't have to, too."

"No." Rosalia shook her head. "He did that so we *all* wouldn't have to. And that's why you have to go."

"Dammit, Rosa—"

"I'm not dead yet. And I don't intend to be. But there's little I can control now, and the more people who are involved, the more variables, the less I can predict the outcome . . . and the harder it will be to make the decisions I might need to. But believe me, Mariko—sacrificing myself is never going to be my first decision."

She had a son. A grandchild on the way. If she had any choice at all, *never* would leaving them alone be her decision.

Mariko let out a heavy, frustrated breath. "And *him*? You can anticipate him?"

"Yes." An ache bloomed in her chest. "He's going to be very, very angry with me."

"But not *that* kind of angry," Mariko said, narrowing her eyes at Conley. Obviously thinking of those bruises again.

No, Deacon wouldn't be that kind of angry.

"Excuse me," Rosalia said, and rose from her chair.

With the sun lightly warming her face, she walked across the brick-paved street. The small table that Conley and Nikki shared had been cleared of their meal. He scribbled on a receipt; Nikki had lapsed into a sulking silence.

Rosalia stopped beside her, and brushed her fingers lightly over the other woman's wrist. "You don't have to stay."

Nikki yanked her hand back. "What the—"

"You deserve better than this," she said.

Conley's chair scraped as he shot to his feet. His hand clamped around Rosalia's upper arm.

A warm hand. Not hot. Not a demon's.

A vein throbbed in his temple. "Get the hell away from her, bitch."

When he shoved, Rosalia didn't move. She addressed

Nikki alone. "I cared for a man who would as soon spit on me as talk to me, and he never changed. No matter what I did, he never changed. What do you owe this man that you haven't paid for, over and over? You deserve better," she repeated.

Nikki's gaze dropped to her wrist, shutting her out. Conley stopped trying to push Rosalia, spinning around and shouting for the management.

Rosalia sighed and turned. Mariko shot her a thumbs-up, which changed to a flip of her middle finger when Conley yelled after her.

"I still say a dog would have been better," Mariko said when Rosalia reached her seat. "One bite, right to the balls."

"Conley is the type who'd kick a dog."

"So, better that he kicks us?"

"Yes. And better than kicking her."

"True." Mariko sighed, and they both watched Conley hurry the woman off, his anger radiating against Rosalia's psychic senses like heat. "She might take a few anyway."

Rosalia wasn't so sure. Nikki glanced back at her. When she looked up at Conley again, a new hardness had entered her eyes.

It wouldn't be that easy. It was never that easy. But at least it was something.

❧

Four hours later, Rosalia sat cross-legged on the bed in Deacon's hotel room, watching him sleep. Afternoon light formed a glow around the edges of the heavy curtains, but didn't penetrate. This was her element. The darkness. Where she was most powerful, most certain.

She did not feel so powerful or certain now.

Like all vampires in their daysleep, Deacon appeared dead. He didn't breathe, didn't move, and she could barely discern his heartbeat. But he *had* a heartbeat. And if she made one mistake, took one wrong step, she risked both their lives.

She should let him go. She should try to carry this out on her own. But even a hint of Guardian involvement would endanger them all—and endanger the vampires, when no Guardians were left to protect them.

Camille could bring the vampire communities together, but Malkvial would be suspicious if she approached him. He'd sniff out Rosalia's presence. But Deacon, who'd betrayed the Guardians? Approaching Malkvial would still be dangerous, but the possibility existed that he'd believe Deacon if the vampire proposed an alliance.

No one else fit. No one else was as strong as Deacon. And there was no one else whom she trusted so deeply.

Leaning forward, she studied his face. She wished he still wore long hair so that she could smooth it back, have an excuse to touch him. Instead, she rose from the bed and vanished all of his belongings into her cache. She retrieved the body bag she used to move vampires during the daytime, and had almost finished zipping him into it when she felt another presence in the room.

Calling in her crossbow, she whipped around.

Jesus, Mary, and Joseph. Rosalia barely recognized Taylor, the new Doyen. Dried blood stained the sleeve and front of her white shirt. Her dark trousers were wrinkled, her bare feet filthy. She stank of nosferatu and a sewer. Her red hair formed a wild tangle around her pale face—and Michael had linked himself to her in some way. Her eyes were fully obsidian, hard and gleaming, deeper than black.

She seemed to be struggling against something, though Rosalia couldn't see anything holding her.

"Are you all right?" Though concerned for the woman, Rosalia didn't lower her crossbow.

Taylor didn't answer right away. Her hands made small, jerky movements, opening and closing—reaching for something, or forcing herself not to.

Finally she spoke, her voice a strange, familiar harmony. Beneath the detective's voice, Rosalia heard Michael's melodic one. "You can . . . protect the vampire from me?"

Protect *Deacon*? Oh, God. Protect him from a new Guardian, yes. If Michael was in there, too, Rosalia wasn't so sure.

But there was no other answer to give. "Yes."

"Good." Taylor's chest heaved, as if she teetered on the verge of crying. "I don't mean to come here. But he brings me here."

"You've come before?"

She answered with a jerky nod. She still hadn't moved from her crouch by the door. Rosalia still hadn't lowered her crossbow.

"How many times?"

"Every day. For a week."

So often? Fear crackled through Rosalia's spine like ice doused with water. Thank God this woman seemed to have some control. "And Michael tells you to kill him?"

Taylor shook her head. "Not . . . words. Not thought."

For six months now, Michael had been tortured in that frozen field. Rosalia couldn't imagine the pain, the terror. But she could imagine how the surface of any human could be stripped away. How Michael's thoughts could be distilled to base reactions, base emotions. "Impulses?"

"Yes." Another chill ran through her when Taylor said, "His impulses are terrifying. Just, *Kill. Kill.* I can't separate his from mine. But I know this one . . . is not me." Those obsidian eyes glistened. "I don't want to kill him. It's not me."

Rosalia nodded. "I'll watch over him."

Taylor closed her eyes. "Thank you."

Quietly, Rosalia regarded the other woman. She'd jumped into the room without Rosalia sensing it. Was it even Taylor's Gift . . . or Michael's? "Can you teleport?"

"Yes. When I regain control. Then I'll get out of here—"

"Not without us." Rosalia turned and finished pulling the body bag's zipper up over Deacon's face. "There's another hotel room in another city waiting."

And there, Rosalia would face whatever Deacon had to dish out. God knew she was going to deserve it.

CHAPTER 6

If Hell existed on Earth, Deacon imagined it'd look like his dreams while he slept.

Every day for six months, they'd been the same. Lucid memories of the white-hot pain as Caym crushed his bones. The scent of his blood. The terror on Eva's and Petra's faces. And his grief and rage when Caym poured their ashes onto the floor. Over and over, until the sun set.

Waking was a release Deacon wasn't sure he deserved. He welcomed it, all the same—waking every night meant he had another opportunity to make the bastard demons pay.

But when he woke, this time he didn't immediately open his eyes and get on with it. His first shallow breath tasted cool and dry, as if the muggy Paris air had been run through a filter. The sheets smelled of lavender, not the harsh bleach of the bedding he'd fallen asleep on.

He'd been moved. And whoever had brought him to this new room had remained here, heart pounding. His psychic probe touched a familiar mind. Sweetness and sadness rolled up into one.

Rosalia. He should've fucking guessed.

He sat up. "Get out."

In a red dress, she sat on a love seat printed with fat pink roses, her legs curled under her, hair spilling over her shoulder. Her arms were crossed beneath her breasts, her fingers tucked into her elbows. Her eyes, those big goddamn brown eyes, looked for all the world like she'd expected that response from him. Like she'd been waiting to be kicked.

"Let me explain," she said.

How long would it take him to dress and get the hell out of here? He threw back the sheet. "You've got about five seconds, sister."

"The London elders are dead. In two weeks, perhaps a bit more, the rest of the community will be, too."

The nephilim. Shit.

But it had fuck-all to do with him. "Sounds like a problem for the Guardians. I'm not after the nephilim."

"I know. But to get to them, I have to go through Belial's demons. That's where you come in."

No, this was where he got *out*. He found his clothes tucked away in the bureau. Quaint little place. The kind of hotel where porcelain figures of children in lederhosen probably kicked their heels up on the reception desk.

He cleaned out the drawers, throwing his shit on the bed. Spying his weapons, jacket, and bag in the closet, he went for them. Rosalia came up off the sofa, shadowing him, still talking like she had something to say that might change his mind.

"I need to get to Malkvial before I get to the nephilim. But *I* can't do it without putting the Guardians in danger. And if the Guardians are in danger, then every vampire is, too."

"Guardians can't save us anyway."

"We wouldn't know, would we? You didn't ask for help and let us try to save your people."

So she'd stoop to hitting below the belt, would she? His jaw tight, he looked over at her, but she already appeared to be regretting it. But she wasn't giving up. Her lips pressed together before she tried again.

"We stopped the nephilim in Seattle," she pointed out.

"*A* nephil. *One.*" Deacon carried his swords and bag back to the bed. "Maybe if I'd known the Guardians had only stopped one of them, I wouldn't have assumed you could take care of yourselves against a few demons, too."

"You thought that when you made the deal with Caym?" She stopped beside him, her gaze searching his face. "You thought we'd just be facing a few demons?"

Damn his mouth. He hadn't meant to say anything at all about Caym. Fucking over the Guardians hadn't been Deacon's choice, but he also hadn't thought they'd be in real danger—especially not Irena. Hell, even the novices could handle themselves pretty well. He sure as fuck hadn't known Irena and the others would be facing a posse of nephilim instead of a few of Caym's friends.

And now Rosalia was probably thinking that maybe if he had known, he'd have done things differently. Screw that. When Caym had put a knife to Eva's throat, nothing else had mattered but trying to keep her, Petra, and the rest of his community alive.

Without answering her, he shoved his extra clothes into the bag, stripped off his shorts. She sucked in a breath. When he glanced up, he saw a faint blush stained her cheeks. Her gaze didn't lift to his.

"Got a good look, sister?"

She averted her eyes—and just in goddamn time, too. Knowing she looked was making him big, hard. Hunger stirred, a building ache in his fangs.

"You still have that demon blood for me?"

Deacon saw hope rise through her expression, a gentle lift at the corners of her eyes and her lips. She thought his asking for the blood meant that he was agreeing to her plan for tonight—whatever it was. Better to set that straight now.

"That's all I'm taking." He hauled on his jeans, reached for a shirt. "Then I'm heading out after Theriault."

"We're in Budapest."

He froze, the shirt bunched in his fist. One look at her face told him she was dead serious. She'd brought him to Hungary. "You'll take me back to Paris. Now."

"There's a demon here to kill. One of Belial's."

"I don't give a fu—"

"He goes by the name Benedek Farkas. He's made himself part of the vampire community, pretending to be one of you. Tomás hasn't caught on. Soon, Farkas will slay him and take over the community to strengthen Theriault's bid for leadership."

Goddammit. Deacon liked Tomás Lakatos. He led the vampires in Budapest well.

"It's a Guardian's job to protect him." Not Deacon's.

She offered a brittle smile. "And so a Guardian has brought *you* here."

Fuck. Now, that was a neat answer, wasn't it? He pulled on his shirt, then slipped into the harness that held his swords against his back. "How do you know this?"

"My surveillance on Theriault." Rosalia moved closer, and while he buttoned up the front of his shirt, she began straightening the material that bunched around the harness straps. "I know Farkas will be at Tomás's club with the rest of the community tonight. You won't have to wait outside his apartment. You won't have to hide from humans. You can just slay him."

He barely heard any of that. Just felt the warmth of her fingers through cotton. What the hell was this? She was smoothing out his wrinkles? *Touching* him, when he was pissed and hungry, and for six months had been wondering how she tasted.

Touching him was the surest way of finding herself shoved up against a wall, his fangs in her throat, and fucked until his knees gave out.

When she reached for his collar, he caught her wrists. Startled, her gaze met his.

"Don't," he said.

For an instant, her face became still, her eyes flat. Then she nodded and pulled her hands away, tucking them into her elbows and moving toward the corner of the room. Almost, Deacon thought, as if she was searching for somewhere to hide, which made him feel like the biggest asshole on Earth.

Which was exactly what he needed to be: a bastard, so that she'd leave him the hell alone.

He picked up his jacket and bag. "You're looking at the wrong guy, sister, but you'll find another easy enough. You're gorgeous, desperate, and lonely. Some sap out there will be panting to kill demons with you."

She looked over her shoulder, her brows arched. And she said just dryly enough that he couldn't help but like her for it, "Thanks."

He turned for the door before he ended up smiling or some shit. Christ.

"By the time you reach Paris, you'll have wasted the night," she said after him. "At least here, you'll accomplish something."

Another low fucking blow. Did she think he'd just take that? He dropped his bag and stalked toward her. To his gratification, she retreated until her back was up against the wall.

He slapped his palms to the wall on either side of her head and got in her face. "So the fuck what? What happens if I don't, sister? No skin off your nose."

The gentle brown of her eyes darkened, so goddamn sad. He hated that, wanted to make everything better for her. He hated wanting *that* more.

"Then people die," she said softly.

Jesus. Trapping him with people's lives—the same fucking thing that Caym had done to him.

Anger exploded inside him. He pulled back and slammed his hands against the wall again. Plaster cracked. She flinched, and it felt good. He didn't give two shits about her reasons for playing him. All that mattered was that she played like a demon, and he needed to make her pay.

He pushed in closer, until he could feel the warmth coming off her. Her perfume smelled like flowers. He wanted to breathe in that scent while he drank her down.

"Offer your neck," he commanded.

Her eyes widened. Her gaze flicked to his fangs before lifting to his again. "I have blood for you."

"But I want to get into your head. To know your reasons. And make sure you aren't fucking with me the same way Caym did."

"I'll *tell* you my reasons—"

"That's not good enough." He didn't care what they were anyway. He was just tired of being used.

Her heart began racing. He could hear desperation in every wild beat. "What about your bloodlust?"

His laugh was bitter. It wouldn't matter. The bloodlust wouldn't take over a vampire unless the women he drank from wanted him. And Rosalia was . . .

Breathing hard. Her moistened lips had parted, as if expecting a kiss. Her nipples formed hard bumps beneath red silk. A slight tremor shook her hands before they fisted at her sides.

She wanted him?

Ravaging need tore through his blood. Rosalia, soft and sweet—so perfect a man would be glad to beg at her feet—wanted *him*?

Yeah, right.

More likely, she just got off on fear. Or on playing off *his* fear of losing control. Deacon imagined the bloodlust taking him over and forcing him on her.

Like the nosferatu probably had.

His stomach seemed to crawl up into his throat. He could still picture how Irena had found Rosalia in the catacombs, her body crusted with her own dried blood, her skull gaping open where the spike had been shoved through it. Rosalia's brother and Belial's lieutenant had made a bargain, and as a result, the nosferatu got their claws on Rosalia. They'd fed on her for over a year.

And now she was trembling after he threatened to drink from her. Fuck.

He ripped away. "Give me the blood."

She held out a plastic bag. After being close to her, hungry, his cock felt like heated stone. Dark and rich, the demon blood soothed some of that hunger. Rosalia waited by the window while he drank, looking out into the night, her arms around herself again.

What was she holding in?

Why the hell did he care? "So the demon is at Tomás's club?"

Her smile came out on a relieved breath. She could save it. This was a onetime thing, and only because he liked Tomás.

"Yes," she said. "I'll go with you."

No need for that. Deacon had been there several times. He'd find his way. "I thought you didn't want anyone to know a Guardian was behind all of this."

"I'm going as a human. Vampires can't get beneath my psychic shields to see the difference."

"The demon can."

Her smile widened. "But he'll be dead."

He looked her over. That red dress skimmed her knees, and the sleeveless cut was relatively modest—except that it covered her incredible body. The fairy-tale princess with thick dark hair, perfect ripe tits, and lush crimson lips, which needed to be kissed. Any human man who looked at her would have but one thought in his head: getting Rosalia under him. Pampering her, taking care of her—but mostly just getting her in a bed with her legs wrapped around his hips and her nails digging into his back.

But if she walked into a vampire club, they'd treat her like a whore. Simply for showing up on his arm.

All right then.

She'd see what it meant to accompany a vampire that everyone considered a traitor. She wouldn't be a princess, then. And tomorrow, maybe she wouldn't be so eager to stick her nose in his life.

❧

Deacon had agreed to come, but Rosalia knew she hadn't won him over. She suspected he'd only capitulated because he thought that her plan would come back and kick her in the face.

Did he mean to reveal her as a Guardian to the vampires?

She squashed that uncertainty. No. Deacon was upset with her, but he wouldn't do anything that might endanger the other vampires if demons discovered that a Guardian had been a part of this.

But when he'd made his deal with Caym, Deacon had thought the Guardians could take care of themselves. That no matter what he did, the Guardians could handle it. He might assume she would handle herself now, too—even posing as a human. And although he might use the knowledge against her, she had to let him know she couldn't.

She waited until they crossed a street, still busy with evening traffic. Cooler than Paris, but still warm enough for short sleeves and sundresses, humans strolled along the sidewalks, looking into shop windows, stopping at cafés and restaurants.

"I can't protect myself."

Deacon threw a hard glance her way. They weren't going to pass as the most loving couple, were they? It didn't matter. The vampires would just assume he was using her as food.

"I'm supposed to be human." She wouldn't have to worry about breaking the Rules with vampires if she *was* forced to defend herself, but if she wanted to maintain the appearance of a human, she couldn't whip her crossbow out of her cache, either. In a club full of vampires hostile toward Deacon, Rosalia would be vulnerable.

"I'm here for the demon, sister. Not saving your ass." His voice was colder, harsher than usual, like the scrape of a blade over broken concrete. "And if you're *human*, that means you can't save my ass, either. So we're even."

She would, though. If it came to that, she'd drop her human mask and save him. She'd risk ruining everything. But she couldn't blame him for not doing the same. He didn't owe her anything.

Her chest tightened. "All right. That's fair. You don't have to help me. Just please don't expose me."

Deacon glanced at her again, but whatever he saw he didn't like. He swore under his breath and looked away.

＄

When he'd been an asshole at the chateau, Rosalia had hit back at him. Deacon kept expecting her to snap at him again. What had changed between now and then that she just took his shit?

Maybe she felt like crap for forcing this on him. She didn't strike him as the type to go against a Guardian's principles, and pushing a man—even a vampire—into something against his will. So if she was still pushing the issue, whatever she was planning must mean a lot to her.

Not that it mattered. Whatever her reasons, the fact remained that she was grabbing his strings and trying to play him.

The club lay a few streets off from any main thoroughfares. Surrounded by buildings more run-down than the tourist-friendly parts of the city, the façade appeared flat, gray, and industrial. Nothing interesting to see there, except when someone was looking for it.

Twenty years ago, after slaying the head of the community and stepping into his position, Tomás had taken care to give his people a place to run if threatened—by humans, by demons, even by Guardians. The back of the club hid a reinforced chamber that even a nephil would have difficulty breaking into.

It also offered the vampires a place to gather. Tonight, if they'd heard about London, many of the city's vampires would probably already be here.

As they neared the entrance, Rosalia's fingers slipped into the crook of his elbow. She looked up at him, and in her eyes

Deacon could see the expectation that he'd shrug her off, combined with her silent request for him not to.

All right. He'd play this her way. It didn't hurt him to walk in with a gorgeous woman on his arm.

He'd been right: The place was full. Even before they opened the doors, he could sense the number of vampires inside.

"They've heard about London," she said softly.

"Yeah." He could feel their panic and their helpless anger from here. They'd be looking for someone to take that out on. Deacon would be an obvious target, but Rosalia would be, too. This riled up, they might not just leer and give her a hard time. They might take it further. "So you wait here while I—"

A male vampire with long dark hair and lined eyes swung the door open and held it while another passed through. He glanced at Deacon, then looked again before stopping his friend in the entrance. The friend caught sight of Deacon. His lips drew back over his fangs.

No doubt they'd recognized him. So leaving Rosalia out here alone wasn't an option anymore.

"Just keep on walking, traitor." The first vampire's gaze ran over Rosalia. Snakelike, he slid his tongue between his fangs and licked his upper lip. "She can stay."

Any other time, that would have been enough for Deacon to take him down. But a demon waited inside, and Deacon didn't want to reveal the one advantage he had—his speed—while teaching this pissant a lesson. And if he started a fight out here, he might not make it into the club.

And these vampires might talk about fighting, but they wouldn't make a move against him without Tomás's permission. Gripping Rosalia's hand, Deacon pushed past them and through the door.

The two vampires followed, flanking them. Rosalia looked up at Deacon with a smile.

Wouldn't a human be showing a little more fear? But she was pretending that having him at her side filled her with confidence. Shit. Even knowing she was acting, that felt damn good.

Inside, the setup was more like a gentleman's club than the dance club preferred by a few other vampire communities. Amber pendant lights hung from a high ceiling, casting warm light on the paneled walls and wooden floors. Two billiard tables sat on the right side of the large, open room. Multiple groupings of velvet sofas and leather chairs encouraged pockets of conversation. The smaller tables ringing the floor held laptops or hosted several varieties of poker games.

One by one, the vampires quieted and turned to look at them.

From a table at the back of the room, Tomás frowned and rose to his feet, a big man with blond hair pulled back into a queue and a bushy yellow beard. Rosalia hadn't given Deacon a description of Benedek Farkas, but the demon wasn't hard to spot. Dark-haired and slick, he'd shape-shifted into a good-looking bastard, like they all did. Seated on a sofa in the middle of the club, he was the only one not giving Deacon the evil eye. He looked amused, even. And he was the only man who hadn't looked Rosalia over twice.

Maybe she had a good reason for wearing that dress and her current form, and it wasn't just so Deacon would be thinking of sucking her dry. She could walk through the club naked, and a demon wouldn't get hot. *Couldn't* get hot. A demon only faked it.

Farkas wasn't even bothering to do that.

Deacon led her to a small table on the left, a location that would offer him a direct line to Tomás, with Farkas in the middle. The click of her heels echoed in the silent room, and beneath it came the pounding of the vampires' hearts. Almost fifty, by his count. He heard the rustle of clothes as vampires got to their feet. Oh, yeah, they wanted to fight. He felt their psychic probes, aimed at him, aimed at Rosalia.

He got Rosalia into a seat. She smiled at him, a sweet curve of her lips that could have sent a man off to war with steel in his spine, not just heading out to slay one demon.

Deacon turned. Vampires, male and female, faced him with fangs exposed. Farkas just seemed to be smiling. Deacon looked over the demon's head at Tomás.

"This isn't much of a welcome, old friend."

"Just turn around, Deacon." Tall, with a chest to match, Tomás's deep voice carried easily across the club. "Take your human and get out."

Deacon lifted his hands in a conciliatory gesture. "I just want to talk bloodsharing until my woman can—"

"Get *out*."

Fuck. Tomás must be thinking that Deacon was here to kill him, was gunning for his position. So he probably wasn't going to invite Deacon over to his table, fearing that once Deacon got in close he'd try to take Tomás out.

All right. Deacon didn't need to be invited over there. He could do this another way.

One thing about vampire communities: no one interfered if a leader was challenged. Deacon reached back and drew his swords.

Tomás quickly retrieved his own weapons. The vampire kicked aside his table, giving himself room to fight—but as Deacon anticipated, Tomás stayed where he was. A reinforced steel wall lay at Tomás's back; he wouldn't give that protection up.

Deacon stalked closer, his gaze fixed on Tomás. His path took him behind Farkas's sofa.

The demon made it too easy, rising up in his seat so that he could watch the showdown. Obviously, he never once considered Deacon a threat. As Deacon passed him, Farkas turned his head to follow his progress, facing the opposite direction and leaving his neck exposed above the level of the sofa's back.

Deacon struck, fast and hard. His blade cut cleanly through the demon's neck. Shock ripped through the vampires' psychic scents, holding them silent.

Until Farkas's head fell over the back of the sofa, thudding to the floor. Blood spurted. The female sitting next to him shrieked, scrambling back.

With an enraged roar, Tomás charged. Deacon stepped back from the spreading pool of blood. He'd expected this attack. The vampire had remained near the wall when his own life was threatened, but Tomás wouldn't stand for anyone killing his people.

"Listen, Tom—!" Deacon's shout was cut short by the swing of Tomás's sword.

All right. Stop Tomás now. Explain later.

Deacon dodged Tomás's blade and led with a right hook to the vampire's bearded jaw. Blood and spit flew. Tomás staggered. A hammering blow to his chin laid him out. Not unconscious, just stunned. Shaking out the pain in his hand, Deacon placed his boot on the vampire's neck and held him down.

He looked back at Rosalia. Her fingers of her left hand were clenched on the table's edge, her knuckles white. Beneath the table, he saw the glint of steel clutched in her right hand. "Rosie, get over here."

She vanished her weapon and hurried forward, threading through vampires who bared their fangs at her passing. Several abruptly stopped, glancing at Deacon, as if they'd just realized that they might have a new community leader in about ten seconds.

They could rest easy there. Even if he'd killed Tomás, Deacon wouldn't have taken that on.

"Pick his head up," he said as Rosalia passed the demon's sofa.

Gingerly, she grabbed Farkas's severed head by the hair.

"Put it on the floor in front of Tomás's face." He waited until she did, then took her hand and drew her behind him. "Now breathe deep. And tell me what you smell."

He heard the vampire's inhalation and felt the uneasy realization in Tomás's psychic scent. Murmurs of "demon" hummed through the crowd. The others smelled it, too. The scent of Farkas's blood saturated the air.

"He was sent to kill you and to take over your community. I've got no plans to do the same. I'm done here."

Deacon eased his foot off and waited a second, just to make sure Tomás wouldn't leap up. Holding Rosalia's hand, he began backing toward the exit. The vampires moved out of their path.

Tomás rose to his knees and picked up the demon's head. Not much time had passed; Farkas's skin would still be hotter than a human's. As he pressed his thumbs against the demon's fangs, disbelief worked through Tomás's expression. Yeah, the vampire sure hadn't seen that one coming.

Deacon turned for the door. Rosalia slipped her hand into his elbow, and that soft grip felt a little too good for his liking. He shrugged her off.

Outside, the air surrounded him like a heated blanket. His shirt front and jacket sleeves were splattered with blood. He'd planned to ditch Rosalia the second they were done, but now he had to return to the hotel and clean off before going anywhere. No train or plane would take him back to Paris in this state.

He didn't realize how fast he was walking until he noticed Rosalia was running to keep up with him.

He slowed to a human's pace. Not for her sake. Drawing attention never boded well. People weren't blind or stupid.

Vampires weren't supposed to be blind and stupid, either.

It was one thing for a demon to impersonate a human. But although a demon could form fangs and look like a vampire, the fuckers had hot skin. And Farkas might have shared blood, but his bite wouldn't have felt anything like the pleasure of a vampire's. Did *no one* in that community notice that? And if Farkas had tried to explain it away, what idiot would believe him?

"How could Tomás not know? How could he not *see*?"

Rosalia didn't have to ask what he meant. Perhaps she'd been wondering the same, but she came up with a kinder answer than he would have.

"He didn't have the benefit of the friends that you did."

That was true enough. From the very first, Camille had warned him about demons and taught him about vampires.

She'd taught him about fighting in ways that didn't use his fists. Then Irena had taught him more.

Rosalia caught him off guard by adding, "Thank you, Deacon."

For what? The demon had made slaying him too easy to get much satisfaction out of it. "Yeah. Now you can show your thanks by buying me a ticket back to Paris."

His gruff response didn't put her off. She smiled up at him, instead. He couldn't figure out why she seemed to like him despite the shit he threw at her. It bothered him. Like she knew something he didn't, because he couldn't imagine why she wasn't slugging him into next week.

"No need to buy one." She glanced at his shirt, and he felt the sticky wet blood vanish into her cache. Nice trick. "I already have a flight scheduled."

Of course she did. A pair of big, white wings. "You?"

"Yes." She laughed and skipped ahead for a few steps before twirling around to face him. "And you should stay in my hotel room." Before he could say anything, she added, "You can watch Theriault, you can listen to the surveillance tapes, and it's air-conditioned."

He stopped. So she thought it would be that easy? Just fall in with her once, and he was her puppet? No chance.

"What the hell are you doing?"

Her smile wavered. "Failing miserably?"

"Yeah." He started walking again. "So haul off, sister. I'll find my own way back."

He didn't want to owe her a goddamn thing. Not that he would have anyway, since she'd forced him into a position where he *had* to find his way back.

He passed her still form. She'd wrapped her arms tight around herself again. A few moments later, she called after him, "What you did here matters, Deacon. It will make a difference to this community, to everyone."

Maybe so. He didn't care. How many ways could he tell her before she accepted that? He didn't know, and he didn't have much left.

And when he was down to nothing, he only had one response. "Fuck off, Rosie."

Damn him, though, if he didn't look back when he reached the end of the street. Yet she wasn't standing there looking forlorn, looking sad. The sidewalk lay empty. So she'd finally taken the hint and gone.

It didn't feel like he'd won.

CHAPTER 7

Rosalia hadn't witnessed the battle that had made Deacon the leader of the Prague community. She'd only heard the story later that night, coaxing it from a vampire who'd still been shivering in the corner of the club where the fight had been waged.

Much of the city still lay in rubble after the American bombing earlier that year. The war had devastated both human and vampire communities; Deacon and Camille—friendly, but already distant—had traveled from city to city, helping rebuild. Taking over a community of vampires hadn't been on his agenda, and he might have been surprised to find himself in that position. Once she'd heard *how* it had come about, however, Rosalia hadn't been surprised at all.

A vampire female had come to beg help from Marco, the community head. New to the city, her husband had been killed in the bombings, leaving her without a partner to feed from . . . and the infant that she and her husband had transformed twenty years before.

The vampire recounting the story had wept as he'd described the baby boy the female had brought with her: curly-haired, fanged, blue eyes shining with the intelligence of a young man. Rosalia had listened, sick to her heart.

The bloodlust created a powerful sexual drive, even in children—and the reality of feeding them was too horrifying for almost any vampire to contemplate. Every community had rules forbidding their transformation, but Rosalia still knew of a few children who'd been changed. Almost all had been sickly as humans, whose parents couldn't bear to lose them. And although their minds eventually matured, their forms never did—and anyone who desired that form could never be an admirable life partner. Rosalia had pitied both parents and children, and had done what she could to help them . . . but there wasn't much that could be done.

Marco hadn't agreed. Something *could* be done. And when she held the infant out to him, imploring him to help, his solution had been to strike the boy's head from his shoulders.

The woman had still been screaming when Deacon had challenged the older vampire. She'd screamed while their swords had clashed, as their blood fell slick on the floor, Deacon the weaker of the two but driven by fury. She'd been screaming when Deacon had stood over Marco, the vampire's heart in his hand.

Deacon could have chosen to leave the community to someone else. Camille had asked him to; when she finally led a city of vampires, she hadn't wanted that city to be Prague. But he'd chosen the community over her, and his decision had finalized the break between them—a decision that had ended up being better for the both of them.

But Rosalia didn't think he'd planned it that way. No, if she had learned anything about him in those years between the wars, it was that Deacon acted in the moment. Not thoughtlessly, and usually with full understanding of the consequences, he decisively handled each problem as it came his way. If his people were threatened, he'd faced the threat and neutralized it. And if his people—or any other vampire—

stepped over the community rules, he enforced them. But he didn't manipulate his people or maneuver them; he didn't sweeten them up or cajole them. Always straightforward, he told them how something should be, and then he backed up his words.

His approach was so different from Rosalia's. She spent so many hours planning ahead, examining her every move from several angles, trying to anticipate each outcome, and utilizing other people's strengths and weaknesses to achieve the result she wanted. When faced with an immediate threat, she acted quickly, but she preferred a more considered method.

Now she thought it was no surprise that Deacon both fascinated and frustrated her. He simply reacted, sometimes with hardness or anger, at other times with compassion and gentleness. And although Rosalia had suffered through upheavals in her life, her considered approach had helped her weather the bumps and keep everything around her under control. But Deacon's volatility didn't allow her that smooth ride, and she found herself reacting strongly in return.

She'd always been drawn to him. But she hadn't known that once she was close to him, the swing of her emotions would be so violent and wonderful and frightening. And she hadn't known that even when she could predict his reaction, she couldn't control her response to it.

Perhaps she should have seen it, but she'd always been better at anticipating other people's reactions than anticipating her own.

And Deacon . . . She knew he'd keep resisting her.

She could put him in front of more demons who were a threat to vampires, and he'd slay them. She could put him in front of demons who weren't an immediate threat, and he'd slay those, too. She could use his need for revenge to slay every demon that she needed slain.

But she didn't want to *use* him. Rosalia wanted him to see the danger that she saw, and take a stand against it, just as he did against every evil and injustice he'd ever faced. Unfortunately, ninety years had taught her that Deacon didn't take decisive action against hypothetical threats.

Rosalia couldn't let go of this, however. She *did* deal in hypotheticals. And those said that in a few weeks, hundreds of vampires in London would die. Eventually, either Belial's demons would come together to destroy the Guardians—or Anaria and her nephilim would. The nephilim had to be stopped, but they were stronger and outnumbered the Guardians. And Anaria . . .

Above all, the Guardians and the vampire communities needed to be safe from Anaria. She was too strong, and too convinced that she was right.

And so although Deacon would prefer never to see her face again, Rosalia planned to return to him shortly after dawn—and she had even more reason now. Taylor had said she arrived in Deacon's room every day. Though Taylor hadn't noticed any regularity to her arrivals, several hours passed between each one. Once the new Doyen regained control over Michael's impulses, she kept it for a little while—and so Rosalia had a little time before she had to find Deacon.

Time that she needed, so that she could see clearly again. Destroying the nephilim, protecting the vampires—both felt *so* right, but Rosalia couldn't shake the feeling that, with Deacon, she'd been going about it all wrong. She just couldn't see *why* . . . but she suspected that her emotions clouded her vision.

She needed to talk. She needed advice. And she needed to take her heart out of the equation.

Yet another thing that was easier said than done.

Rosalia descended out of the cool, high-altitude air into a hot, sticky Rome night where everything seemed to drip and droop. Humans slept restlessly, sweating. Trees stood with branches outspread and no breeze to stir their leaves. The air smelled both stagnant and full of life—unmoving and stale, yet the fragrance of food and flowers and exhaust wafted through pockets of still air, filling every humid breath she drew.

For a long time, she'd resented this city almost as much as she'd loved it. She'd always thought that once Lorenzo was gone, she'd leave Rome. But in the six months since she'd returned from the catacombs, she couldn't imagine making a home anywhere else. Her resentment had fled, the scales had tipped toward love, and she suspected that humanity's Eternal City would also be hers.

It felt more like home than even Caelum had.

She flew over her abbey to check that nothing was amiss before continuing on to the parish church. For more than two hundred years, the church had been a foundation of the neighborhood—and the priests acted as Rosalia's liaison to the Vatican. Twelve different men had she outlived, and most of them she'd mourned their passing. A few of the priests she'd had to work around rather than with, others merely passed on messages, but others had become her close friends.

The latest, Father John Wojcinski, she counted as a friend and confidant. The priest had been her liaison when the Church had not just quit of her services, but quit of her. She had not even been excommunicated—the Church simply no longer acknowledged her existence.

That rejection hadn't been as hurtful as their first. After Rosalia's transformation to Guardian, the Church had not heard her confessions or allowed her to participate in any other sacraments—and so when they had turned away from her six months ago, the loss had not been so deep. She could not repay them to her satisfaction, but she no longer needed the physical and spiritual support that she'd relied upon so heavily as a human. Nor was it so terrible to say farewell to the faceless priests who'd once directed her activities.

And they could not sever her connection to Father Wojcinski. For almost thirty years, she'd watched the gray thread through his hair, then flourish. She'd watched his laugh lines appear and had helped them deepen. She and the priest no longer worked together, but he was still a dear friend.

Folding her wings, Rosalia landed on the church's peaked roof, facing the rectory. The soft glow in his rooms indicated he didn't yet sleep. Quiet contemplation lay over his psychic scent, but she couldn't mistake an undercurrent of sorrow and anger.

She threw a pebble. It pinged against his windowpane before dropping to the garden below.

Soft footsteps sounded from inside his rooms. When he peered through the window, Rosalia spread her wings. After he lifted his hand, indicating he'd seen her signal, she leapt from the roof and glided to the rectory door.

With drying herbs, strings of garlic and onions hanging from the ceiling, an enormous fireplace built into the wall opposite the large window, bowls heaped with tomatoes and peppers, and the ever-present scent of coffee, the rectory's kitchen reminded Rosalia of the same room at the abbey before Gemma's grandmother, Sofia, had passed away three years before. Sofia had become the abbey's housekeeper shortly after Gemma's mother had been born, and had been as much a part of the family as were any of the vampires. And when Vin had come into Rosalia's life, shortly followed by Gemma and her brother, Pasquale, Rosalia had found Sofia's advice and friendship invaluable.

Rosalia liked to think that she'd picked up good habits from Sofia. One had been that a chat over coffee in a warm kitchen could help ease the worst pain in a heart.

As this kitchen bordered on hot, Rosalia had brought the coffee iced.

Father Wojcinski entered the room wearing his eyeglasses, his clericals, and a pair of slippers. His pleasure upon seeing her deepened when he spied the bakery box on the preparation table.

"Oh, Rosa. Where have you been?"

"Greece." A small detour on her flight here.

He opened the box and smiled. "Baklava? Bless you."

She sipped her coffee and waited for him to choose a towering piece before taking her own. Sticky, sweet, salty. Perfect.

The priest settled into a chair at the large wooden table. "Vincente and Gemma came to see me today."

Her heart leapt. "About the wedding?"

"Yes." He carefully took a bite of baklava. Flakes of phyllo dough drifted down to his plate. Precise in everything, he savored the bite slowly. By the time he swallowed, Rosalia was ready to beg him to continue. "You know I cannot condone their cohabitation without the sacrament of marriage, but I also cannot regret where it has led them. Particularly if it has led them earlier than they might have."

Her chest full, Rosalia rose from the table and walked to the window. Father Wojcinski would never speak so warmly of her son's marriage if he wasn't convinced of the pair's love and fidelity. Yes, her son and his chosen bride shared both. And soon, a child.

Happiness was a poor word for the emotion filling her now.

"I cannot tell you of anything they spoke about, Rosa."

"Of course not." Yet something must be wrong. A softening of his tone alerted her that all was not perfect.

"It would not be amiss, however, if you could clear some time to speak with them. And to *listen*."

She hadn't been listening to them? My God, she could barely get Vin to *talk* to her.

"Do you think I don't?"

"I think that you are so good at shouldering burdens, you often do not see the weight carried by others."

Worry gnawed at her. What weight did Vin and Gemma feel they carried? But she could not press for details. "Do I ask too much of them?"

"No. But remember, now that he will be a husband and father, his world has changed. And his priorities."

Of course they had. "Yes, Father."

He moved to the sink to wash the honey and butter from his hands. "I am glad you have come tonight, Rosa."

Yes, she'd sensed that he was troubled and angry. "Can I do anything to help?"

"No. Unless you can return trust to parishioners from whom it was taken. And if you can make it easier to forgive the one who has abused his position and taken advantage of a child."

Rage swept through her veins like fire. No, she could not make it easier to forgive such a man. Long before Father Wojcinski had brought a five-year-old Vin to her door, wounded by the loss of his mother, then the "care" of one of his mother's boyfriends in whose home he'd landed, Rosalia had been unable to forgive anyone—priest or otherwise—who abused a child in such a way.

"Who?"

He turned from the sink, wiping his hands on a towel. He regarded her gravely. "If you find out, Rosa, I will accept that it was God's will for you to know."

Because he knew she *would* find out, and put the fear of God into the man. She did not know what to think of Father Wojcinski's easy acceptance, however. Always before, he had urged her to reconsider her role in the lives of mankind before using her abilities against them.

And despite his acceptance, she felt no easing of the emotional turmoil within him. "Is this all that has kept you awake so late? Was this man a friend?"

"I have never met him." With a sigh, he sat again at the table. "The first time I heard such an accusation, I thought it could not be true. I believed that a mistake had been made, that a simple rumor had gained teeth, and he would be found innocent of the charges. I believed in his innocence until I could believe it no longer."

"You heard the evidence against him?" When he nodded, she said, "I have seen too many men and women condemned by mere rumor to fault you for that belief."

"Yes, Rosa. But this time . . . my first thought was not of his innocence. I assumed his guilt, instead. I felt resigned to it." Removing his glasses, he rubbed his hand over his eyes. "All men are capable of sin, but only a few are capable of doing that to a child. Yet my first response is condemnation."

Ah. "So the depth of your cynicism has shaken you."

"Perhaps given me a good rattle."

His weary smile aged him, and a feeling akin to panic suddenly roiled through her belly. How long before she lost yet another friend? Fifteen years?

No time at all.

He slipped on his glasses again with another sigh. "But that is my burden, Rosa. I should not lay it on you."

A burden she recognized, from centuries of conversations in this room. She pulled her thoughts together and expelled the fear. "Nonsense. You haven't been the only one to bear it—though you held out against it far longer than the others."

Now his smile lightened his face. "How many before me?"

"All but three."

"And what comfort did you offer my predecessors?"

"To be glad they are not burdened as I am with eternal optimism, because disappointment often follows it. At least a cynic is happily surprised now and then."

"Yet you still possess that optimism."

"And I remain eternally hopeful that I will lose it."

He laughed quietly. Rosalia sipped at her coffee, smiling, and a comfortable silence fell between them.

After a moment, he leaned back in his chair. "Now, tell me why you are here."

Deacon. She looked through the window, out into the dark. "I've developed a plan to slay many demons."

"It is a dangerous path?"

"Yes. But fear is not why I . . ." She couldn't bear her reflection in the glass. She faced him. "I've forced a good man onto that path with me. I can't win without his help. But he hasn't offered it. I'm using him."

"So you are no better than the demons."

Precise in eating and in words. These sliced like a razor into her heart. "I like to think that I have better intentions—"

"I imagine you do like to think that." His solemn gaze didn't waver. "But if the suffering of even one good man is needed to gain victory, it is not a true victory."

She knew that. She *knew* that.

Tears burned her eyes. Though she wanted to turn and run into the shadows, *this* was why she had come to him. He would open her up and expose her, so that she could see herself.

It formed a grotesque picture.

His face softened as he studied her. "And I suspect, Rosa, that it is not just the suffering of one man, but a woman, as well."

Now he was kind, and that hurt almost as much. Her breath shuddered. "It is only that since I have come back, I feel as if every purpose I've had was stripped away." And though she'd been missing for over a year, it had been but a moment to her. A moment in which everything had changed. "Lorenzo is gone. Svetlana and Christina and Giacomo—everyone at the abbey—they are all gone. Vin has returned but is almost unreachable. And the Church has . . . I am nothing to them. Only my duty as a Guardian is clear, and that duty is to slay demons. To protect those that I can. And yet to do *that*, I must force another to my will. That has never been my purpose. That has never been my way."

"So you either lose yourself to this, or you risk losing everyone else."

How clearly he put it. She wiped her cheeks. "Yes."

"That will be a poor victory, Rosa. So either you must quit your plan—"

"I cannot," she whispered.

"Or you must convince this man to walk this path with you."

She laughed. Yet another task that was easier said than done. But he was right. Completely and utterly right.

Father Wojinksi leaned forward. "You say he is a good man and that your cause is noble. So why isn't he convinced?"

Shaking her head, she said, "I don't know. I have told him everything that is at stake, yet he only . . . he only . . ."

She trailed off, losing the order of her thoughts as a new one occurred to her: She *did* know why. She had only given him hypotheticals. Nothing personal. Nothing immediate.

Deacon needed a clear threat or a reason to care. She hadn't given him one.

And she hadn't given Deacon as much as she already had from him. She knew what drove him, knew him through to his soul. She'd seen his suffering. But he had no connection to her. He had a purpose, driven by grief and anger. He had no idea her purpose was driven by the same.

"Rosa?"

A long breath steadied her. "I was wrong, Father. It *was* fear that brought me here."

Fear that if she opened her heart to him, she might finally lose it. But in protecting herself, she had jeopardized everything.

If her plan succeeded, surely all that every human, vampire, and Guardian stood to gain was worth the risk to her heart?

And so she would.

❧

Rosalia called Gemma when she arrived back in her Paris hotel. Vincente answered Gemma's cell, and she heard the faint sound of retching in the background.

She clucked her tongue in sympathy, and tried to conceal how very much that pitiful noise thrilled her heart. A grandchild. Simply incredible. "Morning sickness?"

Vin grunted a reply caught halfway between wonder and terror.

Smiling, Rosalia sat at her computer, checking Deacon's accounts. She wasn't surprised to find that he'd already purchased a ticket and boarded a flight that would arrive in the city before dawn. She'd watch over him after that. Taylor's unexpected presence meant Rosalia needed to adjust her daily schedule.

"I've had to return to Paris," she told Vin.

"Paris? Gemma said that you'd planned to return to the abbey tonight. Did you have problems in Budapest?"

"No. Everything went perfectly." Except Deacon hadn't come back to Rome with her.

"So Deacon is with you now?"

"No."

Vincente's silence said far too much. She'd failed to convince Deacon; now her son doubted if she'd pull off the rest of it, too. "Mother, you're planning to go up against the nephilim. Are you certain—"

"Yes." She could do this. If Deacon helped. And if she discovered who Malkvial was. "Did Gemma finish the preliminary work on St. Croix?"

She heard Vin's frustrated sigh. "Yes. Here she is now."

"Rosa!" Gemma came on, and something in her voice reminded Rosalia of the girl who'd listened so closely to her stories.

"You've found something," Rosalia guessed.

"Oh, you'll never believe this. St. Croix's father drowned in a boating accident when he was eight years old. He owned a small accounting firm, which St. Croix's mother, Madelyn, took over after he died—put herself through classes, bought out the partners, and worked her ass off building the firm into a financial powerhouse, Wells-Down Investments."

Rosalia had heard of it. "Impressive."

"Yeah, but St. Croix, he's something else. He went off the rails. Just as a teen, he's got vandalism, drug possession, breaking and entering, auto theft—you name it, he probably did it. By fifteen, he'd been expelled from three schools, even though his mother donated enough to the third one that they named a library after her. At sixteen, he just drops off the map. Then ten years ago, he shows up again in the States— touted as some financial whiz, five a.m. to midnight, ruthless bastard that chews up failing businesses and shits out gold."

"He underwent a complete personality change?" Just like her father had.

"And that's not all of it. He returned to London and went after Wells-Down."

The bastard. "Did he get it?"

"He did. And five years ago, he just shut everything down, closed up shop."

A cruel bastard. Breaking up the company and selling it for pieces would have hurt less. "And his mother?"

"Disappeared right after. But not just Madelyn—her personal assistant, Rachel Boyle, vanished at the same time."

Rosalia closed her eyes. "That can't be a coincidence."

"The police and Boyle's family didn't think so, either. But there were no bodies and nothing to hang on him, so whatever he did to get rid of them, he got away with it. He went on to eat a few more companies, then joined Legion three years ago. He's based in London, though he travels everywhere Legion is."

"Where is he now?"

"Here in Rome. He arrived today. I've already got the info on his hotel. I'll start surveillance tomorrow."

Rosalia sucked in a sharp breath. Legion didn't have offices in Rome. And that was much too close to Gemma and Vin for her liking. She held the phone to her ear, torn between the impulse to return and her need to stay in Paris.

Gemma easily read her silence. "Stop worrying, Rosa. I have it covered until you arrive."

And she *could* handle it—both of them could. Even though Vin had been gone for ten years, he'd spent that decade building a security and investigations firm. If Gemma needed backup, there were few people with more knowledge and experience than her son.

"All right," she said. "Thank you. I'll try to return tomorrow night. Sleep well."

"No chance of that," Gemma said lightly, but the truth behind her statement struck Rosalia hard. Because of the nephilim, the young woman *wouldn't* sleep well. Perhaps she never would again.

And Rosalia would do everything in her power to make the nephilim pay for that.

❦

Taylor swam up out of the dark, into the sun, and collapsed to her hands and knees in hot white sand. Her body heaved, again and again, as if she tried to expel him, but he was already gone, sitting quietly at the back of her mind, like he hadn't just taken her over and raped her will.

Bastard. The goddamn bastard.

Her breath came in sobs. She sat back on her ass, the lone person on an empty beach, turquoise waves crashing in on her left. Blood covered her hands. A part of her recognized the smell—*demon blood*—and she had a broken memory of crimson skin, of a sweltering jungle, of the sword in her grip. Slaying a demon, just like a Guardian should be. But she wasn't a Guardian. She was Michael's fucking puppet.

Rage and frustration boiled into a scream, but she bit it back. He wouldn't drive her to that. She focused inward and thought, *I hate you*, hoping that he would hear it, hoping he would understand it was for him.

She hadn't wanted to become a Guardian. But when it had come down to the decision between dying or living, she'd signed on. But she hadn't signed on for *this*.

And she was so damn tired of fighting him. Exhausted, down to her soul.

Bracing her elbows on her knees and pushing her hands into her hair, she stared out over the sea. She didn't even know where she was—or why he'd brought her here. But she had to leave soon, find Rosalia, and teleport her and the vampire to another city.

Soon.

She closed her eyes. The waves should have lulled her to sleep. Should have given her a little release. She could only feel him.

I hate you.

A harmonious voice answered her, "I hope that emotion is not directed at me."

Taylor lurched to her feet, her toes flinging sand as she spun around. Only the grigori had voices like that, but the only ones that Taylor knew were Michael and Khavi. This wasn't Khavi, though she had the same bronze skin and black hair, the delicate frame. This one had the regal bearing of a queen, and a soft, understanding expression on her exquisite features. Her dress looked something between a toga and a sari, white cloth twisted at her narrow shoulders, crossing over her breasts. The separate skirt tied at the waist and was fluttering around her ankles in the breeze.

Anaria.

Ohfuckshit.

"Stay," Anaria said, and Taylor's intention to teleport the hell away seemed to fizzle out with that command.

She expected Michael to take over, the darkness to ascend—and though she felt him, tense and watchful, he didn't rise up.

Anaria tilted her head, studying her. "Why did he come?"

"I don't know. I don't even know where we are," Taylor blabbered, then stared at the woman. Jesus. She hadn't meant to answer. But something in Anaria's voice, in her face . . . compelled her.

But Taylor couldn't get angry. She tried. She just couldn't work it up.

And that scared the shit out of her. Human or Guardian, one thing she'd always been able to count on was getting good and pissed when she wanted to. And whatever Michael did, at least he didn't fuck with her emotions.

Anaria sighed. "Don't be afraid."

Taylor almost laughed. Apparently, Anaria couldn't compel *that*, because her heart still pounded and fear raced through her veins.

"Come with me, then," she said.

Taylor followed.

CHAPTER 8

Anaria lived on a private island in the Aegean, complete with a sun-warmed mansion overlooking the sea. Taylor didn't know how Anaria managed to pull that off, until she realized that the almost sixty humans sharing the grigori's home weren't humans at all, but the nephilim. One of the humans that the nephilim possessed must have owned the island before he'd kicked over and gone to Hell.

It was almost like walking through a retirement home—one that drew its residents from every part of the world. Which made a hell of a lot of sense, though Taylor hadn't considered it before. When the Gates to Hell had closed, Lucifer had freed the nephilim from prison so that they could enforce the Rules on Earth, but the nephilim couldn't just fly between the realms. They possessed the souls of the damned as the humans died. And except for a few—the youngest in her early twenties, Taylor guessed—they had a lot of white and gray hairs between them, and quite a few men without any hair at all.

For the most part, they acted like humans, too—eating, talking in little groups, some off by themselves and reading. A bunch of zombies having a big family reunion.

But they bothered her. She thought they bothered the hell out of Michael, too, though he was staying quiet. And it wasn't until Anaria invited her out onto a big, sprawling patio to sit and talk that Taylor realized why: Every one of these bastards had done evil enough that they'd been destined for Hell. Though the nephilim possessed the human and took control, the human's personality still remained.

And one of these fuckers had raped and murdered the vampires in London.

Anaria sank gracefully onto the foot of a lounge chair, studying Taylor's face. She wondered how deep the scrutiny went, but Anaria must not have picked up on the determination hardening Taylor's every thought and reaction. Anaria smiled, and it was beautiful—and Taylor didn't feel the same compulsion to smile back.

"Michael has always been stubborn. I imagine he circled the world trying to find me."

Find Anaria, or the nephilim? "Probably to ask you to spare London."

Anaria's voice gentled, as if she spoke to a child. "We *are* sparing the vampires. People were never meant to suffer the nosferatu's curse, the bloodlust. People were meant to walk in the sun. They are abominations."

One of Taylor's few friends was a vampire. Only years of practice dealing with bigoted assholes kept her temper in check. "Abominations? Have you ever actually spoken to one?"

"I have spoken with many. And I know that next you will say that they are like humans—they love; they laugh. That is all true. But their very existence is a cancer, one that can spread without check, and destroy the protection of free will in every human."

Oh, God. She couldn't be serious. "They destroy free will? They *choose* to become vampires."

"Yes." Anaria's face brightened, as if Taylor had just made a point for her. "You see? It is a disease, one that behaves in the same way as a demon. A demon doesn't force a human to do anything, but preys upon a human's greed, fear, anger until an irrevocable choice is made, and his soul is lost. Vampirism is the same. It preys upon a human's fears: weakness, death—and the human *chooses* to throw away the protection of his free will. What human could reject the lure of immortality and strength, especially as they grow older and death comes closer? Very few. And once they've given up their free will, the demons would easily destroy them all when Lucifer opens the Gates to Hell again. Is not the Guardians' purpose to prevent the destruction of humanity at the hands of the demons? Yet you protect the vampires, those selfsame creatures who will bring that destruction about."

Speechless, Taylor shook her head. And though she tried, Taylor could not find the point at which the argument fell apart. If more humans knew about vampires, many of them *would* choose to become immortal, and demons *could* kill humans after they transformed. It all made a twisted kind of sense, but was so *wrong*.

A layer of Anaria's harmonic voice deepened in sympathy. "I understand why this troubles you. Certainly you have vampire friends. But you should not let your emotions cloud your judgment."

Un-fucking-believable. "And I suppose Khavi's prophecy, which states that vampires will be the downfall of your children, has not clouded your judgment at all?"

"Of course not." Anaria's brow furrowed delicately. "Nothing that Khavi predicts is certain, and moreover, she is a liar. She foresees much more than she tells anyone, and manipulates everyone to her end. Her prophecy concerns me not at all."

That rang far too true. Khavi had predicted Taylor's death at the hands of a vampire, but had not prevented it. For several months, Taylor had wondered and suspected that Khavi had put the events into motion that led to her death, simply so that Michael would have someone as a tether.

Anaria watched her face. "You know this is true," she said.

"I don't."

With a sigh, Anaria shook her head. "Do not try to lie. Truth was once my Gift, and I still see it clearly."

Well, shit. Taylor looked away from her as two of the nephilim strolled by. She glanced back at the grigori, who was smiling at them, her eyes shining with love.

"They will be humanity's saviors. First, from the vampires. And when I take the throne in Hell, they will ensure that humans only choose love and kindness, saving all from the tortures of the Pit. Can you not see them as I do?"

Taylor thought it prudent not to answer that one. "Which one is the savior who killed the two vampires in London?"

"Do you think I would tell you, when you so clearly wish to do him harm? You have nothing to fear from them—I have told them never to slay a Guardian, unless they must to defend themselves. And I have stressed that you in particular are not to be harmed. Can you not make the same promise in return?"

Though her gentle expression didn't change, a note of steel had entered Anaria's voice. The mother, in full-on protection mode. Taylor stepped carefully.

"I don't have enough skill with a sword to harm any of your children."

Anaria relaxed and seemed to take that as a promise. "That is true."

Taylor hesitated, then ventured further. "The humans whose bodies they've taken . . . Do you think that—"

"My children are in control."

Anaria anticipated her, which told Taylor this wasn't the first time the question had come up. All right. So throw something unexpected at her.

"So he *meant* to rape the vampires in London? I thought you only needed them dead. Not violated."

But Anaria's eyes didn't so much as flicker. "My children are new to their physical forms. They have been imprisoned for more than two *thousand* years, and have had little opportunity to experience what humans take for granted." She paused. "And the vampires were not forced or tortured."

"Threatening someone's life until they acquiesce is still force."

"That is not what happened."

Oh, *Jesus.* Taylor felt sick as she realized what that meant. "And you think that is *okay*?"

Anaria gave her that infuriating speaking-to-a-child expression again. "My children are only spirit. They are living proof that a body is only a vessel, and without psychic energy to fill it, that vessel becomes empty. You are letting your emotions and your human sensibilities cloud your judgment again. My child did no harm."

"Except for murdering them."

"*Slaying* them," Anaria said. "Even more necessary to humanity's survival than slaying the demons."

There was no point in arguing there, Taylor realized. Anaria was absolutely convinced that the vampires were a cancer that needed to be eradicated. But to say that a body was just a meatsack, that it meant nothing to violate it? No. And this time, she wasn't left speechless.

"Then why do I have Michael's body in my cache if it is merely a vessel?"

Khavi had explained it to her: His soul manifested as flesh in Hell, but his physical form matched the resonance of his psyche and completed the link between them—like a tuning fork struck and held near a sympathetic string until both vibrated at the same frequency. Every individual's resonance was as distinct as a DNA strand and was the only reason Taylor hadn't dumped his body out of her cache, breaking the link between them. If she did, he couldn't come back. Khavi worked even now, trying to discover a way to bring his soul out of the frozen field—but it would be for nothing if he had no body.

She hated him. But she wasn't a cold-blooded murderer.

And now she'd surprised Anaria. Her brows arched high, her lips parting. She leaned forward. "How did Khavi know to link you in that way?"

That, she'd never explained. "I don't know."

"He inscribed symbols into his body, yes?"

Taylor had been dying, but she remembered that part. Using Irena's flaming knife, the blade heated by the power of a dragon's heartblood, Khavi had carved the demon script into Michael's torso, his back, and his neck.

"Yes."

"And you took his blood from the symbol for 'merge.'"

She hadn't known what the symbol was. And she hadn't known that sucking down a mouthful of the Doyen's blood wasn't a part of the standard Guardian transformation.

"Yes."

"Then he took your blood, and—"

"No." Taylor shook her head. "He didn't take my blood."

Anaria's eyes narrowed thoughtfully. "You tell the truth, but you must be mistaken. The link cannot be completed without an exchange of blood. What did he do, then?"

His lips, always so hard, had been soft against hers. He'd tasted her, kissed her as if he meant it . . . and she'd been completely lost in every deep stroke of his tongue. Her head already spinning from the wound to her chest, and he'd blown through her mind. She hadn't even cared that only a minute before, she'd been unable to breathe and coughing up . . .

Oh, God. Coughing up blood. Her mouth had been full of it.

She didn't know what the other woman saw in her expression, but Anaria's voice was suddenly sympathetic again. "So he took your blood?"

Taylor had to swallow before answering. "Yes."

"He is sometimes so thoughtless and focused only on his goal, he does not see the pain he leaves in his wake." Anaria sighed. "He should have told you that he has kissed many, many women, so that you would know it meant nothing."

It hadn't meant anything, Taylor wanted to say. But she didn't think it'd pass Anaria's truth test. Despite all the dark and cold and screaming afterward, that kiss had been . . . warm. A moment of hope and clarity, after fear and pain and confusion.

She refused to dwell on it, though. There was still so much to do—and two vampires who still needed their murderer confronted and accused. She lifted her gaze to Anaria's.

"If you'd introduce me, I'd love to meet your children."

❧

Deacon didn't need the dry air to tell him he'd been moved. That he was *moving.* Either the Guardians had invested in a private jet, or Rosalia had chartered a plane. He faced a line of oval windows, their shades pulled down. The steady drone of jet engines didn't drown out her breathing and heartbeat. They sounded near and clear—and directly behind him.

So she hadn't taken the hint, after all. Instead she'd laid him out on his side in a half-reclined seat and pulled a blanket over his legs. Now she was probably waiting for him to roll on over, so that she could tell him which demon she'd set him up to kill.

He'd just come fresh out of dreams of a demon crushing him, of killing his partners, and here she was pulling at his strings.

Goddamn her.

He closed his eyes, holding it in. Anger sparked the bloodlust, and he needed to be cold now. When he turned to look at her, he had to be a hard bastard, one who didn't give a fuck about how soft she seemed.

Not that he needed to look. The warmth of her breath touched the back of his neck. She had to be lying just behind him, in the same position as he was. Any closer and she'd be spooning him. And it was too damned easy to imagine these seats as a bed.

He sat up. She remained half-lying in the seat, covered by

a dark cloak that swallowed her body in its voluminous folds. The hood shadowed her face, concealing her expression.

Irritated, he reached over and pulled it back, expecting to reveal her sad eyes and the gaze that saw right through him. She had them closed, instead. Relief helped him even out his voice, smooth out his frustration. "When are you going to quit, sister?"

"I can't quit." She still didn't open her eyes, but she didn't need to. Grief and anger suddenly burst through her shields, both as familiar to Deacon as his face in the mirror. "The nephilim killed my family."

She said that like she'd had family worth saving.

But he couldn't be rough on her while sitting this close. Spotting his clothes piled on the seat facing him, he took the opportunity to grab a little distance before he said, "I'm not crying over that, sister. If any vampire deserved what the nephilim did to him, it was your brother."

"No. I don't mean Lorenzo."

She had other family?

When he turned back around, she'd raised the back of the seat, but still sat half-turned with her legs curled beneath her. A man sitting like that would look broken; Rosalia just looked comfortable.

But was she? Her fingers poked out of the wide sleeves to play with the folds of her cloak. And she'd opened her eyes, but didn't look at Deacon, directing a pain-filled stare at the shaded windows.

"Not *just* him," she continued. "The nephilim slaughtered every vampire in Rome, including friends who'd shared my abbey for more than one hundred years."

Deacon remembered her abbey. She'd brought him there after he'd slain Caym in Prague. He'd stayed in her home for only a few minutes, but that had been long enough. Every piece of furniture and every decoration had told him a family had lived there, filled with warmth and steeped in history.

Walking through that place so soon after losing Eva and Petra had been like a knife to his chest. And he hadn't considered until now why only one woman—a human—had been in the abbey when he'd woken up.

He hadn't considered until now that the empty home might stab through Rosalia's heart every time she walked through it, too.

"Fourteen vampires," she continued softly. "Some had lived with me since their transformation. I trained them. I fought with them. I saw them live and love. But the nephilim came . . . and now almost all of my family is gone."

Those staring eyes glistened with tears. Deacon turned and hiked up his jeans, giving her the moment she obviously needed.

So she'd had her own little community in Rome. Friends, maybe a lover.

No. Scratch that. Any man good enough to be with some-one like Rosalia would have torn Rome apart trying to find her when she'd been in the catacombs. First stop would have been her brother, and Deacon hadn't heard any rumors that Lorenzo had slain another vampire around that time. And Deacon *would* have heard the rumors; Rosalia's brother had liked every other community leader knowing just how strong he was.

"Your friends," he said. "Anyone I know?"

"One, though she had moved away from the abbey before you met her. She wasn't with those slaughtered." Before he could ask who that was, she said, "And I was trapped in the catacombs while they were dying. I still would be trapped there, if not for you."

If not for him? She had her gratitude on backward. Caym had told Deacon to lead the Guardians to the catacombs in hope that the nosferatu waiting there would kill them all. Rosalia's rescue hadn't been a part of it.

"I hate to point out the obvious, sister, but even if you hadn't been trapped, you couldn't have done anything to save them. The nephilim would have killed you, too."

"I'd rather have died trying." For the first time since he'd woken, she looked at him. "Don't you hate being in a position where no matter what you do, it ends badly?"

All right. He'd walked right into that. No matter what decision he'd made while dealing with Caym, it would've ended badly—for his community, for himself, or for the Guardians. She'd chosen a heavy-handed way of making her point, though.

He tried to summon up a little anger toward her. He couldn't. And now that he was on this ride, he might as well see where they were headed. He assumed she had another demon for him to kill.

And he had to admit, as easy as slaying Farkas had been, killing him had been more satisfying than waiting around for Theriault.

When he glanced at her again, she was back to staring at the windows. "So what do you have planned for tonight?"

"We'll be landing in Athens within an hour."

"Sardis's community? He's a prick." His vampires deserved better. "Let the demon kill him."

"Valeotes—the demon—doesn't intend to slay Sardis. At least not yet. He's put Sardis and the community into his pocket. Valeotes promises protection; they give up blood in return."

And how long before the demon asked Sardis to do worse? "Everyone knows the shit Caym pulled on me, yet Sardis is taking that risk and working with him?"

"As you said, he's a prick. An arrogant one."

Her lip curled slightly, as if she'd smelled something foul. So Sardis disgusted her. Deacon couldn't fault her taste in people.

Heh. She must think it unfortunate that her plan included hanging around *him*. "And what'd you think of me when you found out about Caym? That I was a prick? Arrogant?"

Rosalia looked at him. Her smile formed slowly, as if she held secrets behind it that she didn't want to let out too soon.

Or let them out at all. She didn't answer him, but said, "After Caym destroyed your people, the Guardians visited every vampire community and killed any demons leading them. Most were Lucifer's demons, but Belial's demons obviously learned from it. Now they aren't leading the vampires directly—either to avoid notice by the Guardians or because the nephilim kill the vampires' leaders."

"What about Farkas?" The demon had planned to take over Budapest.

"Farkas was Theriault's demon. Not as smart, twice as arrogant. Valeotes follows Malkvial."

Was she still looking for that one? "Are you hoping to get Malkvial's human name out of him, then?"

"No. Taking the time to question him would be too dangerous for you—and Valeotes would just lie. I simply don't want Valeotes's fingers on any of Sardis's buttons when you bring the European communities together."

She really thought that was going to happen? She didn't give up easily. He couldn't decide whether her determination despite certain failure made her foolish or admirable.

But he imagined that his quest for revenge probably looked the same from her end.

"You said Malkvial intends to slaughter vampires once he's taken the lieutenant's position. So why would one of his demons pair up with Sardis?"

"Because Sardis might be useful."

Yes. Vampires could kill humans. God knew what else. "So we kill Valeotes before that happens. Before he can use anyone."

"You'll kill him, yes. We'll be arriving in Athens just after sunset. That will give us time to look over Sardis's compound before you go in."

A compound. Deacon knew the general layout only through other vampires' descriptions. He'd never visited Sardis.

What she'd said finally struck him. "*After* sunset?"

"Yes." She smiled slightly. "I do not imagine that anyone will detect my Gift, unless they are also flying at 35,000 feet."

He still couldn't grasp it. "It's daytime. Outside. Now."

"Yes."

"Bullshit."

Her brows lifted. "Look."

Pulling in a deep breath, Deacon turned toward the windows and reached for the shade. Rosalia didn't stop him. Taking her silence as a sign that he wouldn't burst into flames, he slid the window shade up.

His knees almost buckled. Daylight spilled through the glass onto his hand and arm. In ninety years, he hadn't felt that warmth. Swallowing hard, he looked through the window. A shadow lay across the glass, like seeing through sunglasses, but outside it was unmistakably day. White clouds floated against a blue sky. And . . . the sun.

He'd forgotten how bright it was. Even through the shadow that Rosalia's Gift created, he had to squint. Incredible.

About to say as much, he turned, but the distress on Rosalia's face stopped him. Her skin had paled, and her eyes were tightly closed. Pain bracketed her mouth, held her body rigid.

As if his silence tipped off Rosalia that he was looking at her, she glanced up at him before closing her eyes again. "My Gift isn't . . . compatible . . . with the sun."

And hadn't been since he'd woken up, Deacon realized. Maintaining this shield inside the cabin had been the reason for her blank stare—and obviously the direct sunlight, even the sliver coming through the window, made it worse.

With a final look outside, he lowered the shade, then sat to pull on his boots. Her sigh indicated some relief, but her fingers still clutched the folds of her cloak and her eyes remained closed.

Deacon laced up his boots, feeling a little shaky himself. Though he'd come to accept the differences between living as a vampire and as a human, he had no idea *how* a vampire fell asleep at sunrise and caught fire at the touch of the sun. Natural law couldn't account for it. Obviously something bigger was at work, a force more powerful than nature.

And he'd accepted that the Guardians' Gifts could rewrite natural rules, too. Irena shaped metal to her will. Alejandro could create fire from nothing and control the flames' intensity. Other Guardians could teleport or instantly heal wounds.

But accepting that Rosalia's Gift could rewrite even the powerful *unnatural* rules that governed vampires knocked him for a loop . . . and humbled him.

Leaning back in his seat, he looked down at her. With her legs curled under her, she had to sit sideways. The cushioned seatback pillowed her cheek. Her dark hair hung in tangled waves over her shoulder. The pain had eased from her features, so that she almost appeared to be sleeping.

The princess, waiting for her kiss. Deacon wasn't even close to qualifying for a prince.

And maybe "princess" didn't fit her so well, either. A Guardian's Gift reflected some part of their human life. He couldn't figure out why a woman like Rosalia would have darkness for a Gift.

"So," he said, and saw that a single word opened her eyes as quickly as a kiss would have, "what's the story behind your Gift?"

"I don't know. It could be the manner in which I died—my connection to vampires."

She didn't sound convinced of that. "You must've thought of other reasons."

"Oh, I have." She laughed softly, but it didn't last. Looking up into his eyes, she seemed to hesitate, as if uncertain whether to reveal the rest. Then her mouth firmed, determination slipped into her psychic scent, and she continued. "Perhaps from when I was a girl. My father . . . I do not know if a demon arranged for his death, or if my father died of natural causes and a demon took advantage of the opportunity. But one day, my father was no longer himself."

"A demon took his place?"

"Yes. Lorenzo and I didn't know then what had happened. And my mother . . . she didn't last long."

That had to have been rough. "But you?"

"Lorenzo and I avoided him as much as possible. My father didn't care about us, anyway. Not until we were useful . . ." She stumbled and broke eye contact before finishing quietly, ". . . to him."

Useful. So he'd been right; she didn't like forcing him into this. He didn't like it much, either, but he didn't have the urge to tell her to fuck off. Seeing this side of her had gotten to him.

That didn't sit well with him, either—but he wasn't going to stop her from revealing herself, now that she'd started.

"I challenged him once," she continued. "I told him I knew what he was, and he ordered one of the servants to lock me into a wardrobe. No light, no food or water. He left me there for three days."

He could picture that all too easily. Alone in the dark, in her own filth. Hungry and terrified.

But her voice warmed as she remembered. "Lorenzo was on the other side of the door. He tried to help me, to open the wardrobe. And when he couldn't—he was *so* young then— he sat talking to me. At night, he slept outside the wardrobe doors. That's what I remember best. The dark, yes—but also Lorenzo's voice. They were both comforting. I felt safe. The dark was less frightening than being outside with Father."

Jesus. And that explained why she hadn't slain her brother. Deacon and every other vampire in Europe just knew Lorenzo Acciaioli as a sadistic, tyrannical bastard. But he and Rosalia had probably spent most of their human lives protecting each other.

"But your father didn't let you die."

"No. Eventually I would be useful. He could marry me off."

The revulsion in her expression didn't surprise Deacon, but his own anger did. This had all happened centuries ago. The thought of Rosalia being forced to marry shouldn't feel like a punch to his gut. "Did he?"

"No. I ran away to the convent. I thought Lorenzo would be safe, too—he'd already left our home. But he was not."

"Your father talked him into the transformation."

Acciaioli would have to be convinced. Most humans died after being transformed against their will.

"Yes. He became a vampire and visited the abbey with my

father. And that was the end of my human life—and the end of the demon's life, too."

The way she skimmed over the details told him that it must have been bad. He focused on the good part. "You killed the demon?"

"Michael did." A shadow passed over her face. She adjusted her position, bringing her knees up beneath that long cloak. After a moment, she continued. "When I finished training in Caelum, I returned to Rome, where Lorenzo was already heading a community. I tried to help him—to change him. But obviously I did not; I barely contained him."

Because Acciaioli hadn't just been a vampire. He'd been nosferatu-born, and strong. Unsurprisingly, he'd ruled his community unchallenged. The only surprise was that he hadn't tried to take over the other European communities.

Only recently had Deacon realized that they had Rosalia to thank for that.

Almost seven years ago, Acciaioli had come to Prague looking for a fight. With Acciaioli had been his weird little brother; Deacon hadn't known then it was Rosalia, shapeshifted. In that strange, pubescent-vampire disguise, she'd kissed Deacon—a halting, awkward kiss that had turned his stomach—and Acciaioli, who'd witnessed the kiss, had left Prague as fast as he could charter a flight.

Whether Acciaioli had been embarrassed or disgusted, Deacon didn't know. But Rosalia had obviously known what to do and how her brother would react—and had probably saved Deacon's life.

"Why didn't the other Guardians slay him?"

"He wasn't breaking the Rules, so they left him alone."

And Guardians rarely interfered with vampire communities. "They couldn't have liked it, though."

She shrugged. "Perhaps not, but I wasn't in Caelum or with other Guardians enough to worry about it. When I wasn't trying to manage Lorenzo, I served the Church. I owed them for taking me in."

When she'd been human? Three centuries had passed. She

had a completely fucked-up sense of obligation. "You work for the Vatican?"

"I *did*." She tugged at her cloak sleeves before hiding her hands within the wide material. "Now the Church doesn't acknowledge my existence. Lorenzo is gone, and most of my family has been slaughtered. So I am just a Guardian again. Perhaps it's what I should have been all along."

That bothered him. Whatever she'd been, "just a Guardian" would never fit. From just talking to her for ten minutes, he'd learned that much.

And to think he'd imagined that he had Rosalia figured out, based on the little he knew. But he hadn't guessed any of this about her. He'd been better off not knowing. Pushing her away was easier when she was just a gorgeous face, sad eyes, and a great pair of tits.

Goddammit. She wasn't supposed to matter. But now he knew what drove her. He just didn't know how far she'd take it—or how long she'd drag him with her.

Deacon glanced at her, realized she'd been watching him. Those sad eyes were back, and with a sigh, she uncurled her legs and sat forward in her seat.

"I have to withdraw my Gift. If I wait until we're in Athens, someone might feel it and know a Guardian is near."

Withdraw her Gift . . . and put him back to sleep? Oh, hell. Not yet—

❦

Gritting her teeth against the pain sawing at every nerve, Rosalia reclined Deacon's seat before collapsing into her own. Using her Gift during the day felt like being shredded from the inside out. And like a physical injury, it took time to recover.

Long, shallow breaths helped her focus. After a few minutes, she opened her eyes. Deacon lay in the next seat, his big body motionless, his heart barely beating.

Had anything she'd revealed had made a difference? She didn't know. Though he hadn't been as angry with her tonight, she still felt his resistance.

What if she couldn't persuade him? What would she do then?

Despair followed her uncertainty; she forced them both away. She couldn't afford to consider failure.

But, dear God, she *needed* Deacon to believe that slaying the nephilim was important enough to see his part through to the end. Needed him to see that it wasn't enough to kill as many of Belial's demons as possible before one killed him. And Deacon had to believe that she could pull off the endgame—because after Deacon brought the communities together, Rosalia needed him to make an alliance that he would *never* consider otherwise. Not if he simply walked a path of revenge.

But she had to believe in him, too. She had an advantage, though. She'd known him for so long, had admired his strength, his will, and his heart—and so that belief came easier to her than it would to him.

He'd be angry when she asked him to form that alliance. But if he believed in the necessity of killing them all—demons and nephilim—he'd follow through.

And by asking, she'd lose any chance she might have ever had to be with him. A chance that seemed so vital now. She risked her heart, but she had to hope it wouldn't be broken.

That heart sat heavy in her chest as she studied his profile. So many times she'd watched him, but never from this close. Near enough to touch, to explore the rough line of his jaw with her fingers, to feel the firmness of his mouth. So strong and hard, even while he slept.

Did he dream?

Lightly, she reached out with a psychic touch.

Grief. Agony. They wrapped around her throat like a scream. Beneath them, rage and self-hatred seethed around a deep sense of purpose and an incredible will.

Gasping for breath, Rosalia retreated. All vampires dreamed vividly, fueled by powerful emotion. She had no doubt he relived the murder of his people. Everything that fed his need for revenge—and his resistance to her—she'd felt in that psychic touch.

An incredible will.

She turned away, drawing her cloak tighter around her body. When Deacon saw the necessity of killing the demons and nephilim, when he *wanted* their destruction as badly as he wanted revenge, that incredible will would carry him through.

And she'd probably never had a real chance with him, anyway.

〉

Before he'd lost his community, Deacon had earned his income by restoring classic automobiles. Rosalia hadn't been able to secure one to rent on such short notice, but what the car she'd chosen lacked in age, it made up for in power.

Deacon didn't hide his appreciation as he circled the black Maserati convertible, his fingers stroking its gleaming lines. "If we're going top down, you'd better pull back your hair."

As if she didn't regularly fly with her long hair unbound. "I can withstand a few tangles."

His gaze lifted to her hair as he swung open her door. "At least it'll look like you actually fed a vampire."

Yes. Tangled and mussed, as if he'd taken blood from her, not from a glass. As if they spent the first hour after sunset in his bed.

Her skin tightened and her blood warmed as she pictured it. She wouldn't have him, perhaps, but maybe . . . maybe at some point, she could hold him against her. His lips to hers, bodies aligned. To take him inside . . . She could barely even imagine how that would feel.

But she wanted to know.

Deacon waited, holding the door. His gaze had fallen to her neck. His expression had darkened, as if his words had given him similar thoughts, but they plagued him rather than brought pleasure. Fighting her disappointment, Rosalia slipped into her seat, inhaling his scent as she passed him.

Beneath the clean fragrance of the soap, he possessed the same natural odor he'd had as a human male, but with a metallic undertone that marked him as a vampire. No cologne tonight. He didn't need to conceal his nature from the demon. She did, however.

The engine growled before settling down into a purr. Deacon entered the address for Sardis's compound into the GPS system, and it immediately responded with directions that would take them out of Athens. As they drove out of the lot, Rosalia pulled in a perfume bottle from her cache, spritzing the fragrance on her neck and arms. Deacon glanced at her, his brow furrowed.

"That's not just perfume."

"It contains female human sweat." Most vampires didn't know that Guardians had no odor, but one might look at her more closely if he sensed something missing—even if he couldn't pinpoint what that *something* was. "And my hair is taken care of, but if we want them to believe you are feeding from me . . ."

She brought in one of his unwashed shirts from her cache. Concentrating on her neck and chest, she slid it over her exposed skin, transferring his scent.

Deacon made a disgusted sound. "Give me a little credit, sister."

She lifted her leg, propped her foot up on the dash. She rubbed the shirt over the insides of her thighs. "Feel better?"

His slow, sexy smile appeared and sent her senses purring in time with the engine. "I meant that wouldn't fool me. There'd be a lot more sweat and the scent of blood."

With a smile, she vanished the shirt and settled deeper into the seat. "Most vampires aren't you. And it's 'Rosalia.' "

"What?"

"My name." Until he'd called her "Rosie" the night before, she'd thought he didn't remember her name. He'd certainly never used it. "I'm not 'sister.' Not anymore."

His gaze ran up her legs. "Don't I know it."

A few minutes earlier when he'd held the car door open for her, she hadn't been certain if he *did* know it, but now his dark mood seemed to have lightened. She tried to watch him

through the curtain of hair streaming forward past her face—
not quite like flying, after all—before giving up and braiding
it. He glanced at her, and though he didn't say, "I told you so,"
his eyes glinted with humor, and his fangs flashed in a grin.

Not abrasive, not angry—and reminded her of how Deacon
had once made it so easy to like him. Even when doubt had
driven him out of the clergy and into the boxing ring, when
he'd been battered both body and soul, he'd been quick to take
his enjoyment where he found it. Quick to smile and to laugh,
even with his eyes swollen to slits and his nose bleeding.

She'd thought that Caym had broken that in him. Or, like
so many who blamed themselves for their loved ones' deaths,
he wouldn't *let* himself take pleasure in anything. Perhaps he
made an exception when he controlled a ridiculous amount of
horsepower.

But even as she watched, his expression closed, leaving no
trace of his grin. With a sigh, Rosalia pulled in her makeup
out of her cache, applying a heavy line around her eyes and
black lipstick.

Though he glanced over at her, Deacon didn't say anything
until she changed her clothes, exchanging the sundress for a
black miniskirt, thigh-high stiletto boots, and a top so small
she was thankful she didn't really have to breathe.

"What the hell are you wearing?"

"I'm giving them what they expect." Vampires and demons
too often trusted appearances; Guardians never did. "A whore
looking for a dangerous thrill. Someone you paid and who
doesn't know any better. Who else would deign to be with you
after what Caym did?"

His jaw clenched so hard that his skin paled beneath the
shadow of his beard. "You don't care if they think you're a
whore?"

"Why should I? I am what I am; how someone treats me
doesn't change that."

He cursed. Rosalia stared at him. He seemed more bothered by it than she was—and she hadn't thought he'd care at
all. There'd been every possibility that she'd be treated like a

whore in Budapest, miniskirt or not, and he hadn't been concerned about the vampires' response then.

And he knew what sort of vampire Sardis was. Surely he hadn't expected different? "If I go in as myself, both he and Valeotes will take time to figure me out, so that they can put me in my place. Especially Sardis, because he *likes* to put women in their place. But if I go in like this, they don't have to think about it. They'll assume that they know."

"Right." Though he agreed, it clearly frustrated him. As if trying to get a grip on that emotion, he pushed his hand through his hair with fingers so rigid she was surprised he didn't scalp himself. "Just . . . stay close. We both know exactly where Sardis thinks a woman's place is."

"Yes." On her back, legs open and mouth shut. And most of the women in the community complied. *That* deserved the hair-pulling kind of frustration. "I keep hoping they'll kill him."

"The females?"

"The males, too. Any of them. They must recognize that he isn't the right kind of leader."

His eyebrows shot up. "The right kind?"

"One who understands that he serves the people he leads, and who enforces the community's rules to protect his people. Not to crush them."

The kind of leader that Deacon had been.

He smiled grimly. "You mean, anyone who isn't like your brother."

That, too. "Yes. But Lorenzo . . . I understood why no one rose up and killed him."

"Because no one can go up against the nosferatu-born," Deacon said.

Despite his words, his contemplative tone and the way his hands flexed on the steering wheel told Rosalia that he was wondering if, with his new strength, he *could* have defeated her brother. He'd beaten demons, after all—and even a nosferatu-born vampire like Lorenzo didn't possess a demon's strength and speed. So Deacon very well could have won.

The realization came with a strange sense of relief. Even if the nephilim hadn't killed Lorenzo, Rosalia's obligation toward her brother could have ended by now. Paid in full.

"Would you have protected him from a strong challenger?"

"No. Not from you. Not from anyone."

That answer apparently wasn't what he'd expected. He glanced away from the road to read her face, as if making sure she wasn't lying. "Not even from a Guardian?"

"No."

"You didn't interfere with his challenges?"

"Oh, I did. If I could, I protected the vampires who challenged him."

He frowned. "I thought your thing—whatever you owed your brother from when you were kids—meant you protected him."

"Only from himself." When Deacon still looked confused, she said, "I never tried to save his life. Only his soul. I just tried to undo what our father did, to make Lorenzo see that he should have been a better man. A better leader."

"But you didn't make him see."

"No."

She'd failed Lorenzo, or he'd failed her. Rosalia didn't know which it was—except that, of the two of them, she'd been the only one to make any effort at all.

At the prompt of the navigational system, Deacon slowed to turn, then accelerated up a narrow winding road. A grassy verge rolled down from the road down into a rocky incline, where enormous houses overlooked the sea. The tang of salt flavored every breath. Rosalia savored the taste, the view, until Deacon's voice brought her back into the car with him.

"You ever consider that it wasn't your father who fucked him up?"

Had she ever thought that, even without a demon's influence, Lorenzo would inevitably become a corrupted, power-hungry bastard? "Of course I've considered that. And if I believed it to be true, perhaps slaying him would have been easier."

He stole another glance at her face. "So if he'd turned out the same without your father's influence, you would have killed him?"

"I think so." And wouldn't have begged Michael to give her the opportunity to change him.

Deacon looked away from her, shaking his head in disbelief. "So every vampire he faced wasn't physically strong enough to defeat him. And you were—"

"Too weak?"

"You said it, sister."

"Everyone tells me the same." She leaned her head back, stared up at the night sky. The full moon sat behind thin clouds shredded by the wind. "But I cannot believe that refusing to slay my own brother is a weakness—particularly as his only sin was being a complete and utter bastard. He never broke the Rules *or* the community's rules."

"Except for when he killed you."

She lifted her head to look at him. "And I thought he deserved a second chance."

"Yeah. You're just full of those."

Amusement speared through her as she realized what he meant. "I'm not asking for your help as a way of offering you a second chance."

"Everything I know about your bleeding heart says that it is, sister."

"You don't know enough. A *second* chance suggests that you failed after the first one. And you've never disappointed me."

"Bullshit."

She had to laugh. No, he'd never believe that. He simply couldn't see himself as she did. Ah, well.

His jaw clenched as if he held in a response. He wouldn't have had time, anyway. As they sped around the next curve, Rosalia leaned forward in her seat.

"There it is," she said.

CHAPTER 9

If Sardis's ego hadn't created such a grim reality for his community, the layout of his compound would have invited Rosalia to question not just the vampire's taste, but whether he was secure in his masculinity. But the disparity between the main house—an enormous, templelike structure complete with Ionic columns—and the squat outbuildings that quartered the vampires living on the property was too great to ignore. And Rosalia wished she could believe Sardis's extreme self-love had been the reason behind the marble statues bearing his face that dotted the landscaping, but she suspected that he never wanted anyone to forget who lorded over them.

"Jesus." Deacon pulled the car up to the gates and let it idle. "How many live here?"

"Sixty." And not one of them was out walking the grounds. Even on a night this hot, surely someone would rather be outside than cooped up within a building. "It's a community rule: Anyone transformed has to serve Sardis for twenty years or buy their way out of service. Most can't afford the amount he asks."

Deacon's expression hardened. "That's complete shit. Did he lift that rule from your brother's community?"

"Probably. And, like Lorenzo, he makes it difficult for them to leave after their service is up."

Shaking his head, Deacon punched the gate's intercom button with a stiff finger. None of his disgust leaked into his voice, however; he spoke like a man who expected to attain entrance anywhere he wanted to go.

She wasn't surprised when Sardis let them through. Vampires all around Europe must have heard about Budapest by now. If the community here thought that Deacon posed a threat to Sardis, then refusing to face him could be interpreted as a weakness. So Sardis would meet with Deacon if only to show his people that he wasn't afraid.

As Deacon halted the car in the semicircular drive at the front of the main house, Rosalia called in her fan from her cache of weapons. Black lace stretched over ribs constructed of steel. She deliberately caught Deacon's eye, then pressed the release button. Six-inch blades shot out from the tips in an elegant array. She pressed the button again, and the blades retracted. Casually, she began to fan herself, and weighted her Greek with a heavy American accent. The more stereotypes she piled on, the less Sardis and Valeotes would be inclined to look beneath them.

"Hot tonight, isn't it?"

Deacon responded with a gravelly laugh that she felt down to her toes. When he rounded the car and opened her door, she breathed in his scent again. He'd begun to sweat in the evening heat, but she couldn't detect fear beneath it. She didn't know if that spoke of his confidence, or if he simply didn't care whether he made it out alive.

She preferred to believe it was confidence.

She followed him up the steps. They didn't have to knock. The door opened, revealing a giant of a man.

Dimitrios Maniatis had been a celebrity bodyguard before

his transformation. Sardis had recruited him for his intimidating bulk, but he didn't have too much height on Deacon. As if realizing that, Maniatis drew up a little taller and crossed his arms over a wide chest.

"No weapons. Leave them here, or stay outside."

Deacon hesitated. He must have decided that he'd make use of something inside, with or without weapons, Rosalia surmised. After he gave his short swords over to Maniatis, the big man patted him down.

Rosalia stepped up, fanning her face and neck as Maniatis manhandled her calves and thighs through her boots. His clumsy search continued upward, and he managed to grope her ass and fondle her breasts.

She warned Deacon back with her eyes when he stepped forward, his fists clenched.

The indignity over, she preceded Deacon inside, where an enormous foyer featured a row of Sardis-shaped busts upon marble pedestals. Cold air wafted against her exposed skin. Ah, vampires and their air-conditioning—as predictable as the dawn. As Maniatis escorted them toward the back of the house, she snapped her fan closed and passed it to Deacon.

"Will you hold this for me, baby? I don't have anywhere to put it." With a bubbly laugh, she glanced down at her second-skin shirt. Dear God. Her nipples appeared ready to pop through the material. "Obviously."

Realization skimmed through his expression. Followed, she thought, by a touch of admiration. "You won't need it?"

"Hell, no. It's freezing in here."

He slipped the weapon into his jacket pocket. Smiling, she tucked her fingers into his elbow.

Maniatis led them to a large, open rotunda, capped by a dome painted to replicate the Sistine Chapel's ceiling. Though Rosalia wouldn't have been surprised to see Sardis's face in place of Adam's, the vampire had employed restraint—a restraint that wasn't in evidence anywhere else. A white piano stood near a huge curving window overlooking an infinity swimming pool and the sea. Nude female vampires frolicked in the water, while others lounged at the side of the pool—not facing the sea view, Rosalia noted, but the rotunda, where they lay exposed to the vampires inside.

Kyriakos Sardis waited in the center of the rotunda floor, his hands tucked into the pockets of his white silk pants, his shirt unbuttoned to the waist and revealing the tan he'd sprayed on to conceal a vampire's paleness. Though young when he'd been transformed, the decadent lifestyle he'd led as a human had already begun to show, softening his face and thickening his torso. Five other vampires, equally tanned and unbuttoned, sat around the room on low-slung sofas and chairs, all upholstered in gold fabric. Not one vampire took his eyes off Deacon.

So they recognized Deacon as dangerous. Good.

The demon didn't. Unsurprisingly dark-haired, blade-nosed, and strong-jawed, Valeotes sat on the piano bench with his back to the vampire nymphs. Amid the gaudy opulence, his manufactured beauty appeared understated, and his gaze piercing as he subjected both Deacon and Rosalia to a slow scrutiny—though he didn't delve beneath her shields.

But then, he wouldn't imagine he had reason to. Rosalia wasn't blocked as a Guardian would normally be, just lightly shielded. Hiding in plain sight.

Deacon barely gave Sardis a glance, and looked past him to Valeotes. "I'm here regarding Malkvial."

Rosalia's stomach flopped over at the name. But she saw that Deacon had played exactly the right card. Deacon had the demon's attention, and Sardis apparently didn't know who Malkvial was.

He turned to Valeotes, his brow furrowed. "Who?"

The demon ignored him. He rose from his seat with a lethal, sharp elegance. His voice matched his movements, cultured and dripping with menace. "And what do you have to say regarding Malkvial?"

"I have a proposition for him. One he'll find mutually beneficial."

Though the demon's lip curled, as if to indicate how little

he thought of anything a vampire could offer, he inclined his head in agreement. And, recognizing Sardis's curiosity, was cruel enough to say, "Let us speak in private, then."

Deacon took hold of Rosalia's hand as Valeotes crossed the room. She turned to leave with the two men, but stopped when Sardis called out, "The human stays."

Without bothering to look back, Deacon said, "Not a chance."

Sardis's smile showed his fangs. "We've heard about Budapest. So we'll keep her in here . . . as a bit of insurance in the event you attempt to slay our friend."

Deacon turned to Valeotes. "I'm not interested in killing you. Farkas was one of Theriault's demons, and horning in on a friend's community. I need you to extend a proposal to Malkvial. You can't do that if you're dead."

Valeotes flicked a glance down to their linked hands. "She stays."

When Deacon looked to her, Rosalia shrugged. "Go on. They'll see they're worrying for nothing."

She stood quietly as they left, feeling the vampires' eyes on her. Down the hall, a door closed. The room Deacon had entered must have been soundproofed, because she heard nothing from them after that. Not footsteps, not voices.

Sardis's gaze fastened on her face and slid down. Usually, it amused her when men focused on her chest. But if Sardis was hoping she'd feel as if he'd poured a bucket of sewage over her body, he succeeded.

Instinctively, she crossed her arms over her breasts—the wrong reaction, she immediately recognized, but too late. Sensing vulnerability, Sardis moved in close.

"What does Deacon intend to propose?"

His psychic scent radiated aggression. Rosalia realized this would go one of two ways: bad or worse.

Since *bad* required Rosalia cowing to him and playing stupid, she chose *worse*. "When he's done, perhaps Valeotes will tell you."

With a growl, Sardis grabbed for her neck. She forced

herself to remain still. A human couldn't dodge a vampire—wouldn't even see his hand coming. To Rosalia, waiting, it felt as if he slowly closed his fingers around her throat.

She made a helpless noise and pulled weakly at his wrist.

Laughing, he lifted her into the air, pushed her back against the wall. Behind him, the other vampires watched without expression. The females frolicked and splashed outside.

No help would be coming from them. She had to hope Deacon finished quickly.

Sardis's gaze leveled on her chest again. The aggression in his psychic scent turned sexual. Still holding her up against the wall, he palmed her thigh with his free hand.

"No." She had to force the word past his grip on her throat.

He leaned in close, the bare skin of his belly pressing against hers. She tried not to gag. "No point fighting. Once we get our fangs into you, you won't care who's doing the sucking or fucking."

Damn him. He'd pushed faster than she'd thought he would; he hadn't even repeated his question about Deacon's proposal. But Sardis didn't truly care why Deacon was here. He just wanted to show Deacon's whore her place.

Deacon.

She looked toward the doorway. He wasn't coming yet.

The vampire's cold hand slid beneath her skirt. Rosalia didn't feign her shriek of outrage. He laughed and ripped away her panties, lifting them to his nose and sniffing.

"You're not wet." He looked up into her eyes, and lowered his voice as if relating a confidence. "It doesn't matter. I'll get in."

The bastard. Cold anger swept through her veins. She might be playing a human, but even a human woman had recourse. And she could play a *strong* woman.

She smashed her knee into his groin.

Sardis went rigid, his face purpling. He didn't collapse. Rosalia took advantage of his stillness and rammed her fist into his face. A Guardian could pound through his skull. She pulled her punch, and only his nose crunched.

Blood spurted over his mouth. He whipped his hand around, slapped her. Pain exploded through her cheek and upper lip. She tasted her own blood, felt its effect on Sardis as the scent hit him.

The rasp of his zipper seemed to rip through the room.

Fear rushed over her in a cold wave. She hadn't wanted to make this decision. A human would be unconscious after that slap. A human couldn't fight this. Rosalia could, but she'd have to reveal herself as a Guardian. She'd risk her plan, risk everything.

But she had to. Even if it meant she ruined any chance of defeating the nephilim. She wasn't willing to let Sardis rape her.

One punch, through his head. Her fist curled.

Something thudded against the wall next to her ear. Sardis froze.

Deacon's voice ground through the sudden silence. "Stuff your cock in *this* piehole, you fucking prick. It's still nice and hot."

Rosalia turned to look. Deacon had his hand in Valeotes's hair, holding the demon's head against the wall. Valeotes's slack mouth hung open; his neck was a bleeding stump. Blood spattered Deacon's face and clothes. His grin would have frightened Rosalia if she hadn't been so relieved.

Sardis whimpered. "She's just a whore."

Deacon's grin vanished. He dropped Valeotes's head, grabbed Sardis's below his jaw, and twisted. Steel flashed— her fan. Blood sprayed her face and chest. Sardis's grip loosened on Rosalia's neck and her feet hit the floor.

Deacon tossed Sardis's head next to Valeotes's. "They're in Hell now, so I guess they're both fucked."

Rosalia almost laughed, but the fury in his psychic scent hit her like a blow. He looked around at the other vampires.

"If I *ever* hear of any of you forcing a woman—human

or vampire—I'll do the same to you. And if you ever watch it again without interfering, if you *ever* hear of it happening without holding the prick who did it responsible, then before I kill you, I'll make you suck the blood out of your own dicks."

He turned back to Rosalia, gave her the fan. "Let's go." He pulled her along, and didn't slow until they encountered Maniatis, lurking uncertainly near the door—probably regretting that he'd molested her, wondering if he was next to die.

"My swords," Deacon commanded.

Obediently, Maniatis handed them over. Rosalia looked behind them. Vampires, male and female, stood in the hall watching them leave. They reeked of terror, of disbelief—and relief.

Deacon pulled her outside, pushed her into the car, and slammed the door. He leaned over, looking at her face. With a gentle hand, he touched her lip. The cut no longer bled, but his rage grew hotter.

He vaulted over her into his seat. The tires screeched as he ripped out of the drive. Someone at the house had the sense to open the gates. He tore through them, onto the narrow road.

Rosalia watched him. Only once had she seen him angrier: when Caym had murdered his people. His rage had been mindless then, burning against her shielded psyche. Though not as volcanic now, she didn't know what to say or how he'd respond. He certainly hadn't reacted this way ninety years ago, when he'd rescued her from a similar situation.

"Deacon, I need to thank you—"

As if her gratitude snapped something within him, he slammed the brakes. Rosalia gasped, bracing herself. The car skidded onto the deserted roadside. He cut the engine and got out, blocking his psychic scent. He stalked past the car, into the pool of yellow headlights.

She couldn't feel his anger now, but she saw it. He walked with his head down, his fists clenched. Slowly, she opened her door and moved to the front of the car, where she sat back on the warm hood. She waited, listening to the distant crash of the sea, drawing in the lush scent of the grass crushed by the skidding tires.

After only a few seconds, he pivoted and stalked back. An erection bulged behind his trousers. Rosalia's breath caught. He'd fed on the plane, but a vampire's bloodlust was unpredictable. She could understand why he'd be infuriated if the scent of Valeotes's and Sardis's blood had aroused him. As he came closer, she vanished the blood from his shirt and face, then from her own skin.

He still didn't stop until stood directly in front of her. Bending low, he caged her with his hands. "How far?"

She frowned. How far . . . what? "I don't understand."

"No?" He stepped back. "Stand up."

Slowly, she did. He took her spot on the hood. With his hands on her hips, he pulled her around to stand between his legs. She stared at him, her heart pounding. There was no mistaking this. She didn't know what point he wanted to make, but she understood this. Excitement thrummed through her veins.

"Kiss me."

Anticipation and uncertainty spread through her in equal parts. Rosalia hesitated. His face held none of the softness that she expected to accompany such a command. And she hadn't really imagined it as a *command*.

She also hadn't imagined how thrilling it would be.

Unknowing what to do with her hands, she braced her palms against his shoulders and leaned in. His lips were cool. A shiver started deep in her belly. Would he open his mouth now? Was she supposed to initiate that?

Suddenly, whether she was supposed to didn't matter. She wanted to taste him. Parting her lips, she licked between his, caught the faint flavor of blood and salt.

His shoulders tensed under her hands. His fingers clenched on her hips.

She didn't know much about kissing, but she didn't need a flashing sign to interpret his reaction. She licked again. His mouth opened and she slipped deeper. Her tongue brushed his fangs, cool and sharp. The shiver in her belly raced outward, over her skin. She shuddered, and his grip tightened. She loved that. She wanted to squirm closer to him but he held her still except for the exploration of her mouth.

Without warning, he pulled back, and her stomach sank when she saw his face. His expression hadn't softened. His eyes remained flat and hard; not a hint of the desire burning through her was reflected in them. The kiss hadn't affected him, after all.

The pounding of her heart became a painful thud. "I'm not good at that," she admitted.

"No." His laugh was hard, too. "It doesn't matter. You've got other parts I like better. So lose the top."

She'd misheard him. "Lose what?"

"Lose the shirt, sister."

Why? She stared into his face, wondering what he was driving toward—and realizing that she had only one way to find out. If she refused, that would be the end of this. Full stop. He wouldn't force her to go further. But she wanted to know what had brought him to this point.

And she wanted him looking at her.

She vanished her shirt. Released from the confining material, her breasts swayed gently, her nipples already tightly budded. And when hunger pierced his psychic shields, she'd never appreciated the fullness of her body so much.

"Now feed them to me."

His gravelly command rumbled along her nerves, sparking more heat. Arching her back, she cupped her hands beneath her breasts. Beautiful, and sometimes useful—but she'd never felt this part of her was sexy before. She'd never felt the power in this, but as he lifted his head to meet her, she reveled in it. His big palm smoothed around her hip and flattened against her back. She held her breath, watching his mouth open. His tongue flicked against her nipple, then drew a slow circle around the sensitive tip. Rosalia leaned closer to him, shaking.

His teeth closed over the taut bud, and she froze. Slowly,

he sucked her nipple between his lips. Her head fell back. Oh, God. Oh, Heaven. Every pull of his mouth seemed to set her on fire, a line of heat that settled between her legs. A fierce ache burned there, seemed to pulse outward, so strong. Her hips writhed, and Deacon's hand slid down to her ass as if to hold her in place.

His fingers caught the edge of her tiny skirt. Rosalia stilled again, panting, feeling him everywhere. The press of his fingers nearing her center. The roll of his tongue on her nipple. And still she wanted more. So much more . . . She feared how much more she wanted.

His fingers curled inward and abruptly stopped. He lifted his face toward her, staring in disbelief.

"You're wet. You're *so* fucking wet."

Did he think she wouldn't react? That Guardians couldn't? "Yes."

His voice deepened. "Then come up here."

A push of his hand told her exactly how. She came up on the hood, straddling his thighs. Her heart wouldn't stop pounding. She had Deacon between her legs. The thickness of his erection formed a hard ridge against her sex.

"Kiss me again."

She did, and this time she kissed him as she wanted to. Hungry, deep. And didn't stop, even when she felt the probing between her legs, the separation of her wet folds. Pressure at her entrance was followed by a faint pain. Oh, God. He was . . .

He stopped, barely inside, and pulled his mouth from hers. His voice was ragged.

"God, Rosie. You're so little."

What was she supposed to say? She didn't know. His gaze locked with hers and the penetration continued, ever deeper, Deacon slowly working himself into her. It felt good. And strange. And she couldn't stop herself from tensing up, not quite so aroused now, but . . . uncertain.

He must have sensed it. "You want me to stop?"

She shook her head. She just wanted to know what to

do. To be a part of this again, because somewhere along the way, she'd become lost. Distant. But she knew the mechanics, didn't she? She'd *seen* this so many times in her life. She knew how it worked.

But when she moved her hips, she felt him slip out of her. No, she didn't want to quit now. It had felt lovely and she'd never—

She looked down. It took a moment for her to realize that she'd gotten it all wrong. His trousers were still zipped, the fabric wet. She rode his hand between her thighs. His middle finger glistened.

"Oh," she whispered, then half laughed. "That wasn't— I thought—"

"That I was fucking you?" Anger returned to his voice. "You'd go that far?"

"Yes." Obviously, yes. She'd thought they already *had*.

And maybe Deacon meant to now. He took her mouth again, his tongue pushing past her lips. She felt his fingers working between her folds again, and pressure inside—so deep. His thumb slid up, began to circle.

And that quickly she was back in it, wanting too much, no longer lost. Deacon scraped his fangs down her neck, then sucked the tip of her breast into his mouth. Rosalia's head fell back, her eyes closing, her fingers clenching as if she could hold on to something, hold something in. Need and excitement swelled within her, growing too fast, too big. She hadn't thought it would be *this*. Rough. Hot. Urgent. She'd thought it would be sweet, and soft. Not . . . not this . . .

Out of control.

"Deacon—"

She cried out as the pressure increased. A second finger joined his first, thrusting slowly. She hadn't known the burn, the pain could be so good. *Too* good.

"Stop . . . Oh, God. You've got to stop. Before I come."

And she couldn't stop herself. She was still moving on his hand when he pulled it away. He watched her, not speaking, his face still hard. Almost sobbing, she quieted her body.

It took a few more moments before she could breathe steadily enough to explain. "I don't know if I can shield my mind. Sardis's compound is too close. The vampires there might sense my presence."

His eyes narrowed. "How can you not know? You've come before."

"Yes. But only alone. Cocooned in the dark." And that sounded . . . pathetic. She put on a smile and tried to turn it around. "When I'm desperate and lonely."

Something in his expression changed. She couldn't read it. And she couldn't stand not knowing, but wouldn't ask.

She pulled off. Stumbling to the grassy verge, she sat heavily, her hands covering her face. The pressure inside her built up again, but this time she felt no pleasure. Only panic. She'd come so close to not caring whether she revealed herself. To losing control at his touch—and loving it. This wasn't the risk she was supposed to be taking.

Behind her, Deacon cursed, and Rosalia steeled herself. She recognized the harshness of his tone. It always appeared in his voice just before he told her to fuck off.

"At least now we know how far you'll go. You'll let yourself be raped. You'll fuck me because you want my help. But you won't let yourself come. That's some sick shit, sister, any way you twist it. And you can count me out of your goddamn plan, because I'm not going to be a part of this."

This was what he'd meant by *How far?* And he'd asked her to kiss him to find out. Not driven by his bloodlust or his arousal, but driven to prove a point.

And he'd missed it by a mile.

She glanced over her shoulder, found him standing rigidly beside the car. The tightness in her throat and chest almost choked her, but she spoke past it. "I wouldn't have let him rape me. When you arrived, I was a moment away from punching through his head—and for that, I'm disappointed in myself. I thought I'd sacrifice more. But when it came down to a poke between my legs and saving everyone from the nephilim, I tossed the world away."

His brows drew together. She felt his astonishment, saw the darkening of his expression as surprise turned to rejection. "That's fucked-up, Rosie."

An almost hysterical laugh bubbled up. She swallowed it down and turned away from him again. "Maybe."

"So what the hell were you doing with me? Were you proving to yourself that you could sacrifice and take that poke between your legs?"

He hadn't considered that she might want him? What was lower—his opinion of her or of himself?

"I was doing what I wanted to since I met you. What were *you* doing?"

He didn't answer. His silence stabbed at her. God, she'd been so stupid. To think that he might feel any desire in return. No matter the reason he'd commanded her to kiss him, she'd believed something had changed along the way. But while she'd been losing control, he'd been . . . testing to see if she'd whore herself for the cause.

She'd said it didn't matter what anyone thought of her. But she did. And it hurt.

Pale yellow light began to shine against her legs. Her eyes, glowing as she lost control to her emotions. She *never* did that. She suddenly, desperately needed him to leave, before he witnessed that, too.

So he'd managed to do one thing: *She* had discovered how far she would go.

"All right, Deacon," she said, and almost didn't recognize her own voice. She felt as if dirty rags had been shoved into her chest. "Count yourself out. I'll figure out another way."

She heard his sigh, and the regret in it. "Rosie—"

"Go. I'll call ahead. The plane is yours. I won't even check to see where you went. You're free of me."

"Goddammit. At least let me—"

"Apologize? Fine. I accept it. You don't owe me anything else, so go on." She didn't hear him leave. Maybe he needed words he could understand. Words he'd thrown at her before. "We're done. So get the fuck out of my face."

Still no movement behind her. Only the beat of his heart.

"Haul off, Deacon." To her horror, her voice broke.

But it got him moving when words alone could not. She heard the crunch of gravel beneath his feet as he walked onto the road. The car started, and a moment later, he drove away.

Oh, God. What had she done?

She closed her eyes, which had begun shining like a beacon. Hugging her knees up to her chest, holding on to the darkness, she prayed. *Oh, God, oh, God.* The refrain remained the only light in her mind, and she begged Him to help her bear the pain, to help her formulate another plan.

She had no idea what she was going to do now.

CHAPTER 10

Rosalia couldn't sit and cry forever. Prayer steadied her, but she'd already been gifted with strength of heart and mind so that she could help herself. And putting a new plan into motion would take time—but the vampires in London didn't have much.

With a deep breath, Rosalia gathered herself, and brought in her satellite phone from her cache. She had to contact the plane's charter service. No doubt Deacon would want to head to Paris and continue on with Theriault.

The alert for a waiting connection sounded as soon as she opened the phone. The number linked to the surveillance van. Panic fluttered in Rosalia's chest. Gemma had been watching St. Croix. Had something happened?

The phone transmitted video in addition to audio. She engaged both, and a moment later, Vin's face filled the screen. He wasn't supposed to be there.

She couldn't keep the fear out of her voice. "Is Gemma all right?"

"Yes. But she's been throwing up and decided to stay at

the abbey. So I've taken over the van until you return. . . ."
He frowned and peered more closely at the screen. The indifferent mask she was so accustomed to him wearing cracked. Concern bled through. "Mama, are you all right?"

Oh, curses. Her lipstick and heavy eyeliner had suffered though kisses and tears. She must appear horrid. "Oh, that." She vanished the makeup, gave a soft smile. "I'm fine."

He stared doubtfully at the screen for a few more seconds. "All right. I just wanted to ask you to check in on Gemma if you return to the abbey."

That hadn't been what he'd intended to ask. "You be with Gemma. I'll take over surveillance."

"No can do, Mama. After we visited Father Wojcinski, Gemma got it in her head that there will be no more cohabitation until the wedding." He shrugged. "Anyway, putting in a late night will be good practice for after the baby comes."

"Vin—"

"I've got a game up on the other monitor. You can keep an eye on me and on the Paris feed in your War Room. And you can take a few hours, take a swim."

"Thank you, Vincente." Fearing that the tears were coming again, she moved on. "What of your surveillance?"

"He's sleeping. Or pretending to."

It had just passed midnight in Rome. A reasonable time for a human to go to bed . . . or a demon who needed to pretend for the benefit of a human.

"Is he alone?"

"Yes."

Odd. Then either St. Croix wasn't a demon, or he was very careful about appearances—just as she suspected Malkvial might be. "All right. I'm en route now. I should arrive in another hour."

"Give me a buzz to let me know you got in all right."

Sweet boy. She disconnected and called the charter service. A few minutes later, it was settled: Deacon would soon be on his way to Paris, and she was heading for Rome.

Maybe it was better this way.

❧

So, that was that. No Guardian using him anymore. He'd known all he had to do was be an uncivil bastard and she'd stop hounding him.

He should have done it before driving away became so fucking hard.

As she'd promised, the plane was waiting for him. So it was back to Paris. Back to what he'd been doing: stalking Theriault, and slaying him. And if slaying Theriault messed up Rosalia's game plan, she'd come up with another. She had to, anyway.

But he couldn't stop staring at the empty seat next to him. She should be there, all curled up in that ridiculous pose. She was done with him, but so what? That didn't mean she had to get back home under her own power.

Too late now. She'd called ahead to the plane, but he didn't have her number. He couldn't tell her to get over herself. So he'd been a bastard. She could still catch a ride and . . . kiss him so sweetly.

Because she'd *wanted* to kiss him.

Christ. He still couldn't believe that, but it didn't matter anyway: She wouldn't want to kiss him again. He'd made sure of that, hadn't he?

Fuck. *Fuck.*

He had Camille's number. If anyone could help Rosalia, it'd be Camille. A strong vampire—though not as strong as Deacon, now that he'd taken the nosferatu blood, but Camille's skills made up for that. She'd taught him everything he knew that didn't involve punching a man.

Yves, though. He was used to Camille manipulating him from behind, but if she came out in front? There was no telling if Yves could handle that. He might accidentally expose both Camille and Rosalia, and send demons running after them both. If Rosalia ended up in the path of demons, she could probably handle that. But she was worried about the nephilim—and their mother, Anaria.

Anaria, who had torn through the Guardians' warehouse, and they'd been unable to defend themselves against her.

Rosalia wouldn't stand a chance against Anaria.

And Yves, the little prick, would fuck it all up. Or Camille would, if she and Rosalia didn't hit it off. Rosalia would have to start over. Again. Probably with some vampire who couldn't hold a sword. Someone who would ruin the perfect setups she gave him.

Hell, even resenting how she'd overrun him, Deacon recognized how perfectly she'd arranged the two kills he'd made. The demons had practically cut off their own heads.

He looked out at the runway. It was an easy decision, to do nothing. To go where he'd intended. He just had to . . . do nothing.

Shit.

❧

Situated near the old walls of the city, the abbey had stood unchanging for hundreds of years, orange plaster over stone, an old warm sanctuary amid the newer construction that came and went. Once surrounded by an orchard, now only a small fenced garden overgrown with roses separated her walls from her neighbors'.

She didn't mind. The abbey's heart had never resided in its stone walls.

Deceptively large from the outside, the building didn't hold nearly as many rooms as its dimensions suggested. An enormous courtyard relegated the living spaces to a narrow string of rooms along the walls, and many of the bedchambers were accessible only from its paths. It was where the family had met, fought, trained, and talked. Abundant with life; with gardens planted for consumption and for beauty; cypresses; fig and orange trees, the courtyard formed the abbey's center in a sense that went far beyond the physical.

Rosalia flew directly to Gemma's room, landing on the gallery that overlooked the courtyard and served as the walkway connecting all of the second-floor chambers. Beyond the door, the young woman slept. Vanishing her wings, Rosalia continued to her own chambers, two rooms separated by a corridor leading from the gallery. After checking in with Vin, she returned outside.

The roses had folded for the night, but the jasmine had bloomed and filled the air with its heady fragrance. The birds rested quietly in the trees, and the tinkling of the fountain was the only sound in the still air.

Fifteen years ago, she'd had a lap pool installed at the end of the courtyard. The scent of chlorine sometimes overpowered the flowers' perfumes, but Rosalia had never regretted the change.

She stripped off and dove in. Though she could swim at extraordinary speeds, she sought only a methodical rhythm: twenty strokes, and turn. She'd have liked to work herself into exhaustion, but Guardians couldn't tire. Peace couldn't be found in sleep. Only the rhythm.

Once she found it, she turned her mind to the daunting task she faced. Of all the vampires she trusted, Camille was the only one who might pull off such a scheme. But Rosalia knew Yves too well. He was a good man, but he'd make a mistake.

And Malkvial would have no reason to believe Camille, anyway.

She pushed away the despair, the doubt. There had to be some way. But she still hadn't thought of one two hours later, when a knock at the front door pulled her out of the water.

She climbed from the pool, wondering if she'd been mistaken. Shaking the water out of her hair and slipping a silk robe on over her naked form, she listened—and the knock came again.

At three thirty in the morning? That didn't bode well.

Typically, she used a psychic probe to discover the identity of the caller. But there was another way, just as simple. She brought in a crossbow from her cache. Forming her wings, she flew up to the roof, where the bell tower at the corner provided cover and offered a view of the door.

Deacon.

Her heart thudded. Her mind raced while she decided what to do. She hadn't thought he'd come here.

Why had he come here?

His fist rose to the door, but he paused before knocking again. As if he'd heard her, his gaze swept her direction, found her atop the roof. He stepped toward her.

Defensive mode kicked in. She fired the crossbow. The bolt stabbed the ground in front of his boot. He froze.

"I can hear you from here. Just say what you've got to say, then leave."

He lifted his hands, as if in surrender. "I'm sorry."

"I've already accepted your apology."

"No. I never had time to give it."

"Well. Now you have." She turned to go, but paused when he said—

"Yves will fuck it up."

God. He could already see where she would go next, the best course of action? "You've stated, very clearly, that you don't care."

"Then tell me why I should. Tomorrow."

Her eyes narrowed. "What?"

"Tell me when we go hunting another demon tomorrow. Tell me another reason why I should care. And if I don't, there's the next day, and the next demon. I know you've got one lined up."

Rosalia sank to her heels. "Are you offering to help me?"

"Yes."

"Why?"

His slow smile caught her off guard, and her heart thudded again. "I'll give you a reason tomorrow, too. But tonight, it's because I was a complete bastard, and I'm sor—"

A scream split the air—from inside the abbey. Oh, Lord. Gemma.

Rosalia dove from the roof and hit the ground running. Across the courtyard, she leapt to the second-floor gallery leading to Gemma's bedroom.

She flung open the door. Gemma was sitting up in bed, screaming. Her eyes were open, but unfocused. Seeing horrors that wouldn't let her go.

Rosalia vanished her crossbow and ran to the bedside. "Baby girl, it's okay; you're safe—"

Gemma shrieked and jumped into an attack, barreling into her and toppling them over. Rosalia took the brunt of the fall against the slate floor, her wings trapped beneath her. Gemma's fist smashed into her cheek, and Rosalia actually saw stars. Hallelujah, she'd taught this young woman to hit hard.

"Gemma, baby, you're safe! Wake up and see that—" She broke off as Deacon rushed into the room, sword drawn. "Get back! She's fine. I'm fine. Just . . . wait. Out there."

Deacon hesitated when she took another blow from the screaming woman. Then Gemma's fist froze midair.

She glanced down, her eyes losing their terrifying emptiness. "Oh, God. Rosa."

"Ciao." Rosalia breathed out a laugh. "You're okay. Yes? We're both okay."

"Yes." As Gemma scrambled to her feet, Rosalia glanced at the doorway. Deacon had gone. She looked back as Gemma put her hands to her face. "Oh, God."

The young woman broke into wretched sobs. Rosalia drew her into her arms, down to the bed, and vanished her wings. Curling up behind the taller woman, she stroked her blond hair, straightening the sweat-tangled strands.

After a while, Gemma quieted. "It's the same. Always the same. Giacomo and Svetlana coming in to protect me. Then the nephilim." A shudder wracked her body. "God, they were so big. Those black wings. Their skin so red . . . and their *eyes* glowing red. Their swords were already bloody. I yelled at Svetlana to get behind me, because a demon couldn't hurt me. Couldn't go through me. But then she and Giacomo were just . . . gone. And everything was covered in red."

Almost every room in the abbey, and Gemma had cleaned it all long before Rosalia had been freed from the catacombs. The young woman had been left on her own for months, until she'd run across Vincente.

Gemma drew a deep, shuddering breath that seemed to rinse her out. "I'm sorry I hit you."

"It's okay. You were asleep."

"Yes. Okay." She tensed. "No, it's not. Let me be sorry."

"Okay."

Gemma growled in the back of her throat. "You always do that. You let people beat up on you, and you never hit back."

Shock held Rosalia silent for a moment. "Gemma, I can't—"

"Hit me, because I'm a human. If you do, you Fall. I get it. I don't mean *me*, and I don't mean hitting." She made a motion in the air with her fist. "I mean that when you love someone, you let them walk all over you."

Realization slipped through her. "Vincente."

"Yes. But not just Vin. You put everyone ahead of yourself, Rosa."

Not everyone, but a few. And she could not be sorry for that. "It gives me pleasure to know that the ones I love are happy. And safe."

"And that's the only thing that gives you pleasure. What other pleasures do you have?"

Rosalia almost laughed. How absurd this was. "Gardening, swimming, slaying demons—"

"Those are solace. Those aren't pleasures."

"My greatest pleasure is you and Vincente." She rested her hand on Gemma's belly. "You will see."

"But we have each other, too. You don't have anyone." She took a deep breath. "Oh, God. I'm sorry, Rosa."

"I do not want to anger you by saying it's okay."

Gemma's short laugh ended on a sigh. "It's just been building up for a while."

"Then I will think on what you've said." She paused. "Would you like me to stay here while you fall asleep again?"

"Yes." But she didn't immediately close her eyes. "I used to be so jealous of Vin for this."

"For what?"

"I remember, even after days when he wouldn't talk to you, when you'd spent an evening arguing, that I would walk by his room and see you on the bed, holding him like this. I always wanted that."

Rosalia's throat tightened. "Your grandmother was—"

"Wonderful, yes. But I was still so jealous of Vin and his sweet, beautiful princess mama, who would always come and cuddle with him, even when he was awful."

It had been all that she could do. "I heard you outside the room . . . but I never knew. I would have asked you to join us."

"And Vin and I would have begun our cohabitation as children. Father Wojcinski would not approve."

Rosalia laughed and squeezed her softly. Lord, but she loved this woman.

Gemma raised her hand to cover a yawn before asking, "Vin must still be out?"

It wasn't really a question. They both knew that if he hadn't been, he'd be in here with her—Father Wojcinski or not. "Yes. He says that the late nights will be good training for when the baby comes."

"And I've told him that since you don't sleep, that makes you the perfect babysitter." The laughter left her voice. "He says it's not a good idea to ask, though. Why is he such a stubborn ass?"

Now Rosalia's eyes did fill. Sometimes, he really was a sweet boy. "Gemma . . . I can't."

"You'll be busy, but—"

"No, it is not that. I cannot hold the baby unless she is sleeping. If she pushes at me, or tries to get away . . . even a baby's free will must be honored. Toddlers are impossible. They always want down, even when it is not safe for them. If I want to remain a Guardian . . . when a child pushes me away, the only time to hold him is while he sleeps."

Gemma lay quietly as she absorbed that. Then sadness and understanding filled her psychic scent. "Oh, Rosa."

"I cannot regret a moment of it, Gemma. So do not be

sorry on my behalf. Just hold your baby and Vincente tight, and celebrate that you *can* hold them. Yes?"

"Yes." Gemma's nod was followed by a quick look over her shoulder. "Did Vin know that you couldn't restrain him?"

"Yes."

"No wonder he was the most spoiled kid I knew." Gemma rested her head on the pillow again.

Rosalia smiled into her hair. "Yes, he was."

❧

His sweet, beautiful princess mama.

Deacon would have agreed with most of that. But the last bit rattled him, like a right hook he hadn't seen coming. And not just a mother, but one whose relationship with her adult son sounded strained at best.

What was wrong with that kid?

He wouldn't find out by continuing to eavesdrop. They hadn't spoken in a while, and he'd prowled through every courtyard path and open room by the time he heard quiet movement from upstairs. Stopping by the fountain, he glanced up. Rosalia closed the bedroom door behind her, quickly found him below, and vaulted over the balustrade. Her wings appeared, spreading wide. She caught air and drifted to his side, the bottom of her silk robe splitting open to flutter like another pair of wings and offering a glimpse of her inner thighs.

A glimpse. He could probably count himself lucky to get that. Christ, what a bastard he'd been. Barely fit to look at her, let alone kiss her.

Yet he knew that was one of the reasons why he'd come back.

She landed lightly beside him. He'd expected wariness, uncertainty—at least defensiveness, considering that he'd just overheard an intimate conversation—but she simply smiled at him before sitting on the bench facing the fountain.

Gardening, swimming, slaying demons. On that short list of pleasures, the last was the only one she wouldn't find in this flourishing paradise. He'd never seen so many flowers open at night, small explosions of red, purple, and orange. Planted for the vampires who'd once lived here, he thought—or because a Guardian didn't sleep either night or day.

He sat next to her, and he felt the brush of her wing against his back before she vanished them. When she half turned toward him, he said, "So I guess I got a jump on tomorrow, and heard another reason."

"You did. And Gemma . . ." She trailed off as her gaze fastened on his neck. Her brow pleated, and a moment later her fingers were on his collar, tucking and smoothing. She continued, "Her nightmares haven't stopped. This was worse than it has been, though. Perhaps hearing of London has brought it back to her. And although slaying the nephilim will not undo what has been done . . . I would like to tell her they are dead."

With a final pat, she finished straightening him up, but didn't remove her hands. Her eyes rose to his. Her lips parted . . . and formed two unmistakable silent words.

Don't move.

He heard it then, over the splashing of the fountain: another heartbeat. Despite Rosalia's warning, he couldn't sit still with a threat behind him. He turned.

The woman—the red-haired detective. Her eyes were blue instead of completely black, and she was sitting . . . just sitting on the flagstone path a few meters away, like a bone-tired traveler. Rosalia caught Deacon's wrist before he could reach for his sword.

The detective's weary gaze sought Rosalia. Her voice was her own, feminine—and she spoke in English. "I didn't come when you wanted me to."

"It's all right, Taylor. We made it there."

To Athens? Rosalia had planned to let this woman teleport them to Greece?

She didn't look possessed now, though. Just lost.

Taylor rubbed her hand over her face. "I feel like I should be tired. But I'm not. I want to sleep. But I can't."

"No. We can't sleep." Rosalia's voice had deepened in

sympathy. "Meditating helps, though. Do you know how to drift?"

"The others have tried with me. But Michael's never gone." She touched her fingers to her forehead. "And I can't push him out."

"Well, we'll try anyway. And maybe it will work both ways, and offer him some peace, too."

Peace? For what? Deacon looked to Rosalia. "What happened to Michael?"

Rosalia hesitated. Not just reluctant to say it, he realized. Reluctant to say it to *him*. What was it, top secret Guardian info?

That was fair. But considering that the man kept trying to kill him, Deacon should probably know what to expect. "What happened?"

Rosalia took a deep breath. "He's dead."

Dead? Christ, no wonder Rosalia was so hell-bent on her plan, then. Without Michael, the Guardians were practically sitting ducks for any force of demons . . . or just a few nephilim.

"Worse," Taylor said. Her gaze settled on Deacon and didn't waver. "He's in Hell, in the frozen field. Anaria accessed Chaos, thanks to info you gave Caym. She made a spell that would have opened a portal between the realms. To close it, Michael sacrificed himself . . . and tied himself to me."

Was this true? Deacon looked at Rosalia. She gave a small nod. So Michael wasn't just dead, he was being *tortured for eternity*—and Deacon was partly responsible.

It had been some time since he'd felt this low.

And he sunk lower when Taylor said, "And the vampire that you created for Caym killed me. That's how I ended up a Guardian."

So that was why she kept jumping into his rooms, hoping to slay him. Deacon had no words. Explaining wouldn't make a difference. *I needed to save my community.* That only mattered to him—and he couldn't say he wouldn't have done it again, or taken another route. He'd sacrificed everything to save them, and that was a reason he could never regret.

But he could regret the fallout, and the innocents caught.

He looked Taylor square on. "I'm sorry."

She nodded. "Me, too."

He glanced at Rosalia and searched for something to say. She turned away from him. "Come with me. I might be with Taylor beyond sunrise, so we'll get you settled in first."

After retrieving the bag he'd left by the entrance of the abbey, he followed her up the stairs to the second level. She turned into a corridor, where a heavy door opened into a long, high-ceilinged chamber. He recognized this room. He'd woken up here sixth months ago, but he hadn't noticed then the personal touches. Propped on a nightstand, a dark-haired boy smiled out of a silver frame. Books lined a recessed shelf in the warm yellow walls. At the far end of the chamber, cream marble tiles and half-melted candles surrounded a tub; pink and white bottles filled the corner niche in an open shower. In the sitting area, a delicate vase holding red roses adorned a carved wooden table. And the art . . . He'd expected pastorals and landscapes, but it was modern, all angles and bright colors.

Recognizing one of Eva's paintings was like a punch to the gut. He walked over to the canvas—had to touch it, feel the rough strokes beneath his fingers.

When he turned, Rosalia was standing beside the bed, stripping back the sheets. A faint blush warmed her cheeks.

"They're clean, but I don't air them enough. So they've become stale," she explained, moving to a wardrobe and reaching in for a new set of linens.

"I don't care."

She smiled and returned to the bed. "I do."

He couldn't argue with that. "This is your room." He said it as flatly as possible. He wasn't making assumptions. Not about her, not anymore.

"Yes." In the space of a breath, she'd changed the sheets and replaced the bedding, then glanced up at him. "With Taylor here, I want you as close as possible."

So she knew about Taylor's darker side. "But you don't sleep. Why would this be close?"

She moved back out into the corridor, opened the door opposite her bedchamber. "I'll be in here."

Though the smaller chamber had the same yellow walls and slate floor, there wasn't any room for personal touches. File cabinets and racks of equipment crowded together at one side of the room, and several computers topped one long worktable. Five TV monitors hung from the walls, running the broadcasts from five twenty-four news stations at a low volume.

"Vincente calls it my War Room. If you want to check in on Theriault and review his tapes, the feed from Paris is there"—she pointed to a computer—"and the surveillance van feed is here."

She moved to another computer and clicked a few buttons. The screen filled with an infrared image of a man sleeping. Another screen lit up and revealed a thirtysomething man in a narrow space, sitting with his chair tilted back and his feet propped up. A soccer game played on a small monitor behind him.

"That's Vincente. Here's the mic if something comes up and you need to be in contact with him."

Deacon couldn't imagine a single reason why he would. "All right."

"I don't know how long I'll be with Taylor. The bedroom is sealed against light; even if I open the door, no sunlight will fall on the bed. You'll be safe sleeping there."

She was worried about *his* safety? Jesus. "Michael's dead. How in the hell can you trust me?"

Her brows drew together, as if for a moment she didn't know what to make of his question. "I have to," she said finally. "I have to trust that you're the man I think you are, rather than the one Caym forced you to be."

He wanted to be that, too. He didn't know if he could.

"Why didn't you throw this at me?" When he saw her confusion, he clarified, "Michael's death. You were after me to help. You didn't bring this up?"

"Why would I? You didn't kill him." Rosalia sighed and came closer, her eyes deep and unreadable. "Deacon, Belial's lieutenant already *had* the information that Anaria used to make her portal to Chaos. He told you that. You were just someone to play with."

And Rosalia knew that because she'd been in Prague, concealed in her shadows. She'd seen that the demon's idea of "playing" meant killing everyone—except for Deacon. The demon had hoped that Irena would be the one to slay him, so that Deacon would die at the hands of his friend.

"He dragged you down and slaughtered everyone in your community *because he could*. Because that's what demons do. He didn't use you to help Anaria. He didn't do it for any other reason than because it amused him, and because it was another blow to you."

Not just him. "And to Irena."

"Irena's pain was a bonus. So was Michael. So if you're looking for another reason why I want to kill all of Belial's demons and take Anaria, too . . . Well, there it is. Michael is my reason. And so is everyone else who died in Anaria's path, and in the path of Belial's demons."

The Guardian healer who Anaria had killed. Vampires in San Francisco . . . and his entire community. Yeah, he could get behind that reason.

"Maybe I'll put that in my column, too."

"No." She shook her head, smiling again and backing toward the door. "Don't tell me now. You aren't supposed to tell me until tomorrow."

Deacon watched her leave. Everything she'd said was true . . . but that still didn't absolve him of his part in it. Grimly, he turned toward the computers.

He'd thought he wasn't fit to kiss her? Truth was, he wasn't even fit to kiss her goddamn feet.

❦

Watching Theriault pretend to sleep from seven hundred miles away wasn't any more interesting than standing outside the demon's apartment and doing the same.

Restless, Deacon left the War Room and stood overlooking

the courtyard. Moonlight silvered the trees and left a sparkling trail across the surface of the pool. Both Rosalia and Taylor floated motionless beneath the water. Rosalia's long hair billowed like a dark pillow, and she'd exchanged her robe for a pale, thin sheath, which clung to her luscious curves. When he found himself staring at the dark shape of her nipples, he went back in.

The surveillance van's monitor flipped on. "Mother, are you—" Vin broke off and peered at the screen. "Deacon?"

"Yes."

The younger man laughed. "So she got her claws into you after all?"

Deacon reminded himself that this was Rosalia's son and that he couldn't pound his fist through the screen. "Do you need her?"

"Not if you're there," Vin said. "The garage watchman is heading into the john, so I'm off to tag our target's car with a tracker. Can you keep an eye on his screen?"

Deacon glanced at the blob of infrared color on the monitor. "I can."

So, now he watched two demons pretend to sleep. Rosalia had the right idea. Killing them was better.

He flipped through the folder next to the computer, got this one's name: Nicholas St. Croix. Yeah, that sounded like a name a demon might make up.

Then the man got out of bed, and Deacon revised his opinion.

After a few minutes, the van door opened and slammed again. Vin's face appeared in the monitor. "So he's awake?"

"I don't think he's your guy. He took a piss."

"If he knows he's being watched, that doesn't mean anything." Vin unwrapped plastic from a take-out plate and shoved it into a tiny microwave, then rolled his chair back in front of the screen. "Mother once told me that she used to find demons just by listening to servant gossip. They're all rich, and a hundred years ago and more they had the servants, the chambermaids. And when a maid started talking about how she never had to empty a pot, Mama would go hunting. So the smart demons think about little things like that if they know there's any possibility the Guardians might be looking at them. And they fake it."

"Fake pissing?" Deacon drank his meal every night and couldn't shake out a drop if he tried.

"They fake it with something else. Before toilets, they used to vanish waste into their cache, and fill up the pot to fool the maid—but that isn't convincing when they're under real-time observation. One demon used his blood and a bulb syringe. He filled it up, squeezed it out. The sound is right, and even the infrared is fooled. And while sitting, he'd cut his dick off—that one managed to stump Mama for weeks."

The microwave beeped. Vin pulled his plate out and dug in, his appetite apparently unaffected. Dinnertime conversation in this abbey must have been a far cry from Deacon's home. Supper in the Knox home had been a serious affair, meat and potatoes and silence, with the Bible coming out afterward. He'd certainly never thought about whether any prophets or saints had taken a piss.

And he'd get along just fine if he never thought about it again. "You can't rely on the infrared?"

"We can for vampires. But with demons, the core temperature isn't so different from a human's. Throw in variations like room temperature, and it's easy for someone to read a few degrees hotter or cooler. On a cold night, with humans for comparison, we'd probably be able to pick a demon out. But basing it on a temperature determined through walls, when he's alone? It's best not to try." Vin paused. "But I'm leaning toward human, too. Another day or two of observation won't hurt, though, until we're certain."

Deacon tilted his chair back, and was wondering if Rosalia's son would be so open to sharing if the topic turned a little more personal when Vin said, "What happened to her in Athens tonight?"

"What?"

"She called around midnight. She didn't look so good."

She hadn't? A knot tightened in his stomach. But Deacon wasn't going to answer to her son. Only to Rosalia.

"We took out Valeotes and Sardis. The vampire gave her some trouble."

"Is she going in as a human?"

"Yes."

Vin looked away from the monitor, his jaw hardening. "Sardis, Jesus. That fucking bastard."

"You know him?"

"I know enough about him to imagine what happened. But I don't know them all like Mother does."

Deacon frowned. "All?"

"Every vampire in Europe. Their names, their history."

He could believe that. She'd known his history, though few others did. "Every one?"

"Maybe she's missed a dozen or two, but she can name every vampire in a community, tell you what he did as a human, all of the aliases he's used and the partners he's had."

"Jesus." That was about a thousand vampires.

Vin shrugged. "She overcompensates for her brother."

"How's that?"

"She couldn't save him. So she wants to save everyone else—and their information is her tool."

He looked at the cabinets behind him. "There's a file somewhere?"

"No. She's got it all up there." Vin tapped his forehead. "You could find some info on the community leaders and a list of vampires within the communities, but everything else about them, she keeps as stories in her head." He stopped to take another bite and swallow. "She tells them now and then. I grew up hearing about you and Camille moving groups of refugees out of Nazi-occupied territory. Her favorite is the night you razed through a battalion of Nazi soldiers."

"She was there?"

"You didn't see her, did you?" Vin seemed to enjoy that. "She set it all up and ran the whole thing with Camille and a few others."

He struggled to keep his surprise from showing. He hadn't known that. So even though Rosalia must already be acquainted with Camille—had run operations with her before—she'd asked Deacon to help her now. That couldn't just be about Yves. What the hell could he do that Camille couldn't?

"She set all of that up?" It hadn't been enough; it could never have been enough—but everything they'd managed to accomplish had pulled through, beautifully.

Just like every demon kill she'd set up so far.

"Yes. Why do you think you were never discovered during the daytime?"

He'd always thought they'd just been lucky. He'd still been in his early years as a vampire—not even twenty years with fangs, and had only just begun to resent how Camille managed him. But now he saw how every person involved had always been in the perfect position, each according to his skill set. How everyone had the information they needed. And how they'd always had a backup plan, so that every human who'd come with them had made it through.

Realizing that Vin waited for an answer, he said, "Camille chose secure locations."

The other man nodded. "Camille *is* good. Mother is better."

Deacon was beginning to believe that.

§

The sun was rising when Taylor disappeared again. Hoping she'd found a little solace, Rosalia left the pool and flew upstairs. In her chambers, Deacon lay on the bed, a sheet draped over his hips, his bare chest unmoving. Even in sleep, his muscles retained their definition. The ridged plane of his abdomen seemed to call her fingers to explore.

She resisted the impulse, marveling instead that he was here. God, she couldn't believe he'd returned, *willing* to help. For some reason, between Athens and Rome, he'd decided that destroying the nephilim and Belial's demons mattered to him. Considering that he'd left Rosalia on the side of a road, that reason probably hadn't anything to do with her . . . but she didn't care. She didn't know what had brought him back, but she thanked God with all of her heart that he'd come.

She watched him for a few moments before shaking herself and crossing into the War Room, where Vincente was still at it—and looking exhausted.

She switched on the microphone. "Go home and sleep."

Vin yawned and stretched. "The tracker's on his vehicle."

"Good. Thank you."

"How's Gemma?"

She's fine. Rosalia almost gave that automatic answer, then realized it wasn't her place to protect him from this. "She had a bad moment. She's sleeping now, but it was a rough night."

His haunted expression tore at her heart. "I don't know what to do. How to help her. I wish to God I'd been here with her that night."

As much as Rosalia wished that he'd never left, it wouldn't have changed anything. The nephilim would still have come. "Just hold her when she needs it."

"I intend to—Father Wojcinski be damned. So don't be surprised when I show up at the abbey in about thirty minutes."

She'd only have been surprised if he *hadn't* come. "All right."

"Good night, Mama." He flipped off the monitor.

Rosalia smiled to herself and moved back into the bedroom. Resisting the temptation to spend a few minutes on the bed, simply soaking in Deacon's presence, she crossed the room and vanished her clothes. Painfully aware that this marked the first time she'd been naked in the same room with a man— even a sleeping one—she showered to rinse off the scent of chlorine. As she dressed, her gaze fell on Deacon again. She could look upon him forever and never tire of the view.

She couldn't help herself. Climbing onto the bed, she curled around him and drew in his scent. She wouldn't sleep. But every day, she took a few quiet minutes to think, to examine and re-examine her plan.

For today, she wanted to do it here.

CHAPTER II

Sunset brought Deacon hard out of dreams. He jacked up to sitting, facing unfamiliar walls, his mind still awash in pain and blood. He fought to orient himself.

Rome. Rosalia's abbey. Her bed.

Jesus.

He threw back sweat-dampened sheets and headed for the shower. Cranking the knob all the way left, Deacon stepped under scalding water. He gritted his teeth and bore it until the rage and pain faded.

He'd be killing a demon tonight. That would help, too. But for the first time six months, it wasn't his only reason for getting up.

He hadn't been going after Belial's demons because it'd been the right thing to do—it'd been the *only* thing to do. It couldn't bring him peace. It couldn't bring his community back. It just made living with himself easier.

But thanks to Rosalia, he had a new reason for taking down Belial's demons and the nephilim. Pursuing Belial's demons could be something useful, something for his community: a vow that they'd be the last. *Never again* would a city of vampires be slaughtered by demons or nephilim.

He'd still take a hell of a lot of satisfaction by slaying them along the way.

The water cooled, the heater tank running low. Deacon lathered up. The pink soap smelled like Rosalia, flowery and delicate. His bloodlust stirred, and he soothed his fangs with his tongue to stave off the insistent hunger. But even after rinsing, her scent remained all over his skin like she'd spent the day wrapped around him.

He wouldn't be kicking her out of bed if she did.

And that was the goddamn understatement of the century. Christ. She hadn't even pulled his strings and he'd come running after her—which just showed how much of a glutton he was for pain. Even if Rosalia was interested in burning up a few sheets, eventually she wouldn't need his help, and he'd have to move on. And in less than a week, she already had a few hooks in him.

He'd loved Eva and Petra, loved them deep—but the hooks they'd had felt different. From their first meeting, he'd liked the two women, and that had grown into affection and a sixty-year friendship. But something else was going on with Rosalia. Even resisting everything he liked about her, she hit him gut-level. She had from the day they'd met. And he wasn't looking forward to knowing what her hooks would feel like if they went deep, because he'd be ripping them out when he left.

Problem was, even knowing what he'd be in for, he'd take any opportunity she gave him. And, hell—maybe he deserved having his heart torn out.

He grabbed a towel. His bag had been moved from where he'd dropped it beside the bed that morning. He glanced around, hoping he wouldn't have to track down Rosalia in his shorts, asking where she'd put it. As hungry as he was, the bloodlust would grab hold of his cock the moment he saw her, and she'd get an eyeful in return.

A second later, he found his clothes piled neatly on the bench at the end of the bed, cleaned and pressed—just as Eva and Petra once had done. Grief hit him out of nowhere. He sat, their absence a dark, yawning hole in his chest.

God, he missed them.

And they'd be so fucking pissed at him. Not for taking revenge, that selfish route—but for being a first-class asshole while going about it. A man could be hard, and he could be ruthless. Leading a community of vampires sometimes called for both, and they'd accepted that in him. Then there was just being an out-and-out bastard. They wouldn't have stood for that.

He had to do better. He had to *be* better.

Resolved, he stood and dressed. When he opened the bedroom door, the ringing clash of metal drew him to the walkway overlooking the courtyard.

Wearing black shirt and trousers, with boots propped by high heels that shouldn't have been anywhere near the soft earth in the garden, Rosalia crossed swords with a tall woman in white fencer's regalia. Gemma, Deacon guessed, though he couldn't see her face behind the mesh mask. Both women used the hedges and fountains as obstacles, leaping after each other, and exchanging a flurry of steel when cornered.

He recognized Vin sitting at a small table near the courtyard's edge, watching the women. Deacon moved down the stairs and joined him.

When the man stuck out his hand, Deacon shook it. "She's going to break her ankle."

Vin grinned. "Father Wojcinski used to caution her about vanity, until she told him how many demons' throats she's slashed open with those heels."

Deacon could believe it. Even holding back, Rosalia put his own bladework to shame. To his surprise, the human might have, too. "Gemma's good."

"She'd have taken gold in Beijing, if she'd gone. But she doesn't compete anymore."

If she'd gone?

Ah. Because earlier that year, before the Summer Games

had begun, the nephilim had killed everyone here, leaving her alone. Yeah, that could have thrown her off stride. Deacon wasn't sure if he knew of anyone who could have bounced back from that in a few months.

"Where were you?"

Vin's jaw tightened. "Not here." He stood as the women finished—Gemma out of breath, and Rosalia with a brilliant smile.

"Deacon." Her gaze ran over him. "I see you found everything."

"Yes." Since thinking back to how he'd found his clothes was bringing his grief up to the surface again, he moved on quick. "What's on for tonight?"

As if she heard a little grief in his voice, she cocked her head and studied him before turning to Vin. "You two are going out?"

"Dinner by candlelight . . . and then a romantic evening in the van."

Rosalia laughed. "The last night, I think—and we should not be too long. I can take over the watch before it grows very late."

Her soft smile remained as she watched them retreat into Gemma's room, and as she looked to Deacon.

"I suppose you will want your dinner as well." A bag of blood appeared in her hand. "I would put them all into the icebox so that you can feed at will, but this is the last one. We should receive another shipment from San Francisco tomorrow."

"And if they don't send it?"

She turned toward the kitchen, and he couldn't read her face when she said, "Then we'll make other arrangements."

He could only hope those arrangements included Rosalia spread out on a table.

With fruit piled in ceramic bowls, and the faint scent of cinnamon and cloves, the kitchen appeared just as warm and lived-in as the other rooms within the abbey, though he assumed only Gemma must have been a regular user.

Deacon discovered he was wrong. After Rosalia set a tall glass in front of him, she pulled out a plate and a peach. A paring knife appeared in her hand, and she sliced around the fruit before rotating it open.

She took a bite, and he couldn't decide which appeared more succulent: her mouth or that peach.

Mistaking the reason for his attention, she said, "Eating became a habit when Gemma's grandmother first came to work for me. By the time Vin, Gemma, and Pasquale arrived, it was a good habit."

Whereas he couldn't even taste food. He lifted his glass. "Well, I appreciate the company. Otherwise I'd be desperate and lonely."

As an apology, it wasn't worth much, but her smile could knock a man off his feet. His weren't all that steady when she gestured to the courtyard.

"Shall we eat out there?"

They didn't have candlelight, but the moon filled in. He followed her to the fountain, where she straddled the stone bench and used the length of seat in front of her to make a table. He swung his leg over the other end, facing her, and took a swig of the blood. Living, it felt like a jolt of electricity across his tongue.

His hunger sharpened. He needed a distraction, and latched onto the unfamiliar name she'd mentioned back in the kitchen. "Pasquale? That's another kid who lived here?"

"Gemma's brother. Vincente's best friend." She looked down at her fingers. "He's gone."

Another vampire? That didn't surprise him. Surrounded by immortals, why wouldn't a young man try to become one? "And another reason for taking out the nephilim?"

"No. This happened more than a decade ago. He was attempting to become a Guardian."

Which meant sacrificing himself in some way. Christ, that must have been one hell of a blow. "But he didn't."

"No. And it was . . . a difficult time. For all of us." He'd become accustomed to seeing sadness in her eyes, but now he heard the same emotion in her voice, almost drowned in it. She fell silent for a moment, then looked up at him again. "So do you go first, or do I?"

"Giving our reason of the day?"

"Mmm-hmm," she hummed around a bit of peach.

He could have said her mouth had been a reason to come back. Her blood. An opportunity to find out more about her. He skipped all of those reasons, and held up his glass.

"This is one."

She accepted that easily enough. "Yes. I imagine that without a partner—partners—it's better than the alternative."

She had that right: Drinking demon's blood from a glass was much better than fucking a stranger almost every night. And he didn't want to think about how finding a new partner would become necessary once the demons and nephilim were gone.

He remembered the stories in her head, wondered if she had two for Eva and Petra. "You knew them?"

"I knew *of* them better than I knew them. I only spoke with them a few times—the latest at Eva's gallery showing in 'ninety-five."

She'd been there? He thought back, trying to remember faces. She hadn't used this one, he was certain. But he recalled the painting in her room . . . and standing in front of the same canvas during the showing. A woman—a human woman, he'd thought—her dark hair streaked with gray and her face gently lined, had come to stand beside him. She'd told him that painting was her favorite, that Eva was both talented and lovely.

Shit. Only fourteen years ago, she'd been close enough to touch—and he hadn't recognized her for the Guardian she was.

"You said I was lucky to have her."

Her brows shot up, as if surprised that he remembered. Hell, so was he.

"You were," she said. Her lashes swept down, but not before he saw the shadows in her eyes. He just didn't know why they were there. "I liked them. And I liked knowing that Prague's leader had such strong personalities behind him. That he had partners loyal to him."

"They gave me hell."

"Because they could. Two women in love with each other at a time when vampire communities weren't open? They went through hell. And women who've been through hell don't play with a man's ego unless they know he won't strike back at them. They don't tease him. But they trusted you. And they *chose* to be with you." Her smile widened almost to the edge of a laugh. "Them giving you hell probably did you good."

Yeah, it had. But he didn't answer. He couldn't. His throat hurt too damn much.

He finished off the glass. His hunger receded, and discomfort took its place. He'd chosen blood as his reason because it would reveal the least, yet she'd managed to peel off part of him, anyway. And he wanted to expose her in return.

"Your son said you overcompensate."

Her brows arched. "He did?"

"Yes. If something goes wrong, you go overboard fixing it."

She pursed her lips. "Maybe so."

"How do I fit into that?"

Her brows lifted again.

"Sister, it's easy to see what you've been doing here. You want to kill demons? You're smart enough you could have made it seem like a vampire was doing it without anyone being the wiser. Hell, you could go in *looking* like me, and no one probably would have noticed anything different. But instead, you're helping me out. Letting me kill them. What I can't figure is *why*. What failure of yours is so bad that you're overcompensating with me?"

"You're wrong. It does have to be you."

"Bullshit."

Laughing a little, she shook her head. "You don't even recognize . . ." She trailed off, her expression becoming serious as she studied him. "All right. You're correct—I am trying to make up for something."

"Then spill it."

She did, but only after a moment, as if she chose her words carefully. "There was a man once. For no reason at all, he helped me . . . and when I've been helped, I feel as though I owe someone."

Her wry smile invited him in. But his gut had tightened up. *A man.* He wasn't sure he wanted to know more. Yet he couldn't stop himself. "Go on."

Her eyes softened. "So I kept returning to him, looking for some way to help him out, to return the favor. And I . . . got to know him."

"Started talking to him?"

"No!" The denial came out on a burst of laughter, and fire swept over her cheeks. "No. I didn't do that. I wouldn't have done that."

So she'd just stalked him. *Didn't see her, did you?*

"You got hot for him." Jealousy brought out the bastard. "I get it."

The look she gave him said he didn't get it. "It wasn't like that. I couldn't be with anyone. Especially not a human. Lorenzo would have killed him, just to hurt me. And I . . . I thought he must be too good to be true. That eventually he'd be a disappointment."

Her color was high again, and she wouldn't meet his eyes. "Was he?"

"No. But I couldn't . . . But the timing wasn't right. It was never right. And it was never going to *be* right. He was human and I was a Guardian, and my brother hadn't changed." She took a deep breath. "But I wanted so much. And I thought, *Maybe one day, it would be right.* So I arranged for him to become a vampire."

Deacon stared at her, struck dumb. That'd been the last thing he expected her to say. And how did she *arrange* for someone to become a vampire? It couldn't have been against the man's will. The transformation had to be voluntary. So the man had chosen a vampire's life for his own reasons.

He could understand that, easily. He remembered Camille, so bright in the darkness of his life. How she'd had a purpose—and through her, he'd had one, too, until he'd found his own again.

This man had probably been seduced by the transformation the same way. "You knew he would accept it?"

"I thought he might."

But Rosalia couldn't be with him and provide the blood he'd need. That meant— "Even though he'd be with someone else?"

So she'd arranged for his transformation, then handed him over to another woman. That was damn cold and calculating.

But the expression on Rosalia's face was neither. "He was with someone else," she said softly. "But he was *alive*."

So his life had made the trade-off worth it. Christ.

She continued. "And I thought . . . At some point, he won't live up to my expectations. And I'll lose interest."

"Did he? Did *you*?"

"Yes, he did. And no, I didn't."

So, some perfect bastard. Someone who might be good enough for her. "So why aren't you with him now? Your brother's dead."

"Yes, well—" She took another deep breath. "Not so long ago, he was forced to make a bargain with a demon."

Now it was coming together. The connection. "Like I did."

She made a strange noise in her throat. "Yes. Like you, he was left with no good choices. Only bad ones. I didn't know it, though. I had no idea what was happening. And while he was away from his community, I thought: Maybe now I'll try."

"And you met up with him. You told him?"

"No." Her gaze locked on his, held steady. "I'd have to tell him how I manipulated his life. I feared his reaction."

He considered his own aversion to Camille trying to

manage him, and his relief that Eva and Petra had never tried. "Yeah, that'd make any man pissed enough to walk away."

Then realize what he could have with her and get over it.

"Yes," Rosalia said softly. She looked away from him. "I probably shouldn't have done it that way. I probably should have been open from the beginning. Maybe it would have changed things." She sighed. "Or maybe it wouldn't have. In any case, the demon got to him, and I should have known. I should have seen, but instead I was trying to flirt. And instead of being able to help him, his bargain with the demon ended . . . badly."

He'd died? Deacon hadn't been around any other vampires the past six months. He didn't know who it'd been—or even if it was a European vampire, someone he was familiar with. And he didn't want to ask around and find out who he was competing against.

Competing against? By the sound of this guy, Deacon wasn't even in the same class.

"So you couldn't help him, and now you're overcompensating by helping me."

And her wanting to kiss him suddenly made more sense. She'd transferred more than her guilt over from this other guy.

"Yes." She lifted her sad eyes to his again. "That's oversimplified, but basically . . . yes. That failure is one of my many reasons."

He'd wanted to expose more of her? Shit. Judging by the jealousy eating at him, he'd exposed more of himself. Her vulnerability was killing him.

He pushed all of that emotion away and said flatly, "So we have our reasons, and now we should be going. What city's on the agenda for tonight?"

She took several moments. Still wrestling with her heartbreak, he guessed. Her answer, when it came, was soft. "Monaco."

Where she'd change her clothes and put on that human-scented perfume, then rub his shirt over her skin. He wanted to put his scent on her. Wanted to mark her as his.

"Did you have all of my shirts cleaned?"

Her puzzled expression said he'd lost her. "Yes."

"Come here, then."

Here, in this courtyard, she was a Guardian, not a human. She'd say no if she didn't want to.

And if she wanted him—even just as a replacement—Deacon wouldn't object to being used. Not when he knew this was the only way he would have her.

He was a bastard again, after all.

"Come here and kiss me, Rosie. You need my scent on you. You'll get it."

Her lips parted. She seemed about to say something, then stopped herself. Leaning forward, she lifted her knees onto the bench and stalked toward him like a cat. She paused in front of him, rising up on her knees between his legs.

Her hair slipped over her shoulder, curling against her breast. Peaches perfumed her breath. For a moment, she looked down at him—maybe through him. Then she lowered her head, and her mouth settled gently on his. The tentative movement of her lips whispered through him, so sweet. He remembered her awkward kiss, his callous response.

You've got other parts I like better.

No. A thousand perfect tits couldn't equal one touch of her lips.

His hand closed around her nape, and he brought her in for a deeper kiss. A vampire couldn't taste, but he could smell her luscious scent. Feel the heat of her mouth.

She moaned softly in her throat when his tongue pushed against hers. She licked his fangs, and the heat of her tongue speared straight to his cock. He strained toward her. Her fingers searched his jaw, his hair, then down over his shoulders. Touching all of him. Her breasts brushed his chest, then pressed harder against his pecs as if she loved the feeling. As if she wanted to surround him, devour him.

He broke the kiss, breathing hard. "Come over me, Rosie. Like this."

Lifting her, he brought her knees forward until her thighs spread wide over his. When she settled back down, her warm center tucked hard against his stomach. Her breath caught, her eyes closed, and then she rocked into him, as if testing the sensation.

His hands found her hips, urged her to rock against him again. Her heart pounded, her breath came fast. She was all heat and softness. And need—as if she couldn't get enough of him. When was the last time he'd felt that? Had he *ever* felt that?

Not like this. She claimed his mouth in a wild, desperate kiss. Sensing the scrape and tear of skin against his fang, he pulled back . . . and stared.

Her eyes glowed. No longer brown but yellow, as if a sun burned within. Her skin had flushed, her hands fisted in his hair. She hadn't noticed the cut, the blood that beaded on her lip.

Temptation gripped him. He'd just fed, his hunger and bloodlust sated. He wouldn't lose control with a taste, and he only wanted to know . . . wanted to know more. Her mental shields couldn't hold when he was in her blood. She closed her eyes as he brought her down. A niggle of guilt made him hesitate, but pausing only fueled his need. Gently, he drew her bottom lip between his.

Just a drop, but her blood was strong, stronger than he'd imagined, crashing into his veins like the crest of an orgasm. His mind hurtled into hers. Longing poured through him, fierce and sweet, and the hectic thread of her thoughts.

. . . *shouldn't have waited so long wish I could hold on forever* . . .

Her lip healed, breaking the connection. Deacon struggled up from the deep psychic well, aware that something had gone wrong. His bloodlust lurked just below the surface, on the verge of taking him over. Rosalia had stiffened against him;

he gripped her hips painfully tight, grinding her sex against his raging erection.

Gritting his teeth, he forced himself to stop. Shock held him quiet, staring up at Rosalia. The bloodlust had never hit him like that before. Not from one drop, taken after he'd already drunk his fill. But he shouldn't have risked it, risked *her*.

Her eyes weren't glowing anymore. She licked her lip, and fear fluttered over her expression. Her voice seemed thick.

"You tasted my blood."

A flash of memory brought him the image of Rosalia, with dried blood crusting her skin. Her shattered skull. The nosferatu, feeding from her. "Christ, I'm a thoughtless bastard. You were in the catacombs for more than a fucking year, and here I am—"

"I don't remember anything that happened to me there." She cut him off, her gaze searching his face as if worried that she'd find . . . what? "Did you hear inside me?"

Just her regret and her need for the other guy. But she didn't need to know that—she looked too vulnerable as it was. He shook his head.

Her relief punched through him. So she didn't want him peeking in, taking her blood? He wouldn't. Not again. Never again.

She swung her leg to the ground and stood up. "We should get started anyway."

Her wings formed, and he realized—"We're flying there?"

"Yes."

So she'd be holding him against her as she flew. By the time they arrived in Monaco, his scent would be all over her.

"You didn't need my shirt." Or his kiss. "Why didn't you say so?"

Her smile appeared, wicked and sly and embarrassed, all at once. She seemed to struggle for a reply, and finally settled on, " 'I sat down under his shadow with great delight, and his fruit was sweet to my taste.' "

She quoted Scripture to explain why she'd come in for his kiss? "I see now why the Church kicked you out."

Her laugh rolled out, light and surprised. She nodded, as if agreeing, then laughed harder, the sound emerging from deep within her.

God, she was beautiful. "Are my lips like lilies, then?"

She wiped her eyes, looking him up and down, and he knew she must be choosing another verse. But when she spoke, he heard reverence in her voice, not amusement.

" 'His legs are of pillars of marble, set upon sockets of fine gold: his countenance is as Lebanon, excellent as the cedars. His mouth is most sweet.' " Her gaze locked with his. A soft smile curved her lips. " 'Yea, he is altogether lovely.' "

He'd heard conviction in her voice before, and he had no doubt that she believed what she'd spoken. But he'd looked in a mirror. His mug didn't qualify for ugly, but he wasn't a prize, either. It only followed that when she looked at him, she saw someone else.

And for now, that didn't matter at all.

CHAPTER 12

The best part of having a vampire computer-genius friend with legal access to many countries' police databases, and illegal access to dozens of others, was that tracking down convictions and dates of death was a damn sight easier. In a conference room at Special Investigations, armed with a computer and the list of names, Taylor began searching for the nephil who'd raped and murdered the London couple.

All of the nephilim had possessed humans who'd been bound for Hell. No one knew exactly how the judgments were made or exactly why a soul went Above or Below, but Taylor preferred to believe that it wasn't for the petty stuff—and considering how much free will mattered, so that even demons had to follow the Rules, Taylor thought that was where the line was drawn. Getting down and dirty with seven naked friends? You still get a pass through the golden gates. Rape? Not so much.

She'd met all of Anaria's children, in their human forms. She remembered faces. And so far, she'd been able to match fifteen of them to convicted murderers, rapists, and one child predator.

The rapists, she scrutinized closely, looking for the same MO as used in London. Facedown, hands behind the backs—and the victim could be male or female. Nothing had popped, yet.

Maybe it wouldn't. There was a good chance he'd never been caught, or he'd be in a database her friend hadn't accessed. Or she'd miss him because the database didn't have a picture, or the conviction was too old. Or he'd been convicted of something else. Taylor knew the chances of nailing him down this way were slim.

But this kind of work was familiar, and Michael was quiet, so she kept on.

As another name matched yet another face, she began hoping that Anaria was right about her children—that they were in control—because otherwise the woman had her own personal village of the damned living under her roof.

And Taylor's mind kept heading back to those body resonances. To possess the body, the nephil had to alter his own resonance until it matched the human's psyche; if it didn't match, the body rejected him. And the nephil possessed all of the human's memories, used the same brain that the human had. So maybe the nephil *was* in control—but Taylor wouldn't be surprised to learn that the nephil had undergone a hell of a personality change.

She was almost through the list when Michael seemed to bristle, and a moment later, Taylor realized that someone was in the room with her. She swiveled the chair.

With black hair in narrow braids, a face sharper and harder than Anaria's, and wearing giant wading boots over jeans, Khavi stood clutching a ten-pound bag of potatoes to her chest. Taylor didn't even ask. After spending two millennia in Hell with only a hellhound for company, Khavi's forays into the modern world had revealed a personality that swung from eccentric to batshit crazy.

As far as Taylor knew, however, that hadn't included necrophilia.

Taylor opened her mouth and Khavi said, "You want to know if the nephilim have become like their hosts. They have."

Ah, yes. At least a conversation with a prophetic grigori was never boring. And despite knowing that Khavi had probably let her die, Taylor kind of liked the woman. As frustrating as Khavi was at times, holding back information and never making any sense until whatever she'd predicted smashed into a person from behind, Taylor never felt the urge to punch her in the face during a conversation, unlike the time she'd spent with Anaria.

Well, okay. Taylor *had* threatened to shoot Khavi in the head once. But Khavi hadn't ducked, so obviously they'd both known it wasn't going to happen.

"I found her island, too."

Khavi dumped the potatoes onto the worktable and began sorting through them. By what criteria, Taylor couldn't fathom. "Yes, yes. Anaria has always loved the sea."

Something in Khavi's easy reply told her, "You knew where she was?"

"Of course. But what good is it? If we move against them—separately, or all together—we will be slaughtered." Khavi stopped sorting spuds long enough to meet Taylor's eyes. "That is not conjecture. I have seen it."

Well, shit. "Rosalia's got her plan, whatever it is. She's intending to kill all of the nephilim. Have you seen that?"

"I cannot see what I do not know."

"Any hint?"

Khavi's mouth tightened. She began stuffing one pile of potatoes back into the sack. "I have seen that we do not lose the balance."

"Uh-huh," Taylor said. Because that made *so* much sense.

Frowning at her, Khavi hefted two spuds, one in each hand. "A balance. There is light"—she lowered her left hand, raised her right—"and there is dark. There is action and consequence." She evened their height again, like a set of scales. "They all must be kept in balance, and that is why the Doyen must punish a Guardian who breaks the Rules, and Lucifer must enforce the Rules for his demons. It is why the nephilim are here, because he cannot enforce the Rules with the Gates closed." She lowered both potatoes. "We do not lose the balance."

Her heart sank—for Rosalia, for the London community. "So the nephilim don't die."

"I cannot see." But she shook her head. "I do not believe so, however."

Dammit. Taylor pushed her hand through her hair. She wouldn't tell Rosalia that, though. The woman was so sweet, and so determined. And maybe she'd slay *enough* of them, even if she didn't get rid of them all. Maybe enough to save London.

"Now you are going to ask, 'What of the vampires in London?'" Khavi shrugged. "I have seen them slain; I have seen them live."

"So how do I weigh the scales toward the 'live' side?"

"Find the nephil who drank the community leaders' blood before he shares the resonance with his brothers." Her gaze flicked to Taylor's desk. "I know you have already started."

Holy shit. "Do I find him?"

"No."

"But—"

"No."

All right. Sometimes she *did* want to punch Khavi in the face. But knowing this was useless, she backed up. "What does that mean, sharing resonance?"

"It is simple. A leader knows all of his people, almost always by psychic scent. That knowledge is stored in the blood—and when a nephil takes the blood, and looks for the right sounds, he can *hear* all of the vampires in the community."

"All of their psychic scents?" Which never felt like scent to Taylor, during those odd times when she recognized another person's emotions. She only heard sound.

"Yes. And nephil are not like Guardians, or grigori, or demons. They are connected. So when the first nephil separates all of the sounds from one another, he can pass that knowledge through his blood into the other nephilim. When they attack a city, there is nowhere for the vampires to hide. The nephilim can hunt down an entire community in a single night—and clean up any strays that they find along the way, vampires who don't belong to the community."

Strays . . . like a family of vampires in an abbey. God. Poor Rosalia. Just bad fucking luck.

"So if I find the nephil who took the blood, I can stop this."

"I've already said you don't."

"Okay, humor me. What happens if I do, and we slay him?" It wouldn't be Taylor. Maybe another Guardian could. Another three or four Guardians.

"Then they will likely choose another community—and the more vampires, the better. One will kill that community leader, and it would begin again."

"But it would buy time."

"Perhaps. I do not see that. But perhaps it will change." She held up a potato, put it in the bag.

All right. Taylor couldn't stand it. "What are you doing with those?"

"I intend to teach Lyta to juggle. Potatoes now, demon heads later."

Lyta, Khavi's hellhound who always remained in Caelum—thank God. Taylor could manage to be around Sir Pup, another hellhound who was often at Special Investigations, because he so often shape-shifted into a Labrador's form . . . albeit a three-headed one. But Lyta remained in her demonic form, standing taller than Taylor did, peering out from glowing crimson eyes, her scaly hide covered with poison-tipped barbs and sparse black fur, three jaws full of giant serrated teeth. Taylor couldn't help it; that hellhound scared the shit out of her.

"You will have to face that fear soon," Khavi said.

Yeah? Taylor preferred to put it off. But at least she could lie to this grigori. "I'll go see her as soon as she's juggling." She glanced at the two piles. "What's the difference?"

Khavi picked up one from the pile on the left. "These reminded me of demon heads."

Ooooookay. "The shape?"

Khavi gave her a strange glance, as if wondering whether Taylor was blind and/or stupid. "No," she said, and squeezed the spud. The potato exploded into a pulpy mess, dripping over her fingers, clumping on the table. "You see? Just the same."

Taylor laughed, and faintly, thought she heard Michael laughing, too. Then the darkness abruptly swept up and grabbed hold of her, and yanked her away.

❧

Watching Deacon approach an unwary demon in Budapest had been difficult. Knowing that he'd been alone in the room with Valeotes had been worse, but Sardis's attack hadn't let Rosalia focus on her fear. Now she knew what it was to wait outside a hotel suite while Deacon talked his way into a seat at a poker table surrounded by six hostile vampires and one suspicious demon.

Terror had her by the throat.

She'd wanted to go in with him, but he'd insisted her presence would make getting to the demon more difficult, and Rosalia went along with it. She'd brought him, but the task of killing the demons fell on his shoulders, and she had to let him take the lead. *This* had been why she'd needed him—one reason among many. He could think on his feet, and knowing his own strengths, find the best way to slay the demon. Deacon didn't need her to hold his hand, guide him through every step. He just needed to see the demon in front of him. And so she was left outside, seeing neither of them, only listening.

She paced in the thickly carpeted hallway, her arms crossed over her chest, holding herself back. Deacon would draw his sword soon, surely. Would she hear it over the pounding of her heart? If he needed help, would he call for her?

She knew he wouldn't.

Fear began to ratchet into panic, nerves stretched to breaking. Oh, Lord, she couldn't do this again. She'd find a way to go in with him.

Only . . . she couldn't. When the endgame with Malkvial came, Deacon had to go in alone. So she had to become accustomed to this terror now.

She didn't know if she ever could.

An alert from her phone startled her. Her heart stuttered, then resumed its quick beat as she read the text message from Vincente.

Target on the move. Will update our location when he stops.

She replied, then held on to her phone, re-reading the message. Deacon, her son, the woman who would be her daughter, their unborn child. She'd pulled them all into this with her, risked their lives, too. She closed her eyes.

Dear God, keep them safe.

Of course, that was what He'd made *her* for. When she opened her eyes, her heartbeat had settled.

Farther down the hallway, the elevator dinged. Wearing sequins and a tuxedo, a middle-aged couple exited, clinging drunkenly to each other as they lurched toward their room. The woman giggled uncontrollably. Diamonds dripped from her ears and throat.

Monte Carlo never slept, which made it an ideal location for vampires; its residents surrounded themselves with wealth and luxury, which made it ideal for demons. And the vampires here were the most moneyed of all the European communities, which made them ideal targets for a demon like Fournier.

Unlike Sardis, this community leader hadn't welcomed him in. Instead, Fournier had killed Henri David and taken over his identity.

But the demon hadn't been careful. Like Theriault, whose bid for leadership Fournier supported, he hadn't taken steps to conceal his nature—and a vampire couldn't attend a state function during the daylight hours. Recognizing David's face in a press photo had tipped Rosalia off, and an overheard conversation with Theriault had confirmed her suspicions, sealing the demon's fate.

She didn't think he'd have had long, anyway. The vampires here feared him, but their hate went deeper. They'd have either worked together to kill the demon or died trying.

Despite that hate, however—and the likelihood that they'd heard rumors from both Budapest and Athens—the vampires hadn't been pleased to see Deacon. They assumed he was here as Fournier's ally, and treated him accordingly.

A year ago, they'd have been honored to host Deacon at their table. For six decades, he'd been one of Europe's most respected leaders—and unlike Lorenzo, he'd earned that respect rather than demanded it—but Caym had trampled that respect into garbage and Deacon had earned the reputation of a demon-loving traitor.

A reputation that Deacon seemed to think he'd deserved.

Now *that* deserved the "bullshit" Deacon so often tossed at her. He had to be the most blind and stubborn man in all of Creation, determined to see himself in the darkest light possible. He couldn't recognize his actions in any description that contained a hint of goodness or painted any positive aspect onto his character.

But his return to her abbey had exposed the truth: that his heart was as good as Rosalia had known. That he couldn't turn his back when lives were threatened.

She'd taken a risk by telling the story behind his transformation. All she'd concealed was a name—and of course he hadn't recognized himself in that, either. But even if she'd revealed all, even if such manipulation would make him walk away, Rosalia didn't believe he would leave until they'd seen the plan through. For now, however, she wouldn't put him in a hurry to walk away once it was done—and she hoped by then he'd have more reasons to stay.

A round of laughter came from within the suite, Deacon's voice among them. Good. They'd all relaxed a bit. The demon wouldn't know what hit him.

It came with the shattering of glass and the sound of scattering poker chips. Rosalia's fingers clenched, her whole being focused on the noise from within. Swords clashed.

Fournier had managed to defend himself? Oh, no. Deacon's advantage depended on speed and surprise. Barely realizing that she'd started forward, she stopped short at the dull thud of bone pounding into flesh. He'd used his fists? *No. Oh, God, no.* He'd lose every advantage in a hand-to-hand fight. She was reaching for the door when silence fell.

Rosalia froze, wanting to scream, but she waited, trembling. A moment later, she heard Deacon's gravelly voice.

"He shouldn't have cheated."

The vampires inside responded with laughter so giddy they reminded Rosalia of the staggering drunk woman. Relief hollowed out her chest. She put a hand to her stomach and backed away from the door.

She heard Deacon take his leave, apologizing for the mess. Almost eagerly, the vampires assured him that the body would be taken care of.

Of course they would. As far as these vampires were concerned, Deacon headed their community now. And even when it became clear that he didn't intend to step into the position, no one here would forget what Deacon had done for them. Whatever his reputation had been entering the suite, he left as a leader—just as he had in Budapest and Athens.

Deacon came into the hall, wrapping a handkerchief around a bleeding palm, an operation made awkward by the use of only one hand. His gaze found Rosalia and narrowed. "You were supposed to wait near the elevator."

She didn't answer. Taking the ends of the handkerchief, she tied it tightly to stanch the wound until it sealed. Long, narrow, and deep—he'd obviously grabbed Fournier's blade as it had been stabbed toward him. If Fournier had swung, Deacon would be missing half his hand.

Frowning, she examined his knuckles. They'd bled, but the skin had already healed. The clenching of his jaw as she prodded told her that he'd hit Fournier hard enough to break them.

"Henri was a good man."

Anger thrummed in that statement—and regret, as if he

wondered whether he could have done anything to prevent the vampire's death. If, by coming here to slay his first demons instead of to Madrid or London, he might have stopped Fournier.

Her response echoed his regret—and his anger. "Yes."

"No more. The demons don't get even one more vampire."

She met his eyes. "Then we've got a lot of work to do. With *swords*. Not your fists."

His grin reopened a split in his bottom lip. So he'd taken a hit, too—and was proud of it. With a sigh, she smoothed her thumb beneath the cut, wiping away the blood.

"You should see the other guy."

Laughing, she let go of his hand, stepped back. He absently licked the blood from his lip, watching her. The amusement in his gaze shifted, became sharp and predatory.

Not bloodlust. Just Deacon.

"Head back to the elevator, Rosie."

No. She wanted to stay right here, and see where that hunger led. Only her awareness of the vampires inside the suite got her feet moving. Deacon followed behind her. Never before had she been so conscious of the sway of her hips, the snug fit of her trousers over her backside.

And she was utterly certain that by the time the sun rose, she'd have taken him into her bed. Into her body. If not for the vampires, she'd have gotten a room in this hotel.

The elevator held four other people. Rosalia barely saw them on the long ride down. Only felt Deacon beside her, his palm pressed into the small of her back to conceal the blood-stained cloth.

Outside, an evening breeze carried the salty tang of the sea. When they'd flown in from Rome, Rosalia had chosen a secluded spot to land, but now she headed toward the still-crowded beach and its softly rolling surf that lay just outside the hotel. As her boots sank into the sand, she turned to Deacon.

"Can you swim?" How strange that she'd watched him for ninety years and didn't know.

"I can." The moonlight glinted against the white of his quick grin. "Is this how we'll return to Rome?"

"Only part of the way," she said, already headed across the beach, where warm water and gentle waves foamed against the shore. "We just have to swim toward the moon."

She stripped off as she walked, letting her clothes lay where they fell. Within a few hours, they'd disappear—Guardian-created garments eventually vanished if they weren't worn. Clad only in her panties and bra, both dark enough to pass for a bikini, she stepped into the water.

"Rosie."

She turned, a small breaker crashing against her calves. Deacon stood on the wet sand, his boots in his hand—but still dressed.

"Your swords?" she guessed. Removing his jacket would expose his weapons to the humans. "I need permission to vanish them. And the rest of your clothes, too."

"You have it."

Leaving the warm water for the cool sand, she returned to him. She watched his gaze slide from her eyes to tips of her breasts, hardened beneath silk. She stepped closer, until only a small space separated their bodies.

"Bring your boots in between us, so that no one can see them disappear."

He did, and she vanished them along with his swords. His gaze focused on her lips. "My jacket?"

"Shouldn't just vanish," she told him. Slipping her fingers beneath the collar, she pushed it back over his shoulders, down his arms, letting her palms linger over heavy muscles. She brought the jacket between them and vanished it into her cache, then reached for his shirt.

Deacon caught her wrists before she touched a single button. He stared at her for a breathless moment, then slowly pushed her hands back down to rest at her thighs.

She tried not to feel disappointment, and failed. "No swim?"

"No taking anything else off, or this crowd will get an eyeful."

His hands slid around to cup her bottom, lifting her against him. Beneath his trousers, his erection rose like a thick steel pipe. Rosalia's lips parted, her heart hammering.

His voice deepened. "Wrap your legs around me, Rosie."

She did, her thighs ringing a muscled abdomen as hard as rock. Her arms circled his neck. He began to walk, his arousal nudging her core with every step. Seawater splashed around his feet, then his knees. When the swirling water swept around the underside of her thighs, tickling the edges of her panties, he dove and took them both under.

The world filled in with a dark rush, stinging her eyes. His mouth found hers, a salty heaven. She tasted him, took him. Kissing him was a pleasure unlike any other she'd known, a twisting ecstasy within her that seemed to break for the surface and dive in deep. He kicked at the water, and then they were arrowing forward beneath the waves, following the path of the moonlight.

His hand slipped between her thighs, where she was as wet as the ocean, and she wondered if he knew that the wetness was her and not the sea. Then his kiss deepened, as if he sought her flavor, and his fingers brushed and teased her sex before withdrawing and leaving her aching.

After a few minutes, he stopped kicking, and they drifted. Rosalia pulled back. Deacon's face was in shadow, his green eyes dark. His shirt collar floated up against his neck, the points touching his jaw. She smoothed it back down.

His slow grin appeared. His eyes seemed to challenge her. Flipping his collar up again, he cocked a brow.

Her laugh bubbled out on her last bit of air. She knew Deacon, but not like this. She enjoyed this side of him: hungry, playful.

And it was difficult not to straighten that collar.

Kicking away from him, she crossed her arms and tucked her hands into her elbows. She hoped her smile looked smug; it wasn't an expression she had reason to use often. He began to circle her, swimming close, keeping her off balance and turning in the water, a shark after his prey.

Two could play that game. With a back somersault to help her gain momentum, she kicked for the surface. She swept her arms down just before she broke through, a powerful stroke that brought her fully out of the water. Monte Carlo glittered in the distance; they'd come too far for anyone to see her. She formed her wings, flew high, and waited.

Below, Deacon's dark head broke the surface of the waves—looking up, but in the wrong direction. Rosalia tucked her wings against her back and dove.

The wind twisted her hair into a wet whip. She timed her speed against the swell of a wave. It lifted just as he turned her direction. She swooped, sliding her hands beneath Deacon's arms and scooping him up.

He shouted a curse, shedding water. Rosalia couldn't stop her wild laughter. She hauled him up, caught her arm beneath his legs, and brought him against her chest. There was no way to carry a man as large as Deacon that wasn't awkward or that produced too much drag, but they'd managed the flight here with him cradled against her.

When she banked southwest, he asked, "Back to Rome, then?"

Eventually, yes. "We can go slowly."

She caught his smile from the corner of her eye, was aware of him watching her face. A strange anticipation filled her, her heart at once heavy and light—half dread, half hope. Dread that she'd fail at this, too. Hope that they could begin to build something.

She vanished the water from his clothes. Her skin had dried, and she created new trousers, a shirt, and boots: Deacon made a disappointed sound.

When her laughter ended, she searched for something to say. On the journey to Monaco, they'd discussed his upcoming fight and the personalities of the vampires within the community. Now . . . Lord, she'd imagined conversations with him so many times. Never had they been fraught with this nervousness. Every topic seemed too trivial and too important.

Deacon had no such trouble. "Your son says you have a file—a story—on every vampire in Europe."

And she overcompensated. Lovely. "He said entirely too much."

"Is he usually that indiscreet?"

"No. But he knows you're different from other visitors." Now *she* had said too much. She saw Deacon's frown and hurried to add, "So you want to know what story I have for you?"

"I know mine. I want to know yours."

That shook her. He was the only one who'd ever asked hers. She'd told it before. But no one else had ever cared to ask.

"Wrong question?"

Her reaction must have shown. She shook her head. "No. It's just not a question I'm accustomed to hearing." When his brows rose, as if he doubted that, she explained, "I'm not out much—not as myself. And I make a point of not drawing attention. So no one cares to ask."

"I'm asking. But you're evading."

"I'm not evading." *He'd cared to ask.* That hope in her heart grew steadily higher, lighter. "I'm formulating."

"A long version or a summary?"

She laughed. "The summary is easy: The girl who believed that good always won learned differently."

Surprised by her own answer, she fell silent. That response had come out of nowhere.

Deacon regarded her with a hint of a smile. "Considering this path we're on, Rosie, one of us needs to be thinking that good will win out."

"It can't be you?"

"I got that beaten out of me," he said. "But there must be some of that left in you, if you're going this way."

She shook her head. "I don't just *believe* anymore that it'll turn out right. The only way it will is if I *do* something. So I'm doing."

He stared at her. "It's a shame you've been hiding so long, Rosie."

"Because everyone could have used me doing before, instead of just believing?" She glanced down, where the moonlight painted a bleak stripe on the dark water. "I know."

"And you're still evading."

She tried to smile. "The long version?"

"We have time?"

She gauged her speed. Not enough time for all of it. "Probably not before we reach Rome."

"Do you have another demon lined up after that?"

"I'll remember that you want two a night," she said dryly. "Tonight, though, I have to take over for Vin and Gemma."

Vincente was convinced that St. Croix was human. Rosalia needed to determine for certain whether he was Malkvial, so that they could either take the next step or move on to another possibility.

And she needed to check in on them. "I'm bringing my phone out of my cache into your hand. Will you look for a message?"

The white glow from the phone illuminated the sudden tension in his expression.

"What is it?"

Deacon read, " 'Target stopped at Lorenzo's place.' "

A chill rippled over her skin. That couldn't be a coincidence. "When did he send that?"

"Four minutes ago. Tell me what that means, Rosie."

She shook her head, trying to think. "I don't know. I sold it a month ago—Lorenzo's house, and everything inside. That monstrosity. It was just . . . I didn't want to see it again, think of it again. And I couldn't believe that anyone bought it. But they did."

"Who?"

"A property developer."

"Not St. Croix?"

Heaviness settled into her stomach. "Not him, personally. Perhaps one of his hold—" Another alert sounding on her phone interrupted her. "Did he text more?"

Deacon's face told her it was bad. "St. Croix has vampires with him."

"How many?"

"At least two." He read more from the screen. "And a human, restrained."

Had the vampires crossed the line and broken the Rules? If so, they might hurt her son. They might hurt Gemma. And she needed to be in Rome, *now*. "Tell him to retreat. We'll arrive in a—"

A small figure appeared in front of them. Steel glinted in her hands. A dark psychic scent swamped Rosalia's mind. She barely had time to register the black feathered wings, the drawn face, and the empty obsidian eyes before Taylor swung at Deacon's head.

Rosalia rolled, folding her wings forward to conceal him. She caught Taylor's strike through her back. Icy steel sliced between her ribs, through her lungs.

Blood erupted into her mouth. Pain ripped through her chest in a hot wave. Rosalia fought past it. One strike couldn't kill her. She just needed to slow Taylor down until the other Guardian regained control. Taylor drew her hand back for another swing.

Still rolling forward, Rosalia slashed out with her foot. Her heel caught Taylor's throat, ripping it wide in a spray of blood.

Holding Deacon tight, she dove. She wrapped her Gift around them, a cocoon of shadow and silence. Gathering the night, Rosalia built it into a massive black wall, and hid within its depths.

Taylor hovered in the sky, searching for them.

Rosalia took a second to look at Deacon. His face was taut, his voice burning with frustration.

"Drop me," he growled.

She shook her head.

"Michael's after *me*, Rosie. You get out of here."

Taylor moved closer to the deep wall of shadows. From outside, it would appear perfectly black and solid, but it was no more substantial than air. Even if she flew into its depths, however, she wouldn't see them within it.

"You can't defend yourself if you're holding me." As Taylor moved closer, Deacon's muscles tensed, rigid beneath her fingers. "And I can't fight."

She knew. Oh, God, how she knew. She'd taken that ability from him by deciding to fly to Monaco. She'd rendered him helpless because she'd wanted to hold onto him.

Taylor flew past them along the plane of the wall, less than ten feet away.

Deacon stared after her in disbelief. "She can't hear us? Our heartbeats?"

Rosalia shook her head again.

"She'll smell your blood and come for you."

Maybe. She had Michael's instincts but not his knowledge. Even now, she only searched with her eyes, not her other senses.

Still, Rosalia wasn't taking any chances. She vanished the blood as soon as it left her body—but she couldn't stop the scent from surrounding them. A breeze the wrong way would reveal their position, and she had to wait until the wound sealed before using her Gift to take them away. She couldn't now. Her blood would leave a physical trail behind them.

Taylor passed into the shadow. Her confusion swirled against Rosalia's mind, a dark miasma of uncontrolled emotion.

Deacon's anger and tension increased. Though he was shielded, she could almost feel how much he hated himself for being in this position, but it was her fault. She'd chosen to travel this way, for no reason other than having an opportunity to keep him close. She hadn't needed the cover of his scent, and the expense of a chartered plane was nothing to her. Now he couldn't defend himself.

She'd been just as bad as a demon: arrogant and careless. She'd taken risks she shouldn't have. She'd had to use her Gift . . . and it was just pure luck that they were over the sea when Taylor had hit them, and no one was nearby to sense it.

Deacon's hand sought her ribs. When he drew his palm back, his skin was red with her blood.

"Is this why you're so quiet?" The gravel in his voice had roughened.

The blade had passed through her lungs. She wouldn't be able to talk for several minutes. Not until she healed.

Her nod made him swear. Helpless, she stared at Taylor. Then, recalling herself, she gestured for the phone.

Awkwardly, she moved Deacon around, holding him against her side. With one hand, she texted Vin, telling him to retreat and wait. Soon, she'd use her Gift to arrive close to Rome, but she couldn't push into the city. She couldn't risk the vampires panicking and killing the human if they felt her coming.

It wouldn't be long. Her wound would seal in another minute or two, and they'd be able to go without leaving a blood trail. Her insides wouldn't have healed—but she didn't need to breathe, anyway.

She put in another message, but not to send. She showed the screen to Deacon.

I shouldn't have chosen flying like this. Our movements are restricted. I knew better.

"Then why take that chance, sister?"

His anger felt like another slice through her chest. But she'd risked his life, and he deserved an explanation, one that didn't use an excuse like needing his scent to fool the vampires. A true explanation, with a reason that came from the heart of her.

I wanted to hold on to you. I shouldn't have. I'm sorry.

His jaw tightened. "Fuck."

Her vision blurred. But she couldn't cry, not while watching Taylor. She vanished the moisture in her eyes.

Taylor's sword hadn't touched her heart. Yet it still managed to ache worse than the injury.

CHAPTER 13

This was a first-class example of overcompensation. Here she was, beating up on herself, when he was the reason Michael was after them.

Christ, she'd gotten a sword stabbed through her chest while protecting him. She shouldn't be apologizing for anything.

Rosalia looked at him. This whole time, she hadn't opened her mouth, as if she was afraid of blood pouring out. Now she nodded, and he realized the scent of blood that had surrounded them had faded. Her wound had healed—at least on the surface.

The shadowy veil around them thickened into an impenetrable darkness. He couldn't see her—couldn't see anything. Then it pulled out from around him, like coming out of a sticky vat of tar. His stomach dropped in a brief sensation of free fall, then her wings pumped and water rushed into the shoreline beneath him. Then they were over land—fields and groves and communities passing in a blur.

Christ. He hadn't known how fast she could fly when she

put effort into it. Within minutes, Rome lay beneath them, and they were diving. His fingers clenched involuntarily on her arm, then she swooped and settled on the ground next to the van. She vanished her wings and set him down, but he still felt like he was dropping, his head spinning.

And he'd kill himself before admitting that.

The van's side door slid opened to the sound of Gemma retching into a waste bin. Rosalia patted her shoulder as she stepped into the vehicle. She stopped by Vin's chair and made a single gesture at her throat.

"You can't talk?" Vin turned to Deacon, standing in the open door. "What happened?"

Rosalia cut him off with another gesture. She poked at the infrared screen, her expression fierce.

Vin got the message. The human mattered now. "We tracked St. Croix here. He went in. A few minutes later, the Davanzatis show up."

"Davanzatis?"

"Vampires," Vin answered Deacon, then turned to Rosalia again. "They drive into the garage and wheel out the human, strapped to a gurney. He's got an IV dripping blood."

"And it's not someone just using it to heal?" Deacon asked. A transfusion of vampire blood could speed healing—or, in the case of terminal illness, strengthen the recipient.

"This guy was struggling. Damn hard. He broke from the restraints once—just his arm—and St. Croix strapped him back in. They registered the same temp."

So that proved St. Croix wasn't a demon. A demon couldn't hold a human down, not without breaking the Rules and calling in one of the nephilim to slay him.

"Now where are they?"

"They're too deep in the house, and the stone walls are too thick. I can't get a reading."

Rosalia looked to Deacon. The question in her eyes was clear: Was he ready to go in?

"Are you still playing a human?"

She nodded.

No worries. Two vampires, he could handle. And a human St. Croix wouldn't likely pose a threat. "Can you give me the layout? Your brother never invited me over for dinner."

She smiled and pulled out a sheet of paper, quickly sketching the floors and rooms. The main floor included several parlors, a study, and a library. The three levels upstairs contained bedrooms and private parlors. Downstairs, her brother had kept a dungeon.

He read that label again. "You're fucking with me. A dungeon?"

Vin shook his head. "She's not. He even threatened to put me down there."

Rosalia's expression froze. She stared at her son before glancing at Gemma. The younger woman gave a weak smile.

Ah, so Vin wasn't supposed to know that. Had this happened when he was a kid?

"How long ago?" Deacon asked.

Gemma sat next to Vin. "About a month before Lorenzo made his deal with the demon, and Rosa disappeared."

Not when he was a kid, but less than two years ago. And after his threat, Acciaioli had gone after Rosalia instead of her son—either trying to get rid of her or make her pay. Deacon looked to Rosalia. "What did you do to him?"

Her lips pressed together and she shook her head.

"It must have been bad for him to retaliate like he did. He risked a bargain with a demon." Deacon had to grin at that. "You must have scared the shit out of him."

After a moment of surprise, her son began grinning, too, but Rosalia wasn't looking. She finished the sketch, then wrote, "Reinforced doors and windows. We'll make noise getting in."

"Do we care if we make noise?"

She shook her head, and a long black cloak formed over her shoulders. She slung a crossbow across her back. A long, thin sword appeared in her head. All she needed was a mask, and she'd look like a female version of Zorro.

That sly fox had always been one of Deacon's favorites.

Vin stood and retrieved a shoulder holster from a locked cabinet. Rosalia gave him another fierce look.

"The trouble is, Mama, you can't stop me. And I know you'll stop him from stopping me." He jerked his head at Deacon.

Judging by her expression, Deacon wasn't so sure that she'd prevent him from chaining her son to his seat. He raised a brow at her. She seemed to contemplate his offer for a moment before shaking her head.

Vin faced her again. "Your hands are tied if the humans in there do anything. And you need someone to watch your back. So does he."

Wearing a headset and rolling her chair along the van's floor, powering up various equipment, Gemma added, "And if something goes wrong between Deacon and St. Croix, the last thing you want is Guardians breathing down your neck, trying to get at the vampire who hurt a human. And they'd love to get at Deacon, wouldn't they? But the Guardians can't touch Vin."

Deacon exchanged a look with Rosalia. The faith these two young people had in them was pitiful. Rosalia rolled her eyes before turning to the other woman and holding out her hand. Gemma gave her a small receiver designed to fit over the ear. She offered another to Deacon.

"If anyone else shows up, I'll yell," she said.

They headed out. A tall, wrought-iron fence surrounded the house. Rosalia had called it a monstrosity, and Deacon had to agree with that assessment. Of black stone, it rose in a solid nightmare of Gothic architecture. Towers stabbed the night sky, and the ornamentation around every narrow window and along the roof was so heavy that the building seemed to be folding in on itself. It was nothing like the open warmth of Rosalia's abbey.

At the side of the property, Rosalia paused and searched the neighboring windows, as if making certain no one could see them. She wrapped her arm around Vin's waist and they jumped over the high fence with an ease that spoke of practice.

That kid must have had an interesting childhood.

Deacon launched himself over and landed beside them. He took the lead, heading for the access point she'd marked above the front entrance. Columns supported the portico roof. He jumped up to the roof, landing heavily on the sloping surface. A moment later, Rosalia crouched beside him, her grip secure on Vin's arm. Deacon found the small oval window tucked between two snarling gargoyles.

He glanced through into an empty bedroom. Dust sheets draped the furniture. Putting his ear to the glass, he listened, but couldn't make out movement or voices from any of the nearby rooms.

Still, there was no reason to bring them running by shattering the window. He drew one of his swords. Irena had crafted the blade with her Gift, and after thirty years, the edge was still as sharp as a diamond-tipped razor. He etched a deep circle in the window near the frame, then thumped the heel of his hand near the cut. The circle popped out and he caught the glass before it fell.

He slipped inside, moved quickly to the door. Rosalia came through, looking around. Her expression was both sad and wary, as if this place didn't bring back good memories.

It probably wouldn't bring back good memories for anyone. Acciaioli had stuffed the rooms full of furniture, great looming pieces covered in sheets. All that white should have lightened the place, but it felt heavy and oppressive, as if one more piece would upset the balance and bury a man beneath the weight.

This second level was clear. Quietly, Deacon used the stairs to the main floor. Muffled voices were coming from somewhere, but he couldn't pinpoint the direction.

A Guardian's hearing was better than a vampire's. Rosalia pulled up next to him, pointed at the floor. The dungeon, then. Probably constructed of thick stone, which usually conducted sound well—but if Lorenzo had used it as a real dungeon, he wouldn't want the screaming and moaning in his living place all the time. Considering how indistinct the voices were, the stone must have been lined with insulation or wood.

She gestured to another room—the library, where they'd find the stairs to the dungeon. Bare shelves lined the walls. Either Rosalia had sold the collection of books, or Acciaioli hadn't been much of a reader.

Someone had been using this room. The chair and desk had been uncovered, revealing ornate carvings in the dark wood, as overwrought as the rest of the house.

Rosalia moved quickly to the stairwell door, calling in a second sword. Deacon heard the footsteps a second later—someone climbing the stairs. *One* person. Gun drawn, Vin stopped next to Rosalia, just behind her shoulder. Deacon flanked the other side of the door. When it opened, Rosalia and Vin would be behind it. Deacon would be the first person he saw.

It was a human—St. Croix. The man's baby blues had barely widened before Deacon's hand closed around his throat, cutting off any call for help. Rosalia shut the door.

To his credit, the man didn't struggle. Vin quickly moved to Deacon's side and patted St. Croix down, coming away with two semiautomatic pistols. Tucking them behind his waistband, he returned to the door. Rosalia moved to the opposite side. If the vampires came through, she could deal with them.

Deacon tossed St. Croix into the chair by the desk. "You've got three words to explain why there's a human tied up downstairs, and why I shouldn't rip your throat out for it."

St. Croix rubbed at his neck, where the marks from Deacon's fingers were still vivid. His psychic scent radiated anger, but not a bit of it showed on his face. A cold bastard. "He's not human."

"Try again."

"He killed vampires in London."

"He killed vampires, but he can't break out of restraints?"

"Apparently not. We've chained him, put him behind those

thick bars. That'll keep even one of them." A London accent clipped St. Croix's words. Not a lofty one, despite the self-satisfaction that bled through the anger. "And once he's in a cage, we won't have to keep pumping him full of the damned vampire blood."

Deacon's veins ran cold. He glanced back at Rosalia, at her wide eyes and suddenly pale face. She'd come to the same conclusion: St. Croix hadn't caught a human. He had one of the nephilim.

Vampire blood weakened the creatures, made it revert to the human form it possessed. Though that form wasn't as weak as a human, a vampire could defeat a nephil before it shape-shifted. But once it shifted into its demonic form, even a Guardian wasn't as strong.

Icy sweat broke out over his skin. Jesus Christ, anyone in this house who wasn't human was in serious trouble. "Are you still pumping the blood into him?"

If yes, they had a chance. Rosalia could get down there and kill the nephil before it shifted.

St. Croix shook his head. "Now that he's in chains, they took the IV line out—"

Rosalia flung open the door. To save the vampires, Deacon guessed.

Too late. Before she could take another step, a scream ripped up the stairs and was cut short by the wet sound of tearing flesh.

Her swords at the ready, Rosalia backed away from the open door. She glanced over her shoulder at Deacon, then lifted her sword to point at the front of the house.

Her message was clear: Get the hell out of here.

Not a chance. Deacon knew she was staying on the thin possibility that the second vampire was still alive downstairs, and to slow the nephil down if it came up and went after him. Nephilim had a hard-on for killing vampires, but they'd also slay a Guardian to get to one. He wouldn't let her stand in the way to save him. They were going to beat this fucker.

Her eyes turned pleading. She tilted her head toward Vin,

standing at the edge of the open door, then pointed at the entrance again.

Not asking Deacon to save her son. A nephilim couldn't hurt a human. She was begging him to take Vin outside so that her son wouldn't see her die.

Goddammit. No one was dying here. He started for her, drawing his swords.

Before he could take two steps, the nephil filled the doorway. Huge, with red skin and feathered black wings that arched behind the height of the door frame, he held two swords, the blades already bloodied. His eyes glowed crimson.

Deacon saw Rosalia's muscles tighten in preparation. An instant later, she was nothing but a dark blur of movement, so fast he couldn't track her. They fought in a whirlwind of crimson and black at the head of the stairs. He heard the clash of metal. A broken sword flew across the room—Rosalia's. Then everything seemed to slow as she skidded backward.

She'd slipped on her blood.

Her stomach lay open.

Deacon had barely been able to run two more steps in that time. She'd be dead before he could cross half the room.

Eight steps away.

She called in another sword. The nephil laughed—*laughed*, the fucking bastard, as if her determination amused him.

Good. The more the nephil dicked around, the more time he gave Deacon.

And enough time for Vin to register what was happening. Then her son was moving, too. Already standing next to the door, he only needed to take one step. One human step.

An eternity.

But Deacon was just six steps away.

The nephil played with Rosalia again. Their blades rang in a furious cacophony of steel. Blood spattered the walls— all hers. She lost another sword. The nephil caught her arm, wrenched it backward. Deacon heard her bones snap.

Just two more fucking steps.

The nephil saw Deacon was almost on him and slapped

her away. Rosalia crashed into wall, her crossbow splintering. The nephilim turn to Deacon and grinned, exposing long fangs.

Deacon braced himself. The creature liked to toy with his prey. Fine.

Anything that gave them a little more time.

The nephil's swords sliced the air. Deacon felt his skin open, the slide of his blood. The blades had been so sharp and quick he hadn't felt any pain. Not yet.

Rosalia cried out. She'd staggered to her feet. The nephil drew his hand back—he wasn't fucking around with Deacon anymore. Not with a Guardian headed his way. The nephil stabbed his blade toward Deacon's heart.

At the last moment, Deacon pivoted to the side. The nephil's sword sliced deeply across his chest.

Vin's hand closed around the creature's crimson wrist.

The nephil froze. They only had an instant. That was enough.

Deacon brought his sword around, up through the nephil's heart. Rosalia leapt, striking the back of its neck. The nephil's head flew. Rosalia whipped around. Her boot smashed into its chest, sending the body flying back to crack against the wall.

Deacon's senses swam, the room spinning dizzily. His legs wouldn't hold. He sat before he collapsed into a heap.

Rosalia dropped to her knees beside him. She held her arm at an awkward angle, her gut still bleeding.

Her face blurred in front of him. His head felt light, empty. He looked down. Oh, Christ. He'd been butchered. His blood was everywhere, pumping from gashes in his chest, his thighs. The nephil had sliced his arteries open—not in one place, but several. His blood pooled on the parquet floor, spreading slowly outward, almost touching Rosalia's knees.

Bleeding out weakened a vampire, slowed the healing—and if Deacon lost all of his blood, it'd kill him. He needed to feed, and soon.

Vin crouched next to Rosalia, his hand gently cupping her face. "Mama?"

She held his palm to her cheek, then glanced over her shoulder. Deacon couldn't read the look she gave her son, but Vin apparently did. He nodded and stood.

The softness left his face as he turned toward St. Croix. "Let's check on your people."

They'd heard only one scream. Maybe the other vampire had made it.

Deacon didn't think there was much hope of that.

Rosalia watched Vin escort St. Croix to the stairs. As soon as her son was out of sight, she clenched her teeth and gripped the wrist of her twisted arm in her opposite hand. She yanked it straight, then curled over, as if stifling a scream. She sat motionless for a few moments, her good arm wrapped around herself, before looking up and meeting Deacon's eyes.

Her gaze turned to worry. Reaching out to him, she touched his neck, where two more cuts spilled blood onto the floor. The slices had been long and deep, and he wasn't healing fast enough.

A plastic bag appeared in her hand—empty. She wouldn't receive more blood until tomorrow, he remembered. The scent rose all around them, dark and luscious. He stopped breathing.

Determination set her face. She pointed to her neck.

Deacon laughed, though he could barely manage it. His vow not to drink from her wasn't so easy to keep now. "No chance, sister."

His voice sounded wet. He felt blood dripping down the back of his throat and coughed it up.

Her expression turned fierce. Grabbing his shirt, she hauled him closer.

He pulled back. Drinking from her was a risk he wouldn't take. When he was this hungry, when he needed to feed this badly, the bloodlust would roar. One taste, and he'd lose control, fucking her in a lake of their blood. She'd have to fight him off with a broken arm and her gut split open.

He didn't need living blood for strength. Any blood would

do. So he had two choices: lick it up from the floor, or drink from the dead nephil.

At least the nephil was still warm.

"Not from you," he told her.

Her hand dropped away. Her expression registered disbelief as he turned toward the nephil. A worried noise sounded from high in her throat.

He paused. A vampire's blood weakened a nephil. Would a nephil's blood harm a vampire? "Will it kill me?"

She lifted her hand, a clear gesture saying she didn't know, before pointing at her neck again. Her eyes pled with him.

He'd had nosferatu blood before, and he'd taken demon blood. Neither had hurt. One had made him stronger. And even if the nephil blood did kill him, the alternative was unthinkable. Just the image of an injured Rosalia struggling under him while he was an animal at her throat, forcing her thighs open and stabbing into her . . .

He shook the image away, feeling sick. No question. He'd risk death.

He lifted the nephil's wrist to his fangs. He pierced the skin and sucked until the lifeless blood flowed over his tongue. Tasteless, just like dead blood, but strong—stronger than a demon's. Already, the lightness in his head began to clear.

Rosalia's face became an unreadable mask, her eyes devoid of emotion. The blood pooled around them vanished. A clean change of clothes dropped to the floor beside him.

She struggled to her feet, looking away from him as if she couldn't bear to watch, and limped toward the stairs.

❧

The bowels of Lorenzo's home were fashioned of crudely worked iron and dark wood. Centuries of blood had soaked the dirt floor, drying as hard as concrete. The air still smelled faintly of rot.

Rosalia had known both vampires. Sally Barrows and Gerald Winn had once been part of the London community, but they'd gone off her radar about three years before, only showing up as blips here and there. Strong and clever vampires, passionate about protecting each other and enforcing the community rules, she'd pegged them as future heads of their own group of vampires. That wouldn't happen now.

After the nephil had broken free, he'd released his anger here. Sally had been slammed into the cell bars with such force that the iron had cut her into narrow strips. Gerald's neck was a ragged stump, his limbs ripped off.

Vin and St. Croix were laying Sally next to Gerald when Rosalia came downstairs. St. Croix crouched beside the ravaged bodies, his face without expression. His psychic scent, anger layered over grief, gave him away. He felt these murders deeply. So deeply that although his mental shields were strong, he couldn't conceal his emotions.

Hopefully, his lies would be just as easy to read when she questioned him.

Though her lungs had pieced back together and filled with air, they still felt too tender to speak. She should wait another five or ten minutes. She could let Vin handle it. He knew everything she'd want to ask, and was capable of handling an interrogation.

But she needed it to distract her from the pain in her arm, her stomach—and her heart. Deacon had risked the nephil's blood rather than drink from her. She should have stopped him, but his decision had felt like another blow from the nephil's fist, and she'd been too stunned to react. Then it had been too late. He'd taken the blood—and now, only her relief that she could hear him moving upstairs, putting on his clothes, was stronger than the ache of his rejection.

She studied St. Croix. Every picture she'd run across had shown him impeccably groomed, his clothes perfectly tailored, but he'd been willing to get his hands dirty. He'd discarded his jacket and rolled up his sleeves to help move the vampires' bodies. Crimson streaked his forehead where he'd pushed his fingers through his black hair, either unaware of the blood on his fingers or too angry to care.

He'd been working for Legion, but she wouldn't yet ask him why. She wanted to see what he'd give her first.

"Two vampires," Rosalia said, coming to stand beside them. "Who were they?"

He glanced up at her, then stood. "Gerry Winn, and his wife, Sally. Both from London."

So he offered the truth to her, then—and apparently *they* had trusted this man enough to offer it to him. She turned to Vin. "Will you bring two dust sheets from upstairs? They ought to be covered. They deserve that respect."

St. Croix's pale blue gaze followed Vin before returning to her face. "Thank you."

"I am sorry we did not arrive earlier and warn them. Who managed to catch and restrain the demon?"

No need yet to call the creature a nephil. First she'd discover how much St. Croix knew. It couldn't be much—and what he had was full of errors. He'd known enough to put a nephil down with vampire blood, but not enough to keep it that way.

"I did." He nodded toward the stairs after Vin. "The same way he stopped the demon upstairs."

By grabbing his arm. The nephil couldn't shake off a human's grasp; he had to follow the Rules.

Rosalia wasn't certain she believed him, however. St. Croix looked at her as someone might a page full of fraudulent figures, calculating where to shift numbers so that the equations would balance—as if deciding what she wanted to hear and giving an explanation he thought she'd accept.

"Where did you capture him?"

"London."

They'd brought him from London in those restraints? "When?"

"Monday."

The day after the nephilim had slain the community elders. "Why bring him here?"

He glanced at the dank cell, his expression tightening. "I'd heard the dungeon was built to hold a demon."

No, Lorenzo had built it to hold a Guardian. But the cell probably could have contained a demon for a short time—or a Guardian whose Gift hadn't allowed her to escape. "You heard that from whom?"

"Gerry."

She could accept that. A vampire might have known about the dungeon. Lorenzo hadn't kept it a secret. "How did you gain access to the house?"

He pushed his hands into his trouser pockets. "How did you?" he countered.

Slowly losing patience, Rosalia thought. Though he'd been going along with her questions, she had the impression that he didn't usually roll over this easily—and that the only reason he answered her was because it would eventually benefit him.

The cold intelligence in his eyes reminded her too much of her father, as if he was constantly judging how useful someone could be. After only a few minutes in his presence, she would have been certain he was Malkvial if she hadn't already known he was human.

She briefly considered whether a human could masquerade as a demon, and rejected the possibility. Demons did not respect humans; they would never follow one, and they wouldn't be fooled by one.

And St. Croix wasn't quite as slick as a demon. His London accent held more river than estate, something no demon would ever allow. And if he hadn't been trying to conceal the rougher edges of his emotions, she would have wondered whether they were a mask he put on to appear more human. Instead, she thought those rough edges were something he hadn't yet filed down—but he'd been trying.

She didn't like him. But he *had* felt something for these vampires, be it friendship or a deeper affection. For that, she could give him something back.

"You'll find a broken window upstairs," she told him.

His brows lifted. He seemed surprised that she answered. Then he nodded and said, "I own the building."

As soon as he made the claim, Gemma spoke up. *"It's true, Mother. I've just confirmed that Willingham Cross Properties belongs to him."*

All right. But why buy it? "Did you need a house where you can lock up a demon, Mr. St. Croix?"

For an instant, his gaze was no longer calculating, but pure ice. "Yes."

"Were you looking for any demon? Or did you just want to keep this one?"

There, she hit a wall. She'd gotten close to something he didn't want to answer. There was a subtle shift of his expression, a suggestion of humor and warmth. And *that*, Rosalia recognized, was his mask.

His gaze slowly traveled the length of her, his interest palpable. Wondering if he could seduce her to get what he wanted? She suspected it wouldn't be the first time he'd done so to a woman. "Maybe I'll keep you."

She supposed he was incredibly handsome—for a human snake. "I don't think so, Mr. St. Croix."

"Then tell me what you are." His focus settled on her mouth. "You have no fangs, and so you aren't a vampire. How can I be certain you aren't a demon? You move quickly enough to be one."

"I could tell you, but if I am a demon, you would be foolish to believe me." Rosalia smiled, though she had to acknowledge the problem: St. Croix had seen her. He knew she wasn't human. And with the wrong word, he could reveal her to the demons at Legion and ruin everything. Which meant she needed to keep him close and slowly dole out information so that he wouldn't go elsewhere to find it. "Now is not the time for telling you what I am, for there is too much to explain. Tonight, you have friends who need to be taken care of."

He glanced down at the bodies again and nodded. His hand rose, as if intended to push it through his hair again, but this time he noted the blood on his fingers. His eyes cooled, losing the warmth—his anger and grief ripping away the mask again, but now joined by the icy touch of hate.

She would have wagered the demon he'd intended the cell for was a very specific one, indeed.

Vin's quick tread descended the stairs, and he was followed by a slower, heavier step. Rosalia frowned and listened more closely. Deacon's gait wasn't hesitant . . . not exactly. And he wasn't limping. But it sounded as if he was being careful as he took every step.

Was he still hurting?

Vin brushed past her, carrying an armful of white cloth. St. Croix stopped him, took the first sheet, took care of his friends.

Rosalia turned toward the stairs. Deacon had almost reached the bottom, and her heart clenched when she saw the way he was moving.

She'd seen it before—more than ninety years ago, when he'd lost himself in a bottle almost every night. She recognized the precision of every step, as if the world was spinning around him, but he'd be damned before he let anyone know it.

But he'd healed well. She'd expected to still see marks on his throat, like a newly formed scar where the blade had sliced his jugular, but not even a hint of pink was left.

Perhaps he hadn't taken as much blood as he'd lost. That might account for some disorientation. Was it just physical, or was it mental as well?

Though the upstairs door had been open and he must have heard every question and response, she told him, "Mr. St. Croix picked up the demon in London."

"That's too bad for the vampires who came with him." To her relief, his reply was clear, his eyes sharp. His gaze ran over her, searching out her injuries—almost healed now. The tightness around his mouth eased. "Where'd he pick the vampires up?"

St. Croix straightened up from beside the covered bodies. "Also in London, three years ago. They are my associates."

"Your associates." Deacon took in the cell, the overturned gurney, the splatters of blood. "In what kind of business?"

"Finding someone."

"A demon?"

Though he stiffened, St. Croix said, "Yes."

But not the nephil, Rosalia thought. So what had St. Croix hoped to gain by bringing him here? "Did you think this demon might help you find the one you're looking for?"

"Yes." His pale eyes narrowed. "How did you happen upon us tonight?"

"We're looking for a demon, too," she said. "But we didn't join Legion to do it."

He hadn't expected her to know his connection to Legion, and in his moment of surprise, she felt his hatred, his determination. This man had no love for demons, she thought. Now he knew that she felt the same—but he didn't know if a mutual enemy meant they shared the same goals. He studied her for a long, calculating moment.

She truly disliked that look. "You're wondering how to use me to get what you need," she said. "So I'll make this easy: If what you need means that a demon dies, I'll offer the help."

"A demon will definitely die."

Dark pleasure suffused his chiseled features. At that moment, St. Croix looked very much like the creature he wanted to kill. Rosalia tamped down her revulsion.

"Then we can share information. With your associates gone, you'll need new ones—the difference being that our information is accurate." The offer sounded cold, even to herself. Gerald and Sally still lay in pieces on the ground. Not being able to vanish their bodies and to take care of them hurt.

St. Croix only took a moment to decide. "That is acceptable."

"Good." Rosalia glanced down at the covered bodies. "Will you make the proper arrangements for them, or shall we?"

"I'll see it done."

Rosalia nodded. "I'll meet with you tomorrow, then." She gave him the name of Father Wojcinski's church. "I will look for you there at eleven in the morning, and we will talk, Mr. St. Croix."

🌶

Deacon hadn't expected her to say farewell to St. Croix so quickly. Although the man didn't know what she was, he'd seen what she could do. Rosalia was so damn set on keeping anyone from knowing about her, yet she hadn't even extracted a promise of silence from St. Croix—or frightened him into keeping his mouth shut.

So Deacon would.

His expression must have tipped her off, though. After telling St. Croix that they'd talk, she'd barely finished turning around before pressing her hand against Deacon's chest, as if holding him back. She looked up at him with warm eyes and an expression that asked him to trust her.

All right. He could do that. But it didn't hurt to smile and give the smug bastard a good look at his fangs before following her up the stairs.

She had the curviest ass he'd ever set eyes on. He wanted to fill his hands with each sweet cheek and take a good bite. He had to settle for just walking up the stairs without tripping.

The first few minutes on the nephil's blood had felt like he'd pounded back a fifth of vodka. Everything around him appeared slowed down, as if viewed through thick water. Climbing up the stairs was easier than walking down had been, but the disorientation wasn't going away. He was just getting used to it.

But he hadn't yet gotten used to the way Rosalia's psychic scent seemed to vibrate with musical notes and sound. Apparently, nephil blood was a drug to vampires. Not a high. Just *more*, like opening a conduit. It brought too much into his head, twisted the input, cluttering his senses.

Deacon made it out of the house without making a fool of himself. By then, he'd realized why Rosalia hadn't threatened St. Croix. The man didn't have anything on her, and he didn't know she wanted to keep the demons from finding out about her. Right now, she had the advantage. But once St. Croix had that knowledge, he could hold it over her head. So she'd given

St. Croix just enough, and then promised more. He probably felt like he'd gained something, but he hadn't gotten anything important out of Rosalia.

St. Croix had been an unexpected complication, but Rosalia had effortlessly put him in a position where she maintained control. Deacon doubted the man had any idea how she'd played him. He had to admire how well she'd managed it—and he hoped to hell she never tried anything like that on him.

Outside, the heat and humidity immediately had him sweating. He could have used another swim, and another opportunity to get his hands on Rosalia, but he didn't think that was on the agenda.

Vin slid open the van door, and was knocked back when Gemma launched into his arms. The woman's eyes were puffy and wet from crying. Christ, hearing the fight with the nephil go down must have torn her raw. Deacon watched them for a moment before turning to Rosalia.

"What's up next?"

"Now we listen to everything he does, and dig deeper to find out what we missed. Then we start looking for Malkvial again." Rosalia stopped next to her son, touched Gemma's arm. "Are you okay, *mia piccola bambina*?"

Gemma unhooked one arm from around Vin's neck and snagged Rosalia in for a hug. "You killed it."

Not fast enough. Over Gemma's shoulder, Deacon saw the loss of the two vampires reflected in Rosalia's expression. He felt it in the deep vibration of her psychic scent.

Since when did anyone's emotions start sounding like that?

Rosalia patted Gemma's arm before pulling away and climbing into the van. "Let's head out. We'll drive by his hotel, and I'll wire it before he returns."

"What about inside the library here?" Vin glanced back at the house.

She narrowed her eyes at him.

"You did it on the way out," he guessed.

"Clever boy." She flicked a curl back from his forehead. "Go on in."

Vin headed for the driver's seat, with Gemma next to him. Rosalia's smile faded as soon as their backs were turned. The engine started, and she sank into a chair, let her face fall forward into her hands.

Deacon rolled a chair next to her. He remembered the desperation in her eyes when she'd faced the nephil. The dread in her psychic scent when she'd begged him to feed from her. And the devastation upon realizing that they'd lost two more vampires.

She looked completely alone. Probably wondering what she could have done differently, what she hadn't seen, obsessing over the mistakes she'd made. It killed him.

And it pissed him off.

"Get over yourself, princess."

She stiffened. Her hands dropped, revealing her face. Just as he'd suspected: Her eyes were sad and tortured. She'd been beating herself up over everything that had happened since they'd stepped into that nightmare of a house.

"So you didn't single-handedly save everyone. So you didn't foresee that they'd take out the nephil's IV, or even why they'd be pumping vampire blood into someone in the first place." He pushed closer to her, got into her face. "Who'd have thought two vampires and a human could bring down a nephil? Who?"

"*I* should have."

"Because you're omnipotent fucking God?" He didn't know whether she flinched at the words or at the hard smile he gave her. "You aren't his bride anymore, and you're not a saint or a miracle worker. And beating yourself up over it won't bring them back."

A yellow glow lit her eyes, and she replied with controlled ferocity, "So you are the ox and I am the ass."

God, he loved it when she slapped back at him.

But this time, she'd missed. There was a world of difference between Deacon blaming himself for what had happened to his community and Rosalia taking the blame for what had happened here. "You can't win everything."

"I have to try, and to believe I can."

"You'll set yourself up for a lot of failure if you take that view."

Her ferocity receded, leaving a bleak smile in its place and her eyes dark. "I know."

A faint noise came from one of the speakers—St. Croix, making a phone call from the bugged library. Rosalia turned away from Deacon, listening close.

Deacon watched her profile, wondering about her last reply. She'd sounded as if she had a close acquaintance with failure, as if she'd fallen down too many times in her life.

In all of that time, why hadn't anyone been there to catch her?

CHAPTER 14

A few minutes before dawn found Deacon in bed, listening to Rosalia working in the War Room. She'd been busy, but not with anything Deacon could help her with. Mostly trailing through financial information, searching for anything about St. Croix they might have missed.

St. Croix had given her more to look at. Over the course of the night, he'd called in several favors. Someone to provide coffins, another to provide transport to the airport. Another to smooth his way through customs, so that no questions would be asked. He took care of the vampires, and each person he contacted was a link to his past. Now Rosalia was discovering how he'd intersected with these people, and why they owed him.

And that was all she'd been doing. Though she hadn't pushed Deacon out of her space, she'd shut down emotionally. He could still hear her, though—that strange new sound, a strong psychic sense. Pain sang a dirge just below her shields, and told him that her shutting down had been a defense.

A defense against what, he had no fucking clue. He posed no danger to her. Christ, if anyone was in trouble, it was him. Every look, every smile, and those hooks she'd gotten into him sank deeper.

Hell, she could probably see it. After years of watching people, she had the ability to read them like no one he'd ever met. No surprise, then, that she was so good at managing a potential enemy and arranging situations to her advantage.

What he wouldn't have given to have someone like her around six months ago, Guardian or not. Caym wouldn't have known which way was up.

Of course, maybe Deacon wouldn't have, either. She might be able to read him, but he couldn't make heads or tails of her—like why she was sitting in the next room, her psyche humming like her heart ached. He only knew that it tore at him.

Christ. As soon as they were done with the demons and the nephilim, he needed to get the hell out of here.

He closed his eyes, waiting for dawn, for that instant drop into sleep. The black would fall over him and the dreams would start. Maybe tonight, they'd be of Rosalia. Her silken skin. Her gorgeous lips and hot mouth.

But if he didn't stop thinking of it now, he'd end up forming a tent of her sheets before he fell asleep and stay hard throughout the day. Daylight had to be coming soon. A few minutes felt like it had stretched into a dozen—the nephil blood, still slowing his perception. Maybe it'd wear off as he slept.

In the War Room, the quiet clacking of the keyboard fell silent. Rosalia's sigh floated across the corridor, and was followed by her approaching footsteps as she entered the bedchamber. She paused, as if she stood near the bed, looking at him.

Unbelievably, Deacon felt the mattress dip beneath her weight. His eyes popped open as her cheek came down on his chest. Her hair spread over his shoulder. She inhaled his skin. Her body pressed against his side, and she seemed to do a fluid roll as if snuggling in as close as possible.

What the hell?

She stiffened. Her head jerked up from his chest and she stared into his face. Shock rounded her eyes. "You're awake!"

Was he? Deacon wasn't convinced he hadn't slipped into daysleep and begun a vivid dream. "Am I?"

"Yes! The sun is . . ." Her eyes darkened. That subtle shift was the only thing that saved him, the only thing that gave him time to catch her wrist before her bladed fan sliced through his neck.

Jesus Christ. He'd reacted fast enough to catch her wrist . . . *and was strong enough to hold it.*

Rosalia still had the advantage of position and leverage. Shaking with effort, she shoved the tips of the blades into his skin.

"Demon! Where is he? Where's Deacon?"

Fear and anger screamed through her psychic scent. She thought someone had killed him, took his place.

"Rosie . . . feel." Her skin was hot against his. His must be cool against hers. Whatever else had changed, he was still the same temperature. *"Feel."*

Her hand trembled. "The sun is up. How are *you* up?"

Realization hit hard. "The nephil's blood."

And afterward, everything around him had seemed slow, but that wasn't right. *He* was faster. His senses were stronger— and his body, too.

Deacon prayed it wouldn't wear off.

Her eyes rounded again. Beyond her amazement, however, Deacon recognized one clear thing: She'd come to hold him while he was sleeping. Using him as a substitute for the other guy, most likely. He didn't give a fuck. If she'd come, she probably wanted someone to grab onto.

That guy wasn't here. Deacon was.

And God knew he wanted her, too.

❧

Rosalia could not wind back her astonishment. The sky outside had been light when she'd come in here. Yet he was awake.

The realization in Deacon's expression shifted into something heated and intense. "You're in my bed," he said.

And he was *awake*. Incredible. So far as she knew, only one other vampire could resist the daysleep—and that vampire could also survive the sunlight. Could Deacon? They'd have to be careful, but they had to try.

She vanished her fan and tugged on his hand, half rising. "Let's see if you can go out—"

His hand closed over hers, pulled her back down. She recalled how he'd caught her before. Not just awake. Strong. Fast.

"You came to my bed. Wrapped yourself around me."

Oh. Now she felt a hint of color in her cheeks. "Yes. But Deacon, you're *awake*."

How could that not overwhelm any other concern right now? But he wouldn't be put off.

"Have you come before?"

"Yes," she said, and tugged again, but he wouldn't let her move.

So he wanted to deal with this first. All right. He did deserve to know. She settled against him again, and with her astonishment fading, became aware of his body beneath hers, the cool hardness of muscle. She looked into his green eyes, focused intently on her face. Waiting for her explanation.

She moistened her lips. How to say this? His body beneath hers *was* the explanation.

"I do it to think," she said.

His eyes narrowed. "To think?"

"Yes. To remind myself why I'm risking so much. It's easier when I can . . . hold on to someone."

He looked doubtful, but it wasn't a lie. Although she didn't just want *someone*. It had to be Deacon, who risked the most with everything she did. Who she had to send into battle over and over. Who she'd almost lost that very night, in a battle she hadn't foreseen.

And who she could have lost again, because he'd turned down the offer of her blood and risked the nephil's, instead.

She'd spent the rest of the night trying to suppress the ache of that rejection—and now, faced with the amazing fact of Deacon awake in her bed, that pain seemed far away.

"You want to *smell* someone, too?"

Her cheeks caught fire. So he hadn't missed that. "I wanted . . ."

To imagine this. That he wouldn't be sleeping. That he'd take her into his arms. That her mouth would find his. That he could know her—know everything she'd felt for him.

"What did you want?"

Her heart seemed to shrink in on itself. When she told him, he could reject her again. But she could show him instead, and take a little first—just a little bit of what she'd wanted.

"Damn you," she whispered, and lurched forward.

Though Deacon was fast enough to stop her, he didn't. His mouth opened beneath hers. Her stomach performed a long, slow dive and she stroked her tongue against his.

He kissed her back as if he'd been waiting for the touch of her lips. As if he was relieved. And so careful with his fangs, though with every lick and taste, she felt her control slipping.

Need rushed over her, like a whirlwind catching her wings, spinning her about. Her fingers framed his face and ran down to clench on his wide shoulders. She couldn't taste him enough, touch him enough. Her heart pounded. Fear crashed into her. She didn't know how to manage this.

She pulled back.

Deacon caught her waist, rolled her beneath him. The linen sheet wrapped her left leg, her knee cocked and trapped by his weight. He settled over her thighs, his heavy erection burning into her awareness through the linen, through her skirt. She clutched at his back to steady herself. Beneath the sheet, he wore nothing, only cool skin over iron muscle. Her short shallow breaths sounded panicked. She made herself stop.

He braced his hands next to her shoulders, his biceps bunching as he lifted to study her face. His mouth glistened from her kisses. A soft yellow glow washed over his features . . . Oh, God. Her eyes.

"Is this what you want, Rosie?" With a deliberate roll of his hips, he rocked against her.

Yes. Rosalia's lips opened on a gasp and her hips rose to meet him. That rush sped through her again, made her feel like crying.

His mouth took hers before she came down. He palmed her left knee, pushed her leg higher. The sheet slid over her thigh, the fabric a soft burn against her skin. Deacon settled firmly between her legs, open to him, and the rhythm of his rocking hips matched the thrust of his tongue into her mouth. Rosalia clung to him, drowning.

He lifted his head. She gasped for air, for control—afraid he'd kiss her again and take her deeper.

Afraid he wouldn't.

"Rosie?"

Concern softened the gravel in his voice. She looked up at him.

"Your nails are tearing up my back."

What? A glance over his shoulder revealed her fingertips, wet with blood. Long gouges striped his flesh. Oh, God.

"I'm sorry." She tried to get up, but he didn't move. She pushed at his chest.

"Hold on," he said, and she did. His dark brows drew together. "You're sorry?"

"Yes."

"I don't care. Rip me up if you want. But if you're saying sorry, princess, it means you weren't trying to get me off of you."

He hadn't stopped because of the pain, but because he'd been worried she wanted out? "No."

Her misery etched into the word. Only a few kisses, yet she'd been scratching up his back. That wasn't supposed to come until later, when he was inside her. She felt her color rise again. How many times had she seen people do this? She knew how sex worked. Yet she was losing control, getting it wrong.

Anger darkened his face. "Don't look like that."

"I don't know how to handle this." She wished he'd been asleep. Holding on to him wasn't as frightening as trying to hold herself back. "It's not safe."

Tension hardened his muscles to steel. "You're not safe from me?"

"No. You from me."

She showed him her fingertips, then vanished the blood. His eyes narrowed as he stared at her, as if he could open her up and peel away the layers. She struggled not to flinch away from that flaying gaze, tempted to recede into darkness. To just let it surround her and take her.

Then his face softened, and his long, slow smile appeared. "You don't have to handle it."

"What?"

"I won't make it easy, but I'll catch you. I'll take care of you, keep you safe. If you'll let me."

His hands found hers, folded over them. The possessive gesture seemed to say, *I'm strong enough*. It promised to give her control that she didn't have . . . by giving control over to him.

Could she? Her fingers trembled.

His grip tightened, pinning her hands to the bed. "Let me show you, Rosie."

Oh, she wanted to. Surely it was no different than the trust she'd put in him the past three nights, when she'd sent him in to slay demons. She'd trusted his strength then, trusted that he would prevail, that he wouldn't expose her, that he would take control of the situation. She had been frightened then, too— but he had succeeded each time. And her heart had been at risk each time . . . as it still was.

Yet every kiss had been worth that risk. This would be, too.

With a deep breath, she nodded.

"Say it."

"I'll let you." *Take control. Take me.*

"Trust me."

A command, not a question. She answered it anyway. "I do."

His heavy-lidded gaze fell to her lips. "Then give me your mouth again."

Her breath caught. Another kiss—but she had to offer it. He didn't intend to let her lie back and take what he gave. He'd still make her lose herself in the rush of every kiss, every touch.

He'd said it wouldn't be easy. But his strength would be her safety net—only if she truly trusted him.

She would soon find out.

Though strong enough to lift her head to his, it was still awkward raising her torso with her hands pinned to the bed. Her nipples brushed his broad chest, and heat blossomed through her stomach, between her legs. She delighted in the sensation before fitting her lips to his.

This time, she took it slow. He wouldn't reject her. She could explore the shape of his lips, firm and cool. She breathed in, found the fragrance of her soap. *Her scent.* With a possessive thrust of her tongue, she deepened the kiss. Deacon's groan rumbled in the quiet chamber. She lifted herself higher, her breasts flattening against the solid wall of his chest, and shivered when he penetrated her lips in return. A give and take, each taste deeper, more vital than the last.

A new anticipation filled her, an urgent, expanding hunger. His weight was a solid pressure between her legs, no longer rocking, yet she was so aware of him, and so wet. This would lead to Deacon inside her. Making love with her. That would be . . . different. She didn't yet know how. But she *would* know.

Releasing her hands, his callused palms slid from her wrists, up her arms. When his weight eased away from her, she threw her leg around his back, tried to lock him against her.

"Rosie . . ." He looked down at her, trailing off—and whatever he saw in her face brought him back for another kiss, then another, before finally breaking away.

She let him go this time, letting her arms fall back over her head. There was urgency in this, but also a wonderful decadence that needed to be savored. While he lifted away from her, she luxuriated in her body's arousal, the liquid heat that her skin couldn't seem to contain. Every sensation seemed like another caress: the linen wrapped around her thigh, her skirt hem flirting at her knees, the warm air rushing in where he'd been hard and cool against her only moments before.

His breathing ragged, Deacon sat back on his heels, his knees spread and the sheet pulled taut over the bulge of his erection. She watched him, the movements that seemed too fluid for such heavy musculature. His pale skin glistened from the heat of her body. Dark hair roughened his chest, and narrowed into a thin line from his navel to the edge of the sheet.

She reached out to follow that trail with her fingers. He caught her hand.

"Come up on your knees."

The low rasp of his voice drew her gaze to his face. His jaw was clenched, the strain visible on his face. Need clouded his eyes like a summer storm. Though he'd taken control, he walked on the edge of his.

Her heart hammering, she rose up, folding her sheet-wrapped leg beneath her. The movement dislodged the cover from his groin, exposing his organ. Rosalia stared. Jutting downward, as if weighted by its heavy length, the wide tip rested against the sheets. She looked at his large fingers still holding her wrist, remembering how big they'd felt inside her—how she'd barely been able to stop herself from riding him, the curling tension that hadn't wanted to let her go. Her hands began to shake.

Deacon nudged her chin up. "Eyes up, princess. On mine. Are you all right?"

She swallowed. "Yes."

"Good." He skimmed his fingers over her shoulder, catching on the halter strap of her dress. "Take this off for me."

Holding his gaze, she reached behind her nape to untie the knotted silk. She knew he liked her breasts, but anxiety and arousal made her clumsy. The strap tore. The bodice skimmed over her nipples, falling to her waist.

She didn't glance away from his face, and watched as his gaze drank her in. Need hardened his expression. She recalled the sweltering night in Greece, that same hungry look

Feed them to me.

She wanted to again. How she'd loved offering herself. Feeling bold, she cupped their soft weight.

"Look at you." It tore from him. Not a command. Something out of his control. "You're beautiful, Rosie."

She'd known she was, but it hadn't mattered. A Guardian could look like anyone. But she *felt* beautiful now, when he looked at her.

He rose up, his hands sliding around her waist and drawing her forward, chests almost touching, his erection a solid weight against her stomach. "Lean back."

Still cupping her breasts, she arched back. Her hair brushed the mattress. His hands flattened along her spine, supporting her upper body almost parallel to the bed. A feast spread out before him, given by her hands.

With a soft growl, he lowered his head. His tongue traced the lower curve of her right breast, wetting the seam of her cupped fingers. Though untouched, her nipple contracted into a dark bead. The ache between her legs intensified. She squeezed her thighs together, feeling the moisture there, the dampness of her panties against her core.

The sweep of his tongue around her nipple made her tighten. The soft scrape of fangs made her gasp. His strong hands held her steady when his lips closed over her nipple. She felt his tongue flick, then soft suction that drew her deep into his mouth. Overwhelmed, she began trembling. Her hips pushed against his, seeking pressure where she needed it most. She imagined his mouth there, licking and sucking, and the need rushed over her in a hot wave, filled her voice when she moaned his name.

Without warning, he brought her up and claimed her mouth again. Lost, drowning, she wound her arms around his neck and held on. She loved this. Loved his urgent murmurs between hot, wet kisses. Loved the muscles that bunched in his shoulders, loved the feel of his erection straining against her belly, the incredible anticipation. His hands slid up her front, cupping, then pinching and pulling at her nipples, until the bedchamber echoed with her cries for more.

Deacon gave her more. His hand stroked down, pushed inside her panties. She moaned into his mouth as his fingers teased, circling her entrance but never penetrating.

He broke their kiss, his breaths labored across her moist lips. "When you come, Rosalia, hold your psychic shields. Hold them tight."

She hadn't even considered that danger. This hadn't been her intention when she'd joined him in the bed. Yet he'd remembered, and hadn't made it a request. She *would* hold them.

"Yes," she said. No question.

He kissed her again, deep and quick. "Lie back."

She sank into the pillows, her feet against the mattress, her knees bent. Deacon reached beneath her skirts, hooked the waist of her panties. He dragged the scrap of silk down, lifting her legs until her toes pointed at the ceiling as he pulled them off. Her skirt slipped up her thighs, bunching on her stomach and baring her sex to his gaze.

"Oh, Christ. Rosie, you're so . . ." Staring, he turned his head and pressed his mouth to her ankle—to kiss or to bite, she wasn't certain. Instead he closed his eyes, gathering his control. After a moment he swallowed and placed her heels on his shoulders. "Vanish your dress."

She did, knowing he felt the tremor in her legs.

His gaze held hers. "I won't bite you. I won't risk the bloodlust taking over. Trust me on that."

She didn't need the reassurance—but perhaps he needed it as a reminder to hold on to his own control. "Yes," she said.

He leaned forward, reaching for a pillow. Weight against her lower belly made her glance down. *Oh, God.* Between her thighs, his engorged shaft extended upward from the apex of her sex, a graphic representation of how deeply she'd take him into her body. Anticipation wound tight. Her fingers dug into the mattress, holding herself still.

Deacon reared back and pushed the pillow beneath her hips. With a soft kiss to each of her ankles, he lowered her feet from his shoulders. "Hands on your knees, Rosie. Hold yourself open to me."

With trembling hands, she pulled her knees up and apart. She looked down at herself, her legs spread, her pink flesh flushed and wet. *Open* was too simple a word. She felt exposed. Displayed.

Until she saw his face. Then she was wanted. Worshipped.

She pulled her legs wider and was rewarded by a growl. Deacon bent, pressed his lips against the inside of her knee. The wet brush of his tongue shivered over her skin. His fangs grazed her inner thigh.

His bloodlust flared hot, an explosion against her psychic shields. Deacon froze. He gazed down at her exposed sex, his hunger burning hotter, his expression predatory. His mouth opened over her thigh.

Oh, God. "Deacon?"

"You're so wet, Rosie. So ready to be eaten. One lick, and I'd bury my fangs into you—" He broke off, closing his eyes.

The image of that gripped her mind, whipped along every nerve. She couldn't breathe. She wanted that so much. She couldn't have it yet.

"Soon," he said, and she wasn't certain whether he made the rough promise to her or himself. Rising up between her thighs, he wrapped his fist around his shaft. His tendons stood out in sharp relief beneath his skin, the effort of holding back. "We're going to take it slow. I'll take care of you, Rosie."

She nodded, then stilled when she felt the first touch against her wet core. Her fingers bit into her knees. She couldn't hold his gaze and looked down. The thick head of his penis parted her folds, teasing through her center, but not entering. Aching with need, she tried to lift toward him and push him inside. His free hand gripped her hip, held her down. Slowly, he rubbed the wide tip against her clitoris, already so sensitive. Rosalia's muscles locked, a cry caught in her throat. She'd have begged him, she needed him inside, to *know* what it would be, but he was already pushing down through her sex, pushing *in*.

Her legs shook, her trembling hands on her knees unable to hold them still. She watched him sink inside. Oh, dear God, she had not taken even half his length and there was so much pressure. Her chest heaved as she tried to manage it, not even certain if what she felt was pleasure, only that she felt *so much*. Too much, and so overwhelming as he pushed more sensation through her, leaving no room inside. She closed her eyes, too late. Tears squeezed from beneath her lids.

Deacon stilled, but the pressure remained, so big and full inside her. "Rosalia?" Her name was agonized. "Do you want to stop?"

Never. She shook her head.

"I'm hurting you. You're so tight, I can barely—"

"No." But more tears came, tears she couldn't explain. She could only choke out, "More."

He withdrew. Her eyes flew open and she sucked in a panicked breath, but then his abdomen flexed and he thrust back in. Rosalia's back arched as her body stretched, yielding to him. Oh, God. This *was* pleasure. He gripped the tops of her thighs with both hands, screwing deeper with short, spiraling jerks of his hips.

Pressure continued to build, winding around ecstasy. Panting, she held her knees still, held herself open. By the time he was seated fully inside, she was desperate to move.

He stopped. Her gaze met his again. His lips had drawn back, exposing sharp fangs. His big body was taut with strain.

"Hold on, Rosie."

He came forward between her legs, bracing his hands beside her shoulders. She cried out as the new position drove him deeper. He bent his head, his lips just above hers, his face washed in the glow of her eyes.

"Slow," he said, the guttural word followed by a slow lift of his hips and the endless drive back in.

Rosalia pulled her legs open farther, almost sobbing. His penetration was slow, so slow—and relentless. Excruciating tension twisted inside her, the rush pushed her higher. But this time, with Deacon holding her, she didn't fear falling. Overwhelmed, but not frightened. Ecstasy filled her instead, until everything within her overfilled. Tears ran a constant stream over her cheeks.

She tilted her head back, each thrust wringing another wordless cry from her lips. Deacon lifted her hand from her right knee. He sucked her fingers into his mouth, teasing his fangs over their wet tips before carrying her hand down between their bodies. With his hand over hers, he rubbed her middle finger over her clitoris. A dark ache bloomed through her body, centered on that tiny movement. She rubbed harder.

"No, Rosie." He held her gaze. His fingers slowed hers. "Not fast. Stay with me."

He withdrew his hand, braced his fist beside her shoulder again, and began another long thrust inside. Gasping, Rosalia forced her hand to match the wet slide of his shaft. Her inner muscles clenched around him with each slow circle of her fingers.

Deacon hissed his pleasure from between gritted teeth. "Christ, Rosie. I'd give anything to have my tongue where your fingers are. To suck on your clit while I fuck you."

The crude image shocked her, wound her tighter. She'd have given anything, too. Her right leg wrapped around his back. She urged him deeper. He caught her knee, spread her wide again. Oh, God. He felt so big, invading, stretching, and yet she couldn't get enough of him. Desperate for his taste, she lifted her head, searching for his mouth.

He gently drew her upper lip between his, circling his tongue over the sensitive flesh in the same rhythm as her finger, as the driving pressure within her.

"It would be soft like this," he said, with another kiss to her bottom lip. "But this isn't wet enough."

He opened her mouth, closed his lips around the tip of her tongue. Rosalia cried out, trying to kiss him, but he only suckled, as if her tongue was the small, slippery bud beneath her fingers. Then Deacon pushed forward, so deep inside. The pressure within her contracted before exploding outward. Caught up in it, her back bowed. Her flesh pulsed beneath her fingertips, and now Deacon was kissing her, his tongue not mimicking her fingers but his turgid length, driving into her deep and hard.

Her body had locked, shaking, but now she was all in motion, clenching and releasing, her breaths sobbing. Deacon slowed, his kiss gentling again. Her tears fell faster.

Her limbs felt weak as he turned her over onto her stomach. He moved to the end of the bed and urged her to her knees, raising her bottom into the air. Her head swimming, she complied.

His hand smoothed over her cheek, followed by a sharp nip from his teeth. Surprised, she started to come up, but at the pressure of his hand on the small of her back, she lowered her torso again, pillowing her head in her arms.

The shocking feel of his tongue lapping slowly through her core brought Rosalia out of her skin. She jolted forward, her hands fisting in the sheets. That was too much. *Too much.* Deacon caught her hips, hauled her back against his mouth. His tongue plunged between her folds, licking deep. Unable to help herself, she rocked toward him, her wordless moans muffled by her arms. Yellow light from her eyes spilled across white linen. Oh, God. She'd known being with him would feel good. She hadn't known it would be like this, so destructive to her senses. She couldn't get enough of his touch. She'd thought she'd reached the edge, the high, and yet when his lips surrounded her clitoris and suckled, she came again, screaming into the mattress. The explosion and release was so fast, so easy—and shook her just as powerfully.

Aftershocks rippled through her flesh. The mattress shifted. Deacon kneeled behind her, pushed deep with one stroke.

Her body clenched around him. Struggling for breath, for thought, Rosalia came up, her back against his chest. His left arm wrapped around her, his forearm buoying her left breast, his large hand cupping her right, catching her nipple between his middle fingers. His right hand slid between her thighs, stroking her as he drove up into her core, as if Rosalia's pleasure was his only goal.

It must have been—he could have taken his pleasure already. He needed blood to come, but it didn't have to be hers. A drop of his own would do it.

But if he didn't finish, she could hold him inside her forever. She would love to.

With his jaw, Deacon pushed her hair away from her neck, placed gentle kisses to her shoulder, the side of her throat. Emotion welled up, choking her. Though his hunger burned hot against her senses, he kissed her with tenderness.

Slipping her arms up around his neck, she held on. His movements became more desperate, his muscles slick with sweat. Her back arched as he struck deep within her, a different angle, just right. And when she shook for the third time, Deacon joined her, with the scent of his own blood on his kiss.

❧

When Rosalia's shudders faded, Deacon slipped out of her warmth and eased her forward, laying her on the bed. He kissed the small of her back, the indentation of her spine, the beautiful curve of her waist. She turned her face into the pillow, softly weeping.

Not bad crying, he understood. He still wanted to get up and walk away. Her tears were ripping out his heart. But walking away now would make him more of a bastard than he was—and more of a bastard than he wanted to be.

He lay next to her, stroking his hand through her hair. Her

pulse still pounded in his ears. The bloodlust raged a storm in his veins. His body had been sated, but his hunger continued to rise. He wanted to go at her now like a ravening beast.

He'd be a bastard for that, too. She'd given him a taste of heaven. She'd been so sweet, so trusting—as if she'd been with a better man than he was, when it had been all that he could do to maintain his control. He'd wanted to mark her, to taste her. To brand her as his.

She wasn't, though. He had her now, but it wouldn't last forever. He'd be gone once she no longer had a use for him. He hoped that happened before going meant ripping out his soul.

And he was afraid it might be too late.

She lifted her head, and he had a glimpse of her smile, her wet cheeks, and her eyes—brown again, instead of glowing yellow—before she buried her face in his shoulder.

"You're hiding?" Battling his hunger, he pulled her astride him. "It was that bad?"

Laughing, she looked up at him and shook her head. "I knew it would feel good, but I didn't know it would be . . . *that*." Her fingers rose to his hair. She began smoothing as she continued. "I thought it might be another failure, that it wouldn't live up to my expectations. But it was *nothing* like them—and so much more."

Another failure? What had her life been, always expecting the shit end of a stick? "You imagined being with me before?"

"Oh, yes." Her grin warned him that it wouldn't be good. "I thought it would just be a suck, a thrust, and a 'Haul off, sister.'"

He pretended to lunge for her. She scrambled away from his grabbing hands, dragging the sheet with her, laughing wildly. He stopped halfway across the bed, staring at her. God, she was so beautiful.

Her laugh faded, and she stared at him as if thinking the same about him. Leaning closer, her mouth touched his in a soft, searching kiss.

He should have left. Now it was too damn late.

She lay down again, snuggling up against him, her head pillowed on his shoulder. Christ, she was so soft. He wanted his hands all over her, his fangs buried deep. He forced himself just to hold her.

"But it's not 'sister' now," she said. "Why 'princess'?"

Shit. That wasn't for her, but for him. But he couldn't avoid answering.

"It's a reminder," he said gruffly.

"To be careful?" she guessed, and sighed. "I'm not delicate, Deacon. Not—what is that story?—the girl on a pea."

No. A reminder that she deserved something a hell of a lot better than the man she was snuggled up against. Someone who hadn't fucked over his own community and his friends—and *her* friends.

But whatever he was, he still had too much pride to lay that out. "You're soft all over," he said.

"I could shape-shift and change that—"

"Don't change a damn thing."

Altering her perfect breasts, her little belly, her curvy ass would be akin to burning a Botticelli. Hell, it'd be worse.

She was quiet, and when he glanced down at her, she was smiling against his shoulder. When she caught his look, she rose up, propped on her elbow. "I was just thinking . . . About thirty years ago, two vampires disappeared from their community. I was worried, so I tracked them down—and when I found them, they were doing this. *Just* this. They went to bed and they never got out of it. They'd already spent a year like that, locked up together."

With two vampires, that was possible. They could feed from each other. As long as they had shelter, they wouldn't need anything else. But there was more to this, Deacon realized, as Rosalia's expression became pensive.

"It's been a long time now since I've subscribed to some of the teachings of the Church—particularly their views on sin. But when I found them, I was appalled. Not by the lust. Their devotion, their need for each other was . . . beautiful, in truth.

But the gluttony of it, and the manner in which they'd excluded everyone and everything else from their life . . . I was disgusted." With a sigh, she began to trace her fingers over his chest. "Now I see why it might be so appealing."

Hell, yes. He could stand to be locked up with her for a year. "But?"

"I'd be disgusted with myself. I have too much to do. Too many people who depend on me."

No, she would never withdraw from her life, from her responsibilities. No matter how often she thought she failed, Rosalia would keep going.

"And if you didn't have too much to do?"

"I admit the thought of them doesn't bother me so much now. They have no responsibility to anyone else, so they've hurt no one." She looked up at him. "They are still at it."

For thirty years? Deacon frowned.

She nodded, as if reading his expression and agreeing with him. "It's uncomfortable to be around. It's primal, it's exciting . . . and there's almost no thought left between them. I couldn't do that. A day, perhaps, or even a week. But I could not close myself off from the world for so long."

And she'd already lost more than one year beneath the catacombs. Coming back, seeing the changes that had taken place and how many of her friends were dead, must have been like a smack to the face followed by a full-body beatdown.

"I could not anyway," she added softly. "That's not what a Guardian does. And I have already done—and *will* do—too many other things that a Guardian shouldn't."

"Like using vampires as a means to an end?"

He wished he hadn't said anything when that familiar sadness darkened her eyes.

"Yes," she said. "I could start with that. Do you want a list?"

So now she was hating on herself. Maybe he wanted to, too—and find any reason that would make it easier to walk away when it was time to go.

"Lay them on me, princess."

She pulled back with a half smile that didn't erase the shadows in her eyes. "I'll give you one a day."

Just like his reasons to stay. Now she was giving him reasons to go. Which would run out first?

He suddenly wished to hell he hadn't asked. But it was too late. She was turning away from him, sitting up.

"Since you're awake, we should find out whether you're vulnerable to the sun."

No. Since he was awake, he should throw her back down on the bed, get his fangs in her. But she was already up, shutting him out. Suppressing a frustrated growl, he grabbed for his pants.

She clothed her body in that black outfit—the one he thought of as her Zorro getup, complete with cloak. Maybe she didn't lock herself away, but hidden within its folds, she sure as hell put as many layers between herself and the world as she could.

And after convincing her to hold on to him, to trust him, he was doing a damn good job of pushing her away.

CHAPTER 15

Deacon was shrugging into his shirt when Rosalia opened the door. Instinctively, he stepped to the side to avoid any light falling into the room, but the corridor was in shadow. She looked back at him.

"There's no direct sunlight beyond the gallery."

So he wouldn't know if he'd burn until they reached the walkway overlooking the courtyard. And he didn't need to jump into it. Pushing a fingertip into the sun's path would do.

He stepped through the doorway. The bright fall of golden light at the end of the corridor was stunning. His eyes stung. Blinking rapidly, he said, "I once knew a vampire who got caught outside near dawn, so he climbed into the trunk of his car."

He walked toward Rosalia, waiting at the intersection of the corridor and gallery. She lifted her fingers into the sun. The light formed a brilliant corona around her pale hand, but he could hardly focus on it. The burning rays overwhelmed his field of vision.

"When he woke up," Deacon continued, "his legs had been cut through below the ankles. The seam of the trunk lid hadn't been tight, and the light had sliced through like a laser scalpel."

Rosalia's face was in shadow, but he could barely see her. Her features were darkening, fading away. "He is fortunate he was not facing the other direction."

"Yes." If it had cut through his neck, the vampire wouldn't have been waking up. Crazily enough, though, if it had cut through *half* his head, slicing his brain in two, he'd have eventually healed. "I don't need to stick my hand out there to see that the sun will fry me, Rosie."

He heard the frown in her voice. "Why?"

"Because I can't see anything now."

In an instant she was touching his face, his eyes. The warmth of the sun still lingered on her right hand. "It blinded you?"

He'd barely finished nodding before she was leading him back into her room. She steered him to a chair, sat him down. He felt her breath on his face, her gentle fingers around his eyes.

"Does it hurt?"

"No."

By her silence, he knew she was looking for evidence that he'd lied. In a few seconds, he thought he'd be able to see her, too. A blurry image was already returning.

"It's healing," he said.

"That quickly?" Now that he could almost focus on her, he didn't just hear the concern in her tone, but saw it in her eyes. Her hands ran down his shoulders. A note of realization entered her voice. "You healed quickly last night, too. And you're stronger. Faster."

She'd begun to frown. As everything she'd just said sounded damn good, Deacon couldn't see what there was to frown about.

"That's a problem?"

"No," she said, though her expression disputed her reply.

Deacon wondered if she'd realized yet that he could see her again. "You'll be safer. The demons will know why you're coming now, and they won't let you talk first. But they still won't anticipate your speed. Especially now."

"But?"

"But you might have to lower your shields. The vampires who see you need to know you're a vampire, not just masquerading as one."

"Because anyone who sees me move that fast will think I'm a shape-shifted Guardian." And that would destroy Rosalia's whole reason for going in as a human. It'd paint a target right on the Guardians' backs, the scenario she'd been trying to avoid. He didn't like the idea of lowering his shields, though, and letting strangers into his head. "Will blood do the same? If a demon or a vampire gets a whiff of it, there's no mistaking me for a Guardian."

She nodded. "You're right; that would be better. It's tangible. Demons might not believe anything vampires say about a psychic scent, but vampires know the smell of their own."

Yeah, psychic scents were too tricky, particularly for untrained vampires. How many had run into Rosalia and had no idea what she was? Hell, even Deacon had, though he'd never make the same mistake again. The feel of her mind was familiar now—though he hadn't gotten very deep into it.

"Your shields held when you came," he told her. "Every time."

Her skin flushed, but her smile was pleased—not a hint of embarrassment there. "You told me to hold them, so I did," she said matter-of-factly, then looked him over. "Your vision is healed now?"

"Yes."

She studied him, saw through him. Her heart beat a little faster. "You're hungry."

Even hungrier now that he was thinking about it, and thinking about how she'd held her shields with her body shattering around him—*because he'd told her to.*

He shoved that away, pushed up to his feet. "Did that delivery come yet?"

"Not until this afternoon," she said. He could feel her watching him stalk between the chair and the bed. "You said you didn't want to risk the bloodlust with me. Was that why you didn't feed from me last night? Was that why you risked drinking the nephil blood?"

Christ, she hadn't realized that by now? "Yeah."

Her face seemed to lighten, and she laughed a little, shaking her head. "I'm truly not so delicate, Deacon. Even with my arm broken, I could have held you back."

But could she now? He stopped pacing and faced her square on. "So are you offering? But know it's not just fucking, Rosie. Do you want me in your head, hearing your every thought?"

Her smile faded as she regarded him, and he realized it didn't matter if she said yes. He'd vowed he wouldn't drink from her. That still stood. Because if he got into her that deep, if she gave him that much more to care about . . .

Who was he kidding? Blood or no blood, he was fucked.

She sighed. "Perhaps not yet. Then you'd know all of my reasons far too early." A dagger and a drinking glass appeared in her hand. She set them on a small table, and held her wrist over the glass. "But I can help you take the edge off."

❧

After filling the glass with her blood, Rosalia headed into the War Room, offering Deacon space to drink it, and taking time to gather her thoughts into something manageable. Into something that wouldn't tempt her to throw the rest of the world away.

She'd wanted him to drink from her. She'd wanted to know if that sensation could shatter her expectations, too. And she'd wanted to feed him, to nourish him with her body. After one time in his bed, she could understand very well how two people could hole up forever.

But if she let him drink from her now, if she let him into

her thoughts, it wouldn't be the world she'd throw away. No, she'd lose Deacon, instead. She wasn't ready for that yet. She wouldn't *ever* be ready for that.

She needed to be, though. Already, she could feel him pushing her away. Guilt, probably, for taking pleasure before his community had been avenged. Or, despite her assertion that she wasn't delicate, maybe Deacon thought he'd already hurt her—or that he'd lose control to the bloodlust. Or he'd been disappointed. Sex might not have been satisfying for him without the blood. Whatever his reason, he'd begun withdrawing before he'd even left the bed.

Would it be the same next time? And the next? How long until the pleasure and anticipation of being with him became dread, as she waited for him to push her away yet again?

With a sigh, she sat at her desk, flicking through St. Croix's file. Now that she'd met the man, another story had begun to form in her mind. A father who died early. A mother who'd taken over their business affairs . . . and raised a son who reminded Rosalia of a demon.

It sounded so very similar to Rosalia's story, and to Lorenzo's—except she suspected that two key players had been moved around.

The door opened and Deacon came in, showered and dressed and smelling like her soap. She loved the scent of her fragrance on his skin. But did it bother him?

His gaze fell to the file open in front of her. "You got something on him. Something bad?"

She wondered what he'd seen in her face to draw that conclusion. But although she hadn't been thinking about St. Croix, she could cover it.

"It could be bad. Or it could mean that he's on our side."

"Your side."

Her side? Uncomprehending, she glanced up at him. He stood with his arms crossed over his wide chest, his features unreadable. Completely withdrawn.

"My only pony in this race is killing Belial's demons, princess. I'm not on one side or another."

"I see." She looked back at the screen. Her throat ached. "Well, what I've found could mean that St. Croix hates demons as much as we do. Look here."

On-screen, she accessed a newspaper article that included details into the investigation of his father's death twenty years before.

"We knew the father was dead," she said. "But until we pulled this out, I didn't know there were questions surrounding the circumstances. It was ruled a suicide, and St. Croix's mother took over his company." She paused, glanced up at him again. His gaze was fixed on the screen. "Many humans still think of men as the superior gender, so demons don't usually take a woman's place. But maybe one did."

"The mother? Shit." Standing next to her chair, he flipped through the file on the desk until he came to the picture of a beautiful woman and her unsmiling ten-year-old son. "A demon raised him."

"I think so. And that is why it could be good or bad. Perhaps he joined Legion because he's just like them. But perhaps he joined them so that he could tear Legion down from the inside."

He stared down at St. Croix's picture for another moment, as if trying to read the soul inside the man. "You aren't meeting him by yourself."

"Yes, I am."

"Say he brings a demon friend with him. St. Croix grabs on to you and holds you for the demon, and you're screwed."

She turned away from him, closing out the newspaper article and bringing up St. Croix's financial data. "I've been doing this for a long time, Deacon."

Humans had often been connected to demons—and some humans had known the Rules she had to follow, while others didn't. It hadn't mattered. *Every* human had been a danger to her, so she knew how to stay out of their grasp.

She had to smile. The one time she hadn't evaded two drunk humans . . . led her to Deacon.

He slammed his hand on the desk. Startled, she looked up.

Anger darkened his face. "You almost died last night, Rosie, because this guy brought in something you weren't ready for."

She was ready for the nephilim. She just couldn't beat them alone.

Deacon didn't wait for her response. As if he had the final word, he said, "You'll wait until tonight. I'll go with you."

"Tonight, we have to be in—"

"Fuck your plan, Rosie. You'll wait."

Fury stabbed through her chest, hot and sharp. "*My plan* means you slay another of Belial's demons. That's what you're here for, remember? Unless, Deacon, you've suddenly got another pony in the race. Do you?"

She waited for an answer, desperately hoping that one reason would be *her*. Even if it was just: *I need you to point me toward the demons, Rosie.* Anything.

She waited . . . for nothing.

Her anger slipped into pain, like a sharp stone lodged near her heart. She had to get out of here. She didn't need to meet St. Croix for several hours, but she couldn't stay and let Deacon continue to shove her away.

She stood, moved to the rack of surveillance equipment along the wall, selecting everything she might need. She could feel Deacon watching her.

"So you're going?"

"Yes." Her voice sounded flat. Good. Maybe he'd think she didn't care. "Vincente and Gemma are here. They'll be in contact with me while I'm talking to him."

"Observing you?"

"Yes, here in the War Room. Stay near them. If Taylor shows, she can't get through humans any more than the nephil could." She turned, offered a humorless smile. "You might be fast enough to beat her now, anyway."

She headed for the door, brushing past him. Deacon caught her wrist.

"Rosie, wait."

She jerked her arm out of his grip. Surprise jolted through his psychic scent. He reached for her again, as if her tearing away from him had been an accident. She stumbled back, calling in her crossbow. She leveled it at his chest. He froze.

"Don't touch me." She wouldn't be able to walk away if he held on. She backed toward the door. "Just . . . don't touch me."

Deacon didn't move. He stared at her, his hand still outstretched. The withdrawn expression in his gaze became determination, and he stepped toward her as if he didn't care whether she'd shoot a crossbow bolt through his heart. She wouldn't—but she didn't wait to see what he'd be throwing at her next.

She turned and fled into the sun.

❦

Jesus. Oh, God.

Taylor ripped up out of the dark, feeling as if she'd gone on a three-day bender. The sun was warm on her back. Waves crashed. No need to guess where she was. Anaria's island, again. All right. So, maybe try to find that nephil from London again. She slowly calmed the heaving of her chest . . . and realized she wasn't alone. She looked up.

Anaria sat in the sand about thirty feet away, sobbing into her hands.

Oh, man. Taylor didn't think any of the sudden ache in her chest had been compelled. Anaria cried like her heart had been broken, and it was so wrenching, so sad. And Taylor didn't have to guess what had happened. She'd knocked on too many doors, told too many people that a loved one was never coming home.

She felt Michael begin to push her toward the sobbing woman, but she held him back. What did he think she was that she needed to be prodded to do this?

On bare feet, Taylor crossed the length of beach and sat next to her, sliding her arm around Anaria's shaking shoulders. The grigori shuddered and looked up, her eyes completely white, glowing brilliantly. "My children . . . they felt him die."

"I'm sorry for your loss," Taylor said. Not sorry the nephil was dead, but sorry for her.

Anaria's face collapsed, and she covered her eyes with her hand, bowing her head. "Did you . . . Do you know who did this?"

"No," Taylor said truthfully, grateful that she could. More than grief had layered Anaria's voice in that moment, a note both bitter and deadly, and even Michael seemed wary . . . ready to take over at a second's notice. "No Guardian or vampire, so far as I know."

Her lips trembling, Anaria nodded. "Thank you." She shuddered again, before looking blindly out over the crashing waves. "I've lost so many. My husband. My brother—though Michael was lost to me long before the others. My friends and my children."

Taylor didn't know what would comfort her. "Do they go to . . ." Heaven? Above? Something else? "Where the angels are?"

"Yes. Of course, yes," Anaria said, wiping her cheeks. "You have seen the angels in his memories?"

"No." Just flashes of nosferatu and demons. Only killing.

"Yes, of course," she said softly, staring out into the sea. "There is too much he would not wish you to see."

Like what? But Anaria was crying again, and Taylor could only hope that whatever he kept from her stayed hidden.

She didn't want to try handling more than she already was.

❧

The church was rarely empty or silent, and this day was no exception. Two women spoke together in a center pew. A man knelt, praying. From the confessional, she heard soft weeping, and Father Wojcinski's compassionate response. Their quiet voices filled Rosalia's mind with warmth, and she let herself take comfort in them.

In a gray-haired, petite form and swathed in a black dress, Rosalia genuflected and made her way to the back pew, where she waited. She didn't wait long.

"He's here," she murmured to Gemma, monitoring the conversation from the War Room with Vin and Deacon. The church's proximity to the abbey meant they had no need for the van today. Even the infrared would be of little use if St. Croix had arranged for any demons to arrive first—the day was already too hot for an accurate reading.

Standing at the chamber entrance, St. Croix observed the room, his gaze skimming over Rosalia and moving on. Though she knew he hadn't yet slept, he didn't appear tired. His handsome face displayed no emotion, and his blue eyes were distant and icy as he regarded each person, but she sensed uncertainty in his psychic scent. She guessed that he didn't know what to do here; a church was out of his element. Finally, he chose a seat on the back pew across the aisle from her, tapping his fingers together between his knees.

Not as cool as he appeared. Good.

She rose and walked toward him. He glanced at her, and she watched a polite mask fall over his features. Preparing to gently tell the old lady that he preferred to be alone, Rosalia guessed. Before he could speak, she sat next to him— and since no one was looking their way, she shifted into her natural form.

St. Croix's eyes narrowed. The curve of his lips suggested amusement, but it was a thin, cold smile, with an undercurrent of anger.

She began, "Tell me, Mr. St. Croix, what have you discovered about me?"

She knew he'd found nothing—there was nothing about her to find.

He was careful not to admit that. "Less than you have about me, I'd wager."

"Yes." And she didn't yet know what she most needed to. "And I'll give you more, but how much more depends on the answer to one question: Did you kill Rachel Boyle, or did your mother?"

It was as if she'd stabbed him. Pain slashed across his face before his expression hardened into a smooth mask. "I think we are done here."

He stood and began to walk away. And because that young woman's death had hurt him, she said, "My mother poisoned my father. She cut his throat in their bed. She paid assassins. She tried everything, and when everything failed, she poisoned herself. I should hate her for leaving us alone with him. A mother should protect her children, don't you agree?"

He stopped. He didn't turn, but he stopped—and so he must be listening.

"A father should protect his children, too," Rosalia continued. "Mine made certain that I found my mother's body. He told me that she was burning in Hell for her suicide. I believed him, because of all people, he would know who burned in Hell. Only later did I realize that they are also liars, and bargainers . . . and it's entirely possible that she killed herself only after making a deal that protected us from him. And so I cannot hate her. I do hate *him*, however—and if he wasn't dead, I'd hunt my father down and kill him."

He finally turned. "So what are you—a support group for demon children?"

Though his tone mocked, he took a step toward her. Good enough, she thought.

"I'm something better, Mr. St. Croix. I'm someone with information. You are looking for your mother?"

"Don't call her that." His mouth twisted. "You know where she is? *Who* she is?"

"No."

"Then you're of no use to me."

But he didn't go. No, he wanted to see what she offered him. Because he *did* lack information, and he knew it.

"Sit down," she said.

After an internal struggle, he did.

"You've gone to Legion. You're looking for her in the wrong place. Legion was created for Belial's demons, but what your mother did—" She broke off when the mask shifted, revealing the ice and hatred beneath. "What would you have me call her?"

"A sopping, murderous cunt."

"Here?" Pointedly, she looked to the altar. "I think not."

Through her earpiece, she heard the muffled hoot of Gemma's laughter and the rumble of Deacon's beneath it. For the first time, she saw humor in St. Croix's expression.

"Perhaps not," he agreed. "Madelyn will do."

His mother's Christian name, but not the name he'd probably called his real mother. At the age he'd lost her, she would have still been his mum.

"What Madelyn did to your family better fits the style of Lucifer's demons," Rosalia told him. "You won't find her at Legion."

She saw the speculation in his eyes, and her pulse jumped when she realized where his thoughts were turning.

"No, Mr. St. Croix. Lucifer's and Belial's demons are enemies, but that does not mean Belial's demons will help you. If you go to them, they will do everything possible to break you, simply because it will entertain them. A demon is a demon, no matter his allegiance."

He nodded. Perhaps he'd seen enough of Belial's demons to believe it. "Where would I find her, then?"

"The Gates to Hell are closed. If she is among those Below, it will be five hundred years before the Gates open again."

"I'll wait."

He probably could. "As a vampire?"

"If hate alone can't keep me going."

"It can't," she assured him, though the hatred seething within him could certainly drive a man for a lifetime. "If Madelyn isn't in Hell, you will probably find her in one of two ways. The first, it's likely she will be doing to another family what she has done to yours."

When he glanced at her, frowning, she said, "Demons are creatures of habit. Rarely do they think or act in an original way. If something succeeds once, they will do it again."

"So I'd look for a family that resembles mine, with a suicide as a red flag."

"Yes. Though it is still a daunting task. Thousands of families might fit the criteria in Europe alone. I can help you there."

Though his sudden suspicion didn't show on his face, she felt it in his psychic scent. He didn't trust anyone who offered him something for free. That was fine. This wasn't an offer, but an exchange.

"How?"

"There are others like me. We search for demons, to slay them—and that is all we do. We're familiar with their patterns, their scents, even the human forms they take. If we come across a woman who fits Madelyn's pattern, I will tell you."

He regarded her without expression for a long moment, but she could sense the wariness and temptation behind it. "And what do you get?"

Smart man. "I need to know who is directing the demons at Legion. Who stepped up after Belial's lieutenant left?"

"The new executive director—"

"No." She'd already looked at that demon, an American, and discarded the possibility. "It'd be someone who isn't as visible. Someone who, for the past six months, has been moving people around and pulling strings. He'd be based in a European office, high-ranking, with a solid foundation of supporters, but not at the top. Not yet."

He frowned. "I can make enquiries—"

"And reveal your interest? No. It has to be done quietly."

His gaze sharpened. He apparently enjoyed a challenge. "I'll get names for you, then, if you do the same for me."

"Mine won't come as quickly, but they'll come," she promised.

"And if Madelyn takes the second route? You said she would likely try one of two things."

Rosalia suspected that he would prefer the second. "She spent twenty years building your father's small firm into a financial powerhouse. When you took it over, you tore her work apart."

"She'll come after me," he realized, and dark pleasure swept through him, so reminiscent of a demon's.

Rosalia battled her revulsion. "Yes."

"If she comes after me, I won't need a name. What could you offer?"

"Knowledge, Mr. St. Croix. To start, how to better guard your emotions." She smiled as surprise and unease suddenly radiated from him. "Like those I'm feeling now. The shields Gerald and Sally taught you to create might have been sufficient to block a vampire. They won't a demon."

His eyes narrowed. "And you?"

She deflected that with a deliberate misunderstanding. "And I'll teach you how to recognize Madelyn if she comes for you. To begin with, she'll have hot skin."

"Hot—" He broke off, his face paling. Repugnance and horror crawled through his psychic scent before hatred surrounded it with ice. "And they can change their human shape, too?"

Oh, dear God. Rosalia stared at him. Her father had been cruel. But he'd never done what she suddenly suspected Madelyn had to St. Croix.

"Yes," she finally said. "And there is more. I will tell you all—but I have something I must finish first."

"And that 'something' is why you need me."

"Yes."

He nodded and stuck out his hand. When she took it, her warm skin the same temperature as his, relief moved through him. "You're not one of them."

"No. As I said before—I'm something better." She left her card in his palm, the paper blank except for a phone number. "I look forward to your call."

She watched him leave, shaken by the depth of Madelyn's depravity. Nothing a demon did surprised Rosalia anymore, but she was still sickened by it.

And St. Croix . . . She could pity him, but she could not

like him. Where another man—like Deacon—might be angry and withdrawn, and just as determined to have his revenge, he didn't resemble the demons he wanted to destroy. Deacon had suffered, but he was still a good man, and a generous one. He didn't look at others simply to see how they could be used.

Perhaps when St. Croix found Madelyn and took his revenge, he would change—but Rosalia feared the damage had been done. Not everyone could be repaired.

Lorenzo hadn't been.

"Rosa?"

She looked toward the aisle, where Father Wojcinski stood, wearing his short-sleeved clericals. Smiling, she rose to her feet and joined him.

"When I saw your companion leave, you were looking very much as you did in my kitchen three nights ago." He studied her face, as if trying to read behind the smile. "Are you still conflicted about using the man in this quest you spoke of, or have you convinced him to help you?"

Her heart seemed to drop into her stomach. Keeping her dismay from her expression, she murmured, *"Piccola bambina,"* before vanishing the audio receiver, to let Gemma know she hadn't been cut off.

"I have convinced him." Though she couldn't forget how he'd withdrawn that morning—or how the worst was yet to come. Deacon must have noticed how she was positioning him at the head of so many communities. Focused on his revenge, he hadn't yet asked why, but eventually he would. "Partially."

The priest sighed. "You cover it well, but I suspect I have just revealed something I shouldn't have. Will this jeopardize what you've done?"

She shook her head. "He will not leave before we've finished."

Of that, she was certain. But that didn't mean Deacon wouldn't be angry—and wonder if he'd been manipulated. That would not rest easy with him.

"But now he will think you've misled him."

"And I will tell him I have not—and that is truth, Father. So do not fret. You have jeopardized nothing."

He regarded her closely, and he had known her too long and read her too clearly. Leading her to a pew, he sat. "Nothing, Rosa?"

"Nothing that was not already in jeopardy." Like her heart. She knew her smile was brittle. "A demon destroyed everyone he cared about. He's a good man, and a brave one—but I don't know if he will risk happiness again, Father, or even if he feels that he deserves it. How can I be with a man who will not let himself love me without hating himself for it? *I* deserve more."

"If he's as good a man as you say, Rosa, then so does he."

They were in agreement about that. Deacon deserved more, even if he didn't believe it. But what could she do if he would not take what she had to give him?

She would not quit yet, though.

"Ah, I see your determination. I know now that all will be well." Smiling, he squeezed her hand. "And as we are discussing matters of the heart, it would not be amiss to mention that I am meeting with Vincente and Gemma tomorrow to discuss the wedding ceremony. I assume the reception will be held at the abbey?"

She had just assumed, too, but now she realized that neither Gemma nor Vincente had said a word about it. "I'll ask them."

If Father Wojcinski thought it strange that she didn't know, she couldn't read it in his expression. He appeared tired, she realized—probably still losing sleep over an abuse and depravity that was almost worse for having been committed by a human . . . someone a child should have been able to trust. She would take care of that, soon.

And perhaps it would be tomorrow's item on the list of things a Guardian shouldn't do.

CHAPTER 16

Rosalia took the long way back to the abbey, winding through the streets, shifting into several different forms. She walked through her front door as a young boy, spooning the last of a pistachio gelato into her mouth.

She could hear Deacon in the War Room. He'd likely been there all day, listening to surveillance from Theriault and St. Croix—the inactivity must be wearing on him. As amazing as his walking around during the day was, it wouldn't take long before he felt trapped by the sun, limited to moving between two rooms.

In any case, surveillance was her responsibility, not his. She'd have to find something else for him, something he'd enjoy and that would keep both his hands and his mind occupied.

Gemma's soft snores were audible through her bedroom door. Relief lightened Rosalia's heart. The young woman hadn't slept after the nephil's attack last night. Perhaps a nap would erase the tiredness from her eyes. Vincente's, too. Although, judging by the sound of pacing coming from Gemma's room, Vincente wasn't sleeping with her.

Rosalia sighed, stopping by the kitchen to toss the gelato cup. Never had she imagined having to ask her son whether his wedding dinner would be here. And never had she imagined the possibility that the answer would be no.

But it needed to be asked, and so there was no use delaying. She started across the courtyard, her footsteps over the grass like a scrape in her ears. And a heartbeat, strangely muffled.

No . . . that *was* a heartbeat.

Whirling around, Rosalia called in her sword. Her gaze searched the empty gardens. If the person had a scent, it was covered by chlorine and roses, lavender and the lemon tree. A soft ripple drew her to the swimming pool.

Taylor floated beneath the water. She'd removed her shoes, but still wore a jacket and trousers. Her eyes were closed. Meditating—or trying to.

When had she come? Rosalia's heart pounded, and she listened again to the sounds from the War Room. She hadn't been mistaken. Deacon was up there, alive.

Vanishing her sword, Rosalia retraced her steps through the courtyard, but didn't head upstairs to Gemma's room. Stopping at the fountain, she sank onto her favorite bench, cradling her head in her hands.

Last night's encounter with the nephil, St. Croix, even Taylor . . . So much had begun to spin out of control, and Rosalia felt as if she was holding it all together with her fingernails. What would be next? And what would she do if it was *worse*?

The sun shone hot and bright overhead. In Caelum, the sun was the same—always the same. It never moved from its position, never clouded, never darkened with the night.

Her first years there had been like a dream. Everything had been so clean, so bright. And there'd been so much to learn . . . Guardians from parts of the world she'd never heard of or imagined.

She'd been so filled with hope, and she'd let herself forget her life before Caelum, to forget everything but Lorenzo. And so she'd never thought about how her father had railed at her nurse because Rosalia hadn't been clean enough, and had ordered the woman to hold her face in a basin. She'd let herself forget how the woman had cried, but complied. The nurse had left afterward, and Rosalia had been the one who'd made certain Lorenzo never had a speck of dirt on him, never a hair or a collar out of place—always remembering her desperation, the nurse's hand on the back of her neck, the dark blooming spots in front of her eyes . . . and the relief, the dizzying, overwhelming relief when she'd been able to breathe again.

Those years in Caelum had been like that: Gasping for air, so dizzying and so full of hope that she'd felt faint. Now she sat, feeling as if her face was back in that basin, desperately trying to lift her head, blinded and unable to breathe.

But she didn't know if the hand on the back of her neck was the nephilim's, the demons', or her own.

She heard a door open upstairs, but didn't look up until Vin's shadow crossed her face. Heavens, he was a mess, as if he'd slept in his clothes—even though, like everyone else in this household, he hadn't slept at all. She suspected, however, that he wouldn't welcome her straightening him up. She tucked her hands into her elbows, and remembered the advice that Father Wojcinski had given her three nights before. For now, she would only listen.

"Gemma needs to leave the abbey," he said.

Rosalia frowned, but didn't reply. With a tilt of her head, she invited him to sit next to her.

Vin shook his head and remained standing. "Her nightmares are worse when she's here. They always have been. But she stayed, even after everyone was killed, because she felt obligated to keep up the abbey after you disappeared. And she hasn't told you, but she can't walk through these rooms at night without seeing them drenched in blood."

Rosalia closed her eyes. Oh, God. How it hurt that the woman she considered her daughter was going through this. It hurt that Gemma hadn't said something. And it hurt because Rosalia couldn't make it better for her.

But Vin had known. No wonder he'd been so adamant about not living here. But he hadn't told her about Gemma then, either. Why was he now?

"I need you to convince her, Mama. It has to be you, or she won't leave."

"Okay." If he said so, she believed that. "I'll try."

"Thank you." With a short nod, he turned away.

"Vin." When he looked back, she said, "It would help if I knew why you can't convince her, and I must."

Suddenly agitated, he pushed stiff fingers through his rumpled hair, as if this was more difficult for him than anything he'd said earlier.

"All right." His hand dropped to his side and he seemed to brace himself. "She's staying for you. So you won't be alone."

She stared at him. "Why does she think I shouldn't be alone?"

"Because you never have been, Mama. *Ever*. When you were human, you had Lorenzo, and then the nuns. After that, you had the Guardians and the vampires here, your family. Even when you came back from beneath the catacombs, most of our family was dead . . . but Gemma and I were here. She's worried about you. About whether you can handle it if there's no one here."

Not just Gemma, she realized. Vincente thought this, too.

Astonished, Rosalia could only shake her head. She'd never imagined that they had this view of her. Since returning from Caelum two hundred years ago, Rosalia had been alone—almost *always* alone. Hiding, listening, managing . . . but rarely participating in the lives of those she watched and watched over. Her friends and her family had been bright spots . . . deep breaths, in all of the darkness. It had made them all the more precious.

Deacon barely knew her, yet he had seen it. Lonely and desperate, he'd called her. He hadn't been wrong, but she'd made it through centuries of *alone* rather well, all things considered.

"I'll convince her," she said.

Vincente nodded again, but this time he didn't turn to go. "What did you do to Lorenzo?"

Oh, no. "Vin—"

"He threatened me, but went after you. What did you do?"

Rosalia's jaw clenched. He was obviously determined to hear this. She couldn't imagine why, unless he wanted to pick apart another failure. A Guardian should have slain Lorenzo after the threat. But she hadn't been able to kill her brother in cold blood.

"I woke him up with my Gift," she said. "I took him outside, and kept him awake while he burned. I fried him almost completely through, and told him that the next time he dared to *think* of my son, I would bring all of his community out to watch while I burned him to ashes, then take his place and lead them."

Vin stared at her, mouth parted in shock. No, that was not the mama he knew. She'd never let him see the darker side of living with a Guardian.

But the shock quickly faded, his eyes narrowing. Rosalia braced herself. She'd taught him to look not only at actions, but at the reasons behind them. And Vin knew her too well—she never had just one reason for anything.

"You threatened his position. You *knew* he would retaliate. You couldn't bring yourself to outright kill him, so you forced his hand—made him come after you—because you could slay him if you had to defend yourself."

"Yes. I just didn't expect that he would make a deal with Belial's lieutenant, and that I'd be facing seven demons instead of my brother," she said wryly.

Unamused, Vin shook his head. "You should have just killed him, Mama."

"I couldn't."

"Then you should have left it alone."

After Lorenzo had threatened her son's life? "I couldn't do that, either."

"God!" Vin spun away from her, throwing up his hands. "What *can* you do? Are you a Guardian or a sister?"

That knifed deep into her heart. "I am a mother, too. I couldn't take the chance that he'd follow through on his threat."

"He wouldn't have touched me. He wouldn't have risked breaking the Rules."

Rosalia hadn't been so certain. Lorenzo had wanted to hurt her enough to make the threat. He might have hated her enough to take that risk. And she had no doubt he'd have been arrogant enough to think he might get away with it.

Studying Vin's rigid back, she sighed. Her son shielded his mind too well for her to detect his emotions, but it wasn't difficult to read through his anger and frustration to the fear and concern beneath. When she'd chosen to make Lorenzo come after her, she'd made a decision that had almost cost her life. Combined with last night's attack from the nephil, her mortality had been thrust into her son's face—after decades of never letting him see her bloodied by so much as a scratch.

"Perhaps I protected you from this part of my life too well."

With a hollow laugh, he turned to face her. "Do you think so? Instead of the Guardian fairy tale, you should have given us the version where you have a spike shoved through your brain while nosferatu feed from your neck. The version where a nephil butchers you until you're sitting in a pool of your own blood."

She couldn't argue. She'd hoped that he would never see it, that the violence in her life wouldn't touch him—but by protecting him from that, she'd left him vulnerable. "I should have prepared you."

That is, if anything in the world could prepare a son to see his mother broken and bleeding. She didn't know if it was possible. *Nothing* could prepare her if she ever saw Vincente that way.

He looked ready to contradict her before closing his

mouth. He pushed his hand through his hair again. "Pasquale wouldn't have been so quick to throw himself on a murderer's knife if he'd known what being a Guardian really was."

Sweet, dreamy Pasquale. "Perhaps. But he was a brave boy, Vincente. He might have tried to save that woman's life even if he'd never heard of the Guardians."

Grief tightened his face, closed his eyes. She wanted to reach out to him, but he held himself so far away, she knew he wouldn't welcome it. That he'd step back from her. For all of his emotional strength, grief knocked his legs from under him—and she didn't know how to make that easier.

And she didn't know if making it easier for him merely made his inability to handle it worse. She could only try to reassure him as best she could.

"You probably imagine that this happens to me often—but it does not. In all my three hundred years, last night was the worst it has ever been. And even though I wish that you hadn't seen it, I thank God you were there, and that you knew how to stop him." She sighed. "But I am also sorry, because it means that I have failed you, and turned around what *should* be: A child should never have to protect his parent."

"Mama . . ." He shook his head. "You're a Guardian. 'Should be' has been flipped around from the day I was brought here. Nothing is as it should be. And it will always be turned around." He looked at her, and the pain in his eyes was so similar to when he had looked at her ten years ago, just before he'd left. "When I came back I found Gemma, and now the baby—and I thank God every day for that. But Mama, you and me . . . Sometimes I think it would be easier for both of us if I'd stayed away."

The knife in her heart twisted. "I do not think it would be easier. And I *know* it would not be better."

As if he had nothing left to say, Vin only shook his head again and turned away. She watched him climb the stairs to Gemma's room. When the door closed behind him, she looked at the sunlight sparkling in the fountain, and tried to lift her head.

❧

Deacon could feel her out there. Desperation had been weighing on her—now there was just pain. Like a dirge, howling through her soul.

He was going to kill that thoughtless fuck she called a son. Force the selfish little bastard to have it out with her, whatever his problem was, not flay her like this, piece by piece.

But he was trapped in here. His blood pumping rage and frustration, Deacon stalked between the War Room and the bedchamber. He couldn't go to her. He would have, not caring if the sun blinded and burned him, but that would only add to the weight she bore. God, he wanted to bear it for her. He *needed* to bear it for her.

But he couldn't bear *this*, waiting and listening as she drowned in hurt. He stopped in the door to the bedchamber.

"Rosie," he said.

She came. He felt her shields thicken, muffling the howling pain, burying it under layers of mental steel. By the time she appeared in the doorway, he only sensed the concern that softened her gorgeous brown eyes.

"Deacon? Is everything all—"

She broke off as his hands came up, cradling her jaw. She stared up at him, and he tried to remember what he'd intended to say. But now he touched her, and he could only think that her bones felt so fragile . . . her lips so soft. His thumbs swept across her cheekbones, searching the beautiful shape of her face.

"I need this," he realized.

Her brow pleated, her concern deepening. "Tell me."

Show her.

He claimed her mouth. His tongue thrust past her lips, seeking her response. She stiffened in surprise before her hands clutched at his shoulders. He shut the door and steered her back against it, lifted her, ripping her panties away. Unzipping, he lodged the head of his cock against her moist entrance. He waited for a protest. When it didn't come, he pushed into her tight channel.

She wasn't ready. Tension gripped her, and when she began to lift away he remembered what he'd meant to say.

"I've got you, Rosie. Just let me catch you. Let me take it all."

Her head dropped back and she gasped, breathed deep like a swimmer coming up for air. Then she was snug and slick around him, sheathing his length with the wetness he loved, the smoldering heat.

"Wrap your legs around me— Fuck yes, just like that." He almost lost his mind when her thighs tightened around him, drew him farther inside. Shaking, he dropped his forehead against hers. "Hold on, princess."

It had to be hard. He drove deep so that she could feel his strength. He kept his fangs from her throat only to keep his promise. Her body bucked against his, riding him. Tears rolled over her cheeks, wet her lips. Then she was trembling in his hands, her thighs squeezing his sides, her pussy clenching around his cock, so tight. She buried her face in his neck, crying out in agonized pleasure.

He'd helped her take the edge off—but it wasn't enough for either of them.

Her soft lips searched his jaw. Still buried deep inside her lush warmth, he carried her to the open shower in the far corner of the chamber.

"Vanish our clothes, Rosie."

The fabric separating them disappeared. He stepped beneath the hot spray, feeling the burn that drew his skin tight.

She lifted her head, met his gaze. "Is this what it will be, then? I did not follow your orders when I left this morning. But you know that when you have me here, naked, I will do as you say." Her fingers pushed the wet hair out of her eyes. "When I haven't obeyed your directions, will you always have me against the wall when I return, with commands to follow?"

Don't touch me. God, how that had shaken him—more than the crossbow she'd aimed at his heart. After the sweetness of her bed, the control and trust she'd offered him, her rejection had been a punch to his gut. Now he was shaken again, realizing what she'd meant: She had difficulty saying no to him when he touched her.

Did she hate that?

He couldn't. And he realized that he'd done exactly as she'd said: He'd pushed her against the door and asked for control again. *Taken* control—because it came with her trust. And he'd needed that as badly as he needed to ease her burden.

But although the answer might frighten her, he couldn't lie. "Yes," he said. "It will always be this way."

She smiled. "Good."

Astonished by her response, he didn't stop her from sliding off. With her hands on his shoulders she turned him about, so that the scalding spray hit her back instead of his. Her fingers traced his biceps, and her gaze drifted over his stomach, lingering on his thick arousal.

She looked up. "You've had me kiss you. But you've never told me to put my mouth anywhere else."

Need surged through him. His cock throbbed painfully at the thought of her mouth, her lips . . . Jesus Christ. No, he'd never asked. He'd been thinking of her pleasure, not his. But the look in her eyes said the pleasure would be hers. That she wanted it as badly as he did.

Hunger roughened his voice. "On your knees, Rosie."

She sank down on the marble tile. The shower spray cascaded over her head, leaving her hair slick as sable. Water rushed over her face, dripped from her erect nipples. She stared at his arousal, as if imagining what came next. She circled her lips with a luscious stroke of her tongue.

God. Anticipation gripped him hard, like a fist around his shaft. If he'd been human, he'd have come. The sight of her tongue sent shudders through him. He braced his hands against the shower wall, palms flat against cream tile. His cock had never felt so heavy.

"Taste me."

Opening her mouth, she stretched forward. Her tongue found and circled the thick head of his shaft. So hot. Deacon gritted his teeth, his stomach flexing as he fought not to thrust. His cock bobbed against her mouth. As if to steady it, she sucked the tip between her lush lips. His eyes rolled back.

Christ help him. He was supposed to hold on to his control through this?

Her tongue circled and stroked, a lick of flame against his skin. Fire swept through him, burning away his mind. He groaned another command—*Deeper*—and her hands came up, her nails sinking into his flanks, pulling him toward her. Heat slid down his cock. He looked at her and almost lost it.

She was staring straight up at his face, thick lashes spiked around eyes glowing like the sun—watching his reaction as her mouth slowly destroyed him. Her hair lay in a wet curtain over her breasts, with beaded nipples peeking through. Water streamed over her belly, running in rivulets to the slit between her thighs. Her arousal melted against his psychic shields like hot syrup.

Fisting his hands against the tile, he battled for control, his labored breaths sounding like a choked-up steam engine. *Control.* Jesus, who was he kidding? She might be following his lead, taking direction—but there was no question who had more power here.

Did she even know the hold she had over him?

She took him deeper, her fingers digging into his ass, her eyes slowly closing as she drew harder on the length of his shaft. The suction seared up his spine. Need pounded through his cock. His fangs ached for the taste of blood, with the need to come. He needed to be inside her.

"No more, Rosie."

He groaned as her mouth released him. The shower's hot spray battered his stomach, his cock, painful against his sensitized shaft. She looked up, her eyelids heavy and irises glowing with her arousal, her lips swollen. He had to take her. *Now.*

Catching her around the waist, he hauled her up, slammed his back against the tile, and shoved her over him. Her sex closed around him like a silken fist. Her nails clawed his shoulders. The scent of his blood exploded through his senses, making his head swim. God, she was losing her control. Knowing that almost destroyed his. He hefted her knees higher, forcing himself deeper. She clutched at his arms for balance.

Her spine abruptly straightened. Her eyes widened with horror, trained on the marks of her nails.

He palmed the back of her head, brought her lips to his. "I love being inside you. So rip me up, Rosie. Let me know you love it, too."

The way she kissed him, her mouth open and hungry, said that she did. He pumped deep, holding her still for each of his thrusts, until she was writhing and crying against his chest, her hips working in ragged circles. When she stiffened, began to come, he buried his face in her neck, stabbed his tongue against his fangs. Blood flooded his mouth, shot through him like an electric shock. He surged up, shook through his release.

Slowly, he came back down. His legs wouldn't hold. He slid to the wet marble floor, Rosalia limp against him. Her eyes were glazed, their glow fading. The water ran cold. Neither made a move to turn it off.

"Christ, Rosie. What you did to me."

"Just following orders," she mumbled against his shoulder.

Though completely wrung, he managed to laugh. "You took revenge for this morning."

"Not revenge. Therapy. *Really* good therapy."

For him or for her? He didn't ask. Lifting her up, he headed for the bed.

Now it was time to savor her.

❦

She felt wonderful.

Rosalia didn't know how. Deacon was the source of so much turmoil within her. But the simple truth was . . . she loved being with him. Loved lying against his shoulder as she lazily explored the ridges of his muscles with her fingertips.

Loved the deep sound of his heartbeat when she pressed her ear to his chest. Loved that the heat of her body and his sweat had strengthened his scent, until hers was a faint undertone.

He lay at ease beside her, his thumb traveling up and down the length of her spine. His eyes were closed, as if he was resting, and a faint smile softened the corners of his mouth.

She wouldn't let herself hope this would last. But for now, for this moment, everything was perfect. It was everything she'd imagined.

Her fingers passed over a long, thin scar above his pectoral. Oh, how she remembered that fight. Another boxer had taken a grudge into the ring. Only a few seconds after the opening bell, the boxer had pulled out a razor hidden in his boot. Horrified, Rosalia had jumped to her feet, yelling out a warning that was lost amid the shouts of the crowd, and the man had lunged forward and slashed Deacon open. Deacon had simply looked down at his bleeding chest, then hammered a knockout blow to the bastard's jaw.

Though no one would have blamed him if he'd taken it further, he'd stopped after that one hit. She'd admired him for that—his control, his restraint. He'd done what he'd needed to do, and left it there.

A sigh escaped her. She had things that needed to be done, too.

His eyes opened. "Does that sigh mean you're getting up?"

"Yes." She sat up, letting the sheet fall to her waist. When Deacon's gaze fell, too, she smiled and brushed her hair back over her shoulders, giving him a better view. "How long has Taylor been here?"

"About three hours."

"Did you have any problems?"

"No. I didn't see her. I only felt her."

"Felt her? Can you now?"

"Yes. Though she's quieter now than when she showed up."

Quieter? Without reaching out, Rosalia couldn't sense the

new Doyen at all. Either Deacon had been performing strong psychic sweeps—a dangerous move, as it might alert anyone to his presence—or he'd become more sensitive. "Are your psychic senses stronger?"

"It's different." His came up on his elbows, his gaze still leveled on her chest. "There's noise mixed in."

How strange. Most of the time, emotions manifested as a taste, a smell, or a physical sensation. Rosalia only knew of a few Guardians and vampires who'd ever registered emotions as sound.

"Does it interfere with your hearing?"

He tapped his temple. "It's all inside, just like before: You feel it, but you know what you're feeling isn't yours—that it's just in your head. Same with this. I'm hearing the sound, but I'm not *hearing* it. And I've still got what I had before, backing it up."

Relief slipped through her. He wouldn't have to adjust to a completely new way of using his psychic senses when he fought the demons. "Are you disoriented?"

"No."

"You'll be faster, stronger," she mused. "But we'll need to practice before we head out tonight, so that you can test how *much* stronger and faster."

"And we need to slay more nephilim and feed them to vampires. Demons wouldn't be so quick to try taking over communities, then."

Maybe vampires could be strengthened that way, though it might not be so simple—Deacon had been changed by nosferatu blood before he'd taken the nephil's. Yet it was possible that they could all become as strong as Guardians . . . perhaps stronger.

Uncertainty pinched her mouth.

"No?" He was watching her face now.

"Not every vampire is like you." And unlike Guardians, vampires didn't have to follow the Rules. "It would be difficult to hand them that much power."

His eyes narrowed. Yes, she recognized how unfair that

was. But power often changed men—and vampires, too. If they were stronger than Guardians, if they didn't fear the consequences of breaking the Rules, some vampires would begin taking advantage of humans, simply because they were weaker.

For all their strength, Guardians didn't truly have much power. There was so much they couldn't do. Vampires wouldn't have those limitations—only what the sun denied them.

Deacon repeated flatly, "Not like me?"

"Trustworthy," she said, but still felt uncomfortable. From a Guardian perspective, her answer was about protecting humans. But Guardians weren't prevented from denying a vampire's free will, or even from slaying them. So from Deacon's perspective, Guardians possessed all of the power that she said vampires shouldn't have over humans.

"That's bullshit. We could kill people now if we wanted to. You Guardians would just have a harder time policing us if we were stronger, because we could defend ourselves better."

She nodded. He was right. She knew he was right. And she knew most of the vampires in Europe, yet could only think of a few she *would* fear giving the blood to.

She knew all of that. She still felt sick at the thought of passing out nephil blood.

"We wouldn't all be your brother, Rosie."

"No. No, I know that. But it would be . . . unfair. No matter how we distributed the blood, it would create too much conflict within the communities. There is not an unlimited supply of nephil blood." Though if she and Deacon were successful, she would soon spill *all* of the nephilim's blood—but even that amount would not be enough for every vampire in the world. "And who would choose who received it? The Guardians? The community elders? What would it mean if some got it and others didn't? What kind of division would that make?"

"Would it matter so much if it meant the vampires didn't have to get on their knees for demons? If they weren't scared shitless that the nephilim were finally coming to their city?"

"It'd matter to you if you were the vampire who didn't get any." She sighed. "At most, it could be a onetime distribution, and there's not enough for everyone. What if I wanted to hold some back? What if Vin and Gemma decided to become vampires? Wouldn't I want to keep some for them so that they wouldn't be . . ."

Like a normal vampire. Like Deacon had been before the nosferatu blood, before the nephil blood.

He didn't let her trail off and take the easy way out. He finished for her, "One of the weaker ones."

"Yes. Right or wrong, that's how I would feel. If what I am brings violence into my son's life, then I want him to have the defenses to handle it. Right now, as a human, his best defense against demons and nephilim is the Rules. He wouldn't have that as a vampire. So I'd want him to be one of the strong ones, too."

"Right or wrong?" He shook his head. "You think I'd blame you for that? Who wouldn't want it?"

"Exactly. Everyone would want it, but not everyone could have it. What happened to you—or when one of the nosferatu-born is made—that difference in strength almost always comes by luck or chance, and it doesn't happen often. But for Guardians or vampires to gather the blood and distribute it *creates* a difference. It creates widespread envy and superiority in communities where there is none."·

"Except for what is already there from when we were human."

"Well, yes. Because vampires, Guardians—in many ways, we're still all human." She paused, holding his gaze. And despite every claim she'd just made, despite the reasons behind her uneasiness, she had to admit, "And because of that, I would have given anything for my friends to have been strong enough to fight the nephilim. Or for you to have been strong enough to fight back against Caym."

"So, if you could, you'd let vampires have the nephil blood."

"Probably. But the better solution is: Slay all of the demons and the nephilim. Then vampires won't need it."

His wide grin exposed his fangs. "One thing's for certain: When you have a plan, Rosie, you stay focused." His gaze dropped again. Leaning forward, he cupped her breasts in his large hands. "But when you're sitting naked like this, I can't say the same for me."

She breathed slowly, fighting the urge to throw herself against him. "I'll hang bells from them, next time."

"And win every argument we might have." His thumbs stroked her nipples, and he smiled when she shivered. "Are we still getting out of bed?"

"Yes." And with another sigh, she made the effort. Aware that Deacon was watching her, she formed her panties and put them on as humans did, a long slow glide up her legs.

"Rosie," he warned.

Laughing, she pulled in a brassiere—a scrap of lace that supported very little and displayed too much.

"I'm going to rip that off with my teeth."

Oh, she hoped so. "Later," she said, and to remove temptation, covered the lingerie with her black trousers and shirt. As she walked across the room, the hunger in his gaze told her that she hadn't buried temptation very deep.

He reached for his jeans. "If you did have to choose vampires to give the blood to, who would it be? Community elders?"

If Deacon hadn't already been strengthened, he'd have been at the top of her list. She didn't think he'd believe her, though.

"No, not necessarily the elders. I'd find vampires who would fight with the Guardians—like those vampires who've begun training at Special Investigations. God knows we need the help."

"*Guardians* need the help?"

"Considering that there are only fifty of us left . . . Yes, we do." When he stared at her, she said, "I thought you knew. That Irena or someone—"

"No. She didn't."

"Oh. Well, the Ascension happened ten years ago, and even I didn't know until six months ago. The Guardians have kept it quiet, so that the demons don't find out. They don't know about Michael, either."

Deacon still looked slightly stunned. She couldn't blame him. Fifteen years ago, there had been thousands of Guardians. She couldn't even imagine how empty Caelum must seem with so many gone. Just sun and stone and water—beautiful, but more like a tomb than a city.

In a low voice he said, "So Belial's demons could wipe you all out."

"If they knew, yes. And unfortunately, Taylor is the only Guardian who can transform humans and create more of us . . . which *also* depends on a human sacrificing himself to save someone else from a demon. So we haven't been able to rebuild our numbers." She opened the bedchamber door. Early afternoon light spilled into the far end of the corridor, but it wouldn't touch Deacon as they crossed to the War Room. "So there you have another reason for my focus. If the demons find out how small our numbers are—and I can't imagine that they wouldn't realize it, eventually—both vampires and Guardians are in danger of being destroyed. So I have to stop them before that happens."

He followed her into the War Room, wearing only his jeans. Heavy muscle and hard flesh invited a long, slow look, but it was his face that fascinated her. So strong and uncompromising, so often unreadable, yet the irregular lines revealed so much of his life. His features told the story of a man who hadn't come through every fight unscathed, but he'd *come through*—and despite the hardness, he could still soften with a laugh or a kiss.

She wanted to kiss him now. She wanted to touch him. Not to straighten, and not to lead him to bed, but the kind of casual caresses that she'd seen between lovers and friends. The kind that said, *I love that you are here.*

Pulling out her chair, she sat at her desk instead. She could touch him that way while lying in bed. She did not know how to here.

"Theriault spent the morning telling his pregnant wife she is a fat whore." Resting his shoulders against the wall, Deacon leaned back, arms crossed over his broad chest. "I'd have considered killing him even if he wasn't a demon."

And if Deacon had, Rosalia would have considered not stopping him.

"It's unfortunate his wife cannot do it." Of course she wouldn't. Humans had rules, too.

"Unfortunate that she won't fight back?"

The sudden edge in his voice made her look up. Warily, she took in his rigid stance, his dark brows drawn together over a hard stare. "What?"

"I don't know what pisses me off more, Rosie. That Vin said all that shit to your face, or that you took it without calling him an ungrateful little—" He clenched his teeth, cutting himself off.

"You tell me to my face that Lorenzo deserved to die, but won't call my son a . . . ?" She raised her brows, inviting him to finish it.

"You didn't love your brother. Only felt responsible for him. Your son's a different matter." While she dealt with her surprise that he saw that so clearly, he narrowed his eyes and said, "Didn't you turn that neatly?"

Stalking forward, he grabbed the chair next to hers, flipped it around, and straddled the seat. "You just deflected me away from you sitting out there, your son's hand holding your bloody heart, and you letting him squeeze it."

"Deacon—"

He lifted his hand, cutting her off. "I didn't believe it, you know. That first night here, I heard Gemma say you don't fight back. And I was thinking, *Rosie's put me in my place so many times, snapped back at me—Gemma's got it all wrong.* But she was right. And you sat out there, just taking it."

And that had upset him? It must have. Anger rolled off him, dark and hot. "Is that why you called me up here?"

"To fuck it out of you? Yeah." His jaw clenched. Grabbing her seat, he hauled her close, until only inches separated their noses. "You did it again. Deflected me away from you and Vin. You don't want me to push on this? Fine. Tell me to back the fuck off. Or convince me that you deserved it, because the next time Vin throws that shit at you, I'm not going to sit—"

"He was right." Her own anger boiled up. He wanted to know? Fine. Another item for the list of things a Guardian didn't do. "Everything he said was true. A Guardian has no business being a mother. It flips everything around. So back off."

"No business . . . You *believe* that?"

"I know it."

His voice lowered, all gravel and frustration. "Oh, I get it. You beat him. No, you can't do that—you had a human do it. And you didn't care for him, didn't feed him or clothe him, didn't kiss him good night, and you never made sure he had support when he needed it." He paused, watching her. With a shake of his head, he spread his arms out wide. "Do you see why that makes no fucking sense? If you were anything like the mother I imagine you were, he should be on his knees thanking you for what was probably the best childhood any kid could want."

Rosalia couldn't remain angry when he said things like that. But it didn't change the facts.

She stood, began to pace the room. "Vampires and Guardians . . . we can't have children after we're transformed. *Can't*. Don't you think that's for a reason?"

"I don't know what the big guy Above was thinking. But if you're about to argue that it all has a *purpose*, my response is that I don't give a fuck what He plans."

Though she'd suspected he felt that way, she had to catch her breath at such blasphemy. But she understood why: His community had been slaughtered. Thinking that their deaths had a purpose didn't offer any comfort. The opposite, in fact.

But in Rosalia's opinion, that hadn't anything to do with

those Above. What happened to Deacon's community, what happened to her friends . . . that was on the shoulders of the demons.

"No. That's not what I mean. We can't take care of them. Not as babies. Who would care for a vampire's child during the day? A Guardian has to follow the Rules, and has responsibilities that often take her away from home. But it is more than that, and it is not just babies. There are times when a child must be led where it doesn't want to go, just to keep it safe." She turned to him, spreading her hands, hoping he'd see. "I had Gemma's grandmother to help me. Thank God I had her. But I should have known better. I *did* know better. But Father Wojcinski brought Vin here, and he was so small, and so afraid and angry and I just . . . fell in love. I didn't want anything more than to see him happy."

And she'd loved that little boy so fiercely—so unexpectedly. She'd never dreamed of being a mother. The others had called her "Mother" as a joke, because she'd had the habit of straightening their clothes. She'd never thought a child would come into her life and change everything.

"And you think you were wrong to take him in?" He remained sitting, but his green eyes followed her every move.

"I think that the moment I decided to be a mother, I should have stopped being a Guardian. I should have Fallen and become human again, so that I could have been what he needed. Not always holding myself back. Not always finding ways around him." She sighed when he shook his head, and repeated, "I should have Fallen. But before I Fell I would have to kill Lorenzo, just to be safe . . . and I still had hope that he could change. I still wanted to work with my vampires. I wanted to be both mother and Guardian—and I loved Vin, so I kept him. But I should have chosen one or the other. It was a selfish decision."

"Because you didn't Fall? Jesus, Rosie. Are you telling me that if he'd been standing in front of a bus and wouldn't move, you wouldn't have pushed him out of the way to save him?"

"Of course I would. But motherhood and love aren't the

grand, hypothetical gestures. They are the little, everyday ones."

He shook his head again, but she cut him off before he could argue.

"And you *must* see that it is more than that. He said everything is turned around . . . and it is. He's not immortal, Deacon. And even if I became human again today, I'd be younger than him." She saw the understanding in his face. Good. Just knowing that one day she would experience what no mother should squeezed her heart into nothing. She couldn't have explained without breaking down. "Every day, *every single day*, I realize: I should have Fallen when I took him in. But now I have to live with what I've chosen. And so does Vin."

His chest lifted on a heavy breath. "Would it do any good to tell you that you've gone overboard punishing yourself?"

"No. Some burdens cannot be taken away with words."

Deacon gave a short laugh. "Don't I know it."

He would. No words could take away what he bore, thanks to the demons and the decisions he made.

Smiling, she returned to her chair. "But I cannot regret for a moment that he is mine. Even when he is a . . . whatever you would have said he is."

His laugh became a grin, and her heart turned over. She could regret nothing here, either. And no matter his reaction when he learned her part in his past, she would live with the decisions she'd made.

"Did you want children?" she wondered.

"You don't keep that in your story file?"

"No." And she loved that there was so much still to learn about him. "Did you?"

"Yeah. I wanted kids."

"You did?" Anxiety rushed through her; she hadn't really expected that answer. "Did you know that choice would be gone? Did Camille tell you?"

"Yes. She laid it all out. Everything."

"Oh." It came out on a breathy laugh. "Good."

Leaning forward against the back of the chair, he put his

hands on her knees, squeezed gently. "That's a lot of relief. You didn't make that choice?"

"I did before taking my vows. But vampires . . . so many are disappointed later. It's best that they know before they transform."

Wicked humor lit his gaze. "Maybe the nephil blood changed that. We should test whether I'm fertile now. Test hard, and test often."

Her laugh came out in a rush, and she thought: *This* was when lovers touched, and showed affection for the person with them. Her stomach in knots, she leaned forward, brushed her mouth over his.

He palmed the back of her head before she could pull away. "You want me to try now, just give the word."

Oh, how she did. She wanted him inside her all the time, her body against his, overwhelmed by emotion and release. She wanted to lie against him afterward, stroking his skin.

But she thought of those vampires, in their little world for thirty years. And sighed.

"I'm beginning to hate that sound," he said, kissing her briefly and letting her go. He sat back. "You did good with St. Croix."

And so, back to work. "I hope so."

"He could have been a wild card."

"He still is." But hopefully he'd wait to play until they'd finished.

"You reeled him in with that story about your mother." When she looked at him, he asked quietly, "You think that's true—that killing herself was part of a bargain?"

"No," she said, and could see his surprise. "But it's possible that's what *his* father did."

His green eyes pierced her, as if trying to see into her. He thought she was deflecting again, she realized. He didn't want to hear about St. Croix's father—he wanted to know about her.

"My mother was a strong woman," Rosalia explained. "But he beat her down, and she gave up."

He nodded, as if she'd just confirmed something he'd thought. "And now you *can't* give up. And it's why you can't get back into bed when you have work to do."

He thought he'd pinned her with that one thing? "It's not that simple."

"No? Don't tell me you haven't thought how different your and your brother's life would be if she had stuck in there and protected you, or gotten you out of there."

Rosalia *had* thought about it. A thousand times. And just as often, she'd ruminated on how evil a demon must be, that he could take a strong-willed human and break her down so that death seemed a better option than living and protecting her children. Rosalia had her own child now. She couldn't fathom the depth of evil that would lead her to leave him unprotected.

Her mother had faced that evil and lost; Rosalia would fight until her last breath to destroy it. But she wasn't stronger than her mother. She just had more knowledge . . . and a better plan.

"My life would have been different, but it could have been better or worse. I only know what *is*—and now I'm a Guardian. Perhaps my mother's suicide shaped me, but my mother is not the only reason I cannot give up. Vin, Gemma, you . . . my Guardian friends, the vampires I've watched and known for centuries. You are all reasons. And, if Anaria has her way, every human's free will is in danger—perhaps their lives. I have many reasons not to quit. It's not as simple as my mother."

"So you're a woman with a mission." His expression remained serious, his gaze still penetrating. "A mission you meant to convince me to join. London forced you into doing it faster."

Her stomach sank. He *had* heard Father Wojcinski. "Yes."

"You didn't like the idea of using me, so you convinced me instead. And I'm here, willingly, so you must have. Hell, I came running back after you. What did you do?"

"Deacon—"

"What string in me did you pull?"

"That you're a good man. That you've *always* been a good man, and a strong one."

He shot to his feet. "Cut the bullshit, Rosie. Specifically."

It wasn't bullshit, but the truth. Because if it hadn't been, nothing she'd done would have made a difference to him.

"I made myself a person to you, because you can't ignore a person in need. And instead of asking you to do it for humans or vampires . . . I gave you me."

Deacon stared at her, as if he didn't recognize the woman before him. "So when I woke up in that plane, you weren't exposing yourself to me. You weren't confessing your guts. It was calculated, designed to get me to go along with you."

"Yes." Though it made her more vulnerable to him. Though it meant he could tear her apart.

Her heart ached. She tried to brace herself. He could tear her apart now, with a few words. He looked angry enough to do it.

He shook his head, looked away from her. "At least you didn't know I was awake."

That cut deep. He would have believed that she'd gotten into bed with him just to keep him here? Her chest hurt too much to speak, but she managed, "No. I didn't."

"And it's the only thing that's keeping me from walking out that door right now." He strode toward her instead. With two fingers, he lifted her chin until she met his unyielding gaze. "Don't fuck with me like that, Rosie. Not again. Caym used me, manipulated me, and he got the response he wanted. But I never liked it even when Camille was doing it. So don't play me again."

She nodded. She wouldn't need to. He was here now.

"That includes those sad eyes."

She frowned up at him, confused. "I don't know what—"

"I know you don't." Deacon sighed, then leaned over and kissed her hard. "Now, what's going on for tonight?"

CHAPTER 17

Deacon couldn't get a bead on her. Just a few minutes ago, she'd been sitting in her chair, looking like she was facing a firing squad. Now she was all business, outlining that evening's schedule.

He couldn't make perfect sense of that, either. Her plan was simple enough—have Taylor teleport them to Lisbon, he'd slay one of Theriault's demons, then pay a visit to the vampire community's leader—but it didn't fit the same pattern. They weren't targeting a demon who'd taken over a community, but one who lived in the same city. The demon had put some minor pressure on the community leader to come under his protection, but the community had seen what had happened to Deacon after falling in with a demon, and declined his offer. That had been the end of it. No threats, no immediate danger. So why this one?

By the time Rosalia finished up, Deacon still didn't know where she was going with it. "How is this going to establish me as head?"

She glanced away from her computer, brows lifted. "It's not."

"No? I'm not blind, Rosie. You've brought in three large communities under me in as many days. Why is this one different?"

"You're not taking over the communities. Unless you want to?" When he shook his head, she smiled, just a slight curve of her gorgeous lips. "Why did I ask? In any case, there's no reason to displace José Carvalho. He's a good leader, just as Tomás is."

"Then what have I been doing, aside from killing demons?"

Deacon didn't believe for a second that she wasn't working up to something else. They'd been hopping all over Europe, and when they'd been heading for communities in trouble, that had made sense. Lisbon seemed random—and he had a feeling that nothing Rosalia did was random.

And he sure as hell didn't think the sudden nervousness he detected in the pale set of her mouth was leading up to anything good. She was worried about this next part, but she didn't back away from it, or try to deflect.

Looking him square on, she said, "You've been regaining their respect and confidence, so that when we find Malkvial, you've got them all behind you."

What did respect and confidence have to do with Malkvial? But he didn't get a chance to ask. From behind him, a ragged breath sounded, followed by splashing water and the sharp scent of chlorine.

Taylor.

Rosalia leapt to her feet, calling in her swords. She tried to block him from Taylor's sight; Deacon didn't let her push him back. He turned around and got right in front of her again. He didn't have shirt or weapons, but he'd be damned if Rosalia ever took another hit for him.

But the Taylor who'd teleported into the War Room wasn't the empty, possessed woman who'd attacked them the night before. Though her clothes were soaked and her red hair plastered to her skull, her blue eyes were sharp and clear. This woman, Deacon recognized from when he'd first met her—this was the detective.

A dismayed detective. She looked down at her dripping clothes, the puddles on the slate tile. "Sorry about the floor. I can't get my head around the water to vanish it. And . . . I'm a mess."

"Don't be sorry." Rosalia spoke in English, her accent matching Taylor's American one. The water vanished from around the other woman's bare feet, from her clothes. "We're informal here."

Taylor glanced up, focused on Deacon's naked chest. "I see."

Rosalia laughed softly, but Deacon was grateful when she handed him a white T-shirt. He liked Rosalia looking at him. And maybe it was just his 120-year-old Victorian sensibilities kicking in, but he preferred that *only* Rosalia did the looking.

He dragged the shirt over his head. "Are you all right, then?"

"I'm better than usual." She looked to Deacon, then back to Rosalia. "First, I apologize for eavesdropping on your conversation. You said my name, and after that I couldn't *not* hear it."

"Understood." Rosalia vanished her swords.

So Taylor could listen in on their Italian, but she only spoke English? Deacon said in Czech, "Something you heard here brought you?"

Taylor caught on quick. "It's Michael," she explained. "What you just said sounded like nonsense to me, but once it's in my head, I know what it means. It freaks me out."

Then Deacon would switch to English, too. "So what brought you up here?"

"Hearing that you've all but taken over a couple of communities, which means you're painting a target on your back for the nephilim. And that's just bad juju."

Rosalia shook her head. "No. Deacon isn't actually leading any communities. I wouldn't take that risk."

"And if that was how it worked, you'd be okay. But it's not, and neither Anaria nor the nephilim will stop to consider whether he's *actually* leading the communities. If they hear he's bringing several cities under him, they'll think: Here's our chance to kill a bunch of vampires in one go. They'll end up disappointed when his blood doesn't have all of the resonances they're looking for . . . but by then it'll be too late."

Deacon looked to Rosalia, saw the same confusion on her face—and a lot of worry. He turned back to Taylor. "You've got to explain this."

♦

Taylor told them how Khavi explained the blood and the resonance to her, and she couldn't decide what horrified Rosalia more: that her plan painted a target on Deacon's back, or that Taylor had been visiting with Anaria.

When Taylor finished, she looked at Deacon. "I couldn't figure out was wrong. You're awake."

He wasn't the only vampire that Taylor knew who could resist the daysleep, but the other one had been infected with dragon blood through Michael's sword. Only Anaria and Irena had weapons of similar power now.

Deacon glanced at Rosalia. He waited until she nodded before saying, "We killed a nephil last night. I drank its blood."

Darkness flashed through her mind. Taylor rocked back, fighting it. When Rosalia took a step toward her, her face lined with concern, she held up her hand. "I'm okay. He's just . . . worried. That's really bad news. If she finds out, she'll gun hard for you. And for you"—she glanced at Rosalia—"for protecting him. And anyone else who was with you, or in her way."

Rosalia paled, her hand clutching over her heart. "Vincente and Gemma."

Her son and daughter-in-law-to-be. Oh, damn. He was human, but the Rules wouldn't stop Anaria.

Deacon moved to Rosalia's side. She turned her face into his chest. "One other person knew," he said to Taylor. "But he's not talking. He has his own agenda."

Taylor nodded. The big take-away here obviously was: don't go anywhere near Anaria for a while, if she could help it. If Taylor couldn't lie, Rosalia, Deacon, and quite a few humans would be in some serious shit.

From somewhere outside the room, a bell rang. Rosalia looked up, seemed to steady herself. "That's your blood being delivered. I'll return in a moment."

Taylor watched her go, then turned back to Deacon, who was still looking toward the door with his concern hanging all over his face.

She had a sudden flash of a different expression: his surprise. Of Rosalia, bleeding. Of pain through her throat, and a long, dark shadow. She shook her head, trying to clear the dim memory. "I seem to remember . . . Did I attack you last night?"

He stared at her for a long second, then broke into a sudden laugh. "You sure as hell did."

God*damn* Michael. "Shit. I'm sorry."

"For me? No. Rosalia got tore up some, though."

She felt sick, almost seeing it now—her sword, striking the other woman's back. The give of flesh as the blade slid through. "I'll try to make it up to her. Somehow."

Deacon nodded, then Rosalia was back, handing a glass of blood over to the vampire and turning to Taylor with a warm, gorgeous smile.

Holy hell. Taylor could have described Rosalia's every feature a few seconds after seeing the Guardian for the first time, but it just now hit her how freaking *beautiful* she was. Not a fragile beauty, like Anaria had. And not like a supermodel, but closer to one of those Waterhouse paintings, where ladies gave favors to knights and lay amid flowery fields. Just all over soft and welcoming, but solid—like this was a woman who could shoulder anything, even when she'd been torn down and her heart completely vulnerable.

Taylor glanced at the vampire, who couldn't quite hide the admiration and longing in his eyes. All tangled up. Taylor wasn't much of a romantic, but she hoped like hell they pulled it off.

"I actually can think of a way for you to pay me back—and practice cleaning yourself up at the same time," Rosalia said. "Are you busy this afternoon?"

❦

When Deacon emerged from the Lisbon apartment carrying the demon's head in a black leakproof bag, Rosalia finally let herself take pleasure in how smoothly the evening had gone. She and Taylor had cleaned the garage until Gemma had woken from her nap, and Rosalia spent an hour with the young woman, first persuading her that she wouldn't be lonely and then helping Gemma gather her things. When the sun set, she and Deacon still had to wait a little more than an hour before it set in Lisbon; they spent it in the courtyard, testing the range of his new speed and strength. More skilled, Rosalia could still defeat him with weapons and hand-to-hand combat, but he was stronger and faster than her—and in the first fifteen minutes of practice, he'd been clumsy with surprise at *how* fast and strong.

That had worried her. From the moment Taylor had teleported them to Lisbon and left Rosalia and Deacon alone, her heart had been pounding and her lungs tight with fear. But the practice had served him well, and within a second of Deacon entering the demon's apartment, the fight had been over.

His grin flashed when he saw her waiting beneath one of the palms that lined the quiet street. Crimson darkened his black shirt, and the Atlantic breeze that had cooled the city brought her the scent of the demon's blood . . . and Deacon's.

"Were you hit?"

Stopping beside her, Deacon showed her his hand. A faint pink line crossed the center of his palm. Even as she watched, the scar faded. "I slung some of my blood around. If the demons come across that, they'll know it was a vampire that killed him."

It was better than that. "They'll know it was *you*."

"And that's just the way I want it." He hefted the bag containing the demon's head. "So do we go bowling?"

Oh, he made her laugh. When she finally managed to shake the ridiculous image from her mind, she said, "We walk. José Carvalho's home isn't far."

They started out—two miles through the city, on a warm and quiet night. It was inevitable that her memory would recall Brussels and their first walk. She could barely recognize herself—the dame in distress, curious about the man who'd rescued her. Yet here she was, ninety years later, needing his help and still wondering about his every thought, fascinated by everything that drove him.

So much the same . . . and yet completely changed. Compared to now, ninety years ago her feelings toward him had been like a puddle to an ocean—and she'd only begun to fathom the depths.

And ninety years ago, she hadn't feared that she'd drown.

She glanced over at him, and a cold hand seemed to squeeze at her chest. She'd been quiet as they walked, and so she hadn't thought much of his silence—but now she saw that his silence was a hard thing, like the stone set of his jaw.

As if noticing her sudden attention, he stopped and seemed to brace himself. "The demon is dead. So tell me why we're headed to Carvalho's."

To gain the vampire communities' respect and confidence. He knew that; she'd told him. But she hadn't had time to tell him the rest. Taylor had teleported into the War Room, and Rosalia had been thankful for the respite.

But she'd already delayed so long. Once, she could have called the delay prudent. Now it was just cowardice.

Knowing that didn't make telling him any easier. She met his eyes, and wished the pounding of her heart wasn't so loud. "To slay the nephilim, we need demons to break the Rules."

"So a nephil teleports wherever the demon is."

"Yes. If it's just one demon, however, the nephil will probably kill it. But if Malkvial gathers *all* of his demons together and they bring in the nephilim one at a time . . ."

Something like amazement softened his features as he looked at her. The frigid hand around Rosalia's lungs squeezed tighter. He hadn't heard the rest yet.

"A slaughter," he realized. "And so fucking simple."

Only simple when all of the pieces were in place. "But they've never thought of it. Perhaps they *can't* think of it; they're all too entrenched in thousands and thousands of years of being the same. And a Guardian can't propose it to Malkvial."

"But a vampire can?"

She nodded, and Deacon's eyes went cold and hard. Rosalia had to do the same, or break down. Calling upon three centuries of hiding, she wrapped herself in her reasons, until they were all she saw.

"Not just any vampire," she said. "A ruined one, who'd already made a deal with a demon and betrayed the Guardians. Vampires and Guardians were once human, so they can forgive—and they can understand the choices you made, even if they don't agree with them. A demon can't imagine forgiveness and understanding. So when you approach him, he'll be suspicious, but he won't truly think that you're with a Guardian."

"With you?" His laugh was bitter. "And look where I am now. After what Caym did, you want me to make another bargain with a demon?"

"Yes. He's trying to win their support and the lieutenant's position. Arranging for the slaughter of their enemy and fulfilling part of Belial's prophecy will secure it for him."

"And you want me to make a bargain with a demon?"

"The appearance of a bargain. In reality, this will destroy them. And you'll have your revenge."

That didn't move him. He stared at her, his jaw clenching. "Jesus fucking Christ, princess. You don't ask much, do you?"

"I know how much I ask." If they lost, if this went wrong . . .

they would both be destroyed, too. Perhaps they wouldn't be dead, but to every other Guardian and vampire, they might as well be. And even if they succeeded, Rosalia still might lose everything. "The demons need humans to break the Rules, Deacon. I'm already arranging who it'll be . . . and they won't be coming of their free will."

He turned his face away from her, staring blindly down the street. The gravel in his voice sharpened. "Another reason you need a vampire?"

"Not just one. They're all going to get behind you and help."

Another bitter laugh escaped him. He shook his head, and looked down at the bag in his hand as if a poisonous snake lay curled inside instead of a demon's head. "So it's not just me, Rosie, is it? You're playing everyone."

The disgust in his voice tore away the layers she'd wrapped herself in, speared straight into her heart. She struggled against anger, against tears—and above all, to make him understand. "I'm *not* playing. I'm trying to save them. And I don't think it's too much to ask for them to put a hand in."

"You're asking them to *help*?" He lifted the bag, and for an awful moment, she thought he would hurl it down the street. But he only looked at her again, face unreadable, his gaze flat. "Then why this? Why not just ask them?"

"Because I need *you* to lead this and to bargain with Malkvial, and they won't help *you* without it. They need something to hold on to, something tangible, because they can't just *believe*. They don't know you like I do."

Her impassioned response only made him withdraw further. "You don't know shit, Rosie."

The words pierced like arrows. *You don't know shit.* He'd said that to Belial's lieutenant, at the end. Trying to save his people, Deacon had almost nothing left in him. He'd still been fighting, but he'd been scraping the bottom, and that reply was all that remained.

This time, she'd brought him there—right back to Caym and Belial's lieutenant, and Eva and Petra poured out in ashes onto the floor. A bargain with a demon was a nightmare for Deacon.

She understood that. And she knew that her understanding didn't help; if anything, it must seem worse to him, that she'd *seen* what he'd gone through . . . and yet asked him to do it again.

"So this is what you've been leading up to all this time," he said softly. "You find Malkvial, and then send me his way."

"Yes." Her throat worked, but she couldn't get any more out.

"Jesus, Rosie."

It was barely a whisper under his breath. She waited for more—anything—but he only looked down the palm-lined street again, and began walking. Uncertain, she watched him go, and with his every step, her vision blurred.

After a few seconds, he said without stopping or turning around, "Come on, princess. We've got a head to deliver."

His statement didn't bring any relief. Even if she'd heard humor in his voice instead of flat resignation, she couldn't have laughed. Her chest ached. He hadn't left, but she'd gotten a taste of what his leaving might be like.

What it *would* be like, after he discovered how she'd influenced his life. She hadn't been playing him, but he'd surely see it that way. And after the demons were slain and his revenge complete, he wouldn't have any reason to stay.

She took her time catching up to him—long enough that her tears had dried and she'd been able to tuck her despair beneath her emotional shields.

As soon as she fell into step beside him, he said, "When we arrive, how should I explain you?"

"I'll be Anna Vanek's sister, Eliska." She named one of his community members in Prague. If anyone had a reason to help Deacon take his revenge, it would be one of the vampire's relations. "My general description matches Eliska's records."

"Anna didn't have a sister."

Not anymore. Rosalia wouldn't paint a target on a living

human. "Eliska had childhood leukemia. Anna was twelve when she passed."

He glanced at her in surprise, his face tightening with emotion. "Anna was one of our youngest."

"Well. She began seeking immortality a little earlier than most people do."

"And thanks to Belial's demons, only got five years of it." The grief in his voice hardened, his mouth flattening. "So, your plan: The demons are all together, knocking off the nephilim one at a time. What happens to the demons when they're done?"

"They die." Just as she'd promised him.

"Goddammit, Rosie. *How?*"

"I don't know yet. But I'll figure out a way." Hopefully a way that didn't kill anyone but the demons.

Deacon's jaw clenched, as if he barely held back his response. When he finally spoke, it was only, "Fuck."

❦

Rosalia would have preferred to remain outside in the dark when they arrived at the vampire's house. The front walk led through a walled garden, designed with both day- and night-dwellers in mind. Palms and eucalyptus trees sheltered camellias and rhododendrons. Beside the verandah, water bubbled over Moorish tiles and splashed into a small pond stocked with fat gold and white koi.

Deacon rang the bell and announced his name through the speaker. A few seconds later, she caught his fleeting surprise when they heard the locks disengage. He hadn't expected that the vampire would open the door to him.

Tall and dark, José Carvalho wore buff trousers and a loose white linen shirt. Gray peppered his hair, and faint lines fanned around his eyes and bracketed his mouth. Behind him waited his wife, Maria, her blond hair loosely gathered at her nape, looking cool and elegant in a vintage sleeveless dress.

They'd been middle-aged when they'd transformed, with

two grown children. One had become a vampire. The other was now a grandparent.

She didn't want to be here. In this house, she couldn't escape what it meant to be an immortal with children who weren't—and it hurt her heart.

José smiled. "Come in, my friends, before the heat does."

The couple led them to a comfortable room, lined with books and a large-screen television. Games were tucked away in a shelf. A small stuffed animal was caught between the cushions of a sofa. Not just a room—a *family* room. Too easily, Rosalia could imagine gatherings in this room, of humans and vampires.

Focusing on Deacon instead, she watched him set the bag on a low table and open it. José took a look. Satisfaction flashed over his expression. He didn't show his fear, but Rosalia sensed it.

"The demons won't retaliate? The other communities are worried."

Deacon shook his head. "They won't stoop to retaliation. Any demon who admits that a vampire could do this would seem weak."

Nodding, José looked to Rosalia, and she felt his gentle probe against her psychic shields, followed by Maria's. Rosalia pretended not to notice.

After a moment, Maria smiled at her. "Would you like coffee?"

Rosalia glanced at Deacon, her brows lifting. The less she participated in the conversation, the better. It would be simpler all around if she just didn't speak, but knowing that neither José nor Maria understood Czech was the next best thing. *"Nerozumím."*

"Dáš jsi káva?"

Rosalia turned to Maria, shaking her head. *"Neděkuji."*

"No, thank you. We won't be here long," Deacon explained, and when their curiosity didn't lessen, he added, "Her sister, Anna, was a young member of my community."

"I see." Nodding, José returned his attention to Deacon.

"We'd heard that a human was with you, though no one knew who she was. But yes, that makes perfect sense. Do you plan to turn her?"

Deacon laughed. "No. She's far too good for the likes of me."

José smiled before turning serious again. "What are you intending to do? Kill them all?"

"What do you think my chances of that are?" Deacon smiled faintly when José didn't answer. "I'll find some other way of making certain we're safe from them."

With an elegant wave, Maria gestured toward the bag. "We're already safer than we were."

"It's never enough," Deacon said, then looked to Rosalia. "And we have more to do. We should go."

José extended his hand. "Thank you. If you need a community, Deacon, you will always have a place here."

Deacon stared at the other vampire for a moment before slowly taking his hand. His voice had roughened. "I'll keep that in mind."

At the door, Rosalia managed to butcher a simple *adeus* and left, satisfied. Almost satisfied.

She frowned at him as soon as they reached the street. "*I'm* too good for you? What were Eva and Petra—dog meat?"

"I sure as hell didn't mean that." Deacon's mouth flattened. "They were too good for me, too. They deserved a lot better than they got."

Better than a man who destroyed himself trying to save them? But no argument would matter, she knew. This was his burden.

As if he read her thoughts, he said quietly, "It doesn't matter how hard I tried, Rosie. I failed."

Yes. She understood that, too well. It wouldn't matter how hard she worked to destroy the nephilim and Belial's demons, or how well parts of her plan succeeded. If she failed . . . all of the good intentions in the world would not make up for it.

And as many reasons as she had for doing this, she had just as many ways to fail.

❧

A chartered flight waited to take them from Lisbon to Paris. If the demons had begun to track Deacon's movements, Rosalia didn't want to point them to Rome. At the Paris hotel, she checked on her surveillance equipment before taking a train to the edge of the city. From there, Rosalia formed her wings and carried him.

She flew too fast to talk. They were vulnerable in this position—and they'd lost an hour returning east. If she didn't reach home before dawn, Deacon would be making the end of this trip covered by a body bag.

When they arrived, the abbey was empty. Rosalia wanted nothing more than to fly straight to her bedchamber with Deacon, but the ringing of a telephone in the War Room called her there instead. She landed on the second-level walkway, vanishing her wings.

"St. Croix?" Deacon asked.

Rosalia shook her head. The number she'd given St. Croix had a different ring. This was the number she'd given only the vampires within her community.

For a brief moment, she let herself hope that it was someone she hadn't accounted for—a vampire who'd managed to escape the nephilim. But even before she looked at the display, she knew who it must be: Camille, and with Deacon standing by to hear every word.

Her heart thundering, she answered. "Camille."

A brief silence was followed by the sound of someone rushing across the room. She must have been letting it ring over speakerphone for some time. Yes, Camille was tenacious.

"*Bonjour*, Eliska. Yves sends his love."

Rosalia had never officially met Yves, and so Camille was simply telling her that Yves was in the same room—which meant that Camille would be careful how she spoke, as well.

Rosalia couldn't relax, though. Deacon was looking at her, and the thunderclouds on his face weren't promising. Rosalia sank into her chair and turned away from him. She couldn't manage both. Not now.

And she'd promised not to manage him, anyway.

She kept her voice cool. "Deacon might want to pass on such sentiments to Yves, but I won't. I thought your hospitality was lacking when you last met with him."

"At the hotel restaurant? I didn't see you."

"Of course you didn't."

There was a smile in Camille's reply. "But I recognized your touch in recent events."

"I haven't touched anything. Deacon has. He's much stronger than a human, after all."

"I see." Camille digested that quickly. Rosalia wouldn't need to make it any clearer: She didn't want anyone to know that a Guardian was involved. "But tell me, Eliska, what have you planned? He's taken Budapest, Athens, Monaco . . . and now José Carvalho is ready to lay down his life for him. You must appreciate that we need to know whether Paris is next."

Rosalia sighed as she heard a burst of French from Yves in the background. Camille was trying to understand what Rosalia's endgame was. Yves just wondered if his position was being threatened. "No. But I do expect you to welcome him with the respect he deserves."

"If I'd known—"

"You're too clever for that, Camille." Complimenting the other woman always helped smooth over bad news. Rosalia didn't intend to involve her yet—not until all of the other community elders were involved, too. "You don't start moving a queen around the board on the opening gambit. We'll need you, in time. But for now, Deacon has the maneuverability and the strength to set up the game."

Camille made a noncommittal noise—then sighed as, in the background, Yves asked about London and the nephilim.

At his bidding, Camille asked, "Will you take care of that community, as well?"

Not Rosalia. *Another* queen.

Rosalia sat up straight, her mind racing.

Anaria. Michael was gone. But Anaria had just as much power. Possibly more—and if the demons slaughtered the nephilim, no one would have more reason to kill them than the nephilim's mother.

But Rosalia would have to bring in Taylor, too. Oh, Lord. It would be so dangerous for them all.

Failure would be worse.

"Mother? Have you a solution for London?"

"Let us pray so." She heard Camille's delicate snort of laughter, and then another sigh when Yves launched into an invective against the nephilim, opining that the British vampires deserved it, and expressing his anger that the nephilim had only targeted Europe and America. "Good night, Camille."

She hung up, and braced herself before looking up into Deacon's face. His expression was rigid with controlled anger.

"*Camille* is the vampire who left before the others were slaughtered?"

"Yes."

"How long ago did she work with you?"

"The three decades preceding the First World War."

That was earlier than he'd expected, but the surprise didn't abate his anger. He stalked to the wall, and back. "Let me guess: She learned everything from you."

Not everything. Camille had a natural ability with men that Rosalia could never claim. Camille could be funny and lighthearted, with a quick smile and a quicker comeback—talents which had won Deacon over, those many years ago. Talents that Rosalia did not possess.

"She learned many things here, yes. But not everything."

"And there's no question how you knew so much about me. She fed you—"

"No," Rosalia cut him off, and rose to her feet. "She didn't want to work for the Church. But there were other things that needed to be done in those years." And Camille needed her own purpose. In truth, Rosalia had manipulated Camille's life as much as she had Deacon's. Ninety years ago, his need and Camille's had dovetailed, and Rosalia had used that knowledge to bring them together—though doing so had killed her. "But she did not feed me information on you. Everything I know, I saw myself."

"Bullshit. She has your direct number."

"To reach me if she ever needs help. Or if she knows someone else who does."

He didn't believe her. She could feel his distrust, see it in the rigid stance of his body, as if he expected her to drop something else on him. First Malkvial, now Camille.

And perhaps she deserved that distrust. She *should* have told him how well she knew Camille, but revealing their connection had felt too close to losing him altogether. The timing had just always been so wrong.

It still was. Sighing, she glanced at the clock. "It's almost dawn. You don't want to be locked in here all day."

The tightening of his jaw said it best. *Not in here with her. Not now.*

And she had to live with the decisions she made—even when it hurt. "Come on, then."

❧

The garage had been built onto the back of the abbey about forty or fifty years ago, Deacon guessed. The only access was from the outside, though the eastern door. The place hadn't been used often. Some oil scent still lingered, but not much. A man could have eaten off the concrete floors. The glass in the big bay door had recently been painted over to block the light. The tools laid out on the worktable sparkled, unmarred by even a fingerprint. She'd even set up a computer and phone so that he could research parts and order them. The whole setup was like a cleaner, sparser version of what he'd had in Prague.

Rosalia watched him look around, the sadness in her eyes fading and taking on life. She was excited about this.

He was wary. She'd put a hell of a lot of effort and money into this. And he couldn't fault her choice of car currently sitting in the bay. He'd wanted to get his hands on a Ferrari 250 GTL for years—but then, Rosalia knew a lot about what he'd like. Knew that he'd used to do restore and resell cars like this for a living. And he'd made money from it, but he'd loved it, too. His garage and vehicles had been the last things he'd sold before leaving Prague.

But it felt too much like how Camille used to give him gifts to help soften the blow of something she'd done, or something she wanted. She'd hand the gift over, talking about how much she'd appreciated him . . . and then drop a bomb on him a few days later.

He slid his palm over the dull red fender. Solid. Not rusted out, just banged up a little. Tires rotted, upholstery a mess. Overall, not bad shape, but it'd take a lot of work. He lifted the hood and grimaced. She'd been stripped for parts, and what was left had corroded. He'd have to rebuild the engine.

He was already itching to get in there.

"It's the best I could get on short notice." Rosalia came up next to him, her hands tucked in her elbows. "If you'd prefer another vehicle, I can find it for you."

On short notice, because she and Taylor had thrown this together yesterday afternoon . . . just after Taylor had shown up and put a halt to Rosalia telling him about Malkvial. But she must have known that revelation was coming. The timing of this whole damn thing couldn't have been better, could it?

When he didn't answer, she sighed and pointed to the back wall of the garage. "The sparring chamber is on the other side. After I sunproof that room, I can open this wall up. The War Room is right above it. It shouldn't be difficult to construct an access stair through the floor—and then you could move around between here and the second-level chambers during the day."

Wasn't that convenient? "That seems like a lot of work, when your plan should be all finished up within a week and a half. I'll be out of here then."

The excitement in her eyes dimmed. He watched her back-pedal as if she realized the big prize she'd dangled wasn't as tempting as she'd hoped. "Well. It's best that you're comfortable while you're here."

"Comfortable will win you points, sure. But if you want to

give me something to do and keep me comfortable while I'm at it, just put me in your bed and fuck me."

He'd discovered how calculating she could be—but she didn't run cold. Never cold. Her eyes began to glow, a fierce yellow light.

"Yes, you're right. This isn't about giving you something to keep you occupied for the day. It's not about knowing how you enjoy restoring vehicles, and that you sold yours to pay for revenge. It's not about any of that. It's about scoring points, and managing you."

Her anger burned against his shields. The hurt that sounded beneath made him want to reach out.

But maybe that was what she wanted. Maybe she counted on him taking that step toward her. Now she stared at him, as if waiting—for what? An apology? Fuck that. It wasn't like Camille had been a passing acquaintance. *He'd lived with her for twenty-five years.* Longer than many human marriages. That wasn't something a person failed to mention unless there was a reason to hide it. And the only reason for Rosalia to conceal her history with Camille was that she'd gotten something out of it, and didn't want him to know.

Had Camille told her every string in him to pull? God knew, Rosalia's fingers were right in there, right around his heart. He couldn't take a fucking breath without feeling her and the hold she had on him.

Rosalia decided not to wait anymore. Throwing up her hands, she spun away from him. "All right. You think fucking earns points? Then go fuck yourself, Deacon. You're guaranteed to win."

Faint sunlight stung his eyes as she slammed through the door and into the dawn. Deacon turned, resting his palms on the hood, resisting the urge to pound his fist through steel.

Twenty-four hours ago, she'd come into his bed. In less than a day, it'd all fallen apart—and he couldn't even dredge up surprise. He'd never deserved anything she'd offered. And even though he was good and fucked now, he hadn't won.

He'd lost something, instead.

CHAPTER 18

Her leaving set a pattern for the next several days. Dawn found Deacon in the garage, where he'd work until the sun set. Then he'd snag a unit of blood from the kitchen and join her in the War Room. She'd lay out the plans for the evening, and they'd be off. Deacon would slay another demon in another city. Then she crammed yet another city into their nightly schedule, and barely got him back to the abbey before the sun rose again.

During the day, she swam. He heard her as she swam. And gardened. Her hair smelled like chlorine and her hands like earth. He imagined her out in the sunshine, with the War Room doors open and listening to the surveillance on St. Croix and Theriault the same way another woman might listen to the radio.

And she didn't touch him. The first night, he saw the way her fingers clenched when he'd emerged from her bedchamber, showered and dressed for the evening. But she didn't straighten him up.

The next night, he'd deliberately left himself a mess. She'd crossed her arms over her chest and tucked her hands in tight, and he remembered where he'd seen her do that before: with Vin, as if she'd been afraid her son might slap her hands away.

Since then, he hadn't had a hair out of place or a collar bent wrong.

And once he got over being pissed, not a minute passed that he didn't think of taking that step toward her. After Malkvial and Camille, she couldn't possibly have anything else to drop on him. And though she was only a few rooms away, he missed her like hell. Warm and sweet and clever, yet so vulnerable. She looked at him like he was worth something. She truly believed he could pull her plan off. She'd trusted him. And he knew the pleasure they'd found in bed had just been them—no plan, no calculation there. They'd fit together well.

But he didn't go to her, and didn't call her in. It was better this way. Once they'd finished, she wouldn't have a use for him, and he'd be gone. Far easier to make the break now.

And so he stayed in the garage, and the few words that passed between them were about the demons he'd be killing. She put the blood in the refrigerator and told him to help himself when he needed it. She asked him daily if he'd seen Taylor and to send the Guardian to her if he did.

But they spoke only after sunset. During the day, she left him alone. She never came into the garage. He shut off the air-conditioning and let in the heat, stripping to the waist while he worked beneath the car. By afternoon, the garage sweltered. Sweat rolled into his eyes.

He didn't sleep, and no longer had nightmares, but the days were still his own personal hell. A hell of his making, and one he deserved. The small heaven of her, he didn't.

And when Taylor teleported in, both her eyes and her mind dark, empty voids, he realized that he was finally going to pay.

❧

Rosalia's hands were deep in the soil when the psychic darkness rolled into her—the same she'd felt while flying over the Mediterranean.

Taylor. *Oh, God.*

She leapt to her feet and ran. The sparring chamber passed in a blur. Lowering her right shoulder, she rammed into the wall shared by the garage. Stone and plaster exploded around her.

Rosalia stumbled through, her right arm shattered with pain, sword in her left hand. She froze.

Deacon lay on the concrete, Taylor's blade at his throat. She stood over him, her eyes empty, but she was struggling against Michael's hold. Her hand trembled. A line of blood ran down the side of Deacon's neck.

"Taylor." She tried to keep her voice calm. Agony engulfed the arm that she lifted toward the other woman. "Bring your sword here. You don't want to do this."

The other Guardian made a soft sound, a whimper that wasn't just her. Michael's harmonic voice deepened it almost to a growl. Her shaking increased.

Deacon's gaze never left Taylor's face. "Maybe she does, Rosie. Maybe he's just giving her what she wants."

Taylor's life had been taken away. Her will, possessed. They were both reasons to seek revenge . . . if Taylor had been another woman.

But Taylor wasn't seeking revenge. Michael was seeking it *for* her. And Rosalia had been appealing to the wrong Guardian.

"Michael," Rosalia said, and hoped to God that he could hear her. Hoping the tortures of the frozen field hadn't just reduced him to base impulse, but that some semblance of reason was left. "If you make her do this, she'll carry that forever. If you want this, wait until you come back and do it yourself. Don't lay this burden on her."

Taylor gasped and began breathing again, air sawing past clenched teeth. Some of the darkness receded. Either he'd let go a little, or she was taking control. Rosalia pushed harder, striking Michael where it would matter most. No Guardian cared more about honoring free will—not just in humans, but in everyone.

"Michael, she's fighting you. You've taken her free will. Don't use her for this. She's not like us. She doesn't kill for revenge—only for defense or to protect. Don't make her into something else against her will."

Michael's hold on her broke. Taylor's sword vanished. She fell to her knees, retching and coughing.

Rosalia rushed to Deacon. "Are you all right?" She could see he was, but she needed to touch him. His blood slid beneath her fingers when she checked the wound on his neck, but the puncture had already healed. Sweat bathed his skin. "Why is it so hot in here?"

He didn't respond. She looked up at him. His eyes were fixed and staring, like the daysleep . . . or death.

Ice crept up her spine. "Deacon?"

His psychic scent suddenly battered against her shields. Deacon's . . . but not just a vampire's. Dark and strong, it slid over her mind like the scales of a snake. A nephil's psychic scent.

Deacon sat up.

"Deacon?"

He faced her, spoke. His empty eyes sparked terror in her heart, but the words he spoke were worse.

The demon language.

She grabbed his hand as he stood. With frightening ease, he flung her away. Rosalia smashed against the side of the car. Pain ripped though her arm. Glass shattered and rained down. Fighting against tears, Rosalia struggled to her knees. She watched him turn and head for the door.

For the sun.

She caught him halfway across the garage, tried to tackle him to the ground. It was like wrestling with a mountain. Wrapping her good arm around his waist, she tried to dig her heels in.

"Taylor, help me!"

Deacon spoke again, still in that unintelligible language, his voice frighteningly even. He trudged forward, dragging her along, Rosalia's weight nothing to his strength.

Taylor appeared beside them. "He's being called."

Horror gripped her. *"What?"*

But Rosalia understood, too well. Like the nephil whose blood he'd taken, now Deacon was being called to enforce the Rules. He couldn't resist the call—but he couldn't teleport; he couldn't fly. He could only walk out into the sun.

"A demon has broken the Rules," Taylor said, her voice harmonic and her eyes black, and Rosalia didn't know if she was translating the words Deacon was shouting, or if Michael was speaking now. "The demon must be slain."

Taylor reached out, touched them both. And teleported.

❧

Darkness surrounded him. Pain screamed through his mind. But the pain wasn't his. It was *hers*.

The darkness suddenly receded, though the world remained dim, as if viewed through smoked glass. Deacon recognized Rosalia's shadowy veil, her Gift enveloping him in darkness. He saw her, standing in front of him, a sword in her right hand, her left arm hanging limply at her side. The shadows beneath her boots stretched toward Deacon, bleeding into the veil around him. Beyond her, a nephil with giant black wings held a demon's head. The scent of the demon's blood pierced the veil, sparked Deacon's hunger.

Staggering, Deacon rose to his feet. It was so fucking hot here, bone-dry. Not anything like Rome. He smelled human blood—and saw a human male in a white robe, lying facedown on a yellow rock. His shadow stretched unnaturally long and thin toward the veil around Deacon. The sun was high overhead. In the distance, sand formed dunes against the horizon.

He could almost piece it together. A demon had killed the human. The nephil had been called to slay the demon. Deacon just couldn't figure out how the fuck he and Rosalia had gotten here. This sure as hell wasn't Europe.

The nephil's gaze touched Rosalia before moving past her to Deacon. His lips drew back from his fangs as he spoke. Deacon didn't recognize the words, but he felt the creature's rage and grief.

"He wants to know if you killed his brother," Taylor said from beside him. "Rosalia, he can sense the blood in Deacon. He *knows*."

"And if he tells the others, Deacon's as good as dead. They'll hunt him down." Her grim determination resonated through the shadows. "Get him out of here, Taylor."

The detective didn't move. Her expression tightened as the nephil looked at her and spoke again. With a chilling smile, he began to edge toward her. Two swords appeared in Taylor's hands—Deacon wondered if she realized that she'd called them in.

"What'd he say?" Rosalia slipped between them, staying beyond the reach of the nephil's weapon. "Taylor! What'd he say?"

"He said, 'My mother isn't here.'"

Dark humor slipped into Rosalia's voice. "But I am."

She rushed forward. Darkness snaked around her, thickening her form into an indistinct shape, creating shadow limbs, until it was impossible to determine the exact position of her hands and her head. Her sword flashed out of the darkness— the nephil barely managed to block it. He stumbled back against the slashing fury of her weapon before recovering and bearing down on her.

The shadows from the veil to her feet stretched thinner, thinner. The pain of her Gift was a volatile, living agony against Deacon's shields. He had to get closer. Had to help her.

He stepped through the veil, into the sun. Fire erupted from his skin, engulfing him in flames. Instinctively, he dove back into the shelter of her Gift, clenching his teeth against the flaring pain.

Stupid. *Stupid.* Of course she couldn't track both the nephil and him at the same time. He had to stay put.

Taylor joined her, weapons awkward in her hands. Though her eyes were pure black, she was slow—slower than she should be. Not just fighting the nephil, but fighting Michael, too. She dodged the nephil's blade, but not by virtue of her own skill. Each time, she was yanked back at the last moment like a puppet by her strings.

She was fighting Michael . . . but Michael was fighting to save her.

Deacon shouted, "Taylor! Let him have you!"

Rosalia stumbled to one knee, her legs swept out from under. The nephil raised his weapon. Deacon broke out of the shadows, into the dazzling day. Instantly, his exposed skin caught fire. He didn't give a fuck. If a vampire ball of fire barreling toward the nephil could make him hesitate for even a second—

Just before the sun blinded him, the creature fell.

Rosalia cried out his name. Pain engulfed him again, his and hers. He felt something cover his head and shoulders, smelled chlorine and earth and his own charred flesh.

Jesus Christ, it hurt like a son of a bitch. He breathed shallow, controlling it. "What happened?"

"Taylor cut off his head."

Deacon hadn't seen it—not just because his sight had burned out. When Michael had taken over, Taylor had just been that fast. Christ Jesus. He almost laughed. "Then I'm damn lucky she's been fighting him whenever he pops in to kill me."

"Yes."

He felt her shudder against him. "Rosie?"

"I just . . . pulled the bodies into my cache. A few Bedouins have seen." He felt her move, as if shifting around, being careful not to jar him. "Taylor! We have to go."

He heard footsteps, dimly saw movement beside him as Taylor laid her hand on his shoulder. Pain shot down his arm. Rosalia's Gift vanished from around him—then he had hard concrete beneath him instead of hot sand. Judging by the scent of oil and the sweltering heat, Taylor had teleported them back into Rosalia's garage.

The detective's blurry figure backed away from them until her shoulders met the wall. She slid down to the concrete floor, pulling her knees against her chest. Deacon felt Rosalia's breath against his shoulder, the press of her lips to his skin, and the prayer of thanks she whispered.

God wasn't the reason he hadn't fried out there. Rosie was. But before he could pull her into his arms, before he could thank her, she turned away.

"Taylor, don't go yet."

Deacon's sight had healed well enough to see the bleakness of Taylor's expression, her blue eyes shattered and her mouth in a tight line. Rosalia moved to her side, crouched down on her heels next to her.

"He'd have killed Deacon," she said softly. "He'd have killed me. And if Anaria and the other nephilim learned that we'd slain the nephil in Lorenzo's home, her revenge could have taken her to my family. Vin, Gemma, their baby. The Rules do not hold her back. You saved so many lives."

"I know." Taylor pushed her hands through her disheveled red hair. Frustration overwrote the bleakness. "He was going to kill me, too. They aren't completely loyal to Anaria. And she refuses to recognize what they are."

Rosalia had pegged the other Guardian well, Deacon realized. Taylor would only kill to protect or defend. And although slaying the nephil hadn't been easy for the new Doyen, this one wouldn't hang on her.

"This is the wrong time to ask you . . ." Rosalia trailed off. "No, perhaps it is the right time. This has been difficult, and it is a horrible thing that I'll ask of you—and only you could know if you can withstand more than this."

Taylor shook her head, laughing a little. "I already have. So lay it on me."

"Deacon and I have been working to destroy both Belial's demons and the nephilim. But although we have found a way to slay the nephilim, the demons are left to kill. If Michael was alive, I would ask him. I would do it myself, but I might fail. Anaria won't."

"You need Anaria?"

"I need you to teleport with her . . . but you would be bringing her into a nightmare. Into *any* mother's worst nightmare."

"Into a slaughter?"

"Of the nephilim, yes."

"Oh, fuck me." Taylor pushed her hands into her hair again. "And if I can't?"

"Then I'll return to my original plan."

I would do it myself, but I might fail.

Deacon's voice was rough. "Does that original plan involve you dying?"

"God willing, no."

In other words, Rosalia felt she had no choice but to try. And only by the grace of God would she succeed.

"No fucking way am I letting you do that. I'll chain you down first."

Rosalia glanced over her shoulder at him. Not upset by his threat or pulling her crossbow out again, as he'd half expected, but with a soft pleasure—as if surprised that anyone would care enough to forbid her from gambling with her life.

Christ, how that ripped at him.

"We all have to take risks, Deacon."

"You don't. Not this one."

"That's up to Taylor."

Deacon's anger battled with his fear. Anger was on the verge of winning when Taylor lifted her wry gaze to Rosalia's.

"For once, Michael's not pushing me one way or another—finally letting me decide." Her chest rose and fell on a heavy breath. "Would you want *me* to do it, or him?"

"That's also up to you. You're a Guardian, and so you slay demons. But this will be cold, Taylor, and you are new. Michael, Deacon, and I—we have seen enough demons that the burden of slaying them is a light one. And if you hesitated, if you struggled against him at all, you would be in danger." Rosalia held her gaze. "But there will also be humans to protect. After bringing Anaria, they would be your priority. I can't imagine that would be a struggle for either of you."

The detective managed a slight smile. "You'd be surprised how easy it is for me to find something to struggle against."

The warmth of Rosalia's answering smile transformed her features from beautiful to resplendent, hitting Deacon like a punch to the heart, but her smile faded quickly. "I will be taking steps that no Guardian should take, Taylor. You should hear what I have planned before your make your decision."

Taylor laughed. "You've already got me halfway there, just by being the one Guardian who gives a warning before throwing a girl into the deep end."

Rosalia outlined it all. From Theriault, to the first demon had slain in Budapest, all the way to how she saw the end. Christ. Laid all out, Deacon could see how many places it'd could have gone wrong—but hadn't, because she'd considered so many angles, understood the personalities of so many involved. And even though she still didn't know every detail of when or where or how the battle between the nephilim and demons would go down, Deacon believed she could pull it off.

Hell. She'd already pulled off one miracle. Every night, vampires had been greeting him with smiles and handshakes instead of disdain and hatred. If she could do that, then he could easily imagine everything she said would happen here.

Taylor asked few questions until Rosalia spoke of the humans she planned to bring in. Then her eyes became obsidian and her voice a dark, disapproving harmony. Taylor fought him, and Rosalia finished the outline of her plan with her hands shaking.

As she fell silent, waiting for Taylor's response, the phone began ringing in the War Room. Rosalia glanced upward, as if torn. Finally, she rose to answer it, leaving through the hole she'd smashed through the connecting wall. Both he and Taylor remained quiet, listening to her half of the conversation.

Rosalia returned and told them what they'd already heard. "St. Croix's waiting at the church, with possible names."

And Deacon wouldn't try to stop her from going this time. "You'll bring the surveillance equipment down so that I can listen in here?"

"Yes. If you'll turn the air-conditioning back on."

"Consider it done." Air-conditioning wouldn't do much now with a giant hole exposing the garage to the sun-warmed chamber on the opposite side of the wall, but what the hell. He'd burned enough for one day.

Smiling, Rosalia looked to Taylor. "Will you stay? If St. Croix bumbled around at Legion and revealed his interest in Malkvial, he might have brought thirty demons along without knowing it. If I need help, a teleporter would be a big one."

Taylor's eyes brightened. "Listening in on wire surveillance? Just like old times."

"If you enjoy that, you should come around more often," Rosalia said dryly, and turned to go. She paused when Taylor spoke up again.

"Rosalia? I can do this thing. I'll bring Anaria in."

Her eyes shining with sudden tears, Rosalia's face collapsed in that devastating way women had. Relief, pain, dread, joy—Deacon wasn't sure what lay behind it. But a man would have to be stronger than he was not to take that step toward her.

"Rosie."

She waited while he crossed the garage. When he lifted his hands to cup her face, brushed away the tears with his thumbs, she gave him a watery smile. "It looks like we're almost there, preacher."

Almost finished, and it felt like a hole in his chest. God, what he wouldn't give to ride along this way for a few more weeks. Hell, a few more years. But he'd be damned before he screwed this up, so that everything she'd done was for nothing.

"Then go get that demon bastard's name," he told her.

❧

Once again, Rosalia took the roundabout route to the church, using the opportunity to contact the Guardians in San Francisco. Someone would be sent to investigate why the demon had been in the desert when he'd killed the human—although, with the nephil and demon already slain, it was unlikely that much would be discovered. And from what she'd glimpsed of the scene before the nephil had arrived, she suspected the human's death had been an accident. The demon had been desperately trying to revive the man, his shock palpable.

She didn't mention to anyone at Special Investigations how Deacon had been called to the scene. The horror she'd felt when his eyes had emptied and the demon language spilled from his tongue hadn't completely abated. And she didn't know what it meant for him now. Would he be called *every* time a demon broke the Rules? She feared he would be. With so few demons on Earth, it wouldn't happen often—and the chances would be less after Belial's demons were gone—but even a small chance was too much.

He hadn't been released from that call until the nephil had slain the demon. Perhaps with time, he might gain control over his response—but he could only learn that control with experience. He couldn't afford to gain that experience during the daylight hours.

And he couldn't afford to run into one of the nephilim again. That creature had too easily recognized the blood in Deacon's veins. Deacon had become stronger through it, but that blood had come with dangerous strings.

Rosalia hadn't needed yet another reason to carry this plan through, but now she had one, as vital as the beat of her heart: Slaying the nephilim would cut those strings. After that, only Anaria would be left, and as long as she couldn't connect the slaughter of her children to the Guardians or vampires, she'd have no reason to retaliate.

Praying that Anaria wouldn't find out gave Rosalia another excellent reason to visit the church.

She arrived almost an hour after St. Croix's call—primarily to prevent him from pinpointing how far she'd had to travel, but also so that she did not seem in a rush to come at his bidding. She was certain that if he knew exactly how important the information he had was, St. Croix would try to claim power over her. And it was strange, but although he was providing her with something she needed, Rosalia didn't feel as though she owed him. Perhaps, after three hundred years, she'd overcome her tendency to overcompensate and bury herself in obligations.

Perhaps it was because St. Croix only served himself. She didn't like the idea of helping a man such as him—the type of man who, she suspected, would have kept on walking if he'd come across a woman being accosted in an alley. Unlike Deacon, who had helped—and who expected nothing in return.

And who now thought he deserved nothing.

She would fight until he saw differently. But no managing him. No manipulating him. Simply letting him see that he was worthy of her heart. That she *couldn't* love a man who didn't deserve her admiration, her respect, and her trust. He might reject them all. But in her life, she'd never taken any risks. She should with him.

Oh, God, if he felt anything in return, if there was any hope . . . it would be well worth the risk. So she just needed to open herself to him—and pray he would take her as she was.

❦

St. Croix was a patient man. He waited in the back pew, tapping the screen of his multifunction phone. He put it away when she approached.

He didn't bother to greet her. Without a word, he produced a folder from the satchel by his feet. Rosalia flipped through the pages, each complete with a name, financial and vital data, and a photograph.

He'd included Theriault. Good. He couldn't have known that she'd already ruled out that demon, but it said that St. Croix knew what to look for. She flipped to another page—

Baumhauer, a demon who she knew was loyal to Malkvial. The next one made her pause. Karl Geier, a marketing VP in the Munich office. She'd passed over him when his name had come up in Gemma's search. His unspectacular appearance and modest lifestyle hadn't fit the usual demon template.

Hiding in plain sight?

Of course. *Of course.* Oh, Lord but she was the blindest fool who'd ever walked the earth.

St. Croix said, "For Geier, I had to dig deeper. Baumhauer placed your boy Conley in the Prague offices, but it's rumored that Geier's the one who made the decision."

"That's not a marketing decision."

"No, it's not."

She closed the folder, feeling hopeful. She'd look deeper, set up surveillance . . . but from the right angle, Geier fit.

"Thank you," she told him.

His sharp smile said that he didn't want her gratitude—he wanted something else. "Tell me what you plan to do with those names."

"That isn't possible, Mr. St. Croix."

"No? I could make a single call to any one of those demons and expose you."

And she could point out that if he told them that he'd spoken to a woman in a church who'd claimed that her father was a demon, or that he and two vampires had trapped a nephil, they'd probably laugh at him. But she suspected that any type of challenge would force St. Croix to follow through on his threat. He wouldn't be able to help himself—he needed the upper hand.

If she let him have it, Rosalia could keep him where she needed him: out of her way. With St. Croix, that meant keeping him close.

"And if I said that I intended to destroy them all, would you be so determined to expose me? Though I am convinced your mother was one of Lucifer's demons, I cannot be certain. She might be with those I intend to have slain. Do you want to stop me?"

His reply was exactly what she'd expected. "I want to watch it."

"I can arrange that." Deliberately she looked him over, as if calculating his worth. "If you have any interest in moving up through Legion's ranks, there will be several positions opening soon. But you might want to dump them from your stock portfolio for the time being. Consumer confidence is going to take a dive."

His eyes gleamed. "Then I'll have people ready to move in and take over."

"Don't tip your hand."

He placed his palm over his heart and smiled, but his gaze was deadly cold. "Never."

CHAPTER 19

Taylor teleported them high above Amsterdam before disappearing again. Rosalia's wings caught air, her psychic scent spinning a little, and Deacon realized that he hadn't felt the disorientation that came with jumping from one location to another since he'd taken the nephil's blood.

He also realized that teleporting around like this was going to fuck Rosalia's plan up. "I'm getting around too easily. Warsaw last night. Sarajevo before that. Now Amsterdam. Vampires don't get around like this. Any demon with sense will know I have help."

She shook her head, her gaze searching the ground for their target's home. From this height, the canals running in concentric half circles around the city center looked like dark ribbons against the sparkling city lights.

"I've been purchasing tickets that are easily traceable back to you. If they're looking, they'll think you traveled by rail from Rotterdam in a shipping container today, and that you reached Rotterdam by plane from Warsaw last night."

Jesus Christ. "Have you had a trip planned out every night?"

"Of course."

Of course? He could hardly imagine creating a scheme as complex as the one she had going, and now he learned that she probably had more layers to it than he'd realized. How long had she been planning this?

It couldn't have been too long. She'd only discovered that her family had been slaughtered six months ago. How long had she grieved before deciding to act? Deacon's plan for revenge had been simple: tracking down Legion's executives and figuring out whether they were demons, then killing them. Yet he'd still had to spend three months selling everything off and practicing with his swords so that he could take on the demons. How much time had she put into hers? And how long had *he* been part of that plan?

But she must have been thinking of using him from the first, incorporating his strengths. Even now, he was realizing that she'd only sent him to communities where he was fluent in the local language.

He couldn't decide what astounded him more—that she'd considered that detail, or that she'd known exactly which languages he spoke.

"I'm heading down," she warned him an instant before her wings folded behind her back.

Her dive didn't seem so fast now with the nephil blood in him, his stomach no longer swooping up through the top of his head. He watched Rosalia, instead, the dark hair streaming out behind her, the narrowing of her eyes against the wind, the minute adjustments of her wings. She smiled as they landed in a narrow deserted alley, changing from her Zorro getup into a black dress that hugged her curves and skimmed her knees. Her shoes were just sparkly straps, with heels as high and as ridiculous as her boots. At some point in the past few days, she'd painted her toenails a soft pink.

He'd never been a toenail-painting kind of guy, but God

help him, he could imagine spending plenty of time at Rosalia's pretty feet.

As if noticing him staring at her shoes, she said, "We have a bit of a walk."

They always did, though Deacon had his doubts whether landing here or just outside the demon's door made any difference. "Does coming at a demon from a few miles away really mean he's less likely to pay attention?"

"No. It's for me." Her eyes warm and soft with quiet laughter, she slipped her hand into the crook of his elbow, her fingers wrapping around his biceps. "I've always enjoyed walking through different cities."

Hell. He should have realized that was her reason. Even the past couple of days, when they'd passed through the cities with barely a word between them, he'd seen how she'd looked at every building, watched every person, took in everything there was to see and smell and hear—especially any kind of plant or flower, as if she was considering whether to add them to her courtyard.

He enjoyed walking with her, too—but this wasn't exactly helping to keep distance between them, and making that break easier.

But, fuck it. Not that much time was left. He'd take what he could get, and having her holding on to him like this, her fingers gently squeezing his biceps like she appreciated his strength made him feel protective, maybe even necessary. It wasn't much of a purpose, watching over a woman who could wipe the floor with anyone in this city, but it felt damn good.

And for the past six months, every time he'd met anyone's eyes, every time someone had given him a second look, his impulse had been to tell them to fuck off. Now he was watching to see who looked at Rosalia—and judging by the way people's gazes skittered away and their shoulders hunched when they stopped staring at her and took a look at his face, his expression clearly told them to back off, instead.

With effort, he resisted baring his fangs at every man who glanced at her twice. He hadn't ever been possessive, but now he wanted to push Rosalia up against a building and fuck her, just so that anyone looking would know she was his.

So that Rosalia would know.

Christ. He had to stop this shit, and focus on why they were here—and how they'd gotten here. "How long did it take you to put this whole thing together?"

She paused for a moment to examine one of the trees shading the edge of the canal. He half expected songbirds to fly out and land on her shoulders, warbling a sweet little tune while they braided her hair, but she only touched a green leaf, rubbing it lightly between her fingers before answering him.

"I first thought of it the morning after the gala at the chateau. So, ten days ago."

And she'd come to him *only three days later*, with a good portion of her plan completely worked out. Which meant she hadn't had to take the time to research, to practice, to study personalities in order to place everyone where she wanted them. She'd already been carrying all of that around in her head.

Not just carrying it around—she'd known exactly how to use that information.

"Jesus Christ, Rosie." The whole freaking world should be thanking God that she was one of the good guys.

She misunderstood his response. The look she shot him was almost apologetic. "I know I should have taken a few more days, but I had to rush."

"Because of London."

"Yes. And I hope I didn't make any mistakes—any more than I already have. It helps that I've included as few people as possible, and that we have to carry it out on a short timeline. There are fewer variables, and less chance of something unexpected cropping up."

"Like Taylor?"

"And Anaria and St. Croix," she added. "I'd rather have proceeded without them."

He had to ask, "And without me?"

"Yes," she said baldly. "You're taking on such an enormous

risk. I would rather have the risk be all mine." She stopped and faced him. "But you are the key. In no conceivable scenario could a Guardian do this. We could bring together the vampires, perhaps. But the rest? Impossible."

Because he'd been ruined. He'd rather not go over that again, though. Nodding, he took her hand and wrapped her fingers around his arm before starting out again.

❦

The demon was already dead. The body lay near a white sofa, and the head had been propped up on the oversized television. Blood trailed down the flat screen and dripped to the zebra-skin rug. "The Blue Danube" played on the sound system, a surreal accompaniment to the scene.

Deacon crossed the room, crouching beside the body. He couldn't smell anything but demon blood. Guardians wouldn't have left an odor, but they wouldn't have come here—not without first telling Rosalia. A vampire's lingering scent would be detectable this close to the time of death. The body was still warm. Almost hot.

So the demons who'd done this probably hadn't gotten far. Maybe they hadn't left at all, but had been waiting for Deacon to head inside, leaving Rosalia alone.

Deacon hauled ass back outside, breathed his relief when he saw her standing in the shadows beneath a tree. Were they being watched? He pushed out with a strong psychic sweep, hard enough that Rosalia's eyes widened. Her mind felt human, with strong shields. He pushed harder, a hell of a lot harder, until he broke through and sensed the Guardian beneath. That was what he'd need to find a demon. He swept that out wider, searching over thousands of human minds.

A second later, he felt the dark, scaly slide of a demon's psyche. It answered with a psychic probe that tried to pierce Deacon's shields. A slight taunt echoed beneath it, the message clear. *Come find me.*

It wasn't hard to guess where to go. That taunt originated in the same direction as the vampire community's club.

He told Rosie what'd been left in the demon's home. "Someone knew I was coming," he finished.

She frowned. "I didn't expect him to make this move."

"Malkvial?" he guessed. And killing one of Theriault's demons was a bonus.

Her brow creased, and she stared up into his eyes, but not looking at him. He could almost feel her mind working as she tried to fathom a demon's.

"If he just wanted to kill you, he could have waited here. Is he trying to make a bigger statement by doing it in front of vampires?" She shook her head, talking her way through it. "No. No, that would make a statement to the vampires, but it says to other demons, 'Deacon's dangerous and he's stepping on my toes.' You're not, though. You're doing him a favor. All of Theriault's demons look like fools now. For God's sake, they've been slain by a *vampire*."

Deacon grinned. She'd said that like a demon might, as if a vampire was a piece of shit that a demon had to scrape off his heel.

"Maybe he's delivering a message?" Putting the vampire back in his place. "Though he could have done that here, too."

Her eyes cleared, hardened. "That's it. He's testing your resolve. You're killing demons, but you're taking them by surprise. Now he'll see if you run—because if you do, he'll paint you as a coward and a failure, and drive *that* home with another message."

"By killing the vampires here?"

"That would be perfect, wouldn't it? 'Deacon's arrogance destroyed another community.' So if you confront the demon waiting for you, he delivers his message—probably by slaying you and making you pay for your arrogance. But if you run, he delivers another message to his demons and to every vampire community: Deacon is a coward. Either way, he wins."

"So how does this fit into your plan if I have to kill him?"

"Oh, *Malkvial* isn't waiting for you. He's challenging you, but he wouldn't want to give the impression to any other demons that you're important enough to bother with himself."

"I have to kill the messenger," Deacon realized.

"Yes." She laughed softly, shaking her head. "Demons can be clever, as Malkvial seems to be, but they are rarely original. The only time they surprise me is when love enters the mix. But it isn't here."

Deacon's gaze searched her face. She laughed, but worry and a touch of panic whistled through her psychic scent, a cold wind past a jagged cliff.

And he could have told her that she was wrong: Love *was* here.

But he had to push it away.

❧

Rosalia hadn't expected this. She'd imagined many other scenarios, but not this particular one.

Deacon could handle this, no doubt. But it served as a reminder of how much could go wrong, how quickly everything could fall apart. One missed step. One wrong move. The dreaded possibilities rushed in on her without cease, spinning through her mind. Like falling from the sky, unable to form her wings.

"You all right?"

She had to be. They'd almost reached the club. "Yes."

He wasn't convinced. His gaze searched her face. "You're scared. You've been worried since we left the demon's place."

"I'm not *scared*." Her pride stinging, she frowned at him. "Not of this demon. Just . . ."

"You don't like not being in control. Or letting someone else dictate events."

He saw her so well. Knowing how he disliked her maneuverings, she wasn't sure if that pleased her or not.

"Trust me. I'll pull it off." He grinned, and her heart flipped over. "Then you've got to fix your inner control freak. Just let go."

"I can't."

His grin turned wicked, showing plenty of fang. "You did in my bed."

She had to smile. So she had, and loved it. And she trusted him to carry this through now, just as she had then. But— "If everything goes out of control there, no one dies."

"I came damn close a couple of times, princess."

A laugh burst from her, but she couldn't make it last. She'd come close, too—but not for several days. Barely touching, rarely talking, never kissing. She hated it. But today had been better, giving her hope that they could take another step forward.

She glanced up at Deacon, but he was no longer smiling. He stared ahead, his jaw set.

"You hear that?"

Only the puttering of motorboats on the canals, voices and appliances and televisions within the residences. Listening close, she looked toward the club, a tall, narrow building topped with steep gables. No lights shone through the windows. All was quiet. She didn't dare try a psychic probe to find out why.

And she hoped to God that the silence didn't mean they'd been too late.

But his senses were different, she remembered—stronger now. "What are you picking up?"

"Vampires, blocking their minds. At least, they're trying to. Their fear screams."

Anger wound up inside her, hot and hard.

He glanced at her. "They're pissed, too."

"Good." Fear without anger too often led to subservience. If they got the chance, Rosalia suspected these vampires might fight.

No one met them at the entrance. The heavy wooden door opened easily, and they passed into a large foyer, empty but for the paintings that filled the walls. Pastel landscapes, bold modern pieces, religious scenes that dated back to the Renaissance era, they all shared one feature: the sun. Rising and setting in shades of orange and pink, or high and brilliant in its full glory.

"I've never been able to decide whether Stefan put these up

as a welcome or a warning," Deacon said. Though his voice was casual, Rosalia had never seen him as focused.

Listening for sounds deeper within the club. Waiting to see if the demon came for him.

Rosalia adopted the same easy tone. "Perhaps he does neither, but uses them to gauge a visitor's personality. A cynical or suspicious vampire sees the sun that destroys him; an amiable and hopeful one sees a generous gift from their host, a room bursting with beauty and memory."

And though she said "perhaps," Rosalia knew it for certain. A strong and thoughtful vampire, and a good friend of Tomás Lakatos, Stefan had come to Amsterdam from Budapest ten years before. He'd renovated this building, formerly a small hotel, into a club and boardinghouse for both community members and visitors, with his own suite on the top level, and in the basement, a reinforced chamber designed to keep out demons. In the public areas, he'd created meeting spaces much like those in Budapest, with billiards and game tables, surrounding everyone with warm woods, soft lighting, and comfort.

Deacon pointed to the double doors leading to the community's meeting room, formerly the hotel's dining room and kitchen. Yes, Rosalia heard it, too—hearts thundering, and a small moan, almost like a whimper, as if someone was holding back a scream through clenched teeth.

Deacon drew one of the short swords from the harness beneath his jacket, approaching the meeting room. "I told Stefan that since he'd included one of Eva's paintings, it showed he had damn good taste. What do you think he made of that?"

That Deacon was incredibly loyal to those he loved. But she said, "That you were only pleased that Eva had sold the work because you depended on her money. And that she was your sugar mama."

He choked back a laugh, but was still grinning when he opened the door. The effect was exactly what she'd hoped—the vampires saw confidence, and the demon saw a cocky male that needed to be put down.

And though the vampires crowded into a three-deep circle around the room had been shielding too well for Rosalia to sense their fear, now she felt their hope, rising like warm air. They parted, giving Deacon a clear path to the demon.

In the center of the darkened room, the demon stood in his natural form, a grotesque combination of goat, snake, bat, and man. Leathery wings stretched over a skeletal frame. Black horns curled back from his forehead. Red scales gleamed over bulging muscle. His taloned hands were empty of weapons—he didn't need them. At his feet, Stefan lay on his stomach, his cheek against the polished wood floor and facing the door. With backward-jointed knees, the demon lifted his split-hoofed foot onto Stefan's head, applying enough pressure that the vampire's face distorted with pain. The demon's threat was clear: one wrong move, and he'd crush Stefan's skull.

As threats went, it was a poor one. Painful and gory, certainly—but it wouldn't kill the vampire. When Deacon destroyed this demon, Malkvial wouldn't be losing a particularly clever ally.

And Malkvial must have known what he'd sent.

Rosalia's gaze searched the vampires' faces as Deacon steered her to the left. She recognized all the vampires, except for two standing near the doors. Not blocking the exit, but just close enough for the vampires here to realize that they wouldn't make it through.

Not vampires at all, she thought. Demons, shape-shifted.

But probably not here to kill Deacon. Malkvial had sent a challenge, testing the vampire. What good would that be if the messenger was killed and no one reported the results to him?

Deacon pushed her toward the line of vampires. "You all watch over her. If one hair is harmed, you'll pray for the sun."

The vampires nodded. Cool hands welcomed her in, urging her behind them. Good. Their protection made her seem weaker than anything else could have. The demon barely looked at her.

Everyone was looking at Deacon, who came to a stop less than ten feet from the demon. "You're wasting my time."

"Am I?" His leg flexed, and Stefan's skull cracked. Blood gushed from his nose.

Around her, the vampires sucked in breath. From the circle at the left side of the room, Stefan's lover, Gilles, screamed and tried to leap toward the demon. Two others caught the auburn-haired vampire, dragged him back into the circle. The demon glanced at the male, his pleasure at Gilles's distress evident, before returning his attention to Deacon.

"A complete waste of time." Deacon absently tapped the side of his blade against his leg, as if the demon concerned him not at all. "See, I've come across a demon like you before. He got off on pain, too."

That description pleased the demon. He grinned. "I do love it so."

"Except Caym only beat up on those weaker than him, and he couldn't take any pain himself. I think you're like that, too. The second I cut into him, he started screaming."

That was a lie. Deacon hadn't given Caym time to scream.

But it was effective, sparking the demon's anger. Rosalia smiled. Anger could act as fuel in a battle, but didn't help thought—and this demon needed all the help he could get.

"And he was dumb as a brick," Deacon added. "He always had to be told what to do, where to go, who to kill."

The demon didn't like that much, either. His grin had vanished, replaced by a sneer. He opened his mouth, but Deacon didn't give him a chance to speak.

"So, you're of no use to me. You don't have the brains to pull off what I have in mind. But run back home and tell Malkvial that I have a proposition for him, and that I'll expect he's got brains enough to find me tomorrow at midnight. And I won't waste *his* time."

"I'm not a vampire's messenger boy."

"All right. You're not a messenger boy. You will *be* the message, instead." Deacon's voice hardened. "And you'll tell Malkvial this: We vampires won't be fucked with. We won't be your pawns. And when you crush our head, two will rise up in its place. In this case, it'll be me and Gilles." Deacon flipped his sword around, holding it by the blade and swinging it toward the circle of vampires. "So come on up, Gilles. We'll send this message together."

Deacon tossed the weapon in a slow high arc toward the other vampire. The demon looked to the side, his gaze following the path of the sword. Deacon whipped out his second blade from the sheath beneath his jacket.

Dumb as a brick.

The demon's head fell that heavily, too, thudding to the floor beside Stefan.

When the cheers erupted, Rosalia was already pushing through the vampires. She sprinted to the center of the room. As Deacon turned, she leapt up and flung her arms around his neck. Pressing her mouth to his ear, she breathed, "Two by the door."

Holding her at the waist, Deacon swung around. "Run back to Munich," he called out. "If he finds me at midnight tomorrow, we'll negotiate."

She watched them slip through the door. "They're going."

He looked down at her. His gaze focused on her lips, and Rosalia's heart began to race. The arm around her waist tightened, lifting her to his mouth. Then the vampires were on them, jostling Rosalia hard from behind, celebrating, hugging Deacon, shouting—and forgetting their strength. A human shouldn't be in the middle of this.

"Deacon." She pulled away. "I'll wait by the exit."

She turned at the wrong time. A shorter vampire coming in for an embrace whacked her forehead against Rosalia's mouth instead. Pain sliced her bottom lip. She tasted—*smelled*—her Guardian blood.

Oh, no no *no*. Not in a room full of vampires.

"Oops!" The vampire laughed, finished the embrace, and danced away.

The vampire hadn't noticed the difference. She couldn't have known how Guardian blood smelled. Or that Rosalia's cut was going to heal, very quickly. But others might notice.

Deacon did.

He swung her back against him. She saw his fangs slice his tongue. His thumb gently pulled down her bottom lip.

"I'll heal you up."

And cover the scent. His head lowered. She rose up to meet him. Just like a kiss.

God, she wanted him to kiss her so much.

He licked across the wound. Pleasure flashed through her body—deep, more than a kiss. A vampire's ecstasy at the taste of blood, echoed back through her veins. Deacon stiffened, his big body going utterly still.

His bloodlust flared hot against her shields. The cheers went silent as the vampires all felt it—as they all realized what it meant.

He'd had a taste of her blood. The bloodlust wouldn't let him stop until he'd quenched his thirst, and even if she ran, he'd come after her.

Deacon flung himself away from her, vampires scrambling from his path. He slammed his back against a wall, holding on, trembling. Every muscle in his body straining, he fought the bloodlust.

He was going to lose.

Deacon met her eyes. "Run."

"It won't matter—"

He reached out, yanked the nearest body next to him, shoved the vampire to Rosalia. *"Get her out of here!"*

The young female obeyed, scooping Rosalia up. She hesitated, seemed uncertain where to go.

There was nowhere this vampire *could* go. Deacon was faster and stronger. And he would be coming after her soon.

"The safe room," Rosalia reminded her.

The vampire's eyes brightened. Carrying Rosalia cradled against her chest, she turned and sprinted to the stairs. Rosalia's teeth rattled with every step. The chamber door was unlocked. The vampire swung it open, several inches of solid steel. The interior was bare, utilitarian. Vampires didn't need much. Two supply cabinets stood side by side, a porcelain sink hung from the wall, and a shower filled one corner. The rest lay empty.

As soon as the vampire set her down on the concrete floor, Rosalia told her, "Go."

"Are you sure—"

"I'm sure."

The vampire left—probably more fascinated by the idea of watching outside as Deacon tried to slam his way in until morning than waiting here.

Rosalia closed the door, silencing the noise from upstairs. The chamber had been soundproofed. Perfect. No one would know anything about what went on in here. They'd assume. They wouldn't know.

She vanished her shoes and stood beside the entrance with her back against the wall, waiting. Her heart pounding.

Deacon wouldn't have control. And if she lost hers, he couldn't promise to catch her. But she wouldn't need him to. If she gave him her blood, he would feel every emotion that she'd tried to contain. He would hear the thoughts she hadn't spoken. He would know what she'd hidden from him. She'd only needed the control so that she wouldn't expose herself to him, give everything away.

But now . . . if he wanted it, she'd let him take it.

A moment later, Deacon slammed into the door, the impact shuddering through the reinforced wall, his bloodlust burning against her mind. Then the handle turned—and she felt his shock and despair beneath the hunger. He'd thought it would be locked.

As if she would ever let him batter himself bloody on a door she could open.

He burst through, his momentum carrying him past her position against the wall. She swung the door closed again. Locked it.

Deacon spun around, his eyes narrowing on her, predator sighting his prey. Growling her name, he launched forward, reaching for her.

Grabbing his wrist, Rosalia stepped to the side, yanking

him around and slamming her foot against the back of his knee. He fell, and she shoved him facedown to the floor. Holding his wrists, she pulled upward, pinning him with his arms crossed behind his back, and his spine arched away from her, denying him the leverage to rise. She straddled his waist as he tried to break his wrists free, the veins in his arms standing out against straining muscle. Heavens, he was strong. But she had the advantage here.

A part of him must have realized it. Though his body fought, relief rose through his psychic scent.

"I can hold you," she told him. "But the bloodlust won't fade. And when dawn comes, you won't fall asleep. Until you've been sated with blood, you'll keep trying to come after me."

He shook his head, his chest heaving. *"Run,"* he grated, his voice unrecognizable. *"Get out."*

"Why? I want this. I've hated every single day we haven't touched." Her hands clenched as he roared, his body bucking as he tried to throw her off. She rode it through, and said as he quieted, "But if you don't want me or my blood, I can hold you like this all night, until the vampires fall asleep. By then I'll have thought up a way out of this. Or I can feed you here and prevent you from taking me. It's up to you, but either way, my blood—everything I am—is yours."

"Hurt you."

"You can't. I'm not a delicate princess." She felt him fighting through the haze of bloodlust, his body shaking. She bent and kissed his clenched fist. His hand opened, reaching for her. "My blood or me. Just tell me which you want."

His head fell forward. Self-hatred and longing battled through his psychic scent. Through clenched teeth, he ground out his answer.

"You."

She let him go.

CHAPTER 20

Free, Deacon exploded upward. She slipped from his back, landing hard on the floor, rolling onto her side as if to get up. *Don't let her get away.* Unable to stop the growl tearing from his chest, he caught her slim ankle, dragging her toward him, using his knees to shove her thighs wide. Her fingers clenched on his shoulders and she tilted her head back, exposing her neck.

Mine.

He drove up, fangs spearing into her throat. Rosalia gasped, arching beneath him. Her hot blood poured over his tongue, a frantic rush of sound and light, driving away thought.

His fingers found her wet. Ripping aside her panties, he thrust deep, her silken heat clenching around him, sucking him in. She cried out, and her hips rose to meet his. Her strong blood rushed through his body, her thoughts lost beneath the psychic roar, a raging storm of emotion and thought that battered his mind about, leaving him only pieces of her to see.

Hidden from him. He needed more.

Drawing hard from her vein, he pounded into her, and she took every inch. Her nails shredded his shirt, his back, then scraped downward to dig into his ass, urging him to take more. So sweet and warm and welcoming. She'd given him this, given him the hero's welcome upstairs, where he'd been met with hope instead of the hatred he'd deserved since a demon had poured Eva's and Petra's ashes to the floor.

He didn't fucking deserve any of what she'd given.

Rosalia's legs tightened around his waist, her arms around his neck, repeating his name with every rough pistoning of his hips. Her voice had become hoarse as if she'd been crying out for too long, with pleasure and grief and loss. Maybe they were just his. He couldn't sense her emotions, the blood an overwhelming roar in his head. Then Rosalia shuddered and stiffened, arching back with a primal scream, liquid warmth flooding her sheath. Her orgasm slammed through her veins, into his mouth. The bloodlust shattered and he came hard, jetting into her, thick as the blood that heated him and he could only think that he was cold, cold.

Then sense returned, and the cold became worse.

He'd hurt her. He *had* to have hurt her. Guardians were tough, but not impervious, and he'd used the softness of her throat and pussy like a ravaging beast. His cock still throbbed deep inside her. He lifted his head, began to pull out.

Rosalia caught his face, and he froze. For a long moment, her warm brown eyes stared right through him. He wanted to get up, to take care of her, but *she* wanted him here and so he didn't move. Then, gently, she kissed his forehead. His lips. His jaw. Every kiss felt like a healing balm, soothing his grief, easing his guilt.

Dear God, how he loved her. And he'd have given anything in the world to deserve the comfort she offered so easily.

Her fingers threaded into his hair, and when he looked at her again, tears stood in her eyes. "I miss my friends, too. And nothing we do ever seems to make up for not saving them."

Christ. He hadn't felt anything from her, just that raging psychic storm. But she'd either sensed his emotions or seen them in him, and guessed exactly where they'd come from.

She was always seeing him at his lowest.

Deacon pushed off of her, roughly shoving his erect cock into his trousers as he stood. When he looked down, he had to force himself not to close his eyes. Blood dried in thin trails down her elegant neck. The pale skin between her thighs had been rubbed raw and pink, still wet with his seed. Her ankle was bruised, ringed with impression of his fingers. He felt sick. He'd *bruised* a woman—a Guardian, hard enough that it hadn't yet healed.

She started to get up.

"Stay put, Rosie." He waited until she stopped moving before heading over to the sink. He gripped the sides for a moment, grateful there was no mirror above it. He wasn't sure he could face himself now. And he didn't want to know what Rosalia saw when she looked at him.

He zipped up and wetted a hand towel before returning to her side. She'd come up on her elbows, her gaze searching his face as he wiped her neck. He turned the towel to the clean side before tending to her sex. The rawness had already faded—the bruises gone, too.

And he'd never felt so much like shit.

❧

Where did managing end and love begin?

Rosalia didn't know. She was ashamed she didn't know. And she'd wanted to help him, but she'd promised not to manage him—and so the only thing she'd been able to do was offer her support and strength.

It had been strange and wonderful to be cared for in return, even if that care had only been prompted by guilt.

Now he was far away from her. They'd returned to the abbey early, and he was plowing his way down the length of the pool. But she knew too well that he couldn't outrace anything. Just churn through the water, turn, and try to punish himself against the same length again. Great for thinking. Not so great for escape.

From the walkway overlooking the courtyard, she watched his heavy powerful strokes, as if he could beat himself against the water until it wore him down. A human would be feeling it. A vampire, even one as strong as Deacon, might break a sweat. But he wouldn't tire. He wouldn't ache afterward. He wouldn't feel any pain—and so it wouldn't be a solace for him.

Sighing, she braced her hands against the balcony rail. He hadn't said a single word about what he'd felt or heard as he'd taken her blood, and his silence weighed on her heart like a stone.

She couldn't bear dragging it out. Perhaps it was best just to address it now.

Spreading her wings, she glided to the end of the pool and sat on the edge, slipping her legs into the warm water. Her wingtips bent against the marble tiles behind her, the stone against her feathers gently rough, like the scrape of a cat's tongue. She watched Deacon approach in the next lane.

Instead of turning and kicking off the wall again, he surfaced beside her legs. Standing in the chest-deep water, he braced his hands on the edge of the pool, water streaming over his heavy shoulders and chest.

He pushed the water out of his eyes. "Everything all right, princess?"

"I came down to ask the same thing. But I know it is not. And that you—"

"Don't want to talk about it."

All right, she'd come back to it. "Okay. So I haven't come to discuss that with you, but instead to let you know how my chat with Camille went."

"From what I heard of it out here, your call wasn't so much a chat as a list of things you want her to do."

She marveled. The War Room door had been closed. His hearing was truly spectacular now. "Yes, well. She likes to be useful."

That drew a short smile from him.

She continued. "She'll have the community elders gathered at her apartment the day after tomorrow."

"And I'll be convincing them to go along with me."

"Yes."

After he convinced Malkvial. He'd make a deal with a demon, and the next day, he'd convince every major European vampire community to join in with him.

"That's what I thought," Deacon said, sounding resigned.

Her heart ached. "Where would you like to meet with Malkvial?"

"You don't already have somewhere picked out?"

She shook her head. "You are the one taking the risk. It should be somewhere you know the territory, where you have the advantage of location. And where I can set up surveillance ahead of time."

He closed his eyes, as if trying to picture such a place. "I got rid of my property in Prague. The community meeting places, the house. I wouldn't want to make a deal with a demon there, anyway."

No, not in the house where his partners had been killed by the last demon he'd made an agreement with.

"Should it be a public location?"

"No," Rosalia said. "He'll want to test you. He'll interpret your caution not as prudent, but as a weakness."

He opened his eyes. "I'm going to end up hurting tomorrow, aren't I?"

She nodded. "Yes."

His jaw clenched. "What about the church I found you in six months ago? Your brother owned it. Is anyone using it now?"

On the northern side of the city, Lorenzo's church was situated near his house and had once served the vampire community. Beneath it lay the catacombs where she'd run into Belial's demons. The same lieutenant who'd directed Caym had been the one to drive the spike through her head, leaving her helpless to the nosferatu.

She didn't remember any moment of those eighteen months beneath that church. She still hadn't been able to bring herself to enter it again.

"I own it now," Rosalia said.

He must have read her hesitation. He shook his head. "It's too close. It might lead him to you."

She considered that. "Actually, he'd probably assume that you would choose a city that was only loosely connected to you. He wouldn't think to search for you here, afterward."

"And it fits." His face was grim. "I led Irena there and betrayed her for a demon. Now I'll make a deal with another."

"Making a deal, *with the intent to kill him*," she stressed.

"Betraying a demon instead of a friend is that much different, then? It just erases what came before? I don't think it works like that." His gaze narrowed on her. "And what of you? That's not a good place for you."

"Considering what you have to do, I can make it through." She studied his shuttered expression. "I know how much I'm asking, Deacon—"

"Do you?"

"Yes. Considering the list of humans I'm compiling, I know exactly."

Bringing in the nephilim hinged on breaking the Rules— something that Rosalia would set up. Something no Guardian should do. Fail or succeed . . . what Guardian could respect her afterward?

He was watching her face. "Maybe you do know."

But she'd known all along. Deacon, when he'd agreed to help her, had thought he'd only be slaying demons. The burden of that was a heavy one.

"*Now* you don't look all right." He leaned back, as if to get a better look at her. "Confess, princess."

"Confess what? I'm surprised you don't know. Didn't you hear everything in me?"

"No. Just sound. A *lot* of sound." The corners of his mouth deepened in a smile. "Apparently the nephil blood shouts over everything else."

So he hadn't known? She'd taken that risk, opening herself, but he hadn't heard it.

She wanted to laugh. And she supposed it served her right, for trying to take the easy way out—letting him into her blood instead of telling him. *Showing* him.

"I haven't done this the right way," she confessed. "I'm terrified of a mistake, but the biggest one has not been in execution of this plan, but how I have approached you—and kept so many things from you. I do not know if I can make up for it."

His sigh was a heavy thing. "I didn't sign up for this, no. But I'm here now, and no one's got a knife to my throat. So just stuff your making up for it."

"I just need to—"

"Overcompensate?"

She flicked water at him with the tip of her left wing. "I need to say thank you. And I'm sorry that I didn't tell you from the beginning about Malkvial."

"How about you say thank you when it's over, and I've pulled off this thing with Malkvial." He looked up at her; then his gaze slid over her wings. "Jesus Christ, Rosie. Considering what happened tonight . . . some apologies just got turned around. I should be begging for forgiveness at your feet."

"I could have locked the door," she said.

"Why didn't—"

She cupped his cheek, and he broke off. He tore his gaze from her wings. Leaning sideways, she pressed her mouth to his, a soft graze.

"I wanted you," she said. "And I'm not above taking advantage of an opportunity to have you."

His brows drew together and his mouth opened—she kissed him again, slowly this time, sliding over until he stood between her legs.

His hands came up, curled around her waist. Water slapped the tiles.

Rosalia slipped into the pool. Heavy warmth enveloped her wingtips, saturated by water. Deacon pressed her up against the pool wall, his hands sliding up her back, and pausing when he encountered the base of her wings.

She shivered as his fingers traveled up the soft, downy feathers covering the frame.

His mouth hovered over hers. "That feels good?"

"Yes." Not like the almost unbearable caress between her legs, but like a stroke over sensitive skin. "I'm not used to anyone touching them."

His hand skimmed down her spine. She shivered in the same way, and he laughed quietly.

"What part of you is used to a touch?"

She didn't think it mattered. Even if he did this a thousand times, she would still enjoy it. And enjoy the feel of her hands on him even more.

The thick muscles of his chest, the broadness of his back. She found nothing that she didn't love to explore. The sensitive spot on his side that made him jerk away from her fingers, warning her not to tickle. The ridge of a scar, the coarseness of the hair that drew her fingers down. He kissed her deep when she found him hard beneath his shorts. She wrapped her hands around his length and freed him.

She couldn't resist. "Does that feel good?"

He laughed. Wrapping his arm around her waist, he braced his opposite hand on the lip of the pool, and with a powerful surge, lifted them out.

Her wings drooped, heavy and sodden. She shook them. Her skin prickled in the heat. The soaked silk of her dress clung to her breasts, her stomach, her thighs.

Deacon led her to a patch of lawn, laying back on the grass and pulling her down over him. Straddling his hard stomach, she leaned forward to kiss him, stroking his fangs with her tongue, relishing his groan of need.

"I want these in me, too," she told him.

His body went rigid, and he stared up at her with intense, heated eyes. "You liked that?"

"Yes." Oh, God, yes. When she'd imagined the pleasure

of him taking her blood, she hadn't come close to the reality. "And I don't have anything to hide."

Still, she trembled as he cupped the back of her neck and scraped his teeth against her throat.

"You're shaking," he murmured.

"I want it again. That doesn't mean I'm not nervous."

"Afraid of losing control? Trust me."

"Always."

A faint pain stung her throat. The flat of his tongue swirled against her skin. Pleasure twisted through her, tightening her nipples, a subtle ache in her clitoris that demanded friction. She rocked her hips, grinding her sex against his ridged abdomen.

Breathing hard, Deacon gripped her thighs. "You taste so good, Rosie."

"More," she said. "Everywhere."

He followed a scrape against her collarbone with another lick. She arched back, panting, her blood turning molten, heated through to her core. Beneath her, his stomach flexed as he rose onto one elbow. He offered a wicked smile before he ripped the front of her dress.

His tongue circled her nipple. Rosalia tensed, her anticipation so high it was almost a pain inside her. She worked her hips, pushing her sex in a slick burn over his stomach. He drew the tip of her breast between his lips. Rosalia moaned. His mouth felt so good, he didn't even need to—

The soft bite came as a surprise. She jolted forward, but he caught her. Then he began to suck and she could only feel him, in her blood, hard behind her, beneath her. Crying out, she cupped the back of his head and held him close, her eyes shining across his dark hair.

She wanted to weep. She wanted to laugh. But she only gasped, her face tilted to the night sky, euphoria moving through her, expanding through her veins and tightening her skin, a frenzy of sensation. His left hand slipped between her legs. His fingers parted her, pressed in, began a slow, slow rhythm until she came apart, her body stiffening, her wings flaring out and shaking.

Deacon released her breast, returning for a soothing lick before laying back in the grass and staring up at her. Something in his eyes hardened. "I shouldn't even be touching you, princess."

Rosalia thought she would die if he didn't. Leaning forward, she kissed him. "You should. You truly should."

His laugh held a harsh note. "I'm too damned needy to disagree."

If he needed, then she'd give. She kissed him again, a sweet, wet tangle of lips and teeth and tongue. When she broke away, his eyes were a stormy green, his face harsh with his arousal. He came up on his elbows again.

"Scoot back, Rosie."

It was a guttural command. She slid down his stomach until the steel weight of his erection bumped up against her backside. His breath hissed in as she lifted her hips and reached back for him, dragging his length through her slick folds.

"Take me deep now. Until you can't take any more."

Her wings whispered over the grass as she rose up to her knees. He was hard and big in her hand, soft skin over steely flesh, his pulse beating headily against her palm. Positioning the thick head at her entrance, she slowly pressed down. Her body stretched, accepted.

His teeth clenched. His hands fisted in the grass. "I took you so hard, Rosie."

She remembered how hard, the excitement of being caught up in that maelstrom. Her sex responded in a liquid rush, and she moaned. "Yes."

"I hurt you."

Her eyes flew open. She said fiercely, "No."

She pushed down, taking him to the root. His beautiful body arched, muscles straining as his hips lifted. Bracing her hands against his wide chest, she rode him, watching his face, the clamping of his jaw, the way his mouth fell open and he dragged in air before groaning her name. His hands roamed

her thighs, her belly, pinching her nipples and then hauling
her down to kiss him, hard and deep. His biceps bunched beneath her fingers and he threw his head back, but she followed
him, sensing how close he was, wanting to be there with him.
She drew his mouth to her neck.

He reared up to sitting, shoving her down over his thick
length even as he sank his fangs in her throat. Rosalia cried out
as the orgasm fried her senses, as he pulsed deep inside her.

Panting, she let her wings fall forward, wrapping around
them. Deacon rolled her over so they lay on their sides, tucking her against him, her wings spread out on the grass behind
her. Her head still spinning, Rosalia looked up at the stars.
She used to dream of flying up there. Using her Gift, and seeing how far the darkness went.

Now she was just glad to be here.

"I love you," she said.

He didn't say anything. She lifted her head. His eyes were
closed, his mouth in a firm line, bracketed as if fighting off
pain.

"Deacon?"

"Don't, Rosie. Just— Don't."

"Don't what? Don't love you?"

Too late for that.

He rocked to his feet, leaving her on the ground. Stalking
over to the pool, he swept up his clothes. Anger heated his
psychic scent.

Anger? If he'd been unsettled, she could understand. She'd
said it out of nowhere. They had a lot to deal with. Her timing
might be atrocious. But *angry*?

She stood, formed her black shirt and pants. "Deacon?"

He jerked on his trousers. "Don't manage me, Rosie."

"*Manage* you?"

"Yeah. You've got me where you want me, like I said. No
knife at my throat. I'm in. You don't need this to persuade
me."

She looked at the grass, flattened by the weight of their
bodies. "You think I did this so that you'd meet Malkvial?"

"Not the sex. We're good together that way. But *love*, Rosie? You overplayed your hand."

"I didn't *play* anything."

"But I'm supposed to believe you love me?" He turned his back to her again and scooped up his shirt. "I get it, all right? We're lying there, and you took advantage of an opportunity. You think I have doubts, that I might pull out. So you give me another reason to help you. But I'm telling you I won't pull out before seeing this all the way through."

She never thought he would. "I know. You wouldn't. But you think the only reason that I love you is because you're helping me?"

He whirled on her. "Don't fuck with me like that. Look, just leave it out."

Suddenly, she understood. He didn't doubt her reason for loving him, but just that she loved him at all.

"Why is it so hard to believe?"

"Look at you, Rosie. Fucking look at you! Look at everything you are." He wadded up his shirt as if trying to control his anger. "So don't feed me that line of shit. It's not necessary. I'm in."

She had to try again. She couldn't give up. "That's not why—"

"*I'm in!*"

She stared at him. Rejection, complete and utter, radiated from his posture, from his mind. A gaping hole opened in her chest. She scrambled to breathe, to think, for anything that would get her through the next few seconds.

And found what there'd always been: a reason to keep going. She had millions of them.

"All right," she managed to whisper. "We'll proceed as planned."

"Yeah, we'll proceed as fucking planned." Bitterness roughened his voice. He turned away, as if he couldn't bear to see her face. "No declaration necessary."

CHAPTER 21

For several hours, Rosalia had too much to do to dwell on Deacon's rejection. Arranging his travel, installing the surveillance in the church, and testing it. But as soon as she had everything in place, her mind couldn't let it go. Her gardens needed tending, but she couldn't stand the sun—she felt too exposed, when all she wanted to do was cocoon herself in darkness and figure out what had gone wrong.

She shut herself in the kitchen, instead, closing it up and turning off the lights—and tried to keep busy.

Only her hands were. And so she wondered, over and over: What could she have said that he might have believed her? Perhaps he didn't trust her words, not after learning about Malkvial and Camille. But hadn't she *shown* him? Yet he looked at everything she'd done and had seen something else. Had seen manipulation and lies. *That* was what he believed of her. Not love.

And as long as he believed it, nothing she said or did would matter. She deserved better than that. She deserved someone who would trust her.

It was easy to think so, anyway. She had a harder time convincing her heart.

She heard footsteps approaching, wished it was Deacon to come and tell her that he'd reconsidered his knee-jerk reaction. But the sun was high, and she could hear him in his garage, and the steps were as familiar to Rosalia as her own heartbeat.

Vin came into the kitchen. He flipped on the light, then frowned. "Mama?"

Rosalia looked at the dishes lining the counters. It would take ages to eat all of this. "I hope Gemma's with you."

"She's at the dressmaker's. I'm taking pictures for the caterers so they have a layout of the kitchen and courtyard." He held up a camera. "Unless all of this is you trying to get a head start on the cooking?"

Rosalia frowned, uncertain she'd understood. "You plan to have the reception here?"

"Where else?"

"But Gemma—"

"Is all right during the day, or when she has someone with her."

She took that in, then looked around at the mess she'd made. Breathing deep, she tried to steady herself, afraid she'd burst into tears.

Vin came around the preparation island, peeking under a lid. "Ah, your gnocchi. You can't make it right, but you never give up." He snagged a bite. "A bit heavy, hmm?"

"Yes."

He turned, leaning back against the edge of the counter. "Mama, I've got a shoulder right here."

Now her eyes did fill. That was exactly what she'd said to him as a young boy, so many times. "You shouldn't have to comfort your mama."

He smiled. "If you became human again, I've got about ten years on you. So, this is not only a *should*, but you *will* listen to me and let me make it better."

Laughing, she let him draw her in. But the moment she laid her cheek on his shoulder the tears did come, silent and hot. There was no question of love here. No matter their problems, that was never in doubt.

Had she thought it would always be so simple?

She pulled back, wiping her cheeks. "You do not know how much I appreciate you being here. Thank you."

"I've got to make up for ten years of being a punk, right?"

"No. You had your reasons."

"Yeah, but only half of them were good ones." He snatched a thin slice of prosciutto from a platter. "After Pasquale, I wasn't thinking straight."

Who would have been? "He was your best friend."

He shook his head. "There was that. But I also saw what Sofia went through. No one should have to bury her child—or her grandchild. And I thought: That's going to be Mama in sixty years."

The words were a fist into her heart. She dragged in a deep breath, his face wavering in front of her.

"You see, Mama? You can barely think about it. So part of me thought, It's just easier to take off now."

Oh, God. "You stupid boy. I should slap you."

Laughing, he pushed his hand through his hair. "I know. I get it now. I have Gemma, the baby—and it won't matter when I lose them. God forbid. It'd rip my heart out. Today, tomorrow, a thousand years. It doesn't matter when."

"No, it doesn't."

He sighed. "And all my life, I've never seen you torn up like you were the other night. So it hit me that maybe I'd screwed everything up, leaving. And I'll be the one burying you. Not *once* in my life have I thought that before. And I didn't take it well."

And when facing grief or fear, he became defensive and angry—and he'd lashed out at her. "Gemma has given me a lecture about not saying, 'It's okay.' And so I won't."

It felt good, not saying it.

"Good. Because it's not okay, but I'll do better." He regarded her for a moment, and she felt his grief again—but it was lighter, softer. "Pasquale loved you, you know."

She'd known. "It was a boy's crush."

"A strong one. He wanted to be with you forever."

So he'd attempted to become a Guardian. She saw better why Vin had blamed her. And saw that he didn't blame her now.

"I wish he could have been," she said.

"Well, if he hadn't done that, he'd have become a vampire. And he'd still be gone." His gaze never leaving hers, Vin took her hands in his, squeezed gently. "Gemma and I won't turn. We love you; we never want to hurt you—but we won't turn."

She closed her eyes. "I know."

"I didn't want you to have the hope that someday we'd transform. We won't."

He was right. This was a hope easier to live without, to know that it could not happen. Opening her eyes, she hugged him close. Then she fixed his collar and his hair. His quiet laugh warmed everything in her.

He took another piece of ham, said casually, "St. Croix was outside my building last night."

Her heart jumped. *"What?"*

Though she hadn't moved, he put his hand out as if to stop her. "Don't take off and look for him. He said, 'Tell her that as long as we have the same goals, I won't use this.' "

She put her hands to her head, dragging her hair back. *Oh, God.* Where had she made a mistake? Where had the link been?

Guessing the direction of her thoughts, Vin said, "He's been watching the church."

Damn. *Damn.* Neither Gemma nor Vin regularly attended, but they'd been going in to see Father Wojcinski. St. Croix would have recognized him from Lorenzo's house. "Are you feeling safe? Should I make arrangements for you both to leave?"

He gave her a chiding look. "I own a security firm, and I grew up knowing how to keep demons and vampires out of my home. A human is nothing. I think he just wanted to even things out."

"He threatened you?" She would kill him.

"No. And it didn't even feel like a threat toward *me*. He just wanted you to know that he had something on you." His gaze searched her face, and his brows drew together. "He's not Lorenzo, Mama. You don't have to almost-kill him on my behalf. *Especially* since he's human."

She sighed and patted his cheek to reassure him that she wouldn't. "Oh, Vin. When did you become the levelheaded one?"

❧

When she came into the garage, Deacon immediately recognized Rosalia the Guardian. Her black cloak swirled around her boots, and she outlined the steps she'd taken, buying a plane ticket to Rome so that Malkvial would be pointed right to him, and installing surveillance.

All business. She didn't speak a word of love. The sadness in her eyes almost broke him.

He'd made himself turn away the night before. Whatever he saw in her, it was just wishful thinking. And it had hurt like hell when he'd realized that her declaration couldn't be true, no matter how bad he wanted it, now matter how his heart latched onto it as reality. He'd backed away, faced it logically. And here she was—the woman who didn't give up on anything— carrying on as if she hadn't ever said she loved him.

He wished he knew what was going on in her. Even drinking her blood hadn't shown him. And although he'd hated reading the thoughts of strangers, he'd have given anything to know hers.

Would have given anything if her heart could be his.

But Guardians didn't give their hearts to men like him. Rosalia didn't. He knew the paragon she'd loved before. Maybe she'd transferred some feelings, but they weren't for him. The only reason she'd chosen Deacon for her big plan was because he'd been ruined. And over and over, she'd seen him at his worst. Seen him beaten, seen him fail. And tonight, he'd sink again.

For her.

He knew it was for her. If it was just revenge, he could have it now. With the nephil blood in him, he wouldn't just be slaying demons until they killed him. No, he could take them all now. One by one, and it might take time, but he could destroy them all and come out the other end. He could take off now and avenge his people.

That wouldn't stop the nephilim, and the communities would still be in danger from them—but a part of Deacon still thought, Fuck 'em all. Every vampire in Europe had turned their back on him. He didn't owe them anything. He didn't want to be a hero to them. He didn't care what they thought of him making a deal with a demon—*another* deal.

It mattered to him, though. Even as a trick, the thought of bargaining with Malkvial grated at his soul, churned like vomit in his gut.

But it was important to her. And if he did this, and she pulled off this whole plan, when he left the sadness wouldn't be there. He had two goals now: Avenge his people. Take the sadness from her eyes.

So he was here, listening as Rosalia told him how Malkvial would fuck him up.

"He'll test you, primarily to see if you have someone waiting to save you."

"Like a Guardian?"

"Yes." Her gentle gaze saw right through him. No wonder she'd known a declaration of love would affect him. "You'll have to take it."

"You think I can't?"

"I know you can take anything a demon has to dish out, but your instinct will be to fight back." She lifted his hands, her thumb smoothing over the scars on his knuckles. "Don't. He can't lead the demons if there's an unanswered challenge—so if he feels challenged, he'll *need* to put you in your place . . . no matter what you're offering him."

Too bad he *did* know his place. "What if you're wrong?"

"You'll be able to tell. When he's testing you, he'll wind up to it, try to scare you and pull in any cavalry you've got waiting. If he wants to kill you, it'll be fast."

"Then I fight back?"

"Yes. If it's fast, defend yourself as best you can."

As best he could? "Can I beat him?"

"I don't know. Malkvial didn't get where he is just by laying low and being smart. There's a reason the strong ones haven't challenged him. They must know he's not just brains."

That made a hell of a lot of sense. "All right. So, try not to fight him."

"Yes. And Deacon—" She caught his face between her hands, staring solemnly into his eyes. "There *will* be a cavalry. If you feel the threat is genuine, just say my name. I'll be there. I swear to God on high, I will be there."

"Of course you would. If Malkvial killed me, your plan is shot anyway."

Her mouth hardened. Her hands fell away. Ashamed, he caught them, holding her wrists while he struggled.

She'd been right about his need to fight back—and that had been against the blow she'd landed last night. But she hadn't deserved it. She might not love him, but she was a Guardian. And she was Rosalia. Her heart wasn't his, but it was a good heart. Too big, maybe. He wouldn't have loved her so much if it wasn't.

And if she vowed to be there, she wouldn't give a thought to her plan—her only thought would be of saving him. Deacon believed that, down to his soul.

"I'm a bastard. A sorry one."

She gave a sharp nod. "Apology accepted."

She didn't say it was all right. He was glad for that.

But not so glad when she pulled her wrists from his, and walked away.

❧

Still in his human form as Karl Geier—nondescript and blond, wearing a navy polo shirt and khaki pants—Malkvial arrived an hour early. From an empty apartment in a building flanking the old church, Rosalia watched him leap over the surrounding fence and break the lock at the front doors. Hidden in the high arched ceiling, her cameras covered almost every angle of the interior. Paint-dotted plastic sheets covered the pews, left over from an incomplete renovation. Dust had settled thick on the floor, the altar, on every stained window sill. She'd been careful not to disturb any of it while installing her equipment, but she still held her breath as he crouched to examine the floor, as he quickly checked the chambers beyond the sanctuary.

She checked the time. Taylor had teleported Deacon to Naples after sunset, where he'd caught a flight back to Rome. He'd be arriving within a few minutes.

If he came. He could take off now, if he wanted to. He had strength enough to complete his revenge, and he thought she'd manipulated him at every turn. And this bargain with Malkvial . . . There were very few things that would be worse for him.

"You look awful, Rosa." With a sigh, Gemma sat next to her. "Is it this place?"

"It is many things."

Gemma smiled, watching Malkvial open the door in a chamber floor, revealing the stairwell that led to the underground chambers. "I looked for you here. Not in the catacombs. But I came here."

Rosalia didn't glance at the screen showing the ossuary, where her blood still stained a stone column. "Thank you."

"The others said, *If she hasn't come back, she's not going to.* I looked, though. At Lorenzo's house—"

"You did *what*?" Rosalia burst out, and heard the male echo from her son.

Disbelieving, Rosalia shared a look with Vin. She didn't know who was more horrified.

Gemma rolled her eyes. "I went during the day."

"He could have smelled you. Tracked you back to the abbey."

"I was careful. You'd threatened him; then you went missing. So I had to check. I'd hoped to find you in the dungeon."

Rosalia shook her head, trying to calm herself. She touched Gemma's hand. "You looked for me. That means more than I can say. Thank you." She drew in a deep breath. "I can't remember any of it. But I remember waking up and learning that everyone was gone. For a while I thought you were, too— and I was ready to recruit Vin and track you down."

"You knew where I was after I left?" He glanced at her face. "Okay. That was a stupid question. And I damn well would have looked for both of you."

She'd never doubted that. Smiling, she glanced back at the monitors, and tensed when Deacon appeared. He walked into the church. No hesitation. No bravado. Just confidence.

Malkvial waited, casually sitting back against the altar rail, his hands braced on the top. They stared at each other down the aisle. Rosalia's heart pounded, terror suddenly digging in. She'd have given anything to do this part.

Gemma leaned forward in her chair, her hands clasped in front of her mouth. "What's the script going to be?"

"I didn't give him one." She saw the younger woman's shock, and the same on Vin's face. They both knew she hadn't given up control like that before. She explained, "Deacon has his reasons for doing this. I can't just give him mine. Malkvial would never believe it."

Vin stared at her. "You wouldn't even let *me* go in without a script. And you had vampires with you for a hundred years who still had line-by-line points to make whenever they faced someone."

"Deacon knows what we need to do," she said. "But he can decide how to get there."

She fell silent as Malkvial suddenly smiled. Vin's hands came over her shoulders, and he circled his thumbs over taut muscles.

"Hello, Mr. Deacon."

Deacon's expression didn't change, but Rosalia knew that bothered him. Caym and Rael's lieutenant had called him *Mr.* Deacon.

"Hello, Karl," he replied.

Good. Oh, good. Deacon positioned himself above the demon without a single challenge. Thank God for St. Croix.

"I understand you have a proposal for me." Malkvial spread his hands. "This *is* a place for making vows. Not for leading friends astray."

The demon went straight for Deacon's heart, reminding him of how he'd betrayed Irena. Deacon responded as if it hadn't touched him. "I have a mutually beneficial business proposition. But we aren't friends. Let's not pretend."

Malkvial straightened up, ripping off a piece of the wooden altar rail as he stood. Rosalia hugged herself, and Vin's hands tightened on her shoulders. Not just massaging now. Reminding her to stay in place.

"Yes, let's not pretend." The demon approached Deacon with slow, measured steps down the aisle. The sharp point of the splintered wood dragged along the stone floor. "Let's not pretend that a vampire can be of any use to me."

" 'And the blood that heals shall bring the dead unto judgment, and the judged unto Heaven.' " Deacon quoted from the prophecy that predicted that vampire blood would help destroy the nephilim, and send Belial to the throne in Hell. "It sounds to me that we're of some use."

"Your *blood*. Not you, Mr. Deacon." Malkvial's eyes flashed crimson. "And let us not pretend to forget that you have shed the blood of my demons."

"I brought my proposal to Valcotes, but he wouldn't deliver the message. And the message you tried to deliver in Amsterdam wasn't what I needed to hear."

The demon stopped halfway down the aisle. "And what would you like to hear, Mr. Deacon?"

"That you'll leave the vampire communities alone."

Malkvial struck quickly. Leaping forward, he swung the rail's blunt end at Deacon's head, knocking him sideways. Flipping the wood around, he shoved the point through Deacon's gut.

Oh, God. It should have been her. Rosalia clasped her hands together, shaking furiously. *It should have been her.*

"I can't see that happening, Mr. Deacon." Malkvial twisted the rail and stepped back. "I'll kill all of you, just like this."

Deacon gripped the wooden shaft impaled through his stomach. He yanked out the rail, tossed it aside. "I'll trade the nephilim. Our lives, for the nephilim."

Laughing, Malkvial shook his head. Turning around, he grabbed the end of a pew and swung. The heavy bench hit Deacon in the chest, smashing him back against the stone wall.

Vin was shouting her name. Dimly, Rosalia realized she was dragging him toward the door.

"Mama! You've got to let him finish, or it's all for nothing!"

"Let me go." She couldn't bear this. If she had to Fall, so be it. "It should be me."

He shook her, hard. "You can't always protect us. Do you *believe* he can do this?"

God, she did. And knowing he could was the only thing that might keep her there. She nodded.

"Then *let* him."

❧

She'd warned him. Thank God she'd warned him. He didn't have to prepare himself for the pain—just fight to keep from smashing the demon's head in.

His stomach burned. He pushed his fist into the hole in his gut, holding everything in until it healed. The pew had taken out a couple of his ribs. Every breath shot dizzying pain through his lungs. But he could talk.

"The Guardians are no help to us. Cities of vampires are dead thanks to the nephilim, and the Guardians haven't stopped them. And London is next." Deacon paused to spit out his blood, to take another agonizing breath. "I don't give a fuck about the prophecy or what Belial hopes to take in Hell. I just want to save our asses."

"How do you propose to do that?"

"You break the Rules. You bring those fuckers in one at a time. You kill them."

Malkvial blinked. He stared at Deacon for a long moment, before his lips widened in a smile that chilled his blood. "Thank you for the suggestion, Mr. Deacon. We absolutely don't need vampires for that."

A sword appeared in his hand—to kill him this time, Deacon realized. Faster than the demon, he sidestepped to avoid the swinging blade and said, "You need us to get the humans."

Malkvial paused with his sword raised over his head.

"If your demons break the Rules by snatching people, they'll come at you, one on one, and you're dead." Deacon backed up a step to give himself more room if Malkvial jumped him again. "You've got to bring the humans in—somewhere closed up, so that when the nephil comes he's got nowhere to run. And you better have enough of your friends with you that you can take them all out, even if the nephilim manage to kill some of you. And you know they will."

His eyes narrowing to crimson slits, Malkvial remained silent. Considering it, Deacon realized. He pushed home, calling in every asshole thing that might appeal to a demon.

"Hey, I'll be doing you a favor. You pull this off in front of Belial's other demons, and the lieutenant position is yours, and Theriault is stuck with his thumb up his ass. And all we vampires want in exchange is to be left the hell alone."

"All of us, in a closed area?"

"However the fuck you want to do it. I'm just thinking that those nephilim are goddamn fast, and you don't want them to escape and go running to Mommy." Deacon shrugged. "I won't be the one trying to kill them. You choose the place. I'll meet you here in three days, one hour after sunset. You give me the location, and we'll have the humans there by dawn. Then we clear out. You do your thing."

Malkvial cocked his head. *"We?"*

"The vampires grabbing the humans." Deacon wiped his mouth again. The scent of blood around him was overpowering.

"My communities will be knee-deep in it, breaking the Rules to help you. Each community leader will deliver a human—and you can bet no one is running to the Guardians."

"You've thought this through."

Deacon's laugh was short and bitter. "I got fucked over once by a demon. Then I got fucked over again by Guardians. All I got out of that was a dead community. So, yeah, I've thought this through."

And pulled it all out of his ass.

The demon nodded. "You'll understand that I won't settle for a handshake, Mr. Deacon. I can't afford you betraying me. We'll seal this agreement with a bargain."

He hadn't made one with Caym; he'd just been beaten. And a bargain put his soul on the line, but he felt safer with one—it meant the demon would keep up his part.

"All right," he said. "Here's my part: My communities will bring the humans to the location you choose. After that, you let us live and forbid your demons from killing any of us."

Which didn't really mean anything. The bargain only prevented Malkvial himself from killing the vampires. With every other demon, all bets were off. He could have asked for Malkvial's protection, instead—but there was no way in hell Deacon could bring himself to do that.

If Rosalia's plan went through, all the demons would be dead, anyway.

Malkvial's eyes gleamed. Yeah, he knew he was getting a damn good deal. "And if they don't follow my direction?"

"Then I'm talking to the wrong demon." He let that sink in. "And the humans—no killing them. Slap 'em around, whatever. No killing."

"You ask a lot."

"Yeah, well, you kill them, the Guardians find out, and they'll be after our asses. They'll frown at vampires who push the Rules a little. But if we're connected to people dying, then they'll start hunting us down. We just want to be left alone, not always looking over our shoulders. And you being demons, I think you can come up with ways to have your fun."

"I think we can." If his smile hadn't reminded Deacon that demons were pure evil, then the glee in Malkvial's voice would have. "You have your bargain, Mr. Deacon."

❧

Two hours later, Taylor teleported him out of the catacombs, as arranged. If anyone had been watching the church, they'd assume they had just lost him.

He went straight to the kitchen, found the blood he needed in the refrigerator, pushed back behind a shitload of food. He took the glass out to the courtyard, and that was where Rosalia found him a few minutes later. She sat next to him, holding a rolled-up crêpe that smelled of cinnamon and sweet cream.

"You were brilliant," she said softly.

"I made a bargain with a demon. If I don't bring the vampires together and pull this off, I'll be freezing in Hell with Michael." He took a swig, feeling the electric flavor over his tongue, but no sound with it. "The irony is, if I'd had made a bargain with Caym, I could have said my people weren't to be touched. But I didn't think of it. Everything I knew about demons could be summed up with: If you enter into a bargain, you're totally fucked. But it would have saved my people. Even at the cost of my soul, it'd have been worth it."

She studied his face, silent, looking through him.

He took another drink, then said, "I wish you'd been there at the beginning, Rosie. I have no doubt you'd have seen a way out."

Her eyes glistened, her face crumpling, and she looked away. "I wish it, too."

"Better than being there at the end, anyway." By that time it had all gone to hell, and nothing could have pulled him out.

"I watched you slay Caym," she said. "It was a thousand times more satisfying than watching Michael slay my father."

He had to laugh. "So bloodthirsty, yet you look so sweet."

She smiled at him, then bit into her crêpe. Filling oozed

out the end, and she caught it with her fingers. He couldn't look away from her mouth as she licked it off.

"Apostle's fingers," she told him, her cheeks coloring. "I made *so* many. I've already given half away to the neighbors and to Father Wojcinski's church, but I'll still be eating them for days."

He laughed. Overcompensating for something, no doubt. "You can't save them for the wedding?"

"They won't keep." She grimaced a little. "And they aren't very good. I've never had a talent for cooking."

"But you keep trying?" he guessed.

"To the neighborhood's dismay, yes." She seemed to hesitate, then said, "I want you to know—I realize that you think the only reason I needed you to help me is that you're ruined. And it's true, that's why Malkvial believes you. But I have a hard time letting others do what I want done."

"No kidding."

She didn't smile. "I almost destroyed everything we'd accomplished so far. Even though I prepared myself, even though I knew he'd attack you, I almost went into the church."

He hadn't expected her to say that. "What stopped you?"

"Believing that you could pull it off. And I don't think that I could have sent anyone else in without believing I'd sent them to their death. I couldn't risk someone's life like that— and I'd have destroyed it all tonight. But I knew you'd convince him. And you did."

He couldn't respond. Her trust and her belief in him were humbling.

Now she smiled, a sad little curve of her mouth. "I know you don't see yourself as I do—but you risked everything, including your life, to save people you loved from a demon. The only difference in what you tried to do and the sacrifice I made to become a Guardian is that I was lucky enough to succeed."

That was a nice thought. But the line between a Guardian and Deacon wasn't so thin. "That 'only difference' was a whole lot of lives."

"Intentions have to count, don't they?" She looked out into the garden. "I'm about to ask you and other vampires to break the Rules. That's what demons do. They use others to break the Rules, so they don't have to. In this, it doesn't matter if I succeed or fail, because either way the humans will suffer for it. And so my intentions are the only thing that differentiates me from a demon."

He shook his head. "What else can you do, Rosie?"

He didn't expect a reply, but he should have known she'd already considered it—and had an answer.

"I could Fall, and be the human that the demons torment. I could Fall, and be the one who rounds up the other humans. I should punish myself afterward, and Fall for my part in it." She tilted her head back, looked up at the dark sky. "But I know I won't. Because as sorry as I am, I'd do it again if I thought I could save all of the humans and vampires that the nephilim intend to crush. And because I'm more useful to everyone as a Guardian."

"And *I* should have walked into the sun after my community was destroyed. I know I won't." As sorry as he was for everything that had happened, Deacon would have done it again if he thought he'd save his people. He smiled at her. "We're a pair of sorry bastards, aren't we?"

She laughed through her tears, and he wanted to crush her against him. Her hand found his. "Thank you, Deacon. For being here."

"I have good reasons to be here."

Her wistful smile tugged at his heart. "Tell me one."

Yes. He owed her that. But instead of saying it, he pulled her closer and kissed her. She kissed him back so sweetly, so fiercely, he could almost believe she needed him, that she loved him.

He called himself a fool. But realizing that within three days' time she *wouldn't* need him anymore, he carried her up to her room.

And he let himself believe, for a night.

CHAPTER 22

He didn't leave her bed until sunset. Taylor teleported him to Nice, where he boarded a chartered flight to Paris. He arrived at Yves and Camille's apartment shortly after midnight—and found that she had already done most of his work for him.

Rosalia had obviously fed her the lines. Camille spouted the same bullshit that Deacon had handed to Malkvial the night before, and although Camille must have wondered what the real game plan was, Deacon couldn't have detected it from the conviction of her arguments: The Guardians couldn't save them, Belial's demons had the best chance of destroying the nephilim, and Deacon's bargain with Malkvial would guarantee the vampires' safety afterward. She'd only needed to stress once that Deacon had risked his soul to make the bargain.

But Camille hadn't stopped there. She'd flown a dozen vampires in from London, and only the most heartless among the elders were able to declare to those twelve vampires that they didn't give a shit whether the nephilim massacred their city. And of the three that could say it, each deferred to Deacon when he reminded them that he'd saved their asses and destroyed the demons in their cities that week—and that it would take no effort at all to kill them, and make the decision himself.

He hadn't wanted to pull that crap, but he had no time for assholes who didn't give a fuck.

The loudest objection came when they learned of their obligation to procure a human—until Deacon passed around the files Rosalia had given him. One by one, the objections faded . . . and Deacon noted that some of the vampires suddenly looked eager, every trace of reluctance gone.

Rosalia had chosen their targets well.

By the time the vampires left, each taking a file and a list of instructions with them, Deacon was ready to return to Rome. Camille walked with him to the door, flipping through her human's profile.

"Everyone else was given the name of a human from their city," she said. "But I have a priest from Rome. Isn't that interesting?"

"He's included as a favor."

She arched her delicate brows. "To a friend of a friend?"

He had no idea if Camille knew John Wojcinski, but he wasn't naming names, anyway. "Something like that."

Camille nodded. "And it *would* be these kind of men," she murmured. "Murder is so often called the worst crime, but there can always be extenuating circumstances—and let us be truthful, and admit that some of those who are murdered deserve it. But to hunt a child, to abuse them in this manner . . . it's deliberate, predatory, and there's no question of its immorality or the child's innocence. There can never be an excuse."

He recognized those words. He'd said them to her once.

Glancing up, she interpreted his expression perfectly. "Yes, you've said that to me. But you were not the first I'd heard it from; that distinction belongs to the woman I called Mother. But is this something we can *all* live with?"

She was wondering whether Rosalia could, Deacon realized. Camille knew that this went against the moral fiber of every Guardian who'd ever earned her wings.

But so did letting demons and nephilim slaughter her friends.

"Yes," he told her. "We can all live with it."

♦

She hoped that she could live with herself for this.

As a cop, never in a million years would Taylor have considered bringing even someone as blind and as dangerous as Anaria into a scenario like Rosalia had described. But the rules were different here. And she wasn't a cop anymore.

From the tallest tower in the city, she looked out over Caelum. God, it was beautiful here—a shining marble disk on an endless sea. She'd never imagined anything like this realm, with its towers and domes and temples. Every stone seemed to sing to her, to recognize her presence. When she rested her palm at the edge of the tower's peak, the marble fit her hand, as if reshaping itself to her touch.

She didn't know if it sought her, or Michael.

But she could feel his touch now, rising up almost gently. She didn't trust that. Gentle . . . because he wanted something from her? Up until Rosalia talking to him, he hadn't had a problem taking it.

Her teeth clenched. Her eyes closed. "What the hell do you want from me?"

The memory came on her quickly, not a flash but deep inside, the cold morning air against her bronze skin—and more death. So much more death. But not of demons or nosferatu. The strong scent of human blood saturated the air. Warriors wearing breastplates of bronze and greaves protecting their shins lay near shields cleaved in half.

It had been a one-sided slaughter. All wearing the same colors, no opponents lay next to the fallen. It had been precise and methodic, each man killed with a single blow. It had been terrifying—many had run, but they hadn't been spared. The scattering of the bodies and their positions told her they'd been cut down as they'd fled . . . and so, so many had fled.

And there was Anaria, her sword bloodied, gazing up at Taylor with a soft, slightly disappointed smile, as if speaking to a child who continually failed to understand. Behind Anaria stood the Guardians who'd helped her massacre the human army.

When Anaria spoke, Taylor couldn't understand the words but their meaning was painfully clear.

"These wars they wage upon each other, it makes them like demons! They choose to throw away love and kindness in return for power and fear—and I will stop them before they destroy all of humanity, Michael. I vow to you."

She swore—and Michael knew what he would have to do. The agony of it crushed his heart, stole his speech; he was certain he would never breathe again. Certain he would never be able to bear it, or live with himself for the decision he had to make.

But if he did not, it wouldn't end. Anaria would save everyone from themselves until they were all dead.

"And she always needs an army to stand with her," Taylor said hoarsely. Her throat ached. Her heart ached, as it had been crushed along with Michael's when he'd ordered his sister's execution. "I suppose if you can bear that, then I bear this."

As if satisfied, he retreated into the screams that always lingered in the back of her head, and quieted them.

Taylor began to breathe again. She breathed until the presence of another Guardian drew her gaze up. Irena hovered above her, motionless but for the wings holding her aloft. The serpent tattoos winding around her arms seethed.

"You cow-fucking idiot."

Ah, shit. Khavi must have told her that Taylor had run into Anaria . . . several times.

"I really prefer goats. Or ducks. I would love to hear you say that." But although they'd become friends in the past several months, Taylor could only push the Guardians' leader so far. When Irena's eyes narrowed and began to glow a poison-ous green, she added, "She obviously didn't harm me. And if you're going to worry, add in a couple more: I attacked Rosa-lia, almost killed Deacon, and helped them slay one of the ne-philim. I think I've also slain a demon and a nosferatu, but I'm not certain. And there might be more that I can't remember."

Irena's mouth dropped open, and she landed in a crouch on the tower. "Michael?"

"He asks for permission now. Kind of."

The other Guardian closed her eyes. "Rosalia and Deacon?"

"All right." If you could ignore the heartache and longing wailing from both. "Just getting ready to kill a shitload of nephilim and demons."

"Already?" Irena blinked her eyes open. "I do not know Rosalia, though Alejandro speaks well of her. Do you think what she has done is feasible? Will she and Deacon be safe?"

Taylor hoped so. "Yes."

"Will *you* be safe?"

"I don't think Anaria will hurt me, no."

Irena seemed to choke. "Anaria is involved?"

"Not really by her choice."

The other woman stared at her. Probably debating whether to chain her somewhere, then realizing that Taylor could just teleport out. Finally, she let out a heavy breath.

"You are certain you wish to do this?"

She hadn't been a little while ago. Now she was. "Yes."

"Then take this."

A steel spear appeared in Irena's palms, and Taylor had to stop herself from lurching forward, snatching it from the Guardian's hands. Power hummed from that weapon, which could pierce stone like a blade into water. The heat of a drag-on's blood drew her . . . and drew Michael.

"I cannot make it flame," Irena said as Taylor reached for it. "Michael told me that only those with the dragon blood in their veins can."

So she wouldn't, either. That was all right. As soon as her fingers closed around the shaft, she could feel the power of it burning through her. When she vanished the spear into her cache, she still sensed it, a quiet, warm hum through her mind.

Irena smiled slightly, but the worry in her eyes hadn't disappeared. "When the time comes, I would like to be there with you, Rosalia, and Deacon—if it does not upset her plan. I want you all to have someone watching your backs."

And that right there was why Taylor liked this woman so much. *Watching each other's backs.* The Guardians weren't always so different from the family and job she'd known.

"If it doesn't upset her plan, I'll bring you in," Taylor promised.

❧

Just before dawn, Rosalia forced herself out of bed, and dressed while Deacon laughed at her heavy sigh. She'd have preferred to stay with him, but she'd spent the whole of the previous day—and a good portion of the night—neglecting everything else. She pushed him off into the shower and then to his garage before heading out into her courtyard. The garden needed tending before Gemma's wedding planner arrived for a tour of the abbey.

But when the knock came, she found Irena waiting there instead, dressed not in her outlandish longstockings and rabbit-fur mantle, but simple gray trousers and a long-sleeved shirt.

Rosalia did not even know what to think. Guardians could change their appearance, yet she'd never seen Irena as anything but the barbarian.

But Irena herself wasn't wholly unexpected. The Guardian had known Rosalia intended to use Deacon, but she hadn't told Irena that included his bargaining with a demon.

"I came quietly," Irena said, her Italian marked by a strong Slavic accent. "You will not be revealed by me."

Rosalia nodded, stepping back and inviting her in. She led the Guardian to the courtyard, and when Irena spoke again, she heard the movement from within the garage stop, as if Deacon had frozen in place, holding his breath.

"From the San Francisco community leader, I have heard that Deacon has made a bargain with Malkvial."

Unsurprised that word had already reached the States, Rosalia answered, "Yes."

"You requested him to do this?"

"Yes."

Irena's green eyes suddenly glowed with anger. "You dare risk his soul?"

Rosalia blinked. She'd expected to be called a fool for trusting him, which she would have turned about very carefully. But Irena was concerned for him?

Michael, it seemed, had left them in good hands when he'd passed the reins over to Irena.

"No," she said. "His part of the bargain is not so difficult. He only has to stay alive to fulfill it. And I will fight to my last breath to see that he does. We need but two days more."

"This was of his free will?"

Rosalia gestured toward the sparring chamber, where curtains covered the ragged hole in the wall that opened to the garage. "Ask him."

Irena nodded. "I will return after sundown—"

"No. Ask him *now*."

She led Irena to the garage, where even the air-conditioning couldn't win against the heat coming through from the sparring chamber. Deacon waited for them, his big body tense.

Irena didn't hesitate. She called in her kukri knives, prepared to strike. "You have been fooled by a demon!"

"No, Irena. Feel him," she said, remembering her own reaction. "Look how he sweats in the heat."

Deacon held out his hand. Irena touched his skin, then looked up into his face. Astonishment dropped her mouth open.

"The nosferatu blood did this?"

"No. This was nephilim blood," Deacon said quietly. He

watched Irena carefully, braced as if for a blow—facing his friend for the first time since she'd discovered the truth of his bargain with Caym.

"You killed a nephil?"

"I helped." Deacon wiped his brow, glanced at Rosalia. He was clearly uncomfortable—a discomfort probably made worse by her witnessing it. To her relief, she heard a knock at the door.

"You'll excuse me." She lifted her hands, backing toward the sparring chamber. "A cohabitating couple becomes desperate, so marriage simply can't wait."

❧

Rosalia's parting joke creased Irena's brow. She glanced at Deacon. "You are marrying her?"

A bark of laughter escaped him. He shook his head.

"She smells like you."

That shut him up. What would the Guardians think of Rosalia, fraternizing with him? He knew she was afraid of their reaction regarding the humans. Would being with him, even temporarily, make their reaction harsher?

But Irena didn't seem interested in dwelling on it. Moving to the center of the room, she stood, her gaze skimming over the worktable, the GTL, the engine parts scattered on the benches and concrete floor. Her Gift lay in metal. He'd seen some of the amazing sculptures she'd created with barely a thought. And here he was, sweating over an old car. It probably seemed piddling to her.

When she looked back at him, however, he didn't read any judgment in her expression—and Irena never bothered to hide her feelings, for good or bad.

He should say something. He didn't even know how to begin. There were too many dead. But of those living, Irena was the one he'd hurt the most.

But as usual, Irena did not hesitate to speak her mind. "You've chosen this bargain?"

"I have."

"Of your free will?"

When he nodded, she frowned. Her eyes narrowed and she regarded him more closely, her expression turning thoughtful. "I was certain that when I saw you, I would want to kill you."

Was that why she'd come during the day? "I expected to have taken a few punches by now," he admitted.

And he *would* have taken them. Hell, he'd like her to do it now. It wouldn't make the past go away—but maybe it could make them both feel better.

Maybe. Or nothing could.

"Yes." She looked at her hands, as if imagining them as fists. "And I thought I would be angry. But instead I am sorry. I am sorry it came to this. I am sorry that you felt I couldn't help you. And I am sorry that even though you didn't come to me, I still couldn't save them—any of them. My friends and yours."

"Me, too," he said quietly.

"I wondered if I should kill you then. When we found you."

With a spike through his head, after he'd slain Caym—after Caym had poured out the remains of his partners onto the floor. "Then, I would have welcomed it."

"I know. It is why I did not kill you. I thought it would be worse for you to live."

Was it? He would have agreed, once. This burden would always be his to bear.

But *worse* would have been having no opportunity to pay for his mistakes. No opportunity to grieve. No opportunity to avenge them.

"You should have killed me, then, if you meant to punish me. This is better." More painful than death—even more painful than he could imagine Hell—but better.

She understood. Though coarse and blunt, she wasn't slow. "So you are still fighting."

"I'm trying."

"That is good." She made a vague movement with her

hand. "I have something for you. After Rosalia took you from Prague, I gathered this. It did not seem right to leave them on the floor. I thought I might spread their ashes in Caelum, but you would know of a better place for them."

He came closer, and his chest tightened, filled with an unbearable ache. She clutched an iron box between her hands. The lid of the box had been sculpted like a bed, and atop it, Eva sat laughing and clutching the sheet to her chest; Petra, lying on her stomach, looked over her shoulder with the sardonically amused expression that she'd aimed at Deacon more times than he could count.

"I liked them. I didn't know them well," Irena said. "But this is how I remember them best. I came to you, do you remember? I dragged you from your bed to take you hunting. And they laughed."

"I remember," he said hoarsely, taking the sculpted urn.

The iron was heavy. He cradled it in his arm, tracing his fingers over their likenesses. So perfect. Petra's metal hair moved on a breath, each curl a delicate wire. Eva's mouth almost soft, her fangs sharp.

He could not even voice his gratitude.

Irena must have known. She walked past him, giving him a few moments.

When he turned, she was surveying a fender, running her hand over the dented steel. "I have never understood why you do this. New automobiles are faster and better, and you have money to buy them."

He didn't point out that he had money because he'd restored those cars. And he didn't know why himself. He'd always loved it. He liked reclaiming their beautiful design and function.

"Newer vehicles are faster. I don't know about better."

She smiled and picked up the fender. With her Gift, she could smooth it, strengthen it. He didn't think he'd enjoy restoring anything if the work was that easy.

"And I like to work with my hands," he added.

"I do, too. But only when it is a new weapon."

"You don't fix them?"

"My habit is to throw damaged weapons away." She replaced the fender and looked over at him. "I have been trying to change that habit. With the proper effort, a repaired weapon can also be strong. Perhaps a friendship can be, too."

Christ. That fast, he choked up. He'd never expected this from her. Had never hoped for it, had never even considered it a possibility.

"I'm willing to make that effort," he managed.

"So am I." She came to him, ran her fingers over the urn cradled in his arm. "We have both lost too many friends, Deacon. Let us not lose another."

Speechless again, he could only watch her walk across the garage. She paused at the makeshift curtain they'd put on the wall, and turned.

"I should warn you that I'm more likely to punch friends."

"I know." Her fists had knocked out his teeth more than once.

She narrowed her eyes, as if considering. "Maybe next time."

She passed through the wall, the curtain falling into place behind her. A moment later, he heard Rosalia's soft inquiry, and Irena's accented reply. He moved toward the curtain, and lifted heavy fabric aside.

In the painful flare of light, he saw Irena's fiery hair, the brilliant color in the blooming garden, and Rosalia's beautiful smile before his vision went dark.

A single moment that had been worth ten thousand times the pain.

❧

As soon as Rosalia saw the wedding planner out, she returned to the garage. Immediately she spied the iron urn on the worktable, recognized the beauty of the sculpture on the lid. Tears stung her eyes. Irena was not always the barbarian, and Rosalia could not imagine how much that meant to him.

Deacon slid out from beneath the car on a little rolling plank, and she crouched beside him.

"We have tonight free, if you know of a place you'd like to take them."

Shaking his head, he sat up. His voice was raw. All of him was raw, she realized, down to the core.

"I'll do it after we've finished. And instead of making a promise to them, I can tell them it was done."

"Okay. Are you all right?"

"Yeah, princess. Just fine."

He wasn't, but she let him have the lie. She touched his shoulder as she rose to her feet, and it was as if he broke. Turning toward her, he kneeled on the concrete and buried his face against her stomach, his arms wrapping around her waist. His body shuddered. She tried to sink to her knees, to hold him, but he didn't let her come down to the floor. Her heart aching, she smoothed her hands over his hair, uncertain whether he wept from grief, relief, or a mixture of both.

Irena's gesture had torn him open, exposing a need for forgiveness he hadn't admitted—one he probably had not admitted even to himself. And Rosalia had never thought Irena, hard and unyielding, would give it. She'd never been more grateful to be wrong.

She brushed the wetness from his cheeks when he raised his head, his gaze searching her face.

"Two days," he said hoarsely, then stood, sweeping Rosalia into the cradle of his arms. "Remind me why the hell we're here instead of in your bed?"

Then his mouth was devouring hers, and she couldn't remember, either.

CHAPTER 23

Malkvial chose to use the catacombs beneath the church.

For an instant, Deacon was certain that the demon had found out about Rosalia. Had known that she'd been beneath the church for eighteen months, and a hollow dread filled his chest, as he thought that everything had gone wrong, that both he and Rosalia were fucked now.

But the demon didn't look as smug as when he'd reminded Deacon of how he'd betrayed Irena in this same church. No. The bastard was wary, keeping a good span of aisle between him and Deacon. And Deacon realized the simple reason he'd chosen the catacombs: If Deacon didn't have reason to leave, Malkvial could keep his eye on him throughout the night.

So it was a damn good thing that Rosalia had anticipated the possibility that he wouldn't shake Malkvial until dawn. They could carry this whole thing off without once contacting each other.

Camille stood by in Paris with a chartered plane, the heads of twelve vampire communities, and a dozen bound-and-gagged human monsters. Deacon called her up and told her to haul ass to Rome.

The demons began to gather before the vampires arrived. A little over a hundred, by Deacon's count. Malkvial must have told them to keep their hands off of the vampires, but a few got it in their heads to fuck with Deacon, a couple of hours of trying to shred his soul apart, strip him down to nothing. Deacon shut his ears to their whispers, knowing that any fear or weakness on his part would be pounced on, and then it'd all go to fuck. Rosalia was watching from an apartment next door, and he didn't doubt that if she saw one sign that the demons were thinking of betraying Deacon, then she'd charge through a hundred demons trying to rescue him.

Camille arrived thirty minutes before dawn, as arranged. Deacon met the vampires outside to prepare them, but even telling them how many demons waited inside couldn't halt their shock and terror. The demons ate it up, and Deacon led the vampires and the struggling, whimpering, angry humans down to the ossuary. The chamber was empty of everything but bones and a few of the cameras Rosalia had installed for Deacon's first meeting with Malkvial, each neatly hidden within a skull's staring eye socket. They didn't need the additional cameras that Camille had brought with her, but they quickly placed them, anyway.

Deacon tied the humans to the thick stone columns supporting the ceiling, then removed their blindfolds. He couldn't dredge up any sympathy for humans like these, but he offered them the tiny comfort of knowing they wouldn't die.

Some of them might wish for it afterward.

He hardened his heart and ordered the vampires out of the catacombs, back upstairs. Tomás and Stefan led them; Camille and Deacon took the rear. The only words spoken on the way up came from Camille.

"My friend's brother has a house nearby that we can all use to sleep through the day."

So Rosalia was moving her stuff to Lorenzo's place. That made a hell of a lot of sense. After the demons started breaking the Rules, then Deacon might be called along with them—and nothing in that little apartment next door would slow him down.

Lorenzo's dungeon might.

They reached the main floor. The demons waited silently, each of them with glowing crimson eyes. All of them had taken on their real forms, red scales and leathery wings, horns curling back from their foreheads. At a word from Malkvial, they cleared a path in the aisle to let the vampires pass, and Deacon had to block his mind against the others' terror, piercing his brains like a chorus of screams.

Finally, they were outside. Deacon locked the church doors behind him.

Lorenzo's house wasn't far. Rosalia was probably setting up the new feed in the basement dungeon. He ushered the vampires inside and directed them upstairs to the bedrooms—all of them were going to fall asleep in about three minutes. He got downstairs as quickly as possible, but slowed on the last step, managing his surprise.

St. Croix, he expected—after all, they were using his dungeon, and Rosalia had agreed to let him watch. The human stood near the monitors, his hands tucked casually in his trouser pockets, his psychic scent emitting an almost revolting eagerness. Taylor waited near the steps, nodding at Deacon as he came in. As she'd be the one bringing Anaria into the catacombs and getting the humans out, he'd expected her, too.

But not Irena and Alejandro. Rosalia wouldn't have invited them here. Taylor must have made that call, and brought them. Or maybe Michael had.

They stood together, watching Rosalia connect the monitors to the feed from the catacombs. Rosalia's soft lips had flattened into a thin line; her body was stiff. And as she flipped the power on, he saw her bow her head, as if offering a prayer.

Expecting to be rejected as soon as Irena and Alejandro saw what she'd done.

Irena looked at the screens as they came online. Through

the speakers, sobbing filled the dungeon, soft wails, cries for help.

Aghast, Irena stepped back and turned to Rosalia. "Those are humans?"

"Yes," she whispered. Then, stronger, "You should go. This is not something a Guardian should stand by and watch."

"If a Guardian shouldn't tolerate it, I will stop the demons, and then I will return for you."

Rosalia faced her. "I won't let you stop me."

"Show them who the humans are," Deacon told her quietly.

Rosalia called in their profiles from her cache. She held out the stack, her hands shaking.

Irena passed them to Alejandro, who opened the files. The crime photos were on the top page. The tall Guardian's mouth tightened. He showed a picture to Irena.

She turned sharply toward Rosalia. "All of them have done this?"

"Yes."

"Pig-fucking bastards," Irena spat. "We should let them all be killed."

Rosalia smiled, very slightly. "But we are Guardians."

Irena snorted out a laugh. The two women looked at each other for a long moment, and when Rosalia glanced away, still smiling, Deacon thought they understood each other perfectly. Michael might not like what Rosalia had planned, but the four Guardians here stood in agreement—and they could live with their decision to put human monsters in the path of demonic ones.

St. Croix had been silently following the back and forth. Now he spoke up. "So that is what you are: a Guardian."

"Yes."

"And what does that mean?"

"It means that we have died saving people from demons. And we live again, to save more." She watched the screen. The demons were filing into the ossuary chamber, Malkvial speaking to them in the demon language.

"Saving people from . . ." Sudden hope burst through St.

Croix's psychic scent. "You become a Guardian if you die while saving someone from a demon?"

Rosalia was no longer listening, her attention completely focused on the monitors. Alejandro answered for her.

"Yes," he said.

"Fuck me." St. Croix gave a strange, hoarse laugh. "Five years ago, there was a woman—Rachel Boyle. She became a Guardian?"

Alejandro exchanged a glance with Irena. "No."

"But she *saved* me. Then she died in my arms, and she vanished. Her body vanished. She's not a Guardian now?"

"I'm sorry. None of the novice Guardians was transformed at that time. I am certain of it."

St. Croix ripped his hands through his hair, looking wildly at each of them. Then, like a pricked balloon, he suddenly deflated, his hands falling to his sides.

"They are all in the ossuary," Rosalia murmured. "Several are blocking the entrance. None are left in the corridor. What has Malkvial told them?"

She looked to Taylor, who ticked off the demon's instructions on her fingers. "Don't let the nephilim escape. Don't kill the humans. Don't inflict permanent physical damage. Converge on the nephilim in groups of five."

"Don't kill," Rosalia repeated, and let out a breath. "At least he adheres to that."

"You have a few minutes," Taylor added. "They are choosing which demon within each group will break the Rules." She smiled thinly. "Apparently, they all want to."

Rosalia nodded, then looked to Deacon. Long lengths of chain appeared in her hands. "You are ready?"

He backed up against the cell, pushing his arms between the iron bars and clasping his hands together. "I hope to God I am."

❦

Rosalia wrapped his wrists in the chain, then wound the steel links around his arms and through the bars. She used another to secure him across the neck, chest, and stomach. A final chain bound his feet and legs.

Irena watched her in astonishment. "What is this?"

"He drank the nephil's blood." Rosalia tightened the chains and locked them. "A few days ago, a demon broke the Rules, and Deacon was called. He couldn't resist it. If it happens again—if it happens every time a demon breaks the Rules—he'll be called continually until this is over."

"And maybe I won't," he added. "But considering that the sun's up and I'll head straight for that church, I don't want to take that chance."

Irena's lips parted and she glanced at Taylor. "Khavi did not think Rosalia's plan would succeed because the balance between action and consequence is never lost. Is it *Deacon* who maintains the balance? Is it he who will enforce the Rules in the nephilim's stead?"

"Khavi wasn't sure," Taylor said. "And we won't know until all of the nephilim are dead."

"They are beginning," Alejandro said.

Rosalia wrapped her arms tight around Deacon and looked up at him. His heart pounded against her chest. From the speakers, she heard a smack of flesh against flesh. She felt Irena's instinctive anger in response to the demon's abuse. Deacon's eyes emptied.

He jerked toward her, straining against the chains. The bars groaned, but they held him for now.

She turned her head to look just as the nephil teleported into the catacombs. *One*, she counted.

Swords clashed. A demon was almost immediately killed—the one who had broken the Rules. Deacon went limp. Four demons came at the nephil, and the creature fell.

Deacon looked down at her, his eyes dazed. "It's over?"

"Only one."

The demons jeered. Malkvial kicked the head of the fallen demon. He shouted, and the others shouted back.

"The weak and the dead are unworthy to stand at Belial's side," Taylor translated in a harmonious voice.

Rosalia glanced over and her blood chilled. Taylor's face was pale, her eyes fully obsidian. Her hair had darkened to black.

Just like Michael's.

A human shouted. Rosalia's gaze snapped to the monitor. A demon approached a tethered man, shifting into the form of a little girl with sharp teeth.

"Can I have a lollipop now?"

"Stay away . . . Don't touch me!" The human's shout became a thin, terrified scream.

"Goddamn son of a bitch," Deacon growled. "You'll get what you deserve."

Rosalia wasn't sure if he meant the demon or the human. She wanted to turn away, but made herself watch. She had to count.

The demon-child ripped the human's trousers open and touched him.

Deacon went rigid. On-screen the nephil teleported in, sword raised high.

Two.

The demon-child didn't fall. Deacon didn't stop straining. The demons killed the nephil, but they didn't have time to torture another human. Another nephil teleported in.

Three.

Shouts of surprise came from the demons. Seven died before they overwhelmed the nephil.

Four.

Malkvial began shouting orders, and this time the demons were better prepared. The humans screamed as demons raced around them, swords flashing, blood spattering. The demons' laughter was just as loud.

Five.

The chain around Deacon's right arm snapped. Mindlessly, he flung her away from him. Rosalia flew back, almost smashing into St. Croix but hitting the solid wall instead. Instantly she was on her feet, racing to catch his wrist, trying to force it back against the bars.

Jesus, Mary, and Joseph—he was *strong*.

Then Irena was there, born when a Caesar still ruled Rome, her strength many times greater than Rosalia's. Together, they pinned his arm. Irena brought in a new chain and held Deacon while Rosalia secured it.

She looked back at the screen. Bodies littered the catacomb floor, steeped in pools of blood. "How many?"

"Twenty-three," Alejandro said.

Even as she watched, *twenty-four. Twenty-five*. Malkvial had the demons working in perfect order.

And Taylor had said there were fifty-seven in total. Rosalia glanced over at her. "At fifty-three, go."

Four more nephilim fell in the few seconds it took Taylor to reply. "That doesn't give me much time."

"She's a mother," Rosalia said. "She'll come as fast as she can."

"And I'll get the humans out."

"Yes," Irena said. "But dump them in a sewer."

Rosalia glanced up at Deacon. The cords in his neck stood out sharply, veins popping out against the muscles in his forearms. The bars wouldn't hold much longer, and he'd remain like this until the demon who'd broken the Rules was slain.

She looked to the screen. It had been the demon who'd become a child—but it had already shape-shifted back to its original form. She didn't even know which demon it was.

"Forty-six." Alejandro kept the count. "Forty-seven."

She glanced at Taylor. "Bring her into the corridor, so that none can escape."

"Fifty-two. Fifty—"

Taylor vanished.

"—three," Alejandro finished.

Rosalia held on to Deacon and prayed.

❦

Anaria stood in her mansion, sword in hand, looking desperately around with eyes that shone like halogen flashlights. Oh, Jesus. She'd probably watched each of her children disappear, one at a time—perhaps understanding what was happening and yet unable to do anything to stop it.

She spotted Taylor, and before Taylor could get more than "Belial's—" out, Anaria had sprinted to her side.

"Take me."

Cold and dangerous. Taylor shivered, and then they leapt together.

❧

Fifty-seven.

The last nephil fell. On the monitors, a breathless waiting seemed to take over the demons. All was silent, except for the sobbing and pitiful whimpers of the humans. Then Malkvial raised his sword, and a cheer overwhelmed the speakers.

It abruptly died. As one, the demons turned toward the entrance of the ossuary. Not one looked at Taylor as she flashed in front of the humans, touched two, and was gone.

Anaria didn't show on any of the screens. The demons' eyes were all turned to her, though, and their crimson skin seemed to pale.

Not losing color, Rosalia realized. The shadows behind them darkened as a bright light filled the room. Brighter. A few demons narrowed their eyes and turned their heads away from the brilliant glow. Another stumbled back, as if trying to find a place to hide. His fear acted like an electric prod.

All hell broke loose. Demons scrambled. Monitors darkened in splotches, blood splattering against the cameras. Demons screamed. The light that was Anaria whited out the screens for an instant, a radiant streak. Rosalia couldn't track her.

She strained to see past the light, past the blood and the running demons. She could tell only that there were far, far fewer of them. "Taylor?"

Alejandro pointed to a different monitor. "Only two humans are left."

Almost done, then, and thank God. An instant later, she saw that no humans remained.

Then no demons were alive, either. Emitting a bright light, Anaria stood, her sword bloodied, her white wings saturated with red.

St. Croix's mouth hung open, his face a picture of shock. "What happened? How—?"

Only a few seconds had passed since Anaria's arrival. The massacre must have been nothing but a blur to him.

"Who is that?" He stared at Anaria.

"The worst of them," Irena said.

Chains rattled behind her. Rosalia turned, and horror gripped her throat. Deacon hadn't been freed. He threw his body forward, his lips peeled back from his fangs. Shouting in the demon language, he hurled himself against the chains.

Rosalia whirled back around. "Have any escaped?"

Frantically searching the screens, she spotted the monitor showing the main floor of the church. Sunlight flooded the interior through open doors.

Deacon had locked the entrance when he'd led the vampires outside. Realizing he was the nephilim's target, the demon must have fled before Anaria arrived.

"Irena, hold him," Rosalia said. "Don't let him out."

The other Guardian didn't question her. She took hold of Deacon. Rosalia looked up into his blank eyes.

And let the darkness of her Gift take her.

❦

The sun hung low in the morning sky, and the shadows were long. Still, the pain of her Gift was a sharp, hungry bite as she gathered the shadows, wrapped herself in them, and stretched them toward the church.

Stabbing outward with a hard psychic probe, she felt Anaria, huge and brilliant and bright, like the sun; Taylor, closed and dark; at a distance, Irena, Alejandro, the sleeping vampires, and Deacon's possessed mind; and farther away, the snakelike touch of a demon's psyche.

Her focus narrowed on him. Below her, a thick swath of darkness crawled over the streets and buildings, a long shadow that rose upward in a black ribbon. She caught the shadow, whipped it forward, and rode along. Ahead, the demon's wings beat frantically, terror spilling from his mind like bitter ash against her tongue.

She pushed the shadows forward, surrounding him. He shrieked, whirling about, blindly slashing with his sword. She condensed the darkness into a cocoon, silencing his screams from human ears, and let the black carry her closer.

He had no warning. She erupted out of the dark, her blades slicing through his chest, his neck. She vanished the pieces of him into her cache as they fell, then reached out with another psychic probe.

Deacon's mind was dazed, but it was his own.

But she felt the touch of another mind, brilliant and light, seeking her out. Dismay spilled into her heart, but she'd known that using her Gift would come at this price. She stretched the shadows north again, carrying her back across the city. She couldn't return to Lorenzo's home—Anaria would find them all.

Still enshrouded in darkness, she landed in front of the church. She passed through the doors, wondering if she'd already been noticed on the monitors in Lorenzo's dungeon.

She hoped Irena was still holding Deacon.

On bare, silent feet, Anaria approached from the rear chambers and walked past the sanctuary. Though still soaked with the demon's blood, she glowed. Her radiance ate away at Rosalia's Gift, and the shredding pain was like the agony of Caelum's sun.

Anaria smiled gently. "Do not hide from me."

Oh, God. Rosalia had heard about the effect of that voice, melodic and sweet, difficult to resist. Rosalia proved not strong enough. Obeying, she let go of her shadows and stood trembling, cloaked only in her terror.

She had to turn her face away from Anaria's brilliance, and stared at the plastic-enshrouded pews to her left.

"You have slain the one that fled?"

Rosalia nodded, a sob working up through her chest. Never

had she heard such kindness, such sweetness. Her yearning to reach out to Anaria was almost unbearable. She fought not to drop to her knees.

But she *wouldn't*. Not before Anaria. Her gaze sought the carved figure above the altar, and though it, too, was wrapped in plastic, Rosalia took the strength she needed there.

"You helped me," Anaria said.

No, she hadn't. A terrible ache filled Rosalia's heart. However terrible and frightening Anaria was, she'd acted out of love. It was so much easier to destroy a demon, who relished fear and hate.

But Anaria was no less dangerous, and Rosalia dared not lie. Anaria could see the truth, and so her only chance to survive was to speak it. To *always* speak it.

"No mother should lose her children in such a way," Rosalia whispered.

"No," Anaria said sadly, and tears stung Rosalia's eyes. She wanted to pull the ancient grigori to her breast, soothe the woman's pain. "You are a mother?"

Her teeth clenched, but the answer came anyway. "Yes."

She hated telling this woman about Vin. Hated giving her that.

Anaria sensed it. "Do not fear me. I am not the Guardians' enemy."

Rosalia said nothing.

Anaria sighed, a sound of regret and hurt that almost ripped out Rosalia's heart. She wanted to leap forward, to take the woman into her arms, to comfort her.

She stayed where she was.

"These demons who slaughtered my children, were they all my father's? Did they all follow Belial?"

"Yes."

"Are there others?"

"Yes." Malkvial had not brought every one of Belial's demons. Only most of them. "A few are scattered throughout the other lands. We will hunt them down and slay them."

From the corner of her eye, she saw movement. Taylor,

arriving in the aisle beside Anaria. Rosalia glanced at the Guardian. Taylor was herself again, her sharp blue eyes taking in everything, her hair red.

"Look at *me*," Anaria commanded.

Rosalia did. The grigori's brilliance pulled tears from her eyes.

"Do you swear to me, Guardian, that you would slay them? That you would avenge my children?"

Not Anaria's children. Rosalia would avenge her family. Deacon's community and friends. Everyone else who had suffered at the hands of the demons. It did not matter if those demons were Belial's or Lucifer's.

"They will be slain," Rosalia said. "If not by me, then by the other Guardians."

"And in Hell? Will you slay those in Hell?"

How could she? Rosalia opened her mouth, but knew not what to say. She *could* slay them, if Taylor teleported her to that realm.

But Anaria answered for her. "No. You cannot prevail over his demons in Hell." Determination set her beautiful face. "With my children slain, my father believes he will rise to the throne. But I say to you, the prophecy will not hold."

Rosalia shook her head. "I do not know."

"I do. And there will be no more waiting—only doing. I will see that he who is most to blame for the death of my children will pay the dearest." She turned to Taylor. "You will take me."

Taylor's eyes widened. "To Hell?"

"I will form my army. I will take the throne."

As if asking for help, Taylor looked to Rosalia, who was dumbstruck. This was not what they wanted. No one was safe if Anaria took the throne. Not humans, not Guardians, or vampires. But if Anaria was also unable to return to Earth through the Gates . . . they would all be safer for *now*.

The decision was taken from them. Taylor's eyes turned black. As if shoved from behind, she lurched toward Anaria.

The moment their skin touched, they vanished.

Rosalia stood motionless in the sudden silence. Then her body gave out, and she fell to her knees. Her wings flopped against the floor. Throwing her head back, she gulped in a breath, then closed her eyes, letting the cool air slip in and out of her lungs.

But she could not kneel there forever.

She spoke aloud, knowing they would hear her through the speakers. "Irena, Alejandro—please come. Someone needs to be here when Taylor returns."

If Taylor returned here.

❦

When she arrived at Lorenzo's house, Deacon was waiting at the entrance. He hauled her inside, pushed her back against the door. He crowded against her, his voice a thick growl.

"I could kill you for risking yourself like that."

But an instant later he was kissing her instead, deep and relieved. She clung to him until he pulled away, his chest heaving.

"You did it, Rosie. You amazing, incredible woman. You did it."

She shook her head. "Not just me. And I—"

That was all she could do. Her voice broke, her knees gave out, and it suddenly crashed in on her, a rush of terror and emotion.

Deacon caught her. *Trust me, Rosie. Let go.*

She wasn't sure if he said it, or if she just knew he would hold her. As he lifted her against him, she wrapped them in darkness and carried them home.

CHAPTER 24

Deacon held her through the morning. Hell—he held her, made love to her like a madman, fed from her throat as if starved. When mid-afternoon came and she sighed, the soft sound ripped his heart from his chest.

They were done. He watched as she sat up and scooted to the edge of the bed, his gaze drinking in the beautiful curve of her back, the sway of her hair.

She glanced over her shoulder with a wicked smile, her dark eyes lively. "I am supposed to meet Gemma at the florist's, and then accompany her while she shops for wedding favors. But if you say the word, I will stay here."

He almost gave in to temptation. But dragging this out would just make it harder. Sitting up, he braced his shoulders against the headboard. "Go on and do your thing, princess."

A teasing grin widened her mouth. "Now that I can use my Gift again, you could come with us."

He shook his head. "I'm packing up."

Her grin vanished, and her brow puckered, as if she thought she'd misheard him. "What?"

"Come sunset, I'm hauling off. There's no reason to drag this out."

Her gaze searched his face. Suddenly she turned away from him, and he was staring at the back of her head. A fine tremor shook the hand that grasped at the sheet and pulled it up around her.

His fists clenched. *It was easier this way.*

But she didn't get up and leave him, as he expected. In an even voice, she asked, "What if you're called during the day?"

If a demon broke the Rules? "It doesn't happen often. And it'll happen a lot less with most of Belial's demons dead."

"But it will eventually happen. My Gift can protect you when it does."

So she was going to babysit him every day, hovering over him? Fuck that. And why the hell wasn't she letting this go? Just a few minutes before, she'd been heading out, not giving a thought to any of this.

"And you were going to protect me while you were shopping?"

"I planned to monitor your psychic scent." The words were stiff. "I wouldn't have left without knowing you would be okay."

No. Of course she wouldn't.

The anger that had boiled up only moments before evaporated. She'd worry for him, because she was Rosalia. "I'll figure out something for the days. A cloak, a hood, gloves—and if I'm pulled into the sun, I'm covered."

She shook her head, but didn't say anything.

"We're done here, Rosie. So let's just make it clean and quick."

"Clean and quick," she echoed.

"Yeah. You aren't the type to wallow in bed like this with me. You've got Guardian stuff to do, a wedding in three days—and you don't need me here. Do you have any more reasons for me to stay?"

Christ. He shouldn't have asked. Now he hoped she did. Anything. Any stupid little reason, and he knew he'd stay.

Her sudden, hoarse laugh hit like a sucker punch to his heart. "I've already given you all my reasons, Deacon. I don't have any more."

His throat closed up. All right, then. All right. Needing to move, he got up, hauled on his jeans. She had everything so nicely folded and stacked it took all of two seconds to throw all of his shit in his bag.

He glanced over at her once. She watched him, her eyes dark and sad, and he couldn't bear to look again.

"Where will you go?"

He grabbed Eva and Petra's sculpted urn from the wardrobe. "Paris, first. Theriault wasn't with the demons in the church."

"And then?"

"I don't know. It doesn't really matter, does it?"

"Yes."

With that simple reply, she clasped the sheet over her breasts and rose from the bed. He braced himself as she approached. She adjusted his collar and smoothed his sleeve before looking up at him. Her expression was serene, but he could have drowned in the darkness of her eyes.

"So this is good-bye, then?"

"Yeah," he said gruffly.

She nodded. With a final adjustment of his collar, she rose up on her toes, and he realized she was going to kiss him farewell. Going to break him with her soft lips. She'd given him no reason to stay, but he'd beg, because even trying to leave was killing him.

But he didn't resist it. The moment her mouth touched his, he caved, his hands cupping her face, holding her to him. God, he couldn't let go. She had no use for him now, but she'd become as vital as his heartbeat, as necessary as the night. Her arms circled his shoulders and her mouth opened to his, and her Gift suddenly pressed against his shields, dark and oppressive. She wrapped shadows around them, and if she wanted, he would stay, even here in this darkness, forever.

She kissed him deeper, until his head spun, until he felt pulled in ten directions at once, with Rosalia as the focus. His hands slid down to her waist.

Her body slipped like mist through his fingers. Her lips had softened, the touch of her mouth no more substantial than a breath.

No more substantial than a shadow.

Dread wrapped his throat in a cold hand. His eyes popped open but she was already pulling away, and he was staring through a dark veil at a framed photograph of the Eiffel Tower. His hotel room in Paris. His bag lay at his feet. The urn sat on the bed.

For an instant, the veil held her shape. Then it stretched into a thin string, and snapped.

Clean and quick—and straight through his heart.

He stared at the place she'd been, his gut scraped raw. "Rosie?"

Only the noise from the other rooms answered him.

❧

Curled up on the bed in the hotel room across from Theriault's apartment, Rosalia was crying her eyes out when she felt someone in the room with her. When she smelled the sulphur, the rot. She shot up to her knees, staring at Taylor, sprawled on the floor beside the bed. Red sand trickled from her bare feet onto the white carpet.

The detective stared back, her blue eyes dazed. "It wasn't as bad as I thought. Just a lot of sand. And a giant statue of a Guardian—Anaria started crying all over him. I think that's the same place Khavi hid those two thousand years." She rolled over to sitting, huffed out a breath. "Holy shit. It's done."

"For now," Rosalia said.

"Good enough to catch our breath." She looked at Rosalia for another second. "Are you okay?"

Since the question and the genuine concern behind it almost started her sobbing again, Rosalia forced herself to just stop. Stop thinking of Deacon. Stop thinking of how much it hurt. "Yes," she said, and because it didn't come out with much conviction, went on with something that *was* genuine. "Thank you, Taylor. I honestly don't know if I could have come up with another way out. And I know that I asked a lot of you—and of Michael."

"Well, considering that you gave me a pool to lounge in and a place to regain my sanity, even though I was trying to kill the guy you're in love with, I think we can call it even."

"All right. And you're always welcome to the pool, or a room."

"I might take you up on that." Taylor stood, looked around the empty room. Rosalia had already removed the surveillance equipment. Finally, she glanced back at Rosalia. "He likes you, I think. Not in the same way as the others. Or, not quite the same way. Some Guardians he admires, and some are his friends. Some he just can't figure out."

Rosalia had been lost for a moment. Now she guessed, "Michael?"

Taylor nodded. "I think it's because of Anaria. He sees in you what he wishes Anaria was. You're both full of plans and good intentions. You just do 'good' the right way."

Tears starting to her eyes again, Rosalia shook her head. "What of the humans?"

"I wasn't the one teleporting them out of there, you know. I didn't want to make a rookie mistake, so I let him take over. They didn't end up in the sewer. I'm not sure where it was, but it was the middle of nowhere . . . and he scared the piss out them."

A laugh slipped from her. "That never works like it should."

"Maybe not. But even if he didn't agree with the way you used them, I think he perfectly understood the reason you chose them. Your reason for all of it. Your reasons, actually. I noticed you never have just one."

"I don't think any Guardian does."

Something in Taylor's eyes flickered. "Even Michael?"

"Especially Michael."

With the tips of her fingers, Taylor touched her lips and smiled faintly. "That's good to know." She focused on Rosalia again. "I'm going to head out. You sure you're okay?"

"No." Not right now. Not this moment. But she had hope. "I eventually will be."

Sunset was only thirty minutes gone when some pissant vampire waylaid Deacon on his way to Theriault's. One of those younger shits who wrote poetry to Mother Darkness and thought becoming a vampire would make him sparkle. Hot and hungry and aching through to his soul, Deacon was in no kind of mood to deal with him.

The little pissant could see it on his face. Shifting uneasily in his Converse, he stuffed his hands into the pockets of his skinny jeans. He said in a rush, "Yves and Camille request your presence at their home."

"What the hell for?"

The kid hunched his shoulders a little. "It's about feeding, *monsieur.*"

Oh, Christ Jesus. Feeding. With a single word, he stared bleakly into his future. No Rosalia. And taking his blood from other women.

"I'm sorry, *monsieur,*" the kid whispered, and Deacon realized the vampire had read the despair in his psychic scent.

His anger was suddenly gone, leaving only that huge black hole in his chest. "Haul off, then," Deacon said quietly. "Tell them I'll come."

But not for feeding. Not tonight. Just to pay his respects like any vampire should when coming into a city. Then maybe he'd see how far he could get living off animal blood. It might leave him shaky, stupid, and with a limp dick—but Deacon didn't want to fuck anyone, anyway.

He made his way to Camille's place, then almost stopped

when he realized how many vampires were there, having a party of some sort. But it struck him that there was only one way that Camille could have known he'd returned to Paris—and on the slim chance that Rosalia might be somewhere around, too, he went through that door.

Camille was the first to greet him. She bussed his cheeks, and shoved a flute of champagne into his hand. "We can't become drunk, and we can't taste it—but the bubbles are necessary to celebrate life. Now, come with me."

She led him through a room bursting with vampires, refusing to let a single one stop them. At the balcony overlooking a quiet, tree-lined street, she shooed a couple of vampires back inside.

They wouldn't have privacy, but they had the illusion of it.

She turned to him. "When I woke up today, I found an insulated drink cooler in my home, packed with dry ice, units of blood, and a message to you in it."

Deacon didn't dare hope. "What was the message?"

She produced a folded note from inside her bra. His heart pounding, Deacon took it.

The message wasn't from Rosalia. In Irena's clunky block letters, she offered to deliver demon blood for as long as he needed it, wherever he needed it.

His throat closed up. Deacon stuffed the note into his pocket, feeling Camille's gaze on his face.

"I expected Rosalia here with you. Did you leave her in Rome to clean up after the mess?"

He didn't want to get into this with Camille. She knew him too well. To stall, he threw back a swallow of the champagne—tasteless, but fizzy. Hardly a celebration.

But it gave him an idea of how to answer. "She's busy planning a wedding for her son."

"*Her son?*" Camille's eyebrows shot up. "Oh, Rosa. Good for her."

Deacon frowned at her. That was a little more relief than the revelation seemed to call for.

"It was the reason I left, ninety years ago. I didn't want to be like her: three hundred years old, and never been loved. In any sense." She paused. "Although I suppose now that you and she are—"

"I'm not. *We're* not."

"Oh." Her brow pleated. "You smell like her perfume."

"It's soap." And hours and hours of Rosalia beside him, under him, over him. He hadn't yet washed her off.

"Ah," she said, but her confusion seemed deeper than it should be.

What was the mystery here? "Just have it out, Camille."

She took a few seconds, and he knew she was framing her words carefully when she began, "For two hundred years, she prevented Lorenzo from taking over every community in Europe and ruling us all."

"I know she did."

"And yet, here *you* are—and you're now the de facto head of every European community."

He shook his head. "If that's what everyone is thinking, just tell them I don't want any of their positions."

"I won't tell them. And we aren't expecting you to rule; we're expecting you to protect our communities. This is what you have brought upon yourself by saving us. Will you shun that responsibility?"

His jaw clenched, and he realized this was the reason Camille had requested his presence. She could have delivered the blood. But she'd brought him here, showed him the vampires celebrating—and if he denied his responsibility, he'd have to look each one in the face and essentially tell them they didn't matter.

He wouldn't. He *couldn't*. When a threat showed up, they'd look to him. He couldn't turn his back on them.

Finally, he said, "No. I won't shun it."

Camille smiled as if she'd never had any doubt, and patted his hand. "You won't be locked into a community. In fact, I think it's best if you aren't a part of one, so that you seem impartial. You'll be the one we can all go to, if we need your help. And if ever again another Lorenzo comes to power, you can do what the Guardians—*all* of the Guardians—neglected to do, and slay him."

Shit. He didn't want that responsibility—but he knew that if someone like Lorenzo took over a community, waged the same reign of terror over his people, Deacon *would* destroy him.

As if Camille saw his acceptance, she gave a satisfied nod. Her tone altered, became pensive. "When I heard that Lorenzo had been killed, I called Rosalia up to congratulate her—or to console her. I didn't know which it would be. But I thought, *She'd finally done it*—because no one knew about the nephilim yet."

Not for weeks after Lorenzo had died. And even then, no one knew how the hell an entire city had been massacred until the Guardians had told them.

"So I called her," Camille continued, "and I spoke with Svetlana, who told me that Rosalia wasn't home. I thought nothing of it because she was so often gone. But later, I received a call from a young human woman asking if I'd seen her. And that they hadn't seen Rosa for months, and she was looking for her."

That would have been Gemma. "Her vampires never asked you?"

"Not once." She lifted a shoulder as if it was nothing, but Deacon heard the note of sadness in her psyche. "Rosalia has always been about protecting her family. Her family has rarely offered the same to her."

Deacon would have torn Europe apart looking for her. To *know*, if nothing else. And he'd have given his life to protect her.

"And I'll tell you why Lorenzo didn't just kill her: Without Rosalia standing in his way, he could have taken over all of Europe as he planned. But he hated her too much not to rub her failure in her face. So he'd wake her up and let her see what he'd done." She looked down into her champagne. "That is the one and only thing I thank the nephilim for. If they hadn't killed him when they did, we'd all be dead, and our communities under his rule."

"I don't think anyone shed tears over him. Not even Rosie."

"Who would?" She expelled a disgusted breath. "As it was, even with Lorenzo dead I didn't have much hope once I heard she was gone. Then when Rome was destroyed, followed by Berlin, I had none at all. She's held the balance in Europe since she became a Guardian, and without her, the balance was gone. Everything was spinning out of control. I wasn't even surprised when you turned on the Guardians for a demon."

"But then she came back." If there was any reason to be thankful for Caym, that was the single one. If not for the demon, Rosalia might have still been in those catacombs.

"Then she came back—and I should have known that she would. If there's one thing about Rosa, it's that she won't quit. She won't lose faith, even if she loses hope. And after she loses hope, she still fights on, she still endures." Camille looked up at him with a smile. "And she can be insidiously clever and patient while she's about it. I've learned to never underestimate her. If she told me that she'd planned this ninety years ago, intending to put you in this position as a way to pay you back, I'd have believed her."

Ninety years? "Pay me back for what?"

"You have no idea?" When he shook his head, she said, "I didn't either, not then. I thought it was all for me. She said, *Here is a man who helped me out once. He's a good man. He needs someone to make him laugh, and you need someone who will laugh at you.* And I liked you. We had fun those early years, didn't we?"

"Yes." But he still didn't understand. "*What* was for you?"

"Sending me to you. I simply thought it was her way of helping me. No, that's not fair—it *was* her way of helping me. But Rosa, she never has just one reason. And if she can kill fifty birds with one stone . . ." Trailing off, she took a sip of her champagne. "Afterward, I looked back, and it was true that every single move she asked me to make helped me. But it helped you, too—and I realized, you had always been at the center of it."

Deacon's mind reeled. He knew what this meant—but he couldn't take any of it in. Couldn't believe it. His heart pounded. He set the champagne flute aside, afraid he'd shatter the glass in his hand.

She sighed. "But I suppose that is why you are not with her now. How could you be? She will never trust anyone so much that she will give them her heart. She wraps herself in reasons, and they are all true, but the one reason that makes her vulnerable, she never gives. After what her father was, and Lorenzo—how could she? But what is love without trust? And I know you, Deacon. You could not stay with a woman who has many reasons to be with you, but will never say she loves you."

The admission tore from him. "She did."

Camille stepped back, staring at him as if he'd struck her. "And you *left*?"

She read the answer in his face. Her eyes filled.

"Oh, Rosa," she whispered. Camille averted her face, and when someone called her name, telling her to come for the phone, she went quickly inside.

Deacon stared blindly out into the night. His fingers bit into the balcony railing. Rosalia had trusted him and given him her heart. And he'd thrown it back at her.

What had he done ninety years ago? He couldn't think of anything. Some small act of kindness that had meant so little to him.

And he'd decided to leave, as if she meant so little to him. Nothing could have been further from the truth.

Camille came back outside. "I have a message for you. It says: 'Theriault is alone. His wife has left him.'"

Rosie. He needed to talk to her *now*. "You have her number?"

"It was given to me with the understanding that I would never share it."

"How do I get it?"

She pursed her lips, as if indecisive. Camille was never indecisive—she was manipulating him.

He didn't even care. "How?"

"Perhaps, as leader of the European community, you can apply for protection from the Guardians." Her brows arched. "But do you really need a reason to see her?"

No. But he might need to give Rosalia a reason to see *him* again.

❧

Though he'd hoped to find Rosalia at the hotel across from Theriault's apartment, her surveillance equipment was missing, and humans occupied the room.

All right. So she'd helped him out tonight by giving him that message, but she wasn't hanging around, waiting for him, trying to make it all better between them.

He'd have given anything to see her, but it was good that she was gone. He'd fucked up. He'd hurt her. But considering that she had a habit of overcompensating and trying to fix everything she'd felt she'd done wrong, this meant she wasn't blaming herself for his mistakes. She knew exactly where to lay the blame: squarely on him.

And that meant working his ass off proving to her that she'd never regret taking him back. He'd have to think it out, and plan—and by God, if he had to manage Rosalia a little bit to get her in a place to listen, he'd do it.

But first things first. She'd given him info, and he needed to use it. He crossed the street and pulled his swords from beneath his jacket.

Any demon living in this city was a threat to the vampire community here—and Deacon had a new job to do.

❧

Rosalia took the long route to Caelum, passing over three Gates before diving through a portal in South Africa. She dragged in a breath of warm, dry air.

The city was still beautiful. Domes and towers of white marble reached up against a brilliant blue sky. Graceful arches and columns welcomed her into courtyards, into the temples. But it was just as sterile. No soil softened her steps; her heels clicked against unyielding stone. Nothing grew here. Nothing fragranced the air: no perfume, no rot, so smell of life. And the sun was still too bright.

Ten years ago, she'd stopped coming here, and she'd told herself that Pasquale had been the reason why. That she didn't deserve to be here. Now she wondered if she'd just been searching for a reason not to return. As beautiful as this city was, she didn't love it.

And she loved it even less when it was all but empty.

Mariko's quarters lay at the edge of the city, overlooking the sea, but Rosalia found her friend more quickly than that. The clash of weapons and the pulse of a familiar Gift drew her to a building that speared into the sky. Beside it, at the center of a round courtyard, Mariko spun around, sending a flying kick toward her opponent, a small woman with long black hair, whose only covering were the red scarves binding her breasts and fluttering around her pelvis and backside, and the paint that dyed her skin blue. Radha possessed a Gift of forcing an illusion past the strongest mental shields, and Rosalia didn't know what she'd made Mariko see and hear, but the Guardian's kick missed Radha completely. Mariko slammed into the side of the building, and Radha burst into laughter.

Her laughter abruptly died when she caught sight of Rosalia. Her eyes widened in disbelief. When she shrieked, Rosalia braced herself.

Radha tackled her with a hug, a tiny blue dynamo who lifted Rosalia off her feet and swung her around like a sock monkey. Limping, Mariko joined them.

With a huge grin, Radha set her down and stepped back, clapping her blue hands to a happy beat, quickly picked up by her dancing feet. "Mariko and I were just coming to see you—with this!"

A white satin ribbon dangled from her grip. It held up a

solid gold medal, its face inscribed with Rosalia's name and engraved with a laurel.

"It's plastic and she found it in a discount bin," Mariko said dryly.

"It's the thought that counts." Hopping forward, Radha placed the ribbon over Rosalia's head. For an instant, the Guardian's dark eyes lost their sparkle, and her serious gaze met Rosalia's. "It's the intention, right?"

Rosalia's throat swelled. "Right."

"Just like Radha doesn't *intend* to show everyone her tits. It"—Mariko made quote marks with her fingers—"'just happens.'"

"I'm doing my part to make the world a better place." Radha stepped back. "But I'm going to have to run around naked all of the time if I want to catch up to Rosa. You're our hero now."

"Stop that." Laughing, Rosalia shook her head. She'd worried about their reaction. This might be worse than the cold shoulder she imagined. "There are still plenty of demons and nosferatu—"

"Oh, God!" Mariko threw up her hands. "Shut up, Rosa. Tonight, we party."

"Actually, I have to—"

"Don't even argue," Radha warned her.

"—clean the abbey, and prepare for the wedding."

They gaped at her. Mariko croaked, "To *Deacon*?"

Pain stabbed through her heart, but she swallowed back the tears. She'd shed enough for one day. "No. That's over. It's my son's wedding, three days from now. That's why I'm here—to invite you both."

"Oh, congratulations! Of course we'll come," Radha said sweetly, and immediately followed with— "What the hell do you mean, it's over? Does that mean it started?"

"And *already* ended?" Mariko stared at her.

"Quick and clean," she confirmed.

Mariko shook her head. "That's not your style."

"That's how he wanted it." Her chest was aching. It'd been

aching since she'd left him in that hotel room. She didn't know when it would stop—but it wouldn't be tonight. Probably not for many, many nights.

"Oh, my God," Radha said in disbelief. "Is he stupid? Look at you!"

Yes, look at her. *Look at everything you are.* Deacon's outburst had echoed in her mind for days. It wasn't that Deacon didn't believe she *loved* him, but rather: He couldn't believe that *she* loved *him*. He saw himself as too damaged, too ruined. She'd tried to tell him, to show him that he wasn't—but there was nothing she could do unless he saw it, too. And knowing she couldn't change that ripped her apart.

"He's not," Rosalia said. "And I don't want to talk about it."

Mariko snapped her mouth shut. A second later she opened it again. "All right. I declare girls' night at the abbey, then. We get naked, we swim, we eat until we shape-shift into pigs, and Radha will entertain us with oiled, dancing men. Then we clean up and help you get the place ready."

Rosalia couldn't think of anything better—and she was grateful for any activity that might take her mind from Deacon and the enormous hole in her heart. "All right."

Radha grinned. "And should we spread the word?"

Her abbey, full of laughter and voices again? And she had so much food that still needed to be eaten. "Definitely," she said.

CHAPTER 25

The moment Taylor teleported into Hell, Michael tried to take over—tried to teleport her out. She fought him, stumbling across the frozen faces. Jesus God they were cold, burning her bare feet. Every breath seared her lungs, then billowed out in ragged clouds. Silence reigned. She couldn't hear her footsteps or her heartbeat, but the screams filled her head, the familiar screams, so loud here.

She hadn't known how many of the damned were down here. The field stretched almost as far as she could see, faces packed together with no room between. And rising over them all, their eyes all frozen on its great height, Lucifer's black tower speared against a crimson sky.

And she found Michael, right where she'd known he'd be. His amber eyes were frozen open, staring at the tower, but she saw that he was in there, aware. Crouching beside him, her toes digging into an eye, her heel into a mouth, she blocked his view of the tower with her face.

For an instant, the darkness within her stilled. Then he was pushing again, harder, trying to take her over and take her out of here. She put her hand against his cheek—an ice block, painfully cold. But if she could feel his cold, perhaps he could feel her warmth.

"I figured it out," she told him, but the words didn't emerge, just silence. She thought he understood anyway. "I figured out what I should have told Anaria that day, when she said that vampires would overrun Earth and then demons would just kill them, destroying all of humanity. I should have said: That's not going to happen, because there's going to be whole lotta motherfucking Guardians standing in the way."

She thought his laughter sounded in the back of her head—she knew it came into his eyes. But there was fear, too, rising. A lot more fear than she'd expected. And she was holding, but she wouldn't hold him back much longer.

"So I just want to say, Thank you for watching my back and saving my ass. Multiple times. And as soon as I figure out how, I promise I'll save yours."

Then the darkness almost overwhelmed her, pushing, pushing . . . and she felt the shiver under her feet. *Even if you can't see or hear them coming, you can feel them.*

Taylor whirled around, calling in Irena's spear. Terror sucked her mouth dry, shriveled her heart. A hellhound. Oh, Jesus. So much bigger than any she'd seen, at least three times her height, each of his three heads the size of a SUV. She couldn't hear his growls, but his lips peeled back over teeth as long as her arm.

Not just any hellhound, she realized in horror. Lucifer's hellhound, Cerberus. The master might not be far behind.

The ground shivered again as Cerberus exploded into a run, circling around her, faster and faster, thrashing his heads, exposing his giant maw, as if sensing her fear and trying to twist it to unbearable heights before eating her.

Oh, *hell* no. Anger burst through her, a rush of heat to her hands.

The spear caught fire. Flames leapt along the steel length, roaring high from the tip. Cerberus cringed away from it, turning suddenly, slinking back to watch her with wary, glowing eyes.

Her astonishment forced out a shout, lost in the silence. Cerberus slowly rose to his feet again, his surprise fading. And from the tower, she felt something else—searching, focusing, a dark scream of a psyche that Michael suddenly rose up and blocked . . . pushing her again, his desperation clear.

Taylor finally took Michael's hint, and got the hell out of there. Not out of fear. Of course not. She was a motherfucking Guardian.

And, anyway—she had a wedding to attend.

❧

Unconcerned with night and day and sleeping patterns, the girls' night had spilled over into a second evening, then into the next morning, and by the time they began to ready the abbey for the reception, almost every female Guardian and several of their vampire friends had passed through Rosalia's courtyard, danced and swam. Rosalia fastened Gemma into her wedding dress and straightened Vincente's waistcoat, and although she'd been determined not to cry, she wept through the vows. The reception culminated with more dancing—though the only one to take off his clothes was a neighbor who'd had too much champagne—and had finally wound down in the wee morning.

Now everyone was gone, and Rosalia sat on the bench near her fountain, feeling lighter than at any other moment in her life. For three days, she'd renewed both her friendships and her purpose as a mother, as a Guardian, as Rosalia. Her heart ached beyond bearing, true—but for the first time, she owed no one. All of her debts were gone, her obligations fulfilled.

Perhaps this could be a new beginning for her, as well as her son.

Smiling, she pulled her heel to the edge of the bench seat and rested her chin on her knee, watching the fall of sparkling water. The calla lilies' perfume was strong and heady, the orange blossoms sweet. The house had never been so quiet, but it did not seem empty. After the past three days, the silence felt peaceful and soothing, instead. Not waiting to be filled, but complete.

Over the splashing of the fountain came the click of a door opening. Lifting her head, Rosalia looked toward the abbey's entrance. She could not see it from here, but there was no mistaking the sound of footsteps.

She no longer needed to hide her abilities. Reaching out with a psychic probe, she touched his shields.

Deacon.

Her heart leapt into her throat. Forcing herself to move slowly, she stood and waited for him to emerge from the house. She knew why he had come. Camille had come to the abbey for both the girls' night and the reception, and upon her first visit had expressed her surprise that Deacon wasn't here.

On behalf of the vampire communities, he would be asking for the protection from the Guardians. Of course he would—he was strong, but not so arrogant to assume that he could handle everything alone. And Irena had told Rosalia that she had been providing Deacon his blood.

He did not need her.

But she could not stop her pulse from racing, and the joy that a glimpse of his face brought. She steeled herself against hope, crossing her arms over her chest as if that could muffle the pounding of her heart.

His gaze found her from across the garden, and seemed to take her in all at once, as if devouring the sight of her, hungry for it. And he looked like hell—his shirt buttoned wrong, his collar crooked, his hair in all directions. He came into the courtyard, stopping at the edge of the fountain.

"I'm a fool, Rosie."

Her lips parted. That hadn't been what she'd expected.

Deacon took a step toward her, then stopped himself—as if determined to have it all out first. "I should have listened. I should have trusted. But I didn't believe you loved me. And I almost threw away the best thing I've ever had."

Almost? "You did throw it away."

Though his gaze remained locked on her face, softly searching, his shoulders were rigid and hands curled into fists. "Yes. I did throw it away. I couldn't imagine that the man you'd waited for, the one you'd told me about, could have been me. I couldn't see myself like that. But I swear to you, Rosie, that I will—"

"The man I'd waited for?" Realization swept over her, followed by sudden anger. "Camille told you?"

Uncertainty flickered through his green eyes. His answer was low and rough. "Yes."

"So *now* you believe that I love you? Not because of anything I've done or said in the past weeks, but because of what *was*? What *you* were before Caym got to you? I deserve better than that, Deacon."

She let her anger ride over her, so that her tears wouldn't. She hadn't thought she could hurt more than the day he'd pushed her heart away. But she could.

He took a step toward her, but abruptly stopped when she backed up. He swallowed hard.

"I know you deserve better, Rosie. You deserve the man you loved."

So he could believe she loved the man he'd been, but not the one that Caym broke. He saw himself as a man who betrayed and failed. She saw a man who almost destroyed himself trying to save his people, and then again trying to avenge them.

She shook her head. "I didn't love you then. I hoped I would, someday. I admired you. I liked you. But I didn't love you until the night you returned here to help me." And now she conducted a postmortem on her heart. She couldn't do this; she would break soon. While she could still manage it, she said, "I don't expect you to believe that or to trust it, just as you could not believe me the first time. And so we are at the same place, with no reason for you to stay. You've come to ask for the Guardians' protection. Of course you have it. Now go."

Deacon stared at her, his throat working. Slowly, he fell to his knee and bowed his head. "I did not come to ask for your protection. I came to offer mine."

The hoarseness of his voice scraped her raw. It took a second for his words to penetrate, and still she did not understand.

"What?"

"I came to offer mine," he repeated. "Mine, and the protection of every vampire in whose service I fight. We all pledge to protect you, Rosalia Acciaioli, and to assist you in every mission. Every need you have, we will see it fulfilled. Our swords, our lives—if ever they can protect you or help you, they are yours to call upon. We owe you more than we can ever repay. And I would stay here, to protect and help you."

She could not speak. He wanted to settle a debt. She understood that. But it was unnecessary. "You helped me once, Deacon. Now I have paid you back. You owe me nothing else."

"No. It's not in balance." He lifted his head, and the torment in his eyes ripped at her heart. "You deserve more, but this is what we have to give—this is what *I* have that is worthy of giving. Everything I am now, you gave to me. Without you, I would still have nothing."

"You are welcome to what you have." She had created the plan, but he had seen it through, taken the most risks to his life and his soul. "You've earned it, several times over. But I deserve more."

More than repayment. More than gratitude. Just to be loved in return.

He bowed his head again. "Yes. You do. So much more."

It was so low and hoarse, she barely heard it. And she couldn't bear to hear any more. Her tears were coming now, and she couldn't hold them back.

"I need you to go, Deacon."

His pain slashed against her psychic shields. Through the blur of her vision, she saw a motion that might have been a nod. But he didn't get up.

"Deacon, *please—*"

"I'm trying to think of any reason." Longing and loss wavered through the broken whisper. "Any reason that you might let me stay long enough to prove myself to you."

For God's sake, she loved him! What more proof did he need that he was worthy?

She didn't have this strength. To argue again. To not be believed again. She tried to summon her anger—anything to get her through this. "You don't have anything to prove."

"I *do*. I didn't trust your love. I didn't believe you. And so when I say that I love you, you will have no reason to trust mine." His fists clenched at his side. "So I need time . . . I am *begging* for time . . . so that you can believe."

She could not believe. But she hoped. She flew forward, fell to her knees in front of him, tried to look up into his lowered face. "You love me?"

He raised his head. His body stiffened, as if bracing for a blow. "More than my life."

Oh, God. Oh, God.

She surged upward on a wave of joy, catching his face between her palms, melding her lips to his. Laughing and crying at once, she could barely kiss him, but his mouth was just as awkward, almost unsure, until she felt the acceptance and wonder flooding his psychic scent. Then his strong arms wrapped her tight, his hands cradling her head, and he kissed her deep, hard, as if to convince himself that she was there, that this was real.

She had to convince herself of it, too. Rosalia pulled back, her gaze searching his, her fingers confirming his face, his throat, his hair.

He bent to her again, gently kissed her wet cheeks. "Don't cry, Rosie."

His soft touch, the love she heard in his voice only made the tears fall harder. "I'm happy," she assured him.

He looked into her eyes. "I see you are," he said, low and rough, and his green eyes were suddenly swimming; then he was kissing her again, hard and sweet, and she never wanted him to stop.

But she had to know, had to hear it from his lips. She broke away just enough to say, "You are staying here with me?"

"Yeah. You're stuck with me now, princess."

"Oh, good." She kissed him again, laughing, then teasing his fangs and nibbling at his bottom lip, before taking a deep breath. "I'll always be a little managing, Deacon. I can't help it. I have a . . . a *need* to help those I love."

"The love bit makes it a lot easier." He lifted his head, looked down at her. "Just, not behind my back. All right?"

Perfectly. "Yes."

"And I should tell you—I'd have come earlier, Rosie. But I thought that you might be at your most desperate and lonely right after the wedding, when everyone left. And that I'd have a better chance."

She grinned against his lips. "You manipulative bastard."

He laughed and kissed her, but his gaze was serious when he regarded her again. "No one will ever love you more than I do, or work harder to see you happy. No one will try every moment to be the man worthy of your love."

"You are."

"I'll make certain I always am. I swear it."

She believed him. Laying her hand against his cheek, she promised, "I'll love you no matter what you go through; I'll stand by you no matter what trouble you face. And no matter what *I* face, I'll know you'll love me. That will never be in question."

Deacon nodded, then rested his forehead against hers. His eyes closed, and she felt him breathe her in. "I love you, Rosie."

"Tell me again."

He said it with a soft kiss. His arms, holding her close. Then the words, again, before a wicked smile touched his mouth.

"Unless I've told you to be there, Rosie, I don't like seeing you on your knees." Rising to his feet, he swung her up, cradling her against his chest. His lips touched hers, then deepened into a kiss that left them both breathless, hungry. When he lifted his head, she looked up at him, and he narrowed his eyes. "So what have you got planned for us now? I know you're working something out in there."

She laughed. So she had been. An endless lifetime, new beginnings, and so many possibilities stretched out in front of them. "Short-term or long-term?"

"I'll take care of the short-term." He started toward her bedchamber. "What about the long haul?"

She turned her face into his neck, breathed in his scent. "I'm making a plan for us to live happily, forever—and even after that."

"Happily, forever?" Deacon lifted her left hand and pressed a soft kiss to her ring finger. She heard the smile in his rough voice—and the promise. "I have no doubt we can pull it off, princess."

Keep reading for a special preview of
Meljean Brook's next novel

THE IRON DUKE

Coming October 2010
from Berkley Sensation!

London, England

Mina hadn't predicted that sugar would wreck the marchioness of Hartington's ball; she'd thought the dancing would. Their hostess's good humor had weathered them through the discovery that fewer than forty of her guests knew the steps, however, and they'd survived the first awkward quadrilles. But as the room grew warmer, the laughter louder, and the gossiping more vigorous, the refreshment table set the First Annual Victory Ball on a course for disaster.

Which meant Mina was enjoying the event far more than she'd expected to.

Not that it wasn't as grand as everyone had said it would be. Despite the slowly increasing tension, the great ballroom had not begun to rip at the silk-papered seams; the restoration of Devonshire House had cost Hartington, and it showed. Candle-studded chandeliers displayed everyone to their best advantage. Discreet gas lamps highlighted the enormous paintings gracing the room but had not yet smudged the walls. Musicians played at the opposite end of the ballroom, and the violins did sound sweeter than the mechanical instruments Mina was accustomed to—and *much* sweeter than the hacking coughs from forty of the guests, all of them bounders.

Two hundred years ago, when most of Europe was fleeing from the Horde's war machines, some of the English had gone with them. But an ocean passage over the Atlantic hadn't come cheaply, and although the families who'd abandoned England for the New World hadn't all been aristocrats, they'd all been moneyed. After the Iron Duke had freed England from Horde control, many of them had returned to London, flaunting their titles and their gold. Now, nine years after Britain's victory over the Horde, the aristocratic bounders had decided to hold a ball celebrating the country's newfound freedom, though they had shed no blood to gain it. They'd charitably included all of the peers who had little to their names but their titles.

At first glance, Mina could detect little distinction between the guests. The bounders spoke with flatter accents, and their women's dresses exposed less skin, but everyone's togs were at the height of New World fashion. Mina suspected, however, that forty of the guests could not begin to guess how dear those new togs were to the rest of the company.

And they probably could not anticipate how stubborn the rest of the company could be, despite their thirst and hunger.

At the side of the room, Mina sat with her friend and waited for the entertainment to begin. Considering her condition, Felicity might be the one to provide it. Pale blue satin covered Felicity's hugely rounded belly, which seemed to Mina to require an enormous amount of food, not just the drink Felicity had assured her husband was all she'd needed.

With such a belly, Mina could not see how Felicity wasn't constantly ravenous, consuming everything in her path. If no sugarless cakes were available, she might start with the bounders.

"If it has taken Richmond this long, he hasn't found anything." Beneath intricately curled blond hair that had made

Mina burst into laughter when she had first seen it that evening—and who, thanks to her mother's insistence, wore a similar style in her own black hair—Felicity's gaze searched the crowd for her husband. With a sigh, she turned to regard her friend. "Oh, Mina. You are too amused. I doubt anyone will break into fisticuffs."

"They should."

"You think it's an insult to supply sweet and strong lemonade? To stack cakes like towers?" Felicity rubbed her belly and looked longingly toward the towers. Mina supposed they were to have been demolished by now, symbolic of England's victory over the Horde, but they still stood tall. "Surely, they did not realize how strongly we felt about it."

"Or they realized, but thought we must be shown like children that we can eat imported sugar without being enslaved."

A little more than two centuries ago, the Horde had hidden their nanoagents in the tea and sugar like invisible bugs, and traded it on the cheap. The Horde had no navy, and even though Europe had fled before the Horde, Britain was protected by water and a strong fleet of ships. And so for years, they'd traded tea and sugar, and Britain had thought itself safe.

Until the Horde had activated the bugs.

Now no one born in England trusted sugar unless it came from beets grown in British soil and refined in a British factory—and no one had enough money to pay for the luxury, anyway. The Horde hadn't needed sugar from them, and had left few beet farmers and fewer refineries. Sugar was as precious as gold was to the French, and Horde technology was to the smugglers in the Indian Ocean.

"You judge them too harshly, Mina. This ball itself is goodwill. And it must have been a great expense." Felicity's voice softened at the end, and she looked around almost despairingly, as if it pained her to think of how much had been spent.

"Hartington can obviously afford it. Look how many candles." Mina lifted her chin, gesturing at the chandelier.

"Even your mother uses candles."

That wasn't the same. Gas cost nothing; candles, especially wax tapers of good quality, rivaled sugar as a luxury. Her mother used candles during her League meetings, but only so the dim light would conceal the worst of the wear. Repeated scouring of the walls removed the smoke that penetrated every home in London, but had worn the paper down to the plaster. Rugs had been walked threadbare at the center. The sofa hadn't been replaced since the Horde had invaded England. But at Devonshire House, there was no need for candles to forgive what brighter gas lamps revealed.

"My mother will also make certain that each of her guests is comfortable." Physically comfortable, at any rate. She supposed her mother could not help the discomforting effect that both she and Mina had on visitors. "Goodwill should not stab at scars, Felicity. Goodwill would have been desserts made with beet sugar or honey."

"Perhaps," Felicity said, obviously unwilling to think so little of the bounders, but acknowledging that they could have been done better. "You look to find the worst in everyone, Mina."

"I would not be very good at my job if I didn't." The worst in everyone was what led them to murder.

"You *like* to look for the worst in bounders. But they cannot be blamed for their ancestors abandoning us, just as we cannot be blamed for buying the Horde's sugar and teas. It seems to me, the fault can be laid on both sides of the ocean . . . and laid to rest."

No, the bounders hadn't abandoned England—and if that were the only grievance Mina had against them, she *could* have laid her resentment to rest. But neither could she explain her resentment; Felicity thought too well of them, and she was too fascinated by the New World.

The bounders were part of that fascination—and they were part of the New World, no matter that they referred to themselves as Englishmen, and were called Brits by everyone except those born on the British isle.

Damn them all, they probably didn't even realize there was a difference between English and British.

No matter what the bounders thought they were, they weren't like Mina's family or Felicity's—or like those who'd been altered and enslaved for labor. Bounders hadn't been born under Horde rule. And Mina resented that when they'd returned, they'd carried with them the assumption that they better knew how to live than the buggers did. This ball, for all that it celebrated victory over the Horde, was a reflection of what bounders thought society should be: They'd had their Season in Manhattan City and thought the tradition should continue here. It did not seem to matter that most of the peers born here couldn't dream of holding their own ball. And although the ball provided a pleasant diversion, buggers had more important things to occupy their minds and their time—such as whether they could afford their next meal.

The bounders had no such worries. They'd returned, their heads filled only with grand ideas and good intentions, and they meant to force them onto the rest of Britain.

But their intentions did not mean they'd returned for the benefit of their former countrymen. Not at all. A good situation within Manhattan City was impossible to find, they'd run out of room on the long Prince George Island, and the Dutch would not relinquish any territory in the mainland. So the aristocrats returned to claim their estates and their Parliament seats, the merchants to buy what the aristocrats didn't own, and all of them to look down their noses at the poor buggers who'd been raised beneath the thumb of the Horde.

Or to be horrified by them. Mina's gaze sought her mother. Even in a crowd, she was easy to locate—a small woman with white-blond hair, wearing crimson satin. Spectacles with smoked lenses dominated her narrow face. Wide brass bracelets shaped like kraken circled her gloved arms. Currently, she was demonstrating the clockwork release mechanism to three other ladies—all bounders. Her mother twisted the kraken's bulbous head, releasing the tentacles wrapped around her wrist. The ladies clapped, obviously delighted, and though

Mina couldn't hear what they said, she guessed they were asking her mother where she'd purchased the unique bracelets. Such clockwork devices were prized as both novelties and jewelry—and expensive. Mina doubted her mother told them the bracelets were of her own design and had been made in her mother's freezing attic workshop.

In any case, the novelty of the bracelets didn't divert the ladies from their real interest. Even as they spoke, they cast surreptitious glances at her mother's eyes. One leaned forward, as if to gain a better angle to see the bracelet—and gained a better angle to see behind her mother's spectacles. Her mouth fell open before she recovered.

Rarely did anyone hide their surprise when they glimpsed the shiny orbs concealed by the lenses. Some stared openly, as if the prosthetic eyes were blind, rather than as keen as a telescope and a microscope combined. This particular lady was no different. She continued to look, her expression a mixture of fascination and revulsion. She'd probably expected modification on a coal miner. Not the countess of Rockingham.

But if mirrored eyes still horrified her, chances were she'd never actually seen a miner. Or perhaps she'd heard the story behind her mother's eyes. If so, the lady's gaze would soon be seeking Mina.

Felicity must have caught the direction of her attention. "What is her goal tonight?" she asked. "A husband for you, or new recruits for her Ladies' Reformation League?"

Mina's friend underestimated her mother's efficiency. "Both."

As efficient as her mother was, however, finding new recruits for her League had greater possibility for success. A suitable husband was about as likely as King Edward writing his own name legibly. Mina was approaching thirty years of age—nine of them free from the Horde's control—without once attracting the attention of a worthy man. Only bounders searching for a taste of the exotic and forbidden, or Englishmen seeking revenge for the horrors of the Mongol occupation—and Mina resembled the people they wanted to exact their vengeance on.

A loud, hacking cough from beside Mina turned her head. A bounder, red in the face, lowered his handkerchief from his mouth. His gaze touched Mina, then darted away.

She turned back to Felicity with arched brows, inviting comment.

Felicity watched the man walk away. "I suppose it does not matter, anyway. They will all soon hie off to the countryside or back to the New World."

Yes. Without the bugs, the insides of their lungs would become as black as a chimney.

They'd been made too confident by their success in America. They'd built a new life out of a wild land, taming it to suit their needs. Now, they thought they could return and reshape London—but London reshaped them, instead. The only way to stay alive in the city was to become a bugger, infecting themselves with the tiny machines that their ancestors had run from two hundred years before.

From directly beside Mina came the quiet sound of a throat clearing. She turned. A ginger-haired maid in a black uniform bobbed a curtsy. Though Mina had noted that the servants from the New World usually lowered their gazes, this girl couldn't seem to help herself. The maid studied Mina's face, fascinated and wary. Perhaps she'd never seen a Mongol before—or, as in Mina's case, a mongrel. Only a few of the Horde were left in England, and even fewer lived in the New World. The Horde trade routes didn't cross the Atlantic.

Mina raised her brows.

The maid blushed and bowed her head. "A gentleman asks to see you, my lady."

"Oh, she is not a lady," Felicity said airily. "She is a detective *inspector*."

The mock gravity weighing down the last word seemed to confound the maid. She colored and fidgeted. Perhaps she worried that "inspector" was a bugger's insult?

Mina said, "What gentleman?"

"A Constable Newberry, my lady. He's brought with him a message to you."

Mina frowned and stood, but was brought around by Felicity's exasperated, "Mina, you didn't."

She could determine motives of opium-addled criminals, but what she couldn't do was follow every jump of Felicity's mind. "I didn't what?"

"Send a gram to your assistant so that you could escape."

Oh, she *should* have. It would be a simple thing; all of the bounders' restored houses had wiregram lines installed.

"You mistrustful cow! Of course I didn't." She lowered her voice and added, "I will at the next ball, however, now that you've given me the idea." As Felicity smothered a laugh into her hand again, Mina continued. "Will you inform my father and mother that I've gone?"

"Gone? It is only a message."

Newberry wouldn't have come in person if it was only a message. "No."

"Oh." Realization swept over her friend's expression, brushing away her amusement. "Do not keep the poor bastard waiting, then."

The maid's eyes widened before she turned to lead Mina out of the ballroom. She could imagine what the girl thought, but Newberry was not the poor bastard.

Whoever had been murdered was.

They'd put Newberry in a study in the east wing—probably so the guests weren't made nervous by his size or his constable's coat. Though he must have been alone in the room several minutes, he stood in the middle of the study, his bowler hat in his large-knuckled hands. Mina had to admire his fortitude. Small automata lined the study's bookshelves. If given more than a few seconds to wait, she could not have stopped herself from winding them and seeing how they performed. She recognized a few of her mother's more mundane creations—

a dog that would wag his tail and flip; a singing mechanical nightingale—and felt more charitable toward her host. They might not have provided dessert, but they unknowingly *had* put food on her table.

Newberry's eyes widened briefly when he saw her attire. She'd never worn a skirt in his presence, let alone a yellow satin gown that exposed her collarbones and the few inches of skin between her cap sleeves and her long white gloves. His gaze flicked back up so fast she might have missed his surprise if she hadn't taken that moment to look him over.

Her coat, weapons, and armor draped over his left forearm. She could have no doubt they were leaving now, and he'd come in such a hurry he hadn't taken time to shave. Evening stubble flanked the red mustache that drooped over the corners of his mouth and swept up the sides of his jaw to meet his sideburns. It offered the impression of a large, protective dog—an accurate impression. Newberry resembled a wolfhound: friendly and loyal, until someone threatened. Then he was all teeth.

Not every bounder who returned had a title and a bulging purse. Newberry had come so that his wife, suffering a consumptive lung condition, could be infected by the bugs and live.

"Report, Newberry." She accepted the sleeveless, close-fitting black tunic whose wire mesh protected her from throat to hips. Usually she wore the armor beneath her clothing, but she did not have that option now. She pulled it on and began fastening the buckles lining the front.

"We're to go to the Isle of Dogs, sir. Superintendent Hale assigned you specifically."

"Oh?" The dockyards east of London weren't as rough as they'd once been, but she still visited often enough. Perhaps it touched another murder she had investigated. "Who is it this time?"

"The Duke of Anglesey, sir."

Dear God. Her gaze skidded from a buckle up to Newberry's serious face. "The Iron Duke's been killed?"

She had never met the man or seen him in person, and yet her heart kicked painfully against her ribs. Rhys Trahaearn, former pirate captain, recently titled Duke of Anglesey—and, after he'd destroyed the Horde's tower, England's most celebrated hero.

"No." Newberry glanced around, as if making certain that no servants were around to faint—or to spread false gossip before he could correct them. "It isn't His Grace. He only reported the murder."

Newberry sounded apologetic. Perhaps he hadn't expected her to feel the same reverence for the Iron Duke that most of England did. Mina didn't, though her racing pulse suggested that she'd taken at least some of the stories about him to heart. The news sheets painted him as a dashing figure, romanticizing his past, but Mina suspected he was simply an opportunist who'd been in the right place at the right moment.

"So he's killed someone, then?" It wouldn't be the first time.

"I do not know, sir. Only that a body has been found on his estate."

Mina frowned. Given the size of his estate, that could mean anything.

When she finished fastening the tight armor, the gown's lacings pressed uncomfortably against her spine. She slung her gun belt around her hips; one of the weapons had been loaded with bullets, the other with opium darts, which had greater effect on a rampaging bugger. She paused after Newberry passed her the knife sheath. Mina typically wore trousers, and strapped the weapon around her thigh. If she bound the knife beneath her skirts in the same location, it'd be impossible to draw when she needed it. Driving through East London at night without as many weapons as possible would be foolish, however. Her calf would have to do.

She sank down on one knee and hoisted her skirts. Newberry spun around—his cheeks on fire, no doubt. Good man, her Newberry. Always proper. Sometimes, Mina felt sorry for him; he'd been assigned to her almost as soon as he'd stepped off the airship from Manhattan City.

Other times, she thought it must be good for him. God alone knew what had happened to the Brits who'd fled to the New World. In two centuries, their society had devolved into prudes. Probably because the Separatist pilgrims had arrived first, and they hadn't had the Horde scrub away all but the vestiges of religion. A few curses remained. Not much else did.

She tightened the knife sheath below her knee and grimaced at the sight of her slippers. Newberry hadn't brought her boots—or her hat, but it was probably for the best. She wasn't certain she could shove it down over the knot of hair the maid had teased into black curls. She took her heavy coat from him as she turned for the door, stifling a groan as her every step kicked her yellow skirts forward.

A detective inspector turned inside-out on top, and a lady below. She hoped Felicity did not see her this way. Never would she hear the end of it.

Newberry's two-seater waited at the bottom of the front steps, rattling and hissing steam from the boot, and drawing appalled glances from the attending servants. Judging by the other vehicles in the drive, the attendants were accustomed to larger, shinier coaches, with brass appointments and velvet seats. The police cart had four wheels and an engine that hadn't exploded, and that was the best that could be said for it.

As it wasn't raining, the canvas top had been folded back, leaving the cab open. The coal bin sat on the passenger's side of the bench, as if Newberry had dumped in the fuel on the run.

Newberry colored and mumbled, heaving the bin to the floorboards. Mina battled her skirts past the cart's tin frame as he rounded the front. She resorted to hiking them up to her knees, and his cheeks were aflame again as he swung into his seat. The cart tilted and the bench protested under his weight. His stomach, though solid, almost touched the steering shaft.

Newberry closed the steam vent. The hissing stopped and the cart slowly pulled forward. Mina sighed. Though the sounds of the city were never ending, courtesy usually dictated that one didn't blast the occupants of a private house with engine noise. Always polite, Newberry intended to wait before he fully engaged the engine until after they'd passed out of the drive.

"We are in a hurry, Constable," she reminded him.

"Yes, sir."

The engine roared. Mina's teeth rattled as the cart jerked forward. Smoke erupted from the boot in a thick black cloud, obscuring everything behind them. Too bad, that. She'd wanted to see the attendants' expressions when the engine belched in their faces, but she and Newberry were through the gate before the air cleared.

"Have you met His Grace?"

Mina glanced over as Newberry shouted the question. He often looked for impressions of character before arriving at a scene, but Mina had no solid ones to give. "No."

She'd eaten lunch at Trahaearn's feet, however. Near the Whitehall police station, an iron statue of the duke had been erected at the center of Anglesey square. At twenty feet tall, that statue did not offer a good angle to judge his features. Mina knew from the caricatures in the news sheets that he had a square jaw, a hawkish nose, and heavy brows that darkened his piercing stare into a glower. The effect was altogether strong and handsome, but Mina suspected that the artists were trying to dress up England's Savior like her mother lighting candles in the parlor.

Perhaps all of him had been dressed up. The news sheets speculated that his ancestors had been Welsh gentry and that he'd been taken from them as a baby, but nothing was truly known of his family. Quite possibly, his father had pulverizing hammers for legs, his mother fitted with drills instead of arms, and he'd been born in a coal mine nine months after a Frenzy, squatted out in a dusty bin before his mother returned to work.

Twenty years ago, however, his name had first been recorded in Captain Braxton's log on HMS *Indomitable*. Trahaearn, aged sixteen, had been aboard a slave ship bound for the Americas, and was pressed with the crew into the British navy. Within two years he'd transferred from *Indomitable* to another British ship, *Unity*, a fifth-rate frigate patrolling the trade routes in the South Seas. Before they'd reached Australia, Trahaearn had led a mutiny, taken over the ship as its captain, renamed the frigate *Marco's Terror*, and embarked on an eight-year run of piracy. No trade route, no nation, no merchant had been safe from him. Even in London, where the Horde suppressed any news that suggested a weakness in their defenses, word of Trahaearn's piracy had seeped into conversations. Several times, the news sheets claimed the Horde had him close to capture. He'd been declared dead twice.

Perhaps that was why the Horde hadn't anticipated him sailing *Marco's Terror* up the Thames and blowing up their tower.

"Is he enhanced?"

Mina almost smiled. Even shouting, Newberry didn't unbend enough to use "bugger." *Enhanced* had become the polite term for living with millions of microscopic machines in each of their bodies. *Bugger* had been an insult once—and still was in parts of the New World. Only the bounders seemed to care about that, however. After two hundred years, not a single bugger that Mina knew took offense at the name.

Of course, if Newberry called her by the name the Horde had used for them—*zum bi*, the soulless—she'd knock his enhanced teeth out.

"He is," she confirmed.

"How did he do it?" When Mina frowned, certain she'd missed part of the question, Newberry clarified in a shout, "The tower!"

He wasn't the first to ask. The Horde had created a short-range signal around their tower, preventing buggers from approaching it. Trahaearn *had* been infected, but he hadn't been paralyzed when he'd entered the broadcast area. Mina's father theorized that the frequency had changed from the time that Trahaearn had lived in Britain as a child, and so he hadn't been affected on his return. She'd heard the same theory echoed by other buggers, but bounders preferred to think he hadn't been infected with nanoagents at the time—despite the Iron Duke himself confirming that he'd carried the bugs since he was a boy.

Her father's theory seemed to Mina as sound as any. "Frequencies!"

Newberry looked doubtful, but nodded.

Frequencies or not—it didn't matter to Mina, or to any other bugger. Thanks to the Iron Duke, the nanoagents no longer controlled them, but assisted them. The Horde no longer constantly suppressed their emotions—violence, lust, ambition—or, when the *darga* wanted them to breed, whip them into a frenzy.

After nine years, many who'd been raised under Horde rule were still learning to control strong emotions, to fight violent impulses. Not everyone succeeded, and that was when Mina often stepped in.

With luck, this murder would be the same: an unchecked impulse, easily traceable—and the murderer easy to hold accountable.

And with more luck, the murderer wouldn't be the Iron Duke. No one would be held accountable then. He was too beloved—beloved enough that all of Britain ignored his history of raping, thieving, and murdering. Beloved enough that they tried to rewrite that history. And even if the evidence pointed to Trahaearn, he wouldn't be ruined.

But as the investigating officer, Mina *would* be.

By the time she and Newberry reached the Isle of Dogs, the nip of the evening air had become a bite. Not a true island, the isle was surrounded on three sides by a bend in the river. On the London side, multiple trading companies had built up small docks—mostly abandoned. The southern and eastern sides held the Iron Duke's docks, which serviced his company's ships, and those who paid for the space. In nine years, he'd been paid enough to buy up the center of the isle and build his fortress.

The high, wrought-iron fence that surrounded his gardens had earned him the nickname the Iron Duke—the iron kept the rest of London out, and whatever riches he hid inside, in. The spikes at the top of the fence guaranteed that no one in the surrounding slums would scale it, and no one was invited in. At least, no one in Mina's circle, or her mother's.

She was never certain if their circle was too high, or too low.

Newberry stopped in front of the gate. When a face appeared at the small gatehouse window, he shouted, "Detective Inspector Wentworth, on police business! Open her up!"

The gatekeeper appeared, a grizzled man with a long gray beard and the heavy step that marked a metal leg. A former pirate, Mina guessed. Though the Crown insisted that Trahaearn and his men had all been privateers, acting with the permission of the king, only a few children who didn't know any better believed the story. The rest of them knew he'd been a pirate all along, and the story was just designed to bolster faith in the king and his ministers after the revolution. That story and bestowing a title on Trahaearn had been two of King Edward's last cogent acts. The crew had been given naval ranks, and *Marco's Terror* pressed into the service of the Navy . . . where she'd supposedly been all along.

The Iron Duke had traded the *Terror* and the seas for a title and a fortress in the middle of a slum. She wondered if he felt that exchange had been worth it.

The gatekeeper glanced at her. "And the jade?"

At Mina's side, Newberry bristled. "*She* is the detective inspector, Lady Wilhelmina Wentworth."

Oh, Newberry. In Manhattan City, titles still meant more than escaping the modification that the British lower classes had suffered under the Horde. And when the gatekeeper looked at her again, she knew what he saw—and it wasn't a lady. Nor was it the epaulettes declaring her rank, or the red band sewed into her sleeve, boasting that she'd spilled Horde blood in the revolution.

No, he saw her face, calculated her age, and understood that she'd been conceived during a Frenzy. And that, because of her family's status, her mother and father had been allowed to keep her rather than her being taken by the Horde to be raised in a crèche.

The gatekeeper looked at her assistant. "And you?"

"Constable Newberry."

Scratching his beard, the old man shuffled back toward the gatehouse. "All right. I'll be sending a gram up to the captain, then."

He still called the Iron Duke "captain"? Mina could not decide if that said more about Trahaearn or the gatekeeper. At least one of them did not put much stock in titles, but she could not determine if it was the gatekeeper alone.

The gatekeeper didn't return—and former pirate or not, he must be literate if he could write a gram and read the answer from the main house. That answer came quickly. She and Newberry hadn't waited more than a minute before the gates opened on well-oiled hinges.

The park was enormous, with green lawns stretching out into the dark. Dogs sniffed along the fence, their handlers bundled up against the cold. If someone had invaded the property, he wouldn't find many places to hide outside the buildings. All of the shrubs and trees were still young, planted after Trahaearn had purchased the estate.

The house rivaled Chesterfield before that great building had fallen into disrepair and been demolished. Made of yellow stone, two rectangular wings jutted forward to form a large courtyard. Unadorned casements decorated the many windows, and the blocky stone front was relieved only by the window glass, and the balustrade along the top of the roof. A fountain tinkled at the center of the courtyard. Behind it, the main steps created semicircles leading to the entrance.

On the center of the steps, a white sheet concealed a body-shaped lump. No blood soaked through the sheet. A man waited on the top step, his slight form in a poker-straight posture that Mina couldn't place for a moment. Then it struck her: Navy. Probably another pirate, though this one had been a sailor—or an officer—first.

A house of this size would require a small army of staff, and she and Newberry would have to question each one. Soon, she'd know how many of Trahaearn's pirates had come to dry land with him.

As they reached the fountain, she turned to Newberry. "Stop here. Set up your camera by the body. I want photographs of everything before we move it."

Newberry parked and climbed out. Mina didn't wait for him to gather his equipment from the bonnet. She strode toward the house. The man descended the steps to greet her, and she was forced to revise her opinion. His posture wasn't rigid discipline, but a cover for wiry, contained energy. His dark hair was slicked back from a narrow face. Unlike the man at the gate, he was neat, and almost bursting with the need to help.

"Inspector Wentworth." With ink-stained fingers, he gestured to the body, inviting her to look.

She was not in a rush, however. The body would not be going anywhere. "Mr—?"

"St. John." He said it like a bounder, rather than the two abbreviated syllables of someone born in England. "Steward to His Grace's estate."

"This estate or his property in Wales?" Which, as far as Mina was aware, Trahaearn didn't often visit.

"Anglesey, inspector."

Newberry passed them, easily carrying the heavy photographic equipment. St. John half turned, as if to offer his assistance, then glanced back as Mina asked, "When did you arrive here from Wales, Mr. St. John?"

"Yesterday."

"Did you witness what happened here?"

He shook his head. "I was in the study when I heard the

footman—Chesley—inform the housekeeper that someone had fallen. Mrs. Lavery then told His Grace."

Mina frowned. She hadn't been called out here because someone had been a clumsy oaf, had they? "Someone tripped on the stairs?"

"No, inspector. Fallen." His hand made a sharp dive from his shoulder to his hip.

Mina glanced at the body again, then at the balustrade lining the roof. "Do you know who it was?"

"No."

She was not surprised. If he managed the Welsh estate, he wouldn't likely know the London staff well. "Who covered him with the sheet?"

"I did, after His Grace sent the staff back into the house."

So they'd all come out to gawk. "Did anyone identify him while they were outside?"

"No."

Or maybe they just hadn't spoken up. "Where is the staff now?"

"They are gathered in the main parlor."

Where they would all pass the story around until they were each convinced they'd witnessed it personally. Blast. Mina firmed her lips.

As if understanding her frustration, St. John added, "The footman is alone in the study, however. His Grace told him to stay there. He hasn't spoken with anyone else since Mrs. Lavery told His Grace."

The footman had been taken into the study and asked nothing? "But he has talked to the duke?"

The answer came from behind her, from a voice that could carry his commands across a ship without shouting. "He has, Inspector."

She turned to find a man as big as his voice. Oh, damn the news sheets. They hadn't been kind to *him*—they'd been kind to their readers, protecting them the effect of this man. He was just as hard and as handsome as they'd portrayed. Altogether dark and forbidding, his gaze was as pointed and as guarded as the fence that was his namesake. The Iron Duke wasn't as tall as his statue, but still taller than any man had a right to be—and as broad through the shoulders as Newberry, but without the spare flesh.

The news sheets had shown all of that, but they hadn't conveyed his power. But it was not just size, Mina immediately recognized. Not just his looks. She'd seen handsome before. She'd seen rich and influential. Yet this man had a presence beyond looks and money. For the first time, she could see why men might follow him through kraken-infested waters or into Horde territory, then follow him back onto shore and remain with him.

He was terrifying.

Disturbed by her reaction, Mina glanced at the man standing beside him: tall, brown-haired, his expression bored. Mina did not recognize him. Perhaps a bounder and, if so, probably an aristocrat—and he likely expected to be treated as one.

Bully for him.

She looked to the duke again. Like his companion, he wore a long black overcoat, breeches, and boots. A waistcoat buckled like armor over a white shirt with a simple collar reminiscent of the Horde's tunic collar. Fashionable clothes, but almost invisible—as if overpowered by the man wearing them.

Something, Mina suspected, that he did not just to his clothes, but to the people around him. She could not afford to be one of them.

She'd never been introduced to someone of his standing before, but she'd seen Superintendent Hale meet the prime minister without a single gesture to acknowledge that he ranked above her. Mina followed that example and offered the short nod of an equal. "Your Grace. I understand that you did not witness this man die."

"No."

She looked beyond him. "And your companion . . . ?"

"Also saw nothing," the other man answered.

She'd been right; his accent marked him as a bounder.

Yet she had to revise her opinion of him. He wasn't bored by the death—just too familiar with it to be excited by yet another. She couldn't understand that. The more death she saw, the more the injustice of each one touched her. "Your name, sir?"

His smile seemed just at the edge of a laugh. "Mr. Smith."

A joker. How fun.

She thought a flicker of irritation crossed the duke's expression. But when he didn't offer his companion's true name, she let it go. One of the staff would know.

"Mr. St. John has told me that no one has identified the body, and only your footman saw his fall."

"Yes."

"Did your footman relate anything else to you?"

"Only that his landing sounded just like a man falling from the topsail yard to the deck below. Except this one didn't scream."

No scream? Either the man had been drunk, asleep, or already dead. She would soon find out which it was.

"If you'll pardon me, Your Grace."

With a nod, she turned toward the steps, where Newberry tested the camera's flashing light. She heard the Iron Duke and his companion follow her. As long as they did not touch the body or try to help her examine it, she did not care.

Mina looked down at her hands. *She* would touch the body, and Newberry had not thought to bring her serviceable wool gloves to exchange for her white evening gloves. They were only satin—neither her mother's tinkering nor her own salary could afford kid—but they were still too dear to ruin.

She tugged at the tips of her fingers, but the fastenings at her wrist prevented them from sliding off. Futilely, she tried to push the small buttons through equally small satin loops. The seams at the tips of her fingers made them too bulky, and the fabric was too slippery. It could not be done without a maid, or a mother.

She looked round for Newberry, and saw that the black powder from the ferrotype camera already dusted his hands.

Blast it. She lifted her wrist to her mouth, pushed the cuff of her sleeve out of the way with her chin, and began to work at the tiny loops with her teeth. She would bite them through, if she had to. Even the despised task of sewing the buttons back on would be easier than—

"Give your hand over, Inspector."

Mina froze, her hackles rising at the command. She looked through her fingers at Trahaearn's face.

She heard a noise from his companion, a snorted half laugh—as if Trahaearn had failed an easy test.

The duke's voice softened. His expression did not. "May I assist you?"

No, she thought. *Do not touch me; do not come close.* But the body on the steps would not allow her that reply.

"Yes. Thank you, Your Grace."

She held out her hand, and watched as he removed his own gloves. Kid, lined with sable. Just imagining that luxurious softness warmed her.

She would not have been surprised if his presence had, as well. With his great size, he seemed to surround her with heat just by standing so near. His hands were large, his fingers long and nails square. As he took her wrist in his left palm, calluses audibly scraped the satin. His face darkened. She could not tell if it was in anger or embarrassment.

However rough his skin was, his fingers were nimble. He deftly unfastened the first button, and the next. "This was not the evening you had planned."

"No."

She did not say this was preferable to the Victory Ball, but perhaps he read it in her voice. His teeth flashed in a smile. Her breath quickened, and she focused on her wrist. Only two buttons left, and then she could work.

She should be working now. "Were the dogs patrolling the grounds before the body was discovered?"

"No. They search for the point of entry now."

Mina pictured the iron fence. Perhaps a child could slip through the bars; a man could not. But if someone had let him through . . . ? "Have you spoken with your man at the front gate?"

"Wills?"

She had not asked the gatekeeper his name. "If Wills has a prosthetic left leg, and often saves a portion of his supper in his beard for his breakfast, then we are speaking of the same man."

"That is Wills." He studied her with unreadable eyes. "He would not let anyone through."

Without my leave, Mina finished for him. And perhaps he was right, though of course she would verify it with the gate-keeper, and ask the steward about deliveries. Someone might have hidden themselves in one.

His gaze fell to her glove again. "There we are," Trahaearn said softly. "Now to—"

She pulled her hand away at the same time Trahaearn gripped the satin fingertips. He tugged. Satin slid in a warm caress over her elbow, her forearm.

Flames lit her cheeks. "Your Grace—"

His expression changed as he continued to pull. First registering surprise, as if he had not realized that the glove extended past her wrist. Then an emotion hard and sharp as the long glove slowly gave way. Its white length finally dangled from his fingers, and to Mina seemed as intimate as if he held her stocking.

Her sleeve still covered her arm, but she felt exposed. Stripped. With as much dignity as she could, Mina claimed the glove.

"Thank you, Your Grace. I can manage the other." She stuffed the glove into her pocket. With her bare fingers, she made quick work of the buttons at her left wrist.

She looked up to find him staring at her. His cheekbones blazed with color, his gaze hot.

She'd seen lust before. This marked the first time that she hadn't seen any disgust or hatred beneath it.

"Thank you," she said again, amazed by the evenness of her voice when everything inside her trembled.

"Inspector." He inclined his head, then looked beyond her to the stairs.

And as she turned, the trembling stopped. Her legs were steady as she walked to the steps, her gaze unflinching, her mind focused.

"You were to assist her, not undress her," she heard his companion say. Trahaearn didn't reply, and Mina didn't look back at him.

Even the pull of the Iron Duke was not stronger than Death.

A BRAND-NEW COLLECTION
FROM BESTSELLING PROVOCATEURS
OF THE PARANORMAL . . .

BURNING UP

New York Times bestselling authors

ANGELA KNIGHT

NALINI SINGH

VIRGINIA KANTRA

MELJEAN BROOK

In Angela Knight's *Blood and Roses*, a vampire warrior and his seductive captor join forces to stop a traitor from unleashing an army of demonic predators on their kingdom.

Whisper of Sin is new in Nalini Singh's Psy-Changeling series, in which a woman in lethal danger finds an unlikely protector—and lover—in a volatile member of the Dark-River pack.

Virginia Kantra continues the haunting tales of the Children of the Sea in *Shifting Sea*, the story of a wounded soldier rescued by a strange and enigmatic young woman.

Meljean Brook launches a bold new steampunk series with *Here There Be Monsters* as a desperate woman strikes a provocative—and terrifying—bargain to gain overseas passage.

Coming in August 2010

penguin.com